THE MURDERER INSIDE
THE MIRROR

*Also by Sarah Rayne
from Severn House*

The Theatre of Thieves mysteries

CHALICE OF DARKNESS

The Phineas Fox mysteries

DEATH NOTES
CHORD OF EVIL
SONG OF THE DAMNED
MUSIC MACABRE
THE DEVIL'S HARMONY
THE MURDER DANCE

The Nell West and Michael Flint series

PROPERTY OF A LADY
THE SIN EATER
THE SILENCE
THE WHISPERING
DEADLIGHT HALL
THE BELL TOWER

THE MURDERER
INSIDE THE MIRROR

Sarah Rayne

**SEVERN
HOUSE**

First world edition published in Great Britain and the USA in 2024
by Severn House, an imprint of Canongate Books Ltd,
14 High Street, Edinburgh EH1 1TE.

severnhouse.com

British Library Cataloguing-in-Publication Data
A CIP catalogue record for this title is available from the British Library.

ISBN-13: 978-1-4483-1095-1 (cased)
ISBN-13: 978-1-4483-0643-5 (e-book)

All Severn House titles are printed on acid-free paper.

MIX
Paper from
responsible sources
FSC
www.fsc.org   FSC® C013056

Typeset by Palimpsest Book Production Ltd., Falkirk,
Stirlingshire, Scotland.
Printed and bound in Great Britain by TJ Books,
Padstow, Cornwall.

Praise for Sarah Rayne

About the author

Sarah Rayne is the author of many novels of psychological and supernatural suspense, including the Nell West & Michael Flint series as well as the historical mystery series, Phineas Fox and Theatre of Thieves. She lives in Staffordshire.

www.sarahrayne.co.uk

ONE

The Fitzglens were discussing a new filch when the terrible news came.

They had met on the stage of their theatre, which was usually the safest place to plan any filch, but they were waiting for Great Uncle Montague, because he was the one whose filch this was. They were also waiting for Jack, because it was unthinkable to begin any meeting until Jack was at the head of the table.

The youngest member of the family, who was called Tansy Fitzglen and had lately been promoted to its inner ranks, was trying not to seem overawed. It was difficult, though, because some of the elders of her family seemed almost legends. Opposite to her was the formidable Great Aunt Daphnis, with, next to her, blustery Great Uncle Rudraige, who still affected muttonchop whiskers in the fashion of the Eighties. Tansy gazed at them both with fascination. Farther along were Aunt Cecily, in a dishevelment of woolly scarves and mufflers since it could be *so* draughty on stage, and Ambrose, who – Tansy's father had once told her – was almost entirely responsible for concealing the proceeds of all filches from the prying eyes of officials likely to demand such nuisances as income-tax payments.

Byron Fitzglen, who was nearest to Tansy in age, came to sit next to her, draping himself languidly in his chair, and opening a notebook.

'I'm making notes about a Gainsborough portrait,' he said. 'I believe Uncle Montague's plan is that he copies it so we can make a switch and sell the original.'

'Are you chronicling the filches before they're committed now, Byron?' said an amused voice from the wings.

Several pleased voices said, 'Jack!' and Tansy turned to see Jack Fitzglen standing in the prompt corner, wearing immaculately cut evening clothes, his dark eyes bright, the glow from a nearby gas jet falling across him, turning his hair to pale brown silk. As he walked across to the table, Tansy was aware that in some incomprehensible way the whole atmosphere on the stage had changed.

Augustus Pocket, who was Jack's dresser and collaborator in most of the Fitzglens' work both on and off stage, followed him onto the stage, and reported that he had checked all the doors and everywhere was safely locked. The family nodded, approvingly, because Gus could be trusted to make sure no enterprising prowlers could get in and listen to them – that not so much as an itinerant ghost could sneak its way inside; not that the Amaranth theatre actually had any ghosts, or not as far as anyone knew.

'But I found this posted in the box at the stage door,' said Gus, handing an envelope to Jack. 'It's addressed to "The Fitzglens".'

'That wasn't there when I arrived,' said Daphnis. 'Who would deliver a note at this hour?'

'Ah, midnight, the witching hour,' remarked Byron. 'When orbed is the moon, and the stars glisten and listen.'

'It'll be a bill,' said Cecily. 'It's always a bill.'

'Not delivered at twenty minutes to midnight.'

Jack was already reading the envelope's contents, and frowning. Tansy thought it was extraordinary that someone with golden brown hair could frown so darkly. It was the eyes, of course. Her mother had always said that Jack Fitzglen had the narrow, compelling dark eyes of several of the Fitzglens, adding it pleased her that Tansy had inherited them.

Jack said, in a voice Tansy had never heard him use, 'This is . . . oh, God, this is dreadful. It's from a neighbour of Great Uncle Montague in Notting Hill.'

'We've been waiting for Montague,' said Rudraige. 'He's going to tell us about the Gainsborough he's after.'

Jack looked up from the letter. 'I don't know how to tell you,' he said, 'but it seems—' He made an abrupt movement with one hand, as if pushing something away, then said, 'Great Uncle Montague tumbled down two flights of stairs earlier today, and – well, he broke his neck.'

'You don't mean he's dead?'

'Yes, I do. The neighbour says a doctor was called, but he had died instantly. She says everyone in the street is very upset because they were all extremely fond of him.'

There was a stunned silence. Then Rudraige said, 'Good God,

poor old Montague. He was no great age, either, you know. He always walked awkwardly, of course – that limp – but he was born with that . . .' He shook his head, and pinched the bridge of his nose with his forefinger and thumb.

'He was such a gifted story-teller,' said Ambrose, sadly. 'It's how I always thought of him, you know. A spinner of stories.'

'But aren't we all story-spinners?' said Jack, still staring at the letter. 'What else is acting out a piece of fiction on a lighted stage for an audience, if it isn't spinning a story?'

'Although you never knew quite how much to believe of his stories,' said Daphnis.

'He taught me almost everything I know,' said Byron, his eyes far away. 'I thought he'd go on teaching me. He was the most remarkable forger you'd ever meet. Did you know there's a certain painting in the National Gallery that . . .' He broke off and shook his head.

'And to think,' said Cecily, dissolving in tears, 'that he'll never tread these boards again.'

'But let's remember he trod them a great many times,' said Daphnis, firmly. 'And he never allowed that limp to hamper him. He'll have tripped over something, of course – one of those wretched footstools he kept littered around the house, I daresay. That house has always been shockingly untidy – even for someone with two sound legs.'

'I used to offer to go in with brooms and mops,' said Cecily, 'but Montague would never hear of it. I think he even enjoyed living in all that disarray.'

Ambrose said, 'There'll be a good deal of stuff to sort through. Certainly there'll be things we'll have to search for.'

A sudden silence fell, and Tansy, looking from one face to another, had the feeling that they were all silently sharing something that none of them wanted to put into words.

Then with an air of impatience, Aunt Daphnis said, 'I suppose we all know what Ambrose means.'

She stopped and Jack said, slowly, 'The famous iron box.'

No one spoke for some moments, but Jack was aware of shared memories thrusting forward. He thought, though, that what had always snared the family's attention was not that Montague, the incorrigible story-weaver, had woven a tale around the infamous iron box. It was the fact that he had not. He had merely smiled the slightly mischievous smile, and left it to everyone's imagination as to what the box might contain.

It was Ambrose who finally spoke. 'D'you know, out of all the stories Montague used to spin, the hints about the iron box stayed in my mind more than anything else.'

'Because that was all he would ever say,' nodded Byron.

Daphnis said, 'But did anyone ever believe it actually existed?'

'Of course it didn't exist,' said Rudraige, firmly. 'It was Montague enjoying himself, creating an air of mystery. It was the story he refused to tell.'

Jack was grateful to them all for understanding about this, but he said, 'Are we so sure it didn't exist, though?'

'I always thought it was a myth,' said Byron. 'No more real than – than the armour of Beowulf, or the Glamis monster.'

'In Notting Hill?'

'Yes, but even if the box does exist, would you ever find it in all that untidiness?' said Cecily.

'It probably wouldn't be in the house anyway. Montague would have stashed it somewhere romantic and gothic,' said Byron. 'A crumbling gazebo in the back of beyond, or at the bottom of a lonely lake. Full fathoms five, and suffering a sea-change into something rich and strange.'

'But,' said Jack, 'however untidy the house is, we'll have to go through all his stuff. I think, though,' he said, thoughtfully, 'that we'd better keep the legal profession out of it. At the start, anyway.'

'Of course we will,' said Rudraige. 'When did any of us have anything to do with solicitors? Prying creatures, solicitors – looking into matters that don't concern them—'

'And possibly turning up things we don't want known,' put in Ambrose. 'There'll probably be the Title Deeds to the house somewhere, of course, and we'll have to find out what's to be done about the place – how it's been left and so on.'

'Left to the family, I'd imagine,' said Jack. 'Which would mean we'd sell it and divide the proceeds. Ambrose, you'll be the best person to look into that. Will you come out to the house with me?'

'I will, of course.'

'I'd like to come, too,' said Byron. 'We need to find Montague's notes about the Gainsborough filch before anyone else does, as well.'

'Are we going on with that?' Cecily wanted to know. 'As a memorial to Uncle Montague, perhaps?'

'It would be nice to think we could,' said Byron.

Jack said, 'What do you think about bringing in Todworthy Inkling to help with cataloguing Montague's books?'

There was a thoughtful silence, then Daphnis said, 'Would Tod venture as far as Notting Hill? He hardly ever emerges from that bookshop, and he likes to stay in his own part of the City – Covent Garden, a few streets around St Martin-in-the-Fields and Seven Dials. It's part of his legend.'

'Oh, rot, Tod Inkling goes out and about far more than he lets on,' said Rudraige. 'There are several coffee houses near Drury Lane he frequents. He's been known to eat at Rules as well – get him in the right mood and he'll tell you how he used to see Henry Irving there. Mind you, I used to see Irving there myself on occasions. He'd pop in on matinee days. I've eaten with him, in fact,' said Rudraige, with studied nonchalance. 'Steak and kidney pudding, between his Richard III and his Othello, it was. Jack – tell Tod Inkling we're prepared to pay a fee for cataloguing the books. That'll bring him.'

TWO

Mr Todworthy Inkling, sought out by Jack the following day, emerged from his lair at the back of the Covent Garden bookshop, and expressed himself delighted to see such an esteemed and valued customer.

He dared say it would be a business matter that had brought Mr Jack to the shop, would it . . .? Ah, then in that case they would talk in private, since you could never be sure who might be prowling around.

'Pickers-up of unconsidered trifles, that's what we get here – and I don't just mean the theft of my stock.' He glanced over his shoulder; rather, thought Jack, in the manner of a player in a Feydeau comedy, where suspicious husbands tiptoed along corridors, hoping to catch errant spouses in bedrooms other than their own.

'Scandal-gathering, that's what some people come here for, Mr Jack,' said Todworthy. 'Of course, I never allow a shred of gossip to escape these walls.'

'I'm very glad to hear it,' said Jack, remembering the many extremely confidential pieces of business that had been conducted on these premises, and following Tod between bookshelves creaking under the weight of their contents, and around tables piled with folios of miscellaneous documents. Tod's private room was at the rear of the building, and incredibly had not been liberated to the brightness of gas lights, so that oil lamps stood around the room, and there was a general air of paraffin and old leather. Few of Mr Inkling's customers came in here; Jack thought not many of them even knew the room existed. He noticed, though, that a telephone stood on one side of the desk, which was certainly a recent innovation.

Tod waved his visitor to a chair, rearranged the crimson velvet smoking cap without which he had never been seen, and expressed himself as very much saddened and shocked at the news of Montague Fitzglen's sudden death.

'I knew him very well, of course,' he said, and Jack nodded, because Tod had known the entire Fitzglen clan for a great many years.

'A very astute gentleman,' said Tod. 'Very convivial company, as well. Dear me, this is very sad. I have many memories – even times when . . .' He frowned and broke off, as if stepping back from something he had been about to say. 'Please accept my deepest and sincerest condolences, Mr Jack.'

'Thank you.' Jack was intrigued to know what memories Tod had looked back on, but the shutters had obviously come down, so he said, 'We would like your help with cataloguing some of the contents of his house. It's crammed to the rafters with papers and books and documents, and we would be very grateful for your expert eye.'

Mr Inkling sat back and revolved his thumbs, and Jack waited.

'As you know, I do not, as a rule, often venture very far beyond my own part of the City,' said Tod, at length. 'But for a Fitzglen house – and Mr Montague . . . There's no knowing what might be in those rooms.' Again there was the sense of some memory resurrecting itself in Todworthy's agile brain, then he made a dismissive gesture, sat up a little straighter, and said, 'I don't see why I couldn't travel out to – Notting Hill, isn't it? And if my knowledge will be of any use to your family, Mr Jack, I should be very pleased to place it at your disposal.'

He did not say, 'For a fee', because they both knew Todworthy Inkling never did anything without payment. So Jack only said, 'Could you manage tomorrow? I'll be at the house for most of the day.'

Mr Inkling consulted the pages of a leather-bound diary, and said he could come along at eleven o'clock, if that would suit.

'A very intriguing prospect,' he said, making a note in his diary. 'And now, could I persuade you to drink a glass of malmsey with me in memory of Mr Montague?'

Montague Fitzglen's house, seen by a grey morning light, did not, at first sight, look as if it contained any notable secrets. From the street, it was simply a tall, white-fronted house, whose general demeanour suggested that once inside, the visitor would find himself in a somewhat dusty and probably dishevelled interior. It looked exactly as it had always looked, which was very comforting of it.

As Jack went up the steps to unlock the door, he was remembering how Montague had distributed several sets of keys around the family some years previously – 'Because none of you know when it might be useful for you to have a discreet bolt-hole,' he had said.

Jack felt a fresh pang of loss, and he was glad Byron and Ambrose – Gus, too – were with him. Byron and Ambrose shared the memories of this house, and Gus would find interest anywhere if there was likely to be some benefit to the Fitzglens. Last night, ironing shirts in Jack's dressing room, he had said there was no knowing what they might find in Mr Montague's house. He hoped Mr Jack did not mind him saying that, but he knew all about story-telling – hadn't Pa Pocket spun tales of his own while working Bond Street or the Burlington Arcade, using them to cover the deft lifting of a wallet or purse belonging to some toff. Jack, who always enjoyed Gus's reminiscences, had often thought it was not surprising that Tod Inkling had suggested a much younger Gus might be a useful addition to the Fitzglens all those years ago. And Gus had fitted in as if the situation had been tailored for him.

As Jack unlocked the door, a hansom cab rattled along the street, and Cecily Fitzglen got out, hung about with mops and brushes and dusters.

'She didn't say she was coming, did she?' demanded Jack of Byron.

'No, but we should have expected it.'

As he spoke, a nearby church chimed eleven, and a hansom drew up and disgorged Todworthy Inkling.

'And the famous crimson smoking cap nicely in evidence,' said Byron. 'That should make the locals sit up a bit.'

Todworthy was carrying a large portmanteau of the style made popular by Mr Gladstone some forty years earlier, and it took several journeys to get Tod, the portmanteau, and Cecily's cleaning implements up the steps to the house.

'And now *en avant*,' said Byron, as Jack finally opened the door. 'Cry God for Harry, England and St George, and . . . Oh, my goodness,' he said, as the door swung inwards. 'Uncle Montague's Turkish cigarettes! Doesn't that bring back the memories?'

'Very unhealthy,' said Cecily. 'I should have brought some of my dried lavender.'

The rooms were dim, because the neighbour who had discovered Montague's body had closed all the curtains in the accepted tradition of a bereaved house, but Gus and Cecily were already drawing them back. An uncertain daylight slanted into the house, sending the dust motes dancing.

They agreed that Jack would search the two big rooms at the front of the house, Byron would investigate the rooms at the back, and Ambrose would explore the bedrooms. Tod Inkling had already gravitated to a small room opening off the half-landing, which Montague had used as a book room. Jack considered for a moment whether Tod might quietly slide any choice specimens he found into the Gladstone bag, but although Tod was a shocking old rogue, he was not an outright thief – at least, not when it came to such long-standing friends and clients as the Fitzglens.

Cecily headed for the sculleries, taking Gus with her, and could be heard directing him to light the copper and boil plenty of water.

Jack surveyed the clutter in the main living room with slight dismay, then resolutely began opening cupboards and cabinets and desks. There were memories everywhere – all the years when he and his cousins would come to this house and listen, entranced, to Great Uncle Montague's stories. Rainy Sunday afternoons when they would read the plays he brought out, taking all the different parts in turn . . . Marvellous training, that had been. There had been intriguing glimpses into the past, as well – old posters and playbills and newspaper cuttings of plays staged at the Amaranth by their parents and grandparents, many of them before Jack and Ambrose and the others were born. He would try to find those – the younger members of the family would like to see them. He had a sudden vivid image of Tansy, in raptures over the cuttings and the playbills, and smiled.

Later, growing up, he and his cousins had been included in Montague's evening parties – noisy, relaxed gatherings, often with the slightly more raffish members of the theatre and literary world present, with food and drink circulating freely. It had been in this house that Byron had read aloud the first poem he had ever written – to considerable acclaim, apparently, although Jack had not actually heard it, because he was being given his first real initiation into the mysteries of sex in an upstairs bedroom, with a chair wedged under the door handle. He had only met the lady an hour before, and he had never seen her since. She had been enthusiastic and kind, though, and he remembered her with considerable gratitude, even though he had always felt slightly guilty at missing Byron's first public rendering of his work.

He began to search a tall glass-fronted cabinet, which stretched from the floor to the ceiling, and which was crammed with playscripts and scrapbooks and old newspapers, smiling a little at hearing Cecily from the scullery and the hall.

'—and, Gus, if you could find any Jeyes Fluid, we could scrub down the stairs. I shouldn't think I'd start visualizing poor dear Uncle Montague tumbling all the way down them, should you?'

There was a reassuring murmur from Gus, then Cecily said, 'No, of course I don't believe in ghosts, although as a girl I was very much affected by Uncle Furnival's portrayal of the ghost of Hamlet's father when I was taken to see it. The newspapers said Uncle Furnival gave a splendidly blood-curdling performance, although I didn't really understand much of the Ghost's actual speech at the time.'

Gus said, '"Ay, that incestuous, that adulterate beast . . . O wicked wit and gifts, that have the power so to seduce—" There isn't any Jeyes Fluid, Miss Cecily, but there's caustic soda.'

Jack thought if Montague Fitzglen's shade did walk through this house, it would be a kindly and slightly mischievous ghost. He would be chuckling to see his family searching for his notes about the Gainsborough forgery, and also the fabled iron box, which most likely had never existed.

He reached up to a stack of scrapbooks, pulling into place one of the beaded footstools which were scattered around the house and which Montague Fitzglen used to prop up his weak leg. There were bundles of old cuttings with the scrapbooks, dating to the 1860s; Jack lifted them down then saw, behind them, pushed to the very back, something with a domed lid and a large old-fashioned lock. Something black and deep . . .

He stood very still, staring at it. It would not be the fabled iron box, of course. Probably it was a cash box or a repository for important papers – the deeds of this house, for instance.

There were faint sounds of floorboards overhead creaking, which would be Ambrose exploring the contents of the bedrooms, and Cecily's voice asking Gus to find a stepladder so that they could take down the lace curtains to wash. But the voices seemed to reach him from a long way off, and Jack had to fight off the feeling that something had crept into the room, and was watching him.

He lifted the box from its shelf, and set it on the desk by the window. He was surprised at how heavy it was, but if it was iron, then of course it would be heavy. Would it be locked? It would not matter if it was, because when had a lock ever prevented him – or any of the Fitzglens – from opening a door or a safe or a cupboard? Or a black box, bound with iron strips, with a slightly domed lid studded with brass studs . . .

The box was not locked, but it took several attempts to prise up the lid, because there was an accretion of dust and dirt in the seams. But at last, with a reluctant sigh, it gave way, and the lid folded back.

It was an extraordinary moment. All around him the house's floors creaked as Byron and Ambrose and the others moved around, but the sounds belonged to another world.

Within the box lay a sheaf of papers. They were covered in thin, sloping handwriting, the ink slightly faded to pale brown in places, but the writing itself perfectly readable. And the topmost page was very clear indeed.

THE MURDERER INSIDE THE MIRROR
A Drama in Three Acts of Murder, Revenge and Terror
by
Phelan Rafferty

Phelan Rafferty, thought Jack, staring at the writing. *Phelan Rafferty.* The man acknowledged as one of Ireland's finest gothic dramatists in the last half of the nineteenth century. The play-wright critics said dredged up people's deepest nightmares and placed them on a stage. Spoken of in the same breath as Robert Louis Stevenson, Wilkie Collins and George du Maurier.

He looked at the faded pages again. *The Murderer Inside the Mirror.* Rafferty had never written a play with that title, had he?

In any case, Phelan Rafferty had died five years ago.

THREE

Jack was immediately aware of a strong sense of reluctance to even touch the faded pages, but he pushed the feeling away and lifted the papers out, setting them on the desk. After the title page he expected to see the usual list of characters and scenes, but the second page had only a single stage direction at the top – *The curtain rises on a darkened room, clearly a prison cell. There are stone walls and a barred window.*

Jack glanced over his shoulder to the closed door leading out to the hall, then turned back and began to read.

> *Tomás:* Maran – I'm thankful they let you come in, Maran. You know there are only two days left now – two days for the reprieve to come?
>
> *Maran:* I know it. But there's still time, Tomás. And you do know that if there's no reprieve, I'll be here in two days' time?
>
> *Tomás:* (*Gesture of anger and frustration*). I never thought it would end this way. It was my inheritance I was trying to reach – you knew that, didn't you? Catrina knew it, too. She understood. Maran – was I mad, that night? And on all those other nights when we made those incredible plans?
>
> *Maran:* You're many things, but you were never mad, Tomás. You could never be mad, not even now.
>
> *Tomás:* Not even now – while I'm counting the hours until eight o'clock chimes?
>
> *Maran:* Not even then.
>
> *Lights dim. Curtain.*

The scene ended there, and Jack was about to turn the page, when Byron's voice said, 'Jack – I've found something extraordinary – some of Uncle Montague's notes, and I wanted you to see them straightaway, because . . . What's wrong? You look like a troll that's been caught unawares by daylight and turned to stone.' He walked over to the desk, looked at what lay on it, and said, in a completely different voice, 'My God, that's not—'

'It's Great Uncle Montague's fabled iron box,' said Jack.

Byron said, almost in a whisper, 'Then it really did exist. I never entirely believed in it, you know.'

'Nor did I. But inside it was this.' Jack indicated the script, turning back to the title page.

Byron stared at it, then, in a stunned voice, said, 'Phelan Rafferty.'

'Yes.'

'The man who wrote *The Iron Tongue of Midnight* and *The Twilight Catcher*,' said Byron, his eyes still on the page. 'And who was awarded the Richard Brinsley Sheridan Award – the one they only give every ten years.'

'I remember that award being made,' said Jack. 'I was only eight or nine, but the Amaranth staged *The Iron Tongue of Midnight* as a tribute, and Ambrose and I stole out and went down to the theatre and hid in one of the boxes and watched the entire performance. I've never forgotten it.'

'I know all Rafferty's work,' said Byron. 'I always looked up to him – tried to emulate him, even – and there aren't many people I'd admit that to. Don't mock, will you?'

'I'm not mocking,' said Jack. 'We all need something to aspire to.'

'But I'd stake my life Phelan Rafferty never wrote a play with this title.'

'So would I.'

They looked at one another. Then Jack said, 'We're both remembering Uncle Montague's particular talent, aren't we?'

'The master forger,' said Byron. 'It's what we all called him. Half in fun, but half not. It's what he called himself. Is this a forgery, Jack?'

'I don't know. But if it isn't, then we've found an unknown play by one of Ireland's greatest playwrights,' said Jack. 'A lost play. Montague knew Rafferty, didn't he?'

'Yes, quite well. I don't know how far back the friendship went, but Montague often stayed with him in Ireland.' Byron turned the page to read the start of the first scene.

'"You know we're waiting to hear about a reprieve? There are only two days left now . . ."' He looked up at Jack. 'It's a condemned man – Tomás? – counting down his remaining hours until he's executed, yes? But still hoping for a reprieve.'

'It's what it sounds like,' said Jack, his eyes on the page.

'If we take it over to the window where the light's better, we might be able to read a bit more,' suggested Byron.

Jack again had to push away the feeling that there was something in the pages of the play that would be better left undisturbed. He said, 'Yes, let's do that before anyone comes in.'

Silence closed down as they began reading. The scene was still in the stone room, with Tomás and Maran seated at the table.

> *Tomás:* I'm writing it all down, Maran – what happened that night. What we did – what we found . . . How the darkness was there. There was such a darkness in that place. Waiting . . .
> *Maran:* The darkness you wanted to destroy.
> *Tomás:* Yes. But instead, it's destroyed me.
> *Maran:* You're trying to trap it, though, aren't you? By writing it down? You're almost seeing it as a kind of exorcism.
> *Tomás:* I should have known you'd understand. Maran, when I've written it, will you keep the pages? Don't give them to the world until it's safe, though. For my sake – for Catrina's sake, as well.
> *Maran:* You have my word, Tomás, that no one will know what happened that night.

Jack was turning to the next scene when the hall door opened, to reveal Todworthy Inkling, his pince-nez firmly in place, his sharp eyes looking all around the room. Jack moved instinctively to shield the script, but Tod only said, 'I've made some cursory notes, Mr Jack. Some of those books could be quite valuable. If I could spend a day or two going through them properly, I could provide a more detailed report. Inkling's would be very happy to handle any sales, of course.'

'I'm sure we'd want you to do that, Tod.'

'Good. For now, though, I've come to remind you that a man

cannot live by bread alone, and neither can he live on the dust of antique time, no matter how scholarly or first-edition-noteworthy that dust might be,' said Tod. 'It's already one o'clock, and I am told by the invaluable Gus that there is a very tolerable coffee house along the street.'

Jack said, 'So it is. I hadn't realized how late it was.'

'We'll tidy this away and follow you,' said Byron. He waited until the door had closed and Tod's footsteps had gone down the hall, then turned to Jack.

'I was going to keep this to read to the family,' he said producing a slightly battered notebook from his pocket. 'But I think you should hear it now.'

'What is it?'

'Uncle Montague's notebook, and although there are mostly just brief jottings of ideas for filches, a couple of pages are devoted to Phelan Rafferty.' Byron opened the notebook and began to read.

'*Link between Girdlestones and Phelan Rafferty's family possibly of interest for Girdlestone/Gainsborough forgery,*' Montague Fitzglen had written. '*PR once recounted how family's name was Anglicized to allow a marriage between the families – Girdlestones were scandalized by legend of a 16C Ó Raifeartaigh ancestress who had met mysterious, macabre and probably shameful end. May only be a story – PR a maestro at story-telling! – but now think it worth investigating.*'

'PR is clearly Phelan Rafferty,' said Byron, and, as Jack nodded, he continued reading.

'*Have therefore scraped acquaintance with Lady G – a terrible woman! – and am to visit the Hall in the guise of "Mr Montgomery", a mild-mannered, slightly eccentric art expert.*

'*N.B. Forging and filching the Gainsborough probably still a good idea – will discuss with Jack and family.*'

'It sounds,' said Jack, slowly, 'as if it was the sixteenth-century lady of the macabre legend Montague was after, as much as the Gainsborough.'

'It does. Particularly,' said Byron, 'since we've discovered that Montague had in his possession a play with Phelan Rafferty's name on it. A play that, if it's genuine, must be worth an immense sum of money.'

'And that the theatre world will fight to get their hands on and stage,' said Jack. He frowned, then said, 'Were you able to find out when Montague was going to Girdlestone Hall?'

Byron grinned. 'In two days' time,' he said. 'It was in his diary.'

'Ah. Could two art experts instead of one keep that appointment?' said Jack. 'Associates of Mr Montgomery, perhaps? Polite, scholarly gentlemen they'd be—'

'Perhaps French, which would mean they mightn't understand some of the discussions?'

'And therefore be unable to answer any awkward questions they might be asked,' said Jack, pleased. It was always good to work out plans for a disguise with Byron, who invariably understood what was wanted without it having to be spelled out. He said, 'Ostensibly, they'd be there to examine the Gainsborough, but really it would be to find out more about a mysterious sixteenth-century lady.'

'And discover why Great Uncle Montague hid an unknown Phelan Rafferty work in the back of a cupboard inside an iron box,' finished Byron.

'Dammit, Jack, you should have brought that script out with you,' said Rudraige Fitzglen, angrily.

'There were too many people around,' said Jack. 'Including Tod Inkling, who never misses a thing. I wasn't risking Tod getting scent of any of this, so I put it back where I found it. It looked as if it had been there for several years – another two or three days won't matter.'

'And,' said Byron, 'we haven't been back for it yet, because Jack and I have both been on stage for the last two nights, and Jack's been rehearsing next month's piece during the day. And tomorrow we're going to keep Montague's appointment at Girdlestone Hall. Gus has everything ready for the visit, haven't you, Gus?'

'I have, Mr Byron,' said Gus, producing his notes. 'You're going to be a bit of a dandy. High wing collar and patent-leather shoes with buttoned spats over the ankles. And a handlebar moustache. Mr Jack's to have rimless spectacles and slightly crumpled suit.'

Jack said, 'We think it's important to keep the appointment. That link Montague found between the Girdlestones and the Raffertys needs investigating.'

'Montague certainly thought so,' put in Byron.

'It's a remarkable story that Jack's unearthed,' said Cecily. 'Lost plays and mysterious sixteenth-century ladies – very romantic. Tansy, don't you think it's romantic?'

'It depends what the mysterious sixteenth-century lady got up to,' said Tansy, cautiously.

'Well, one thing I will say,' said Daphnis, firmly, 'is that Gertrude Girdlestone is a selfish and greedy woman, and she deserves to be the subject of a filch. Any filch.' She glared round the table challengingly.

'Yes, but Jack's quite right to say the script will be safe,' said Cecily. 'I'll be going in and out of the house anyway over the next couple of days – there are cleaners coming in, you know, and somebody has to oversee them. Caterers, as well, to talk about serving the food at the wake.'

'I'll get the script out during the wake itself,' said Jack. 'No one will notice if I wander into the study and come out with a few books and papers. Uncle Montague was very well known, so there're bound to be a good many people milling around.'

'Most of them there as much to see if they can unearth any scandals from Montague's past than to mourn his death,' said Rudraige.

'Did Great Uncle Montague have any scandals in his past?' enquired Tansy, hopefully.

'Bound to have, my dear. Everyone has.'

'I thought we'd give the mourners smoked salmon and foie gras,' said Cecily. 'And Byron thinks we ought to serve Amontillado and Chablis.'

'It sounds as if we'll be feeding the marauding hordes,' said Ambrose, gloomily.

'But we do need to put on a bit of a show,' said Rudraige. 'I daresay a few Gilfillans might even come along, and we don't want them saying afterwards that we cheese-pared on the funeral baked meats. I shan't speak to any of them, of course, and I especially shan't speak to that shocking ham Florian Gilfillan if he's there. I hear he's very much back in the Gilfillan fold. He was touring the north with some sort of show, so it's said, although I wouldn't be surprised if he was taking a cure somewhere. He always drank like a fish.'

'There are times when you have to forget feuds and grudges, Rudraige,' said Daphnis. 'Montague's funeral will be such a time. I know it goes against the grain, but you'll have to be polite.'

'I shall be perfectly polite,' said Rudraige with dignity.

'Look here, though, there's still one thing I don't understand,' said Ambrose, leaning forward. 'Why would Montague – who was a man of the theatre to his fingertips – conceal a play apparently written by such a distinguished author?'

'Assuming,' said Daphnis, 'that the play is by the distinguished author in question.'

'Yes, I'm assuming that for the moment. Well, Jack?'

Jack did not immediately reply. Then he said, 'I can only think of one reason why Montague kept that play hidden.' He looked round the room, then said, 'Because it might contain something damaging to this family.'

FOUR

Ethne Rafferty thought it was strange how seeing facts set
out in black-and-white newspaper print could force the past
into the present, and disturb all your feelings of safety.

She had never thought anyone would find out the truth about
her father – or about what had happened five years earlier. She
had thought she had been so clever – that she had allowed for
every eventuality.

But now had come the newspaper article. Ethne's father had
always read his newspaper over breakfast, and Ethne did the
same, because she liked to continue with his ways. It felt like
a link to him. She even had the same newspaper. But this morning
as she read it, the quiet, dim old room that overlooked the tangled
gardens surrounding the house blurred, and fear clawed at her
mind.

*The sudden death of the well-known actor and theatrical lumi-
nary, Mr Montague Fitzglen, was announced by his family earlier
this week in London,* said the article. *Mr Fitzglen – a distinguished
member of the well-known theatrical family – had been a familiar
figure to audiences for many years, and although his appearances
on stage were less frequent in recent years, many theatre-goers
will remember his splendid performances at the family's theatre,
the Amaranth. (See page 6 for reminiscences of Mr Fitzglen's
life and career.)*

*A service and interment will take place at 11 o'clock on the
morning of Friday 14th, at St Martin-in-the-Fields – often known
as the 'actors' church' – after which friends and mourners are
cordially invited to Mr Fitzglen's Notting Hill house for
refreshments.*

It was all conventional and entirely what was to be expected.
The Fitzglens would not miss any opportunity to publicize their
name and the name of their theatre. But what Ethne had not
expected was that a lengthy article about Montague Fitzglen's
career would be published. It was infuriating to discover that her

hands were shaking as she turned to page 6, because none of
this could pose any kind of threat. There would not be anything
that could draw attention to Westmeath – to this house – and
certainly not to Ethne herself . . .

But there was. There was a list of the plays in which Montague
Fitzglen had performed over the years – Ethne skimmed these,
because they were nothing more than the Fitzglens boasting about
their achievements again. But a later paragraph was different.

*Among his many notable colleagues and friends, for many
years Montague Fitzglen was closely associated with the distinguished Irish playwright, Mr Phelan Rafferty, whom theatre-goers
will remember as the author of plays such as* The Twilight
Catcher, *and* The Iron Tongue of Midnight.

*Mr Fitzglen is known to have been a frequent visitor to Mr
Rafferty's house in Westmeath – the house that is believed to
have been originally occupied by the ancient hereditary bardic
family, the Ó Raifeartaighs, and that is said to date back to
around the early fourteenth century. Since Phelan Rafferty's own
untimely death some five years ago, the house is lived in by his
daughter, Miss Ethne Rafferty.*

There it was. The link between Montague Fitzglen and Ethne's
father, clearly set out. Even Ethne herself referred to by name.
The fear gave way to anger, because it was as if whoever had
written it wanted it to be thought that he – it might even be a
she – had actually known Ethne's father. But no one had known
Phelan completely – no one had been as close to him as Ethne.

Her mother had died when Ethne was born, so it had only
ever been herself and her father, living together in this big,
ramshackle house, sufficient company for each other. Of course,
there had been times when Phelan had had to go to Dublin –
even London, sometimes – to meet people to talk about his
plays, and to attend first nights. When she was older, she had
sometimes accompanied him; nervous, but immensely proud to
be at his side.

He often had to accept invitations that Ethne knew he did not
want to accept. Late-night supper parties and dinners – gentlemen-
only gatherings, they were. Brandy and cigars and card games.
He said they were rather tedious, but you never knew when you
might find yourself sitting next to some influential theatre owner

or what was called an angel – a wealthy man who liked to finance the staging of plays. Ethne always remained in the hotel on those nights, of course. Often, her father did not return until the small hours of the morning, but no matter how tedious an evening he might have spent, he was invariably bright-eyed and relaxed, and he always ate a very large breakfast.

But at Westmeath House there did not need to be any late-night suppers or brandy-flavoured discussions with gentlemen. Ethne could shield Phelan from the world – ensure he had uninterrupted peace to work and research and write his plays. There were some interruptions that could not be avoided, of course: the nuns from St Joseph's occasionally called, and they could not be turned away, because they had known Ethne since she was a small child attending the convent's school. Sister Clare, who still taught history to the convent's pupils, was diligent in visiting; she was interested in the house, and in Ethne's family, who were supposed to be descended from ancient Irish bards.

Occasionally people would come to the house to get close to the famous playwright himself – to warm their hands at the glowing flame of his genius, one of the more fanciful ones said. Ethne was always very watchful, because some of them were only wanting to further their own careers.

Mr Montague Fitzglen was one visitor who Ethne did not try to keep away, though. He was a very old friend of her father's, and the two of them sometimes toured theatres, often in England, frequently for Phelan to give lectures to theatre groups or literary societies. Ethne did not accompany them on those trips. Her father missed her, of course, but he said Mr Fitzglen was great company. He often brought him back to Westmeath afterwards, for a week or two's relaxation, which was perfectly acceptable.

The visit of the young actor who came to Westmeath one summer seemed perfectly acceptable as well. When Ethne looked back, it felt as if that had been when it had all started.

The actor had told Ethne that he had wanted to meet Phelan Rafferty for some years – that he was very grateful to be able to do so at last, and that he saw his visit as a pilgrimage. Ethne thought this was a marvellous thing to say, although after she had talked to the actor several times, she realized he might not be quite as young as she had first thought. But it did not matter; he was friendly and interested in everything, and it was clear that he regarded Phelan Rafferty with immense admiration. He told Ethne it was wonderful to sit at the feet of such a man – theoretically speaking, of course; to drink in all the knowledge and the wisdom and the understanding of the stage and the craft of acting. He loved the library, which was where Ethne's father spent most of his day. The actor said it was small wonder that Phelan Rafferty was able to create the extraordinary atmosphere in his plays with such a place in which to work.

After a few days, the actor took to walking with Ethne in the gardens as night was falling. In the soft twilight, you could hardly see that the gardens were overgrown or neglected, nor could you see that the old orchard had run wild, on account of there hardly ever being money for gardeners. Ethne's father always said the important thing was that the land was still theirs. And couldn't you smell the apples from inside the house on a warm autumn day, which was a delight to a man, and it did not matter that the grass often grew to waist-height, partly hiding the sundial put there by Seamus Rafferty a century and a half ago, following his extravagant Grand Tour of Europe.

And, said Phelan, if the occasional courting couple from the village sneaked into the orchard and lay together in the long grass for an hour or two, who was he to object? Seamus would not have objected, either, he said, and his face with the wide, mobile mouth and the vividly blue eyes, would break into the mischievous grin that had caused a great many shameless ladies to try to get close to Phelan over the years. Ethne had seen them on those trips to Dublin theatres, although her father had never looked at any of them, because he was unswervingly faithful to the memory of her mother, and he only needed Ethne herself as companion.

The actor liked the gardens. When Ethne said, a bit hesitantly, that she always thought of them as dreamlike, even enchanted, he at once said, yes, that described it exactly.

She showed him the old sundial, which had carved into its stone surface the words, 'Voyage, travel, and change of place impart vigour . . . *Seneca.*'

Seneca had been a Roman philosopher, although Ethne's father had often said it was a pity that Seamus Rafferty, commissioning the sundial, had not imparted some vigour into the financial side of his life, because his lavish travels to study the architecture of Rome and Vienna and Budapest had certainly hastened the ruin of the Rafferty architecture.

On the fourth night in the old orchard, the actor kissed Ethne – the first man ever to do so. There was no reason not to allow it, although of course she would not permit anything more, and he would not expect it.

But he did. Two nights later he brought with him a flagon of wine, which they drank half-lying in the long grass. There was a scent of pears from the orchard and the wine was sweet and heady, and he said she was inspiring him to make love to her, and he did not think anything – not poppy nor mandragora, nor all the drowsy syrups of the world – could quench his longing to do so. Before Ethne quite knew what was happening, he was pressing up against her, and his hands were sliding beneath her skirts.

She thought at some point she said, 'No,' but she could not be absolutely sure because the wine was making everything spin, and she was not even certain if this was happening to her or whether it was happening to somebody else and she was only a spectator.

He said, 'I won't do anything you don't want, I promise . . . But you're so lovely – such beautiful soft brown hair, and blue eyes that would pierce a man's heart. Just let me feel . . . Ah, that's good, isn't it – isn't that good . . .?'

Ethne had always supposed, a bit vaguely, that you had to get undressed to perform this particular act, but it seemed you did not. It seemed all that had to happen was for someone to unfasten buttons and slide down parts of your clothing and his clothing too.

When he took her hand and pulled it down – down *there* – she gasped, because although you could not grow up in the country without seeing what happened between animals and understanding that much the same thing happened with men and women, it was still a shock to feel her hand being forced to close around him in such a way. It did not feel in the least how she had expected, but he was gasping that she was beautiful, and he could not bear to stop, and didn't this feel so good – and this—

The nuns at school had stressed, very firmly, that there were certain acts you did not allow until after holy matrimony, and that if you did perform them or allow them beforehand, you would have committed a mortal sin. They had not described the act or the sin, of course, but most of the class had a fair idea of what it was, and they agreed afterwards that it could not be as dreadful as Sister Marie, who taught biology, had tried to make out or nobody would ever do it, either before or after holy matrimony. Probably, in fact, it would turn out to be enjoyable, although it would depend on who you did it with, of course.

Even so, Ethne thought it would be as well not to endanger her immortal soul – and her father would be ashamed of her if he found out – so she gasped out to the actor that what he so clearly wanted to do was only permissible after holy matrimony.

He said at once that of course it was only permissible after marriage, but hadn't she realized he had fallen deeply in love with her – from the moment he had seen her, in fact. He quoted one or two lines that Ethne thought were either from *Romeo and Juliet* or possibly *The Taming of the Shrew*, and she was just thinking she would prefer the former to the latter, when he said, 'And I want to marry you. We can be together forever – the three of us, I mean, because I know you wouldn't want to leave Phelan. But we'd all live here together. Wouldn't that be wonderful?'

Ethne wanted to weep at the way he understood about not leaving her father and wanting them all to live together. She heard herself say, 'Oh, yes . . .' on a soft whispering note, and at once he pulled her against him, and said they would be together forever.

'I shall speak to your father in the morning. But now, here – tonight – we can be together properly, can't we . . .? To seal the bond . . .?'

His voice held such a caress, like silk or soft velvet, and Ethne knew her father would be so very pleased at the news of their marriage – and delighted that he would not be losing her . . . There would be a ceremony in church or even in the convent's own chapel, with Ethne wearing white satin and lace . . . And afterwards they would all live together, and her life would be filled to the brim with happiness and contentment.

'And so,' he said, the caress still in his voice, 'you'll say yes to me now, won't you . . .? You'll let me do this . . . And this . . .'

There was a brief confusing sensation of a hard, fleshy warmth being forced between her thighs, and then there was a pain like a deep bruise inside her, but of course it was wonderful and magical – it was what people wrote poetry about and vowed to die for . . . And it was perfectly all right to be doing it – it could not be classed as a mortal sin, or even a venial one, because they were going to be married, and then they were going to be together forever.

They were not even together the following morning, because her father walked into the breakfast room, and said, as if it were the most trivial of matters, that their guest had left earlier, and would not be returning to Westmeath.

'An opportunist,' he said. 'But a sly one. I didn't see through him at first. But he had his plan all worked out – down to learning speeches that he could quote in particular situations. A pity he got some of them wrong, wasn't it, but . . . Is that a new pot of honey on the table? Pass it over, would you? Yes, he was out for his own ends – he believed I could further his career. I couldn't and I wouldn't anyway, for he'll be a very indifferent player, that was clear from the beginning. A villain as false as hell, he was, with no more faith in him than in a stewed prune. Shakespeare and Henry IV had the right of it when they said that.'

He buttered a slice of toast and spread honey on it.

'I wouldn't be surprised to hear he even tried flirting with you, my dear, as part of the plan,' he said, rather vaguely. 'As a way to wheedle himself into my good graces.' He took a large bite of the toast, then said, 'You'd have had the sense to see that for what it was, though.'

Ethne, staring at him, feeling as if the entire world was tumbling in pieces around her head, managed to say, 'Oh, yes, yes, of course I would.'

He considered her for a moment, his head on one side, and for a really strange moment there was a look on his face that Ethne did not recall ever seeing there before. And then she saw it had only been the morning sunlight, because he smiled in the familiar way, and said, 'Good girl. Anyhow, I've sent the wretch to the rightabout, and he slunk away at break of dawn, like the cowardly runion he was.' He stood up. 'And I'll be off to the library now, because if the creature did nothing else, he provided me with inspiration for a splendid new character. A frosty, February-faced fool in Act Two it's going to be – I see it already – so I'll be getting it all down on paper before it slithers away from my mind, and I probably won't appear for luncheon.'

He then remarked cheerfully that they had had a very Shakespearean breakfast and there was nothing like a few touches of the Bard to liven up the day, and went out of the room, his mind clearly already on the February-faced fool in Act Two.

Ethne stared at the crumbled food on her plate, and wondered if she would ever be able to eat another morsel in her entire life. Last night she had committed a mortal sin, and all for what? For a painful, messy experience that had lasted approximately eight minutes – not that she had timed it exactly, but she remembered hearing St Joseph's clock chime the quarter-hour – and really, if that was the act that ballad-makers sung about and lovers vowed to die for then, as far as Ethne was concerned, you could keep it.

When it came down to it, there were only two men she could trust. One was her father, of course. He would never let her down, just as she would never let him down.

The other was a young man who had lived and died more than three hundred years ago.

His name was Thomas Fitzgerald – he had been the 10th Earl of Kildare and his followers had called him Silken Thomas. His portrait hung in a half-forgotten room near the top of Westmeath House, although no one seemed to know how it had come to be in the house – or who had painted it. Ethne's father certainly had never seemed to know.

'It's too far back in the past,' he had said, when the small Ethne, fascinated by the painting, questioned him.

But ever since she could remember, when she was troubled, Ethne almost always went to sit in front of Thomas's portrait, and she did so today, taking her favourite place in the deep window seat with faded cushions. A ray of slanting sunlight trickled through the small window just under the eaves, and fell across the portrait, so that Thomas's hair and the soft beard framing his features glowed like beaten copper.

Telling Thomas what had happened in the orchard helped push away the memory of the man Ethne's father had called a February-faced runion. Thomas would understand and he would be angry on Ethne's behalf. He had never flinched from displaying anger. Sister Clare had taught the girls about him in history lessons, and she had told them how he had been put to death for his beliefs and his rebellion more than three hundred years ago. He had refused to accept what he had called the yoke of Henry VIII of England, she had said – people had often called him the Rebel Earl. But in the end, he had died for his beliefs, slaughtered by the English in the Tower of London for treason.

Staring at the portrait today, fragments of memories – insubstantial as the glimmer of marsh-lights – flickered across Ethne's mind. Things half-heard as a child, never quite forgotten, but never wholly understood. Things passed down in whispers through the generations. Things that had never got into the history books – perhaps had not been allowed to get into them.

But trying to grasp these elusive memories was impossible, and most likely it was simply that romantic tales had been woven around Thomas. Ethne might even have spun childish stories of her own about him.

Ordinary families did not have handed-down secrets about some long-ago ancestor, though. And probably Thomas had not even been an ancestor anyway.

FIVE

The curious thing was that the following day Ethne discovered that there might be a third man she could trust – no, perhaps not trust exactly, but someone with whom she might have found an affinity. Someone she had always thought, vaguely, was irresponsible and arrogant and a spendthrift, but who was suddenly taking on a whole new guise.

It began with Phelan calling her into the library, because he had found something important and she must see it at once. It was impossible to resist him when he was like this – his eyes brilliant with some new enthusiasm or newly discovered piece of the past, delight glowing in his face. Entering the library always felt to Ethne like stepping into a different world. You never knew what you might find or be told about. Her mind flinched from how her deceitful lover had said precisely that, but at least he would not be sharing in whatever had been disinterred from the shadowy corners today.

It appeared that Phelan had discovered several letters sent to Seamus Rafferty, he of the profligate travels and the inscribed sundial.

'I wasn't looking for Seamus,' he said. 'I was working on that villain for Act Two. You remember?'

'The February-faced fool.'

'That's the one. I was scouring the shelves, more or less at random, for ideas, and purely by chance I found these.' He gestured towards the big claw-footed table near the bay window which was invariably strewn with documents and sheaves of notes in his sprawling handwriting.

'They're a bit chewed-looking,' he said, 'but they're from the 1700s, and I daresay I'd look chewed myself if I was that old. Read them.'

The letters were all from the same Dublin address, written in what looked like the same hand, and were all addressed to Seamus Rafferty Esquire. The top one was dated May 1748.

Sir,

I have the honour to send herein the fair copy of your architectural layout for the Clock Tower of Dublin Castle, which you commissioned at our meeting last month, and which has been taken from your own sketches.

I beg to enclose a note of the fee for this work.

Trusting you will find this to your satisfaction, I am, dear sir, yours most respectfully,

E. L. Maguire, *accredited copyist of all manuscripts, written and pictorial works. Est 1536*

The second letter was from August of the same year.

Sir,

I beg to draw to your attention, the fact that my account remains unsettled, and I would most respectfully request that you give this your early attention.

Humbly yours,

E. L. Maguire

The third letter, which bore a date of November, held a note of indignant reproach.

Sir,

Whilst understanding – and, indeed, sympathizing – with your present difficulties, I would beg to point out that I, too, have calls on my finances, but that mine do not include tailors' or wine merchants' accounts (which you have described as 'extremely pressing'). My obligations are for more mundane necessities, and include the rental of my premises here in Dublin, the purchase of such materials as paper, ink, and quills so I may continue in my business as a copyist, and basic requirements of food, candles and clothing.

I would therefore again request that you give your most urgent attention to the outstanding monies for the work provided for you.

Respectfully yours, dear sir,

E. L. Maguire

'Wasn't he the arrogant one, that Seamus,' said Phelan. 'And you'd have to feel sympathy with that poor Maguire, wouldn't you?'

'I wonder if Seamus ever did pay him?' said Ethne, studying the letters again.

'Oh, he probably hadn't the funds to do so – it's always been said he'd go from flamboyant wealth to virtual penury in the blink of a gnat's whisker. I wish I could find the map he commissioned from Maguire – or even Seamus's own original sketches – but I've scoured the shelves and there's no trace. But see here, there's a final letter Maguire wrote to Seamus, and he really does lam into the old reprobate. Read it for yourself.'

Mr Maguire had written:

Sir,

I am in receipt of your most recent missive, which to my grave disappointment did not include a draft for the amount due.

Your threats butter no parsnips with me, sir, as do not your boasts about your ancestry. I do not care how many swashbuckling rebel earls you have in your lineage or how many of them fought for Ireland's freedom. To give you the word with no bark on it, Mr Rafferty, I do not give a fig if you have half the crowned heads of Europe among your ancestors, so please do not hold that over me as a veiled threat.

I ask only that you behave as a man of honour and accept your responsibility to pay your debts. If you do not, I shall be forced to cause to descend on you an army of bailiffs, who will march on your house, brandishing writs.

Respectfully, yours,

E. L. Maguire

'I wonder if Maguire did send the bailiffs out here,' said Ethne's father, as she put down the letter. 'Wouldn't you die of the shame of that?'

Ethne scarcely heard him; she was staring at E. L. Maguire's letter. If Seamus had indeed written about rebel earls in his family, who fought for Ireland's freedom, surely he must have meant

Thomas of Kildare? For the first time she saw Seamus Rafferty not as the spendthrift wastrel he had always been portrayed – a man who had taken his financial obligations lightly – but as someone who had looked into his family's history and found Thomas – perhaps had found the portrait in the upper gallery, even. And then, deciding Thomas could be an ancestor, had been proud of him. She liked this.

She forced her attention back to her father, who was saying there was one more letter he had found.

'It's from the Surveyor General – embossed notepaper, very impressive. It's about the mysterious map again.'

Sir,

We are most grateful for your communications regarding our plans for the Clock Tower in Dublin Castle, and also for your expressed wish to be involved in our work.

It is interesting to hear that you made the Grand Tour and were able to study some of the fine architecture in France and Germany and Italy. That, sir, is a privilege not available to many these days.

I and my committee have studied the map you submitted to us with interest. There are one or two aspects of your proposals we feel have scant relevance to what is intended for Dublin Castle's Clock Tower, but if you find yourself able to attend a meeting at my offices here on the tenth of January next, at which we could discuss this matter more fully, I and my colleagues would esteem it a favour.

I am, good sir, yours faithfully . . .

There followed an elaborately scrawled signature which was virtually indecipherable.

Ethne said, carefully, 'They seem to have taken his suggestion fairly seriously.'

'It may only have been politeness. He might well have met with a courteous refusal when he went to the castle. Still, his travels probably gave him a genuine interest in architecture,' said Phelan. 'I'll bet he romped around the palaces of Europe in high old style – small wonder the family money trickled away. I wish I could get my hands on the letters Seamus sent to Maguire –

and to the Surveyor General – because these only give us half the picture. And,' he said, half to himself, 'on the map itself.'

For a moment his eyes held a strange, faraway look, and Ethne sought for something to say to bring him back. But then he got up and went out of the room, doing so abruptly, almost as if he had lost interest in Seamus Rafferty. But most likely he had been right that Seamus had become interested in architecture after his travels and wanted to be part of the castle's restoration. She would not give any of it another thought.

She would not give the faithless cheating actor another thought, either. He would never return to this house, and Ethne would never need to see him again.

SIX

As Jack and Byron walked out of the small railway halt and went through the imposing stone pillars that guarded the entrance to Girdlestone Hall, Jack was aware that the rush of energy and excitement he normally felt when approaching the venue of a new filch was absent.

His father used to say there was nothing like the moment when you first looked at a house, knowing you were going to enter it stealthily and secretly. And that you were going to take away valuable objects without the owners catching you.

'But,' he had said to the much younger Jack, 'we only ever steal from the very rich – and from people who deserve to lose a portion of their wealth. That's a Fitzglen rule, and it has been all the way back to my great-grandfather – your great-great-grandfather. Highwayman Harry he was called, and he held up the carriages and coaches of the richest lords and ladies, and asked – very politely – for the ladies to hand over their jewels.'

'And they always did,' Jack used to say.

'Oh, yes, always,' Aiden would reply, with a grin. 'I believe there were times where a closer association sometimes resulted, too.' There would be a sideways glance, then some remark about Jack understanding better when he was older.

'But,' Aiden usually added, 'Harry never took from anyone who wasn't very rich, and nor do we. We never ever take from people who have worked to make their bit of money, or people who might be injured or damaged in some way if their possessions were stolen. You must promise you'll always remember that, Jack.'

Jack had promised, of course, and he had never forgotten that promise.

Today, he was intrigued to see if there was evidence of the dishonourable Rafferty lady, and whether Montague could have found links between her and the play hidden in his house. But he could not forget how, when he held the manuscript for *The*

Murderer Inside the Mirror in his hands, he had received the impression of something dark and twisted within its pages. Had Montague felt that? Was that why he had hidden the play where it was unlikely to be found? Or was it more down-to-earth – did those pages hide something damaging – something about the Fitzglen family? Had Jack missed some subtle reference? He reminded himself that he had only read the first scene.

Lady Girdlestone received them with gracious condescension, and led them through the vast old house to its upper floors.

'The Gainsborough portrait,' she said, 'has been in this family for more than a century.'

'So we understand.'

'I met Mr Montgomery a few weeks ago – a private gallery viewing in the Academy, it was. A charming gentleman, and very learned.'

'Very,' agreed Jack, straight-faced.

'We sat together for some while – he appeared to have injured his foot, so I felt it was only kind to sit down with him. He told me about his planned book on Thomas Gainsborough, and how the Girdlestone portrait might add to the research,' she said, as they ascended a badly lit stairway. 'It sounded a very worthy work.'

'It will be a most erudite book, of course,' said Byron. 'It would be a privilege to include your painting, and to tell of its history.'

'And naturally, there would be suitable acknowledgement made to you and to this house in it,' put in Jack.

Lady Girdlestone supposed this would be acceptable.

'And I daresay there will be some form of remuneration . . .? Not that I concern myself with such things, of course— Be careful of that stair. It is somewhat loose.'

'Loose floorboards are frequently to be found in old houses,' said Byron, who had narrowly avoided tripping over the up-jutting floorboard and had, Jack thought, only just managed to suppress a curse that would not have been entirely suitable for the character of a French academic.

The gallery was lined with paintings of a number of somewhat unprepossessing Girdlestones, and Byron enjoyed himself describing the historic chateau of his own ancestors.

'Lost to Robespierre and the sans-culottes,' he said, borrowing from Rudraige the gesture of pinching the bridge of his nose between his thumb and forefinger. Jack hoped he was not going to overdo it.

'Here is the Gainsborough,' said Lady Girdlestone as they reached the far end of the gallery. 'I've always considered it rather pallid, I'm afraid. I like a painting to be rich and colourful.'

'But the use of cooler colours is a distinctive aspect of Thomas Gainsborough's work, madame,' said Jack, and thought their hostess would not have suspected that it was as recently as last evening that he had committed this information to memory.

They considered the portrait solemnly, Byron making use of a magnifying lens he had brought with him, Jack writing in a small notebook.

'You have provenance for the painting, madame?' he asked.

'There is a letter from an aunt of my husband's, referring to it being brought into the family.'

'To see that would be of the greatest value,' said Jack, at once.

'We could wait while you find it,' put in Byron.

'And while you do so, we will study the painting in a different light. You will permit that we open the shutters on those windows . . .?'

'Byron, is it a Gainsborough?' said Jack, as Lady Girdlestone went away in quest of the letter, her footsteps tapping down the stairs.

'No idea. But let's see what else is here while Gertie is foraging for provenances.'

Jack was already unlatching the shutters and folding them back. Sunlight slanted into the dim gallery behind him, and he was just thinking that one of the catches looked satisfyingly flimsy and that there was a section of guttering which could be sufficiently sturdy to be climbed if they had to return, when Byron said,

'Jack. Look at this.'

'What? Where?' Jack looked to where Byron was pointing, and felt as if something had squeezed a hand around his heart.

Hanging in a shadowy recess, almost as if it had been placed there to semi-conceal it, was a small portrait. It was roughly sixteen or eighteen inches in height and some thirteen or fourteen inches wide, and it ought to have been wholly unremarkable – nothing more than a daub by some unknown painter, or perhaps even by a long-ago Girdlestone. But it was not unremarkable at all.

It was a head-and-shoulders portrait of a girl, perhaps seventeen or eighteen years old, and she was staring out at the world with defiance. Her hair and as much of her gown as could be seen were what Jack thought were Tudor style. She had dark hair and vivid blue eyes, mirroring the colour of her gown.

Even to his relatively untutored eye, the painting was poor. The paint looked as if it had been patchily and hastily applied, as if someone had wanted – or needed – to complete the work quickly. The girl's eyes had a faintly skewed look, which might have been due to a slight squint, or might simply have been because the artist had not had the skill or the time to depict them properly. But at the bottom edge of the painting were the words, '*Catherine Ó Raifeartaigh. circa 1536 . . .*'

Jack stood very still, feeling the sunlit gallery whirl about him. Catherine Ó Raifeartaigh. Was this the link Montague Fitzglen had wanted to find? His notes had referred to a marriage between the Rafferty family and the Girdlestones, and to a '16C Ó Raifeartaigh ancestress who had met a mysterious, macabre and probably shameful end . . .'

And here, in Girdlestone Hall, was a lady with the Ó Raifeartaigh name. Was this what Montague had hoped – even expected – to find? Tomás's lines in the play came vividly to him. Catrina had understood, he had said. Catrina . . . And now here was a portrait of a lady called Catherine. Were the names only coincidence, though?

Byron, who was examining the painting closely, said, softly, 'Look there, Jack. In that corner.' He indicated a dim outline on the painting's left-hand edge. 'A lute,' he said. 'It's almost entirely in darkness – deep shadow – but it's just possible to make out what it is. Can you see?'

'I can. But weren't lutes part of everyday life in the 1500s?' said Jack. 'There wouldn't be anything remarkable about a lute being in a portrait in that era, surely?'

'No, except that I don't think that's a patch of shadow,' said Byron. 'I think someone tried to paint over it. D'you see there – and there? A definite line of a different colour. The darker paint almost obscures the lute, but not entirely. Whoever painted over it either didn't do a very good job, or the paint has flaked off in places with time.'

Jack was just wondering if they could take the portrait nearer to the light from the window when Lady Girdlestone's voice, sounding rather annoyed, said,

'I see you've noticed the family murderess.'

The murderess. Jack felt his mind flinch, but Byron said, quite smoothly, 'A murderess? How very dramatic. Who was she?'

'A very distant ancestor of my husband's,' said Lady Girdlestone dismissively. 'Catherine Ó Raifeartaigh. I believe some people called her the Cat. I don't really know why the painting has even been kept here all these years – the connection is a long way back, and it was very tenuous anyway. A cousin acquired the painting through marriage, I believe.'

Jack said, carefully, 'What was the murder she committed?'

'I could not say. I think the story is that the murder – whatever it was – had to be kept a close secret. Strictly guarded within the family.'

'But she was executed?'

'I presume so.'

'All families have one or two bad ancestors,' said Jack, forcing his voice to sound offhand, hoping he was keeping a secure hold of the French accent. 'Is that the letter of provenance for the Gainsborough? So kind.'

'You permit we make notes?' asked Byron, taking the letter.

'Oh, of course.'

'Ó Raifeartaigh is not an English name, I think?' said Jack, as Byron opened his notebook.

'Irish,' said Lady Girdlestone, tight-lipped.

'Ah, of course, the Irish—' Jack spread his hands in deprecatory fashion.

Byron, having completed his notes, took Lady Girdlestone's hand, and bestowed a light kiss on it. Jack contented himself with a plain handshake.

'I wonder,' said Jack, as they walked back to the halt for the London train, 'which came first for Uncle Montague? Did he hear about Catherine during his visits to Phelan, or was there

something in the play that made him suspect there was a mystery
to be uncovered? Although that begs the question as to how he
came by the play in the first place.'

'And who wrote it,' said Byron.

'Yes. But Byron – Catherine's portrait,' said Jack. 'I got the
impression that it had been done hurriedly. It was painted on a
board, wasn't it?'

'Yes, but I think painters often used boards in those days,'
said Byron, as they went onto the platform. 'I don't think that
tells us anything. But I agree it had a hurried feeling about it.
Almost as if the artist had snatched whatever was to hand to get
it done.' He frowned, then said, thoughtfully, 'If she really was
a murderess, could she have been in prison when it was painted?'

'Awaiting execution for a murder the family kept secret afterwards,' said Jack, thoughtfully.

'You might well want to cover up that you'd got a murderess
in your family, though,' said Byron. 'See now, 1536 – she could
have been a martyr. Killed for her religious beliefs.'

'True.' Jack saw again in his mind Catherine Ó Raifeartaigh's
defiant stare. She had looked as if she would have been prepared
to stand up for whatever she believed in, no matter the cost. He
said, 'She didn't look much more than seventeen or eighteen.'

'People commit murder at any age,' said Byron, as the train
appeared at the far end of the track, and puffed its way into the
station, belching out clouds of smoke.

They had a compartment to themselves and, as the train pulled
out, Jack said, 'What was in that provenance letter? I know it
was about the Gainsborough, but did it mention Catherine?'

'Only in passing,' said Byron, producing his notebook. 'It was
from somebody called Augusta Girdlestone, and it was mainly
about how the Gainsborough came into the Girdlestone family
through her uncle. But she did say this:

"If hung in a good light, perhaps near a window, the
Gainsborough should deflect attention from that creature, Catherine
Ó Raifeartaigh. I cannot think why that portrait has been allowed
to remain on view all this time. Neither I nor anyone else knows
the truth about her, of course, but if only half the whispers are
true, to my mind the painting should have been burned long since
and the girl's name expunged from the family's history".'

'That's all?'

'That's all,' said Byron, closing the notebook. 'But if nothing else it confirms Uncle Montague's belief about the link between the Raffertys and the Girdlestones.' He stared through the window at the passing countryside, then said, 'I suppose we can't go through with that Gainsborough filch, can we?'

'Only if you think you could copy the original.'

'Of course I couldn't. And don't grin like that – you know perfectly well that I'm a mere novice – in fact, compared with Montague, I'm not even that,' said Byron. 'It's a pity we can't stage that filch, though. It would have felt like a memorial to the old boy.'

'Speaking of memorials,' said Jack, 'his funeral's going to be quite an event, isn't it? Ambrose is having fits at the cost of the food and wine for the wake. And during the wake, I've got to retrieve the play without anyone seeing, get it out of the house—'

'And read it,' said Byron.

'Yes. I've got to read it,' said Jack.

The funeral and the interment of Montague Fitzglen proceeded much as any funeral and interment. People were solemn, ladies dabbed their eyes with black-bordered handkerchiefs, and everyone told one another what a beautiful service it was – dear Montague would have been pleased. It was all so sad, wasn't it – and a reminder that you should send not to know for whom the bell tolled. And hadn't something been said about refreshments? Whatever else you might say about the Fitzglens, they were always hospitable.

Once at the house people mingled amicably, falling into discussion with old acquaintances, dusting off a few scandals, and calling to mind one or two feuds, including commenting on the remarkable sight of the Fitzglens and the Gilfillans under the same roof.

It was agreed that the buffet lunch was lavish, which was doubtless Cecily Fitzglen's doing; she might not be able to convincingly portray a Lady Macbeth or an Ophelia, but when it came to domesticity, she could not be beaten.

Jack moved around speaking to people, then, when everyone seemed to be in the dining room, he went unobtrusively along the hall to the study. He did not acknowledge – not quite – that he could have come to this house at any time during the last few days and retrieved the script, but he was aware he had deliberately waited until there would be people around. Because his mind flinched from that reference of Tomás's to a darkness? But what was it, that darkness Tomás had wanted to destroy – almost to exorcise?

The study was silent and shadowy, although faint light filtered in from the street. It showed up the photographs on the mantel-piece – several of Fitzglen plays, and a silver-framed one of Montague with Tansy's mother. She was smiling straight into the camera, the narrow Fitzglen eyes strongly noticeable, and Jack smiled back at her, and thought the silver frame was typical, because Montague had had a very great fondness for Tansy's mother – although all of the family had had that, of course. Tansy had a lot of her mother's qualities – the same delight in life, the same energy, the quick intelligence.

He looked round the room, thinking that if the play were to be staged, this was exactly the kind of lighting it should have for the opening scene. A smeary twilight, with uneasy shadows, and then Tomás's words dropping into the listening silence.

There was such a darkness in that place . . . he had said.

But it was important to remember that – whoever had written this play – it was a work of fiction. Whoever had written it . . . Jack looked back at the photograph, and his heart lurched, because for a wild moment it seemed that Montague moved – that he turned his head slightly and looked straight at Jack. Then the moment passed, and Jack's heart returned to its normal rate, because after all it was simply a reflection in the glass of someone standing in the corner. Someone who had quietly come into the room behind him – or had been in the room already when he came in?

'Hello, Jack,' said the familiar, slightly husky voice. 'Were you looking for me or were you in search of a priceless heirloom left by your Uncle Montague?'

Viola Gilfillan.

For a moment Jack did not speak. Then, reaching for compo-sure, he said, 'It's like you, Viola, to make this kind of appear-ance. It's a pity it's so artificial and unconvincing.'

He was glad that his voice sounded slightly dismissive, as if he were brushing away a minor annoyance. He was not actually annoyed, even though it was typical of Viola to add a touch of drama – almost materializing in an empty, shadow-filled room. And, said his mind, within a few feet of a manuscript that must not – under any circumstances – be allowed out of Fitzglen hands.

A small part of his mind registered that she was wearing conventional mourning attire – a silk costume with a small patterned velvet scarf at the throat – and that black suited her. The contrast with her porcelain skin and coppery hair was striking. She was wearing black jewellery – jet? – and her hands were gloved. But her left hand was resting on the edge of the cupboard door – the cupboard in which reposed the document. Had she opened that door? Had she been closing it or been about to open it when Jack came in?

But she said, in what sounded a sincere tone, 'I'm here to offer condolences for the death of your uncle. He was a great figure of the theatre. He should be paid homage. Or did you think I was here purely to look into your bright eyes again, Jack?'

'What I thought was that you might be here to look around this house in case you could disinter any scandal for your family to use against mine,' said Jack, immediately.

'How cynical. But as for scandals, from all I've ever heard, Montague Fitzglen led quite a colourful life. I should think there were a good many secrets in his past. But then which of us doesn't have secrets? And, of course, a scandal or two.' She took a step nearer to him. 'You could certainly tell a few good tales, couldn't you, Jack?'

Jack said, coldly, 'I could, but not to you, Viola.'

'Never?'

'Never. I'll toll out King Lear's five famous "nevers" if that will convince you.'

'Oh, you'd never play Lear,' she said, at once. 'You haven't that melancholy side to your character that Lear had.'

'You'd be surprised,' said Jack. They regarded one another, and then, with a slight effort, he said, 'And having exchanged insults, I shall now remember that you're a guest in this house, and I'll take you into the dining room to have some lunch.'

'Are we playing our Montague and Capulet roles again?' she

said, as he held open the door leading out to the hall. 'And if so, are you taking me to old Capulet's "trifling foolish banquet"?'

'Yes, but it's on the understanding that you don't make a mutiny among the guests,' said Jack, luckily remembering a later line from the scene. He stood back to allow her to precede him. 'If I know anything about my cousin Cecily,' he said, 'the banquet won't be so very trifling.'

The banquet was very far from trifling, but it was fairly short-lived. It was not considered polite to remain too long at such a gathering, and also some people had matinees at which to appear.

Jack waited until the mourners had left and the family had gone into the dining room to finish up the food, then returned to the study. He paused in the doorway, reminding himself that all he was going to do was take some pages of an old document off a shelf, then went in.

The yellowing press cuttings and the scrapbooks were still on the shelf; Jack lifted them down, then reached up for the iron box. He placed it on the table, looked at it for several minutes, then grasped the lid and pushed it up. There was no resistance as there had been when he first found this box; the lid folded back with only the smallest scrape of sound.

The room seemed to tilt and the shadows blurred into rearing outlines. Because the box was empty.

The script of *The Murderer Inside the Mirror* – the undiscovered play that might have come from the pen of a brilliant Irish writer, or that might as easily have come from the pen of a wily forger – had gone.

SEVEN

Tansy was glad the funeral was over. It had been dreadfully sad about dearest Great Uncle Montague, but it did sound as if he had had a splendid send-off, with most of the London theatre world present.

She had supposed she would go to the service and the wake, but Aunt Daphnis had said somebody had to be at the Amaranth for the day, to make sure everything was set up for the evening's performance, and that she and Uncle Rudraige – Jack too – had thought it would be good experience for Tansy to undertake this responsibility. Tansy suspected it was more that they thought the service might bring back the memory of her parents' double funeral – and if so, it was very kind of them and she was grateful. Her parents' death had been just about the most harrowing experience of her entire life. It had been harrowing for everyone, of course – Tansy's mother had been a cousin of Jack's own father and they had been very close. She had married a Fitzglen connection from the Canadian branch of the family – there had been plans for a Christmas visit, which Tansy had been looking forward to.

But this morning, she was helping Bill the Chip on stage. It had been Uncle Rudraige's idea; he had said all actors needed to understand backstage work, and Aunt Daphnis had added that you could never entirely trust Bill not to rearrange a set when no one was watching, and then forget to tell anyone about it, so that folk tripped over unexpected chairs on their entrances.

Bill the Chip, who had been the Amaranth's stage carpenter ever since anyone – even Uncle Rudraige – could remember, was interesting and friendly. As they worked, shunting furniture to and fro, and repairing flats that had become damaged, he related a number of anecdotes about the family, which Tansy greatly enjoyed hearing. Some of them were about quite long-ago Fitzglens, but some were about people like Jack's father – Aiden Fitzglen, who had died when Jack was quite young, which was one of the family's Great Tragedies. Tansy had been very small

indeed when that had happened, but she could still remember
how distraught her mother had been. She had never talked to
Tansy about it, though, and neither had any of the family. Tansy
occasionally had the feeling that most of them knew exactly what
had happened to Aiden, but that they did not want to talk about
it. Because of not wanting to hurt Jack? Whatever the reason,
Aiden was remembered with considerable respect and affection,
and Tansy would like to have known him.

'Although,' Bill said, as they started painting some flats for
the following night's performance, 'I'd have to say, when he was
in the mood, Mr Aiden could be as much of a rebel-rouser as
Mr Jack sometimes is now. But Mr Jack was very young when
he inherited the Amaranth, and it affected him. It's my belief
he'd have grown up very different if Mr Aiden hadn't died,
and . . . Oh, my dear life, we ain't putting that book flat on the
set, are we?'

Tansy turned to look at the flat he was pointing to, which was
painted with rows of book spines to represent library shelves.

'No, no, no,' said Bill, severely. 'We can't allow that on stage,
not like that. That's the flat where Mr Byron painted on saucy
book titles one night while nobody was looking. Pass me that
tin of brown paint – we'd better smudge it all out.' He plied a
paintbrush, then sat back to regard his handiwork. 'That's better.
I've painted out *Fanny Hill, A Woman of Pleasure* and *Casanova's
Memoirs*. I shouldn't think any of the audience will be able to
read any of the other titles, should you?'

Tansy hopped down from the stage to view the flat from the
stalls. 'Paint over *The Lustful Turk* if you can, Bill. I can read
the words from the second row.'

Bill reached for the brush again, then stepped back to view
the result. 'All right now?'

'It is. You've obliterated the Turk altogether,' said Tansy, clam-
bering back onto the stage. 'Bill, tell me some more about the
Fitzglens. You see, I haven't been back from that frightful
finishing school very long, and I only know bits about them.'

Bill liked nothing more than to talk about his beloved Fitzglens,
even though he frequently issued gloomy warnings to them when
they demanded complicated sets.

'Take Mr Rudraige and old Mr Montague – him that's just

died,' he said. 'My word, they were a pair of rascals in their youth, and . . . You know, Miss Tansy, I believe I'd better paint out *The Misfortunes of Virtue* while I'm about it. Where's the paintbrush again? Well now, Mr Rudraige and the rest, they'd go on the town many a night after they'd been on stage. The old cellar clubs they'd often go to – you won't remember those, of course – and the music halls. Why I remember one time—'

Tansy listened, entranced, until Bill realized it was nearly dinner-time, and they sent out to The Punchbowl for mutton pies and cider.

They were finishing the pies when Gus Pocket arrived, to explain he had come to take Tansy out to Notting Hill because a family conference had unexpectedly sprung up.

'And they'd like you to be there.'

Most likely it would be something to do with the intriguing Phelan Rafferty play, and Tansy was pleased to be considered important enough to be included in a conference about it. She scrambled into her coat, assured Bill the Chip again that neither *Fanny Hill, The Lustful Turk* nor *Casanova* could be read from the stalls, and followed Gus down to the stage door and out into Sloat Alley.

Great Uncle Montague's house, which was of whitish-greyish stone, was tall, with long narrow windows on both sides of its front door. Stone steps led up to the door, and there was a scrubby bit of garden and a rather friendly impression that the house enjoyed being cheek-by-jowl with the little shops and coffee houses and part of the bustling life around it.

But when Byron opened the door and took her into what had been Montague Fitzglen's study, Tansy felt as if she had stepped into a swirling well of emotion.

Jack was standing by the hearth, his hair tumbling over his forehead like half-melted amber. Behind him was the wedding photograph of Tansy's mother with Uncle Montague – he had given her away, and Tansy had been promised the photograph. But she only spared it a cursory glance, because Jack's anger was so strong it dominated the room. Uncle Rudraige was here, of course, along with Aunt Daphnis, and Ambrose was seated at a table, studying columns of figures.

Cousin Cecily was sitting in a faded wing-chair in a corner

of the room, shredding a damp handkerchief into ribbons, and saying it was no good people telling her not to be upset, because this was all her fault.

'I'm to blame for what was probably a work of genius being lost to the world.'

Tansy sat down on a small stool near the door, staring at Cecily in alarm. She could only be talking about the mysterious play found in this very house – the play that seemed to have been written by one of the great playwrights of the previous century.

Uncle Rudraige said, explosively, 'Dammit, Cecily, the thing isn't lost, it's been stolen! Filched from under our very noses!'

'We still don't know if it's genuine, of course,' put in Ambrose. 'Byron, Jack – did it look like a forgery?'

'We both thought it looked all right,' said Byron, glancing at Jack, but when Jack only scowled, Byron said, 'It even smelled right. Dust and old wood with a dash of mouse droppings.'

'That doesn't mean anything,' said Rudraige. 'Montague knew all the tricks. He'd imbue a forgery with whatever scents were relevant. I remember him once rubbing horse-hoof oil onto the pendulum of a clock, so he could say it was a Janvier piece smuggled out of Paris in a saddle bag during the French Revolution.'

'Was it a Janvier piece?' asked Ambrose.

'Of course not. Montague picked it up in Spitalfields.'

'Whether the play's a forgery or not, it's my fault that it's gone,' wailed Cecily, who, for once having commandeered centre stage, so to speak, seemed disinclined to relinquish it. 'You trusted me to look after the house and guard the script and I did my best. I was here with the cleaners – oh, and I let Todworthy Inkling in, but he wasn't here long, and I'm sure he didn't come into this room. And I've cheated you all out of giving the world a work of genius.' She subsided in her chair, sobbing, only pausing when Gus arrived with a tray of tea.

'Oh, thank you, Gus,' said Byron. 'Tea and scandal, according to the ancient custom. Splendid,' he said, getting up to take the tray, and Tansy, wanting to justify her place at this very important meeting, went to help him.

'Don't you all think,' went on Byron, 'that if this wasn't so worrying it might be quite interesting to be on the other side of a filch? Also, you can't help thinking of it in terms of a title, can you? The Robbery at the Funeral. The Purloined Play. The Priceless Document stolen in the shadow of the tomb—'

'Montague isn't in a tomb,' said Rudraige, crossly. 'He's in the cemetery, respectably buried. Some sly conniving person got to hear about the script and sneaked along to get it while everyone was scoffing potted shrimps and foie gras. Jack, I blame you. You should have got the thing to a place of safety sooner.'

'No time,' said Jack, shortly, and as if defying anyone to argue.

'It'll turn out to be one of those Gilfillans who took it,' said Daphnis.

'They were actually very friendly and sympathetic, though,' said Cecily. 'Florian Gilfillan came up to me and talked to me for quite a while about Uncle Montague. I hadn't realized he knew him. He was very courteous.'

'Florian Gilfillan is a disgraceful old mumble-mumper,' said Rudraige. 'I haven't seen him for years, and I thought he'd aged shockingly. I dare say he's not much above his mid-forties, but he looks a good deal more. Of course, he drinks like a fish,' said Rudraige, reaching for the decanter and refilling his glass.

'I always thought he had a very attractive voice,' offered Cecily.

'Oh, that's the booze. It's what we used to call a gin and fog voice.'

Tansy committed this expression to memory, along with mumble-mumper. It just showed that you should never ignore your older relatives – they came out with the most marvellous expressions and also produced any amount of spicy gossip. She was rather intrigued by Florian Gilfillan, who sounded as if he might have fluttered Cousin Cecily's sensibilities somewhat.

Then Jack said, 'I'm afraid Rudraige is right.'

'What about?'

'About it being one of the Gilfillans who took the play.'

'We don't know that for certain, of course,' said Ambrose.

For answer, Jack produced from his pocket a folded newspaper article and half threw it onto the table.

The headline was in large typeface, and Byron picked the cutting up and proceeded to read it out.

LOST PLAY BY FAMOUS IRISH PLAYWRIGHT
DISCOVERED

The theatre world is today simmering with the news that a melodrama seeming to have come from the pen of the late Phelan
Rafferty has come to light.

Readers will recall that Mr Rafferty was hailed as the 'Maestro
of Melodrama', and had been the winner of the prestigious Richard
Brinsley Sheridan Award. His death at his Irish home was
announced some five years ago.

We understand the play was found in a house in central London,
and that it will be staged by the well-known theatrical dynasty
of Gilfillan. It is intended to open the much-anticipated four-day
theatre festival in Dublin, which will celebrate the work of various
notable Irish dramatists, including Dion Boucicault and Mr Oscar
Wilde.

Miss Viola Gilfillan, (recently acclaimed for her performance
as Ophelia, about which one eminent critic said she 'took
Shakespeare's tragic heroine to new levels of pure madness'),
spoke to us about the play.

'We can't absolutely guarantee it was written by Phelan
Rafferty, but it bears his name,' she said. 'And the indications all
point to it being his work. It's full of his wonderful eeriness and
darkness, and we're working on the assumption that it is indeed
a lost work by him.'

Asked for details as to the discovery of the play, Miss Gilfillan
gave our reporter her famous mischievous smile, and said she
was sworn to secrecy.

'I will only say it came into our hands by purest chance,' she
said. 'But there is one thing your readers might be interested to
know. Four pages of the script seem to have been disguised by
having been written in a different language – a language we are
still getting translated.'

Asked what language the four pages were, and why Phelan
Rafferty would have disguised part of his work, Miss Gilfillan
said it was thought the pages were in Gaelic.

'Phelan Rafferty was Irish, of course, but it seems there are a
great many variations of dialect and pronunciations within the
Gaelic tongue, and also, over the centuries, fragments of Scottish

Gaelic and Irish Gaelic have become inextricably woven in. We don't yet know the reason for this "hidden scene", but we suspect it contains the core and the climax of the whole play. Perhaps it was part of Mr Rafferty's plan to wrap that in as much mystery as he could.'

EIGHT

As Byron finished reading, Jack said, 'You do see this makes it imperative to find out what's in this play. Even more now than before.'

'Because of what might be in that hidden scene,' said Byron, putting the article down. 'Because it might contain something harmful to this family.'

'What kind of something?' demanded Daphnis.

'Any number of things,' said Jack. 'The truth about any one of our filches – stories of Montague's forgeries—'

'He's right,' said Rudraige. 'There are a great many things about this family that have to remain private.'

'And whoever wrote the play disguised one scene by writing it in Gaelic,' said Jack. 'Doesn't that sound as if something in it had to be concealed? Montague did just that. He kept that play hidden for – well, it must have been years by the look of it.'

Byron said, thoughtfully, 'You know, Montague's action almost mirrors the play – at least, what we read of the play, Jack. In the condemned cell, Tomás was writing his story – he was going to give the story to Maran when it was finished—'

'But he made Maran promise "not to give it to the world until it was safe",' said Jack. 'He said they daren't let it be known.'

'That was only in the play,' said Daphnis. 'Those characters are fiction.'

'Are they, though?' said Byron.

He looked at Jack, who said, slowly, 'Even from that brief scene, I had the impression that Tomás and Maran – Catrina, too – were . . .' He made an impatient gesture, then said, 'That they were masks to hide real people. And don't glower like that, Rudraige. I know it sounds far-fetched, but Byron felt it as well.'

'Byron would find deep meanings and hidden significances in a note to the milkman,' said Rudraige, crossly. 'But I'll accept what you say, Jack.'

Cecily said, 'I still find it difficult to believe there might be something in the play that could be harmful to this family. Hardly anyone knows about our – well, our off-stage profession.'

'That's not entirely true,' said Ambrose. 'A few people know. Tod Inkling for one.'

'Yes, and he was in and out of Montague's house while we were clearing it out,' said Byron. 'He came into the room while you and I were reading that first scene, Jack, if you remember.'

'I do.'

'Don't you trust Tod?' asked Rudraige.

'Not as far as the front row of the stalls,' said Jack. 'And he's becoming very alert to the modern world – he's even had a telephone installed in his shop.'

'Good God,' said Rudraige. 'I wouldn't even know how to use one of those things.'

'They're very useful,' said Tansy, not saying she had been trying to get Aunt Daphnis to have one installed in her house.

'But the Gilfillans might have acquired the play in good faith,' said Cecily. 'Not knowing where it came from. Couldn't we ask them openly about it? Explain it seems to have been stolen from Great Uncle Montague's house? I could write to Florian Gilfillan— There's no need to snort so disgustedly, Rudraige, it's a perfectly reasonable suggestion. And Florian said at the funeral how nice it was to see me again.'

'If you're intending to go cap in hand to the Gilfillans,' said Rudraige, 'I give you warning now that I shall retire from the profession, and in your own grease you can all fry.'

'You mean stew in your own juice,' said Ambrose.

'No, he doesn't, Ambrose. He's quoting Chaucer.'

'Never mind who I'm quoting, I refuse to countenance going humbly to the Gilfillans like – like a parcel of Uriah Heeps,' said Rudraige.

Jack said, 'We aren't going humbly or Heeply anywhere to anyone. Ambrose, were you about to say something?'

'I was wondering if we could infiltrate the Gilfillans' finances to see if there are any payments to translators or even typewriting agencies,' said Ambrose, thoughtfully. 'It could provide a clue we could follow. I know it's sneaky to go into someone's bank accounts, but if they did filch the piece from us, or maybe buy it from someone like Tod, knowing it was suspicious, I don't see we need to have too many scruples.'

'All's fair in love and war,' nodded Daphnis.

Jack said, 'But there might be a different kind of infiltration we could consider.' He paused, and Tansy, fascinated, thought: The Fitzglen Pause. One day somebody will actually call it that in public. It was always immensely effective, and it was now. Even Rudraige broke off in the middle of telling Tansy about somebody called Timon Gilfillan. 'He'd like everyone to think he runs that entire company but . . . Sorry Jack, did I interrupt you?'

Jack said, 'Supposing that – rather than infiltrate their bank accounts – we infiltrate their theatre?'

There was an abrupt silence, then Byron said, 'You don't mean we should – I hardly dare say this – but that we should send in a spy?'

'Someone in disguise?' asked Ambrose.

'That's exactly what I mean.'

'Impossible,' said Rudraige, at once. 'I won't hear of it.' But he looked at Jack expectantly.

'Go into that lair of – of *amateurs*?' said Daphnis, sitting up very straight in her chair. 'Certainly not.'

'But it could mean we'd find out about the play,' said Jack. 'Specifically, about that hidden scene. Anyone who goes in could get a script, or at least watch rehearsals, and we'd know whether there really is anything damaging to us.'

'If there is, what would we do about it, though?'

'Find a way to prevent the performance,' said Jack.

'How? Bribe the Gilfillans? Blackmail them? Blow up their theatre?'

'I don't see how we could get someone into the Gilfillan company, anyway,' said Ambrose. 'We're all known to them – they'd see through almost any disguise.'

'They don't know all of us,' said Jack, and into the silence that came down, Tansy heard, half with panic, but half with excitement, her own voice saying,

'None of them know me.'

It was extremely disconcerting to see them all turn to look at her, but Tansy was not going to withdraw the words, especially when she saw that Jack was watching her intently. It's what he wants, she thought. He wants me to be the one to go into the Gilfillans' theatre, because I won't be recognized. He wants me to find out about the play. She managed not to blush – at least, she thought she managed not to. There were varying degrees of surprise in all the faces, but no one was rejecting the idea. They were examining it, and they were starting to think it might be quite a good plan.

Then Ambrose, speaking slowly, as if he was testing his own thoughts, said, 'But what if they realize who you are, Tansy? Might that be dangerous? To you, I mean?'

'I don't see how they would recognize me,' said Tansy. 'I wasn't at Uncle Montague's funeral, remember.'

Jack said, 'Tansy, would you do it? I don't think there'd be any risk – even if they realized who you were, the worst they could do would be to order you from their theatre.'

By this time, Tansy was so entranced at the idea of solving the mystery surrounding the lost play, and Tomás and Catrina and the wicked Catherine Ó Raifeartaigh, she did not care if she ended in a prison cell or became a dark part of the Fitzglen history so that succeeding generations only ever spoke of her in whispers. 'Tansy Fitzglen,' they would murmur behind their hands. 'She's the one who ruined the family and caused the downfall of the Amaranth itself – we never speak her name aloud in public.'

She said, firmly, 'Yes, I would do it. If you want me to.' Then, in case this sounded half-hearted, she said, more eagerly, 'Actually, I'd love to do it. I'll be subtle and tactful and I'll do whatever you tell me.'

'And you'd emerge triumphant, with the truth about Phelan's play, and probably the identity of the thief, as well,' added Byron. 'And once we know all that, we'll probably know why Montague kept it hidden from everyone.'

'And,' said Jack, 'who the real people behind Tomás and Maran and Catrina were.'

Gus thought that of all the filches and deceits and disguises he had been involved with since coming to work for this family, this was turning out to be one of the strangest.

'She's got to appear to the Gilfillans as a young, rather insignificant girl,' Jack said. 'I'm sorry about that, Tansy, and it's a pity for you, but we can't risk you attracting attention.'

'I understand. I'll be madly insignificant.'

'I've got some of that hair dye left, Jack,' said Cecily eagerly. 'You remember I bought some for a part a while ago? I did have my hair coloured professionally to start with,' she explained to Tansy. 'Just for the play, not as a permanency. I went to a salon in Pont Street, where you'd expect to get a reliable service, but it went disastrously wrong, so I bought some hair dye of my own. I'll let you have it – there's quite a lot left, and it will completely alter your appearance.'

'And,' said Byron, 'you must remember to be very careful that you aren't followed when you come and go from the theatre.'

'Always assuming she gets into it in the first place,' put in Ambrose. 'Tansy, where will you be living while all this is going on? You can't remain in Daphnis's spare room. You might be seen coming or going from her house.'

'Jack's already thought about that,' said Tansy. 'And we've found a sort of garden flat near Russell Square. I'm going to move in tomorrow. It's very small, but it's rather nice. I'm going to write a report every day, and Gus will call to collect it each morning. He'll be dressed as a postman, won't you, Gus?'

Gus was not viewing this prospect with any enthusiasm, but he had not said so, because he had always known it was only a matter of time before he had to don a disguise as part of one of the Fitzglens' mad plans. So he merely said he had found a postman's outfit in a second-hand clothes shop. He did not say it was currently hanging out of his bedroom window to get rid of the smell of boiled cabbage that clung to it.

'And if there's an unexpected development or a crisis,' said Tansy, 'I'm to send a telegram to Jack's rooms and also the Amaranth, from the post office in Russell Square. I could even telephone, if one of you had a telephone,' she said, hopefully.

'However you send for help,' said Jack, giving Tansy the smile that made her feel she would have ridden into the jaws of death and into the mouth of hell if he asked her to, 'we'd come straight in to your rescue.'

'Have we got a name for her?' asked Ambrose. 'As close to

her real name as possible, it should be. That's always been one of our rules, Tansy.'

'How about Tilly?' suggested Daphnis. 'Don't scowl, Tansy, I know it sounds like a kitchen maid, but it's near enough to your own name for you to feel fairly comfortable with it.'

'And scowling results in wrinkles,' said Cecily.

'What about Fendle as surname?' suggested Ambrose. 'That's quite close to Fitzglen.'

'Tilly Fendle,' said Tansy, slightly dismayed. 'I'll sound like something out of Charles Dickens. A scullion, black-leading the grate and scrubbing the steps – twisting my apron nervously between my hands if the master casts a roguish leer my way—'

'And meeting the fishmonger's boy on the scullery steps on your afternoon off?' said Byron, enthusiastically joining in this promising conversational thread.

'Don't be flippant,' said Daphnis. 'This is serious. Tansy, you aren't going to be a scullion, you're going to be an eager young girl, wide-eyed at the chance of working in a famous theatre, and anxious to do whatever they want.'

'And as for roguish leers,' said Rudraige, 'watch out for Florian Gilfillan.'

'I always found Florian to be a perfect gentleman, Rudraige—'

'Also,' said Rudraige, ignoring this, 'if you can't convincingly play a stage-struck young girl, Tansy Fitzglen, then you aren't fit to walk the boards of the Amaranth, or any other theatre if it comes to that.' He beetled his brows at her, then, in an unexpectedly softer voice, said, 'Your mother would have done it to perfection.'

'She would, wouldn't she?' said Tansy, grateful for this very nice comment from dear Uncle Rudraige, and managing not to look back at the memory of her dead parents. Instead, she thought how extremely lucky she was to be part of this family, and how marvellous it was to be involved in this very important plot. She said, earnestly, 'I'll do it to perfection, as well. I won't let you down.'

It was worth blushing, even though it probably made her face look like a radish, to see them all smile approvingly and nod to one another.

Jack said, 'I know you won't let us down, Tansy.'

'And we'll await your reports with the greatest anticipation,' said Byron.

'Dear Jack and Family,' wrote Tansy three days later, covering the page with an eager scrawl, parts of which Jack had to read twice to decipher.

> I feel as if I am sending dispatches from a war, like the newspapermen did from the Battle of Waterloo and the Crimea, although of course there aren't any artillery or rifles here, or things that could explode at your feet – although if there are secrets in this play, they might explode disastrously, and this might all end with the Gilfillans flinging me unceremoniously out into the middle of Covent Garden, and you'll probably disown me.
>
> I'm writing this late at night by candlelight, which you'd think would be romantically secretive, but isn't, because the candles are tallow and they splodge onto the paper without you noticing. I'm sorry about the splodges, but it seems that if I want the luxury of gaslight in the garden flat, I have to contribute to something called the City of London Gas, Light and Coke Company. I haven't done so, because it means paying for an entire month's supply at a time, and I shouldn't think I'll be here for that long. So it's candlelight in company with a mug of cocoa.
>
> It was extraordinary how easily I was accepted into the Gilfillan fold, although it was nerve-wracking to walk up the steps of their theatre and request an interview. But nobody seemed to find it peculiar, and a rather distinguished gentleman, with hair like expensive cashmere and a voice like warm honey, took me to a small rehearsal room. He said they could always find a place for a keen young lady who wanted to study stage management, rather than actual acting. (Please thank Byron for that very good suggestion.)
>
> 'We usually train people within our own family,' said the distinguished gentleman, 'but most of them have their eyes on treading the actual boards – standing in the limelight – not that we use limelight any longer, but you take the

point. And so I think we'd be very pleased to have someone who doesn't want that, and from what you've said, you've taken the trouble to understand a fair amount about backstage work.'

At that point, Jack, I was very grateful for the hours spent with Bill the Chip – also with Gus. I hadn't realized how knowledgeable Gus is about backstage, and I shall tell him so in the morning when he calls in his postman role to collect this note. But you tell him too, will you?

The cashmere-hair gentleman said he thought I might be a kind of assistant to the assistant stage manager, which would be rather a lowly position, but I would be learning, and working my way up. He said it was a friendly company and they would all make me welcome. At that point, I found myself hoping I wouldn't actually end up liking any of the Gilfillans, which would be dreadfully disloyal.

'You can meet some of them tomorrow,' he said. 'We're rehearsing a new play which we've just acquired, and which we're rather excited about. Oh, and my name's Timon Gilfillan, and I'm by way of being the manager of this place.'

So I've met Great Uncle Rudraige's Timon, and he isn't at all what I expected – and I shall be attending a rehearsal of the first scenes of *The Murderer Inside the Mirror* tomorrow.

I doubt I'll sleep a wink tonight for excitement, although the rumble of omnibuses outside my door isn't likely to be conducive to sleep, anyway. If I had realized this street was on a main omnibus route, I might have looked for somewhere else, but I can put up with far worse than omnibuses, and anyhow they stop at midnight.

Fondest love to you all,

Tansy

NINE

Dear Jack and Family,

I'm two days into the quest, and the Gilfillan theatre is already becoming familiar. It has the same scents of paint and timber and glue-size as the Amaranth – and the same noises of hammering and people scurrying hither and yon. But it isn't as *nice* as the Amaranth, of course. The stage is smaller, and the auditorium isn't nearly as large. I expect you'll know that, but I thought I'd mention it.

The company are only being given the pages for each day's scenes. I don't know if somebody wants to keep as much of the play as secret as possible, or if it's only that it's still being typewritten from the original handwritten script. I was expecting a dim, faded manuscript, curling at the edges because of having lain in dark hiding for a long time, but the pages are typewritten. I've been put in charge of hand-props, and so far I haven't been given any pages at all, just a couple of props lists and notes of rehearsal times and scenes. But they're using the stage to rehearse, and I've got a table in the wings so I can see most of the rehearsals. I'm trying to scribble down the dialogue while nobody's looking.

So that you can visualize the scene properly, I'll explain that I wear a hideous kind of wrap-around overall, and I found a butcher-boy cap in the props room which hides most of my hair – although please tell Cousin Cecily the ginger streaks from the dye are hardly noticeable and only at the back anyway, so I think I'm very unobtrusive.

This afternoon, while I was diligently counting props and pretending to make lists and trying to work out how a lantern in a street scene could safely be lit, a man came up to the table. He smiled, and said how good it was to see a new, young face, and that he liked the butcher-boy cap, which to his mind gave me a certain gamine charm.

He said, in a very grand way, 'I'm Florian Gilfillan,' and put out his hand. There was the inference that I would be sure to know his name, and would be humbly grateful to be noticed.

I mumbled that I was Tilly Fendle – it still sounds horrid to say it – but Florian Gilfillan said, 'A charming name for a charming lady,' and went ambling off towards the stage.

I'm sorry if these next comments upset Cecily, but I have to say I think Florian Gilfillan is nothing more than an ageing roué with a very good opinion of himself. When rehearsals started it was a shock to realize he was playing Tomás – goodness knows why. I know we've only heard a few of Tomás's lines from that opening scene Jack read, but that was enough to know Tomás shouldn't be portrayed as someone with a thickening waistline, slightly bloodshot eyes, and broken veins in his cheeks. I suppose Florian could cover up the veins with greasepaint, but he won't be able to cover up his mediocre dramatic abilities. I cringe at his acting. Actually, I think Timon cringes at times, too.

Timon is playing Maran – I suppose he's a bit old for that, too, but I think he'll convince an audience. Viola Gilfillan is Catrina. There are a few smaller roles – a pair of inquisitive sisters who keep trying to find out what's going on in Tomás's house, and a couple of lamplighters, clearly meant to give a slight comedy touch and lighten the darkness here and there. Like the grave-diggers in *Hamlet* – 'playing down to the groundlings' didn't Will Shakespeare call it? And there's a match-seller girl who helps Maran. Her scenes are quite short, but they're very good – showing how she's fascinated by Maran, who exerts a kind of Svengali-type beguilement over her – although it's quite a benevolent Svengali, if that isn't a contradiction in terms. Somebody called Chloris is playing the match-seller – I think she's a distant Gilfillan cousin – and Florian is already shepherding her cosily into corners, murmuring about a little private coaching, my dear. She hunches a shoulder in a giggly kind of way.

This morning they rehearsed what I think is an early scene, with Tomás and Maran at a table in Tomás's house, studying a plan and discussing the details of what's clearly a hugely important crime they're planning. I don't know, yet, if it's the crime that ends in Tomás being in the cell with the barred windows. It was difficult to follow it, because people kept coming up to my table to ask about props. Also, they're still working from the loose pages of dialogue, and Florian Gilfillan kept losing his place. At one point, Timon told him, quite sharply, that if he couldn't read what was printed, he should wear spectacles.

As for Viola Gilfillan – I know none of you like her, but I have to say she is *good.* And she's so graceful – she makes me feel clumpy and hobnailed-bootish. I'm trying to see how she achieves it – it seems to be the placing of hands and the way she sets each foot on the ground when she walks. I'm going to practise it in front of a mirror— And speaking of mirrors, there are one or two quite elaborate ones lying around, so it looks as if the 'mirror' of the title plays an important part in the plot.

Very best love to you all,
Tansy

Dear Jack and Family,

At this rate of letter-sending I shall soon rival those prolific Victorian lady letter-writers, or maybe that family who wrote reams to one another in the 1400 and 1500s – the Pastons, wasn't it? They used to send hundreds of letters, chronicling the progress of the Wars of the Roses and grumbling about the price of bread and how the curate had an amorous eye for Cousin Wilhelmina's daughter, or how somebody's groom had been hailed off to jug for saying Henry VI was weak in the head and better removed from the throne anyway . . .

But to our muttons, as the French say (at least, I think it's the French), and with today's muttons are details about an early scene in the play which was rehearsed this morning.

Chloris – who's playing the match-seller who helps Maran to find the way to Tomás's house – had been allowed yesterday off to attend a wedding. (We had to listen to endless descriptions of what she was going to wear and the important people who would be attending.)

But this morning she sent a message to say she was *too* exhausted to leave her bed after the ceremony and we would have to manage without her. It was annoying, because two of her scenes were to be rehearsed.

Timon was clearly very annoyed, but he only said, 'We'll do the scenes anyway. Who's on the prompt book?'

I was on prompt duty, as it happened. The cast have progressed to working without scripts, but I discovered yesterday that Florian has sneakily hidden a few of his own prompts in various places on the stage and has twice worn flowing jackets with deep cuffs and pockets, in which he hides reminders and cues.

When I called out that I was prompter today, Timon said, 'Ah. Good. Read in for Chloris, will you, Tilly?' (I have to force myself not to grind my teeth when anyone uses the name.) Then he said, 'You've got the scenes, haven't you? And you do know what I mean by reading in? You just have to come in with the lines where it says *Mimi*.'

'And sing the lines out, dear girl, so we can all hear,' added Florian, which, coming from him, was a bit much, because Great Uncle Rudraige was perfectly right when he called Florian a mumble-mumper. You can only hear about every fourth line he utters.

I didn't – of course – say I had more or less grown up with reading scripts or that I had had the necessity of speaking up impressed on me by people like Aunt Daphnis, because the audience in the back rows had paid to see and hear a performance as well as those in the stalls and the boxes. I just said, quite meekly, that I did have the two scenes, and I would do my best.

Jack, I'm slightly worried about disclosing this next part to you, but I'd better do so. The thing is that, as soon as Timon asked me to read in for Chloris, I forgot about being a spy in the camp and a Fitzglen in disguise, and I dived enthusiastically into being Mimi.

It was a good scene for diving into, as well. It's Maran's first significant encounter with Tomás. He meets Mimi under a streetlight and asks her where Tomás lives. It's hugely atmospheric – cobbled pavements and flickering gaslights.

The backstage crew are a bit mutinous about that, and they've been demanding to know whether anyone has thought about fire regulations.

However, here the scene is. I put on a very slight Cockney accent – not overdoing it, as Chloris always does. My father used to say 'character *not* caricature', and I try to remember that.

Mimi: Yes, I know where Tomás lives, sir. Sometimes, at night, I go to the courtyard near his house, and sit down in a doorway where nobody can see me – just to make sure he's all right. He don't belong here, you see. Not in this tumbling-down place with the houses in tatters and most of the folk in tatters, too. But he's been good to me, so I try to look out for him.

Maran: That's generous of you. I'm glad he has a good friend nearby.

Mimi: I got taken up by the peelers for pilfering food once, and he helped me.

Maran: I'm sorry to hear that. Life can be very hard at times.

Mimi: When you're hungry and you got little brothers crying for a bite of bread – well, you sometimes do what you know ain't right. But Tomás, he came to the police station and he spoke up for me, and he paid for what I took, and I was let go. He's a gentleman. Folk don't understand him, though. There's two old women on the other side of the square – always trying to find out what he's doing and who he is, but he don't pay them any heed. And if I'm around when they come prying and snooping I tell them to leave him be. I don't put it so polite as that.

Maran: I'm sure you don't. But I'm not prying – I'm an old friend of Tomás's and he wrote to me – although it's taken me a while to find this place. Will you trust me and tell me which is his house?

Mimi: I do trust you, sir. Funny, ain't it, how you sometimes trust people soon as you meet them? The house is through this alley, and beyond the stone archway.

They walk towards the archway.

Mimi, pointing: That's his house – see the light burning in the window?

Maran: I see it. Thank you. May I know your name?

Mimi: Mimi.

Maran: Mimi. A name for an elfin waif. For a sprite of London Town. But also the name for a doomed soul. *La Vie de Bohème* – resonances of doomed lovers in a garret in a Parisian street . . . But you don't know what I'm talking about, do you?

Mimi: No, but I hope I ain't a doomed soul.

Maran: I hope so, too, Mimi of London Town.

He hands her a coin, and tips his hat to her, and she pockets the coin, then exits, stage left.

Maran plies the door knocker, and the door opens to reveal Tomás.

Tomás: Maran?

Maran: It is.

Tomás: You had my letter.

Maran: I did. Although I'm only here courtesy of a street sprite who showed me the way – and who likes to think she looks after you.

Tomás: Mimi, of course. The one who says she looks out for me. My guardian angel of the streets.

Maran: Strange little soul. Rather appealing, though.

Tomás: Well, Maran? Have you been able to do what I asked?

Maran: I have. I've found it, Tomás.

Pause.

Tomás: So it's found. After all this time, it's found.

Lights fade.

All very evocative, isn't it, Jack? There's a scene break after the dialogue about finding whatever it is, then the lights come up to show the interior of his house, with the two men seated at a table, poring over a large map. On that score, I think I'm expected to produce the map, although I have no idea how large they want it, or what it should look like. You'll see, though, that Maran uses our word, 'filch' – it was a bit of a shock to hear it.

Maran: You do see, Tomás, how we can get inside the castle quite safely?

Tomás: I do. It's a splendid map, as well, but then you always had the way with a sketch. I don't know that all of your sketches were always entirely convincing, but this is beautifully clear. Will it work, though, this wild plan you've conjured up? And will it be safe?

Maran: Tomás, did you ever know me to get caught?

Tomás: Not so far.

Maran: I never have been caught, and I shan't be caught now. This is going to be the finest filch I've ever attempted.

After the second reading, Timon thought I had better walk Mimi's scene through on stage with him, which he said would make it easier for the others. I abandoned the overall, because I didn't think a street waif would possess such a garment, but I didn't have time to discard the butcher-boy cap. I did my best to imitate Viola's graceful movements, and Timon thanked me afterwards, and, out of hearing of the rest of the company, said he was beginning to think I had unsuspected depths.

'And,' he said, 'in that extraordinary cap you look exactly the way I think Mimi would look. Like a hopeful street urchin. If we were in the Victorian era, when young ladies often played the parts of boys, you could have walked on to any stage as the Artful Dodger.'

And although nobody wants to be told they look like a street urchin, or the Artful Dodger, somehow it felt like a compliment. Also, I had trimmed my hair a bit the previous night, hoping to make Cecily's hair dye blend in, but I didn't cut it very straight, so it's resulted in a kind of spiky look, and the remark about looking like a street urchin was probably justified.

I said, 'If anyone ever writes a stage version of *Oliver Twist*, I would love to be the Artful Dodger. Or even the hapless apprentice to Sweeney Todd – Tobias Wragge in *The String of Pearls – The Fiend of Fleet Street*.'

At once, Timon said, in a pouncing kind of voice, 'You

know that piece?' and I remembered, too late, that *Sweeney Todd* isn't a play that's especially well known these days. But I managed to mumble something about having heard somebody mention it, and escaped to my props corner.

Jack, I really am sorry to have succumbed to that fit of 'stageness' and 'Fitzglennery', never mind displaying knowledge about *Sweeney Todd*, but I don't think Timon – or anyone else – has the least idea of who I am. Anyhow, I'll bet any one of you would have behaved in exactly the same way in my place.

Tansy

'Byron, how far-fetched is it to wonder if the theft Tomás and Maran are planning is an account of one of Montague's own filches?' said Jack. 'Something he planned with Phelan Rafferty, and that we never heard about?'

Byron, who had been reading Tansy's letter again, said, thoughtfully, 'Or something that went wrong?'

'Yes, that's possible, too. And afterwards, Phelan set it all down. Think about it. In the play, Tomás is writing something in the cell – something he insists must be kept secret. He asks Maran to hide it when it's finished. Supposing Phelan extracted a similar promise from Montague?'

'But why? The play is a work of fiction. Tomás and Maran aren't real.'

'Catherine Ó Raifeartaigh isn't fiction,' said Jack. 'She was real.'

'True. And there was that impression we both had, of three people standing behind Tomás and Maran and Catrina. But, Jack, we always knew about Montague's filches. He shared them with the whole family. We'd have known about anything significant.'

'Would we, though? There seems to be something in Phelan Rafferty's family that's been kept secret for a very long time,' said Jack. 'And just over three centuries ago, Catherine Ó Raifeartaigh is supposed to have committed a murder that was so shocking that it – and her existence – have been suppressed ever since.'

He paused and Byron said slowly, 'And at some time during

those three hundred years, somebody tried to cover up part of her portrait. The lute, you remember?'

'I do.' Jack paused, then said, 'Byron, how difficult would it be to get back into Girdlestone Hall and find out what else is hidden in Catherine's portrait?'

TEN

It was two weeks after the obituary notice of Montague Fitzglen appeared – when Ethne was starting to believe that life was safe after all – that the second blow came.

It was in the form of a letter from Miss Viola Gilfillan. It was courteous and informative, but it sent Ethne's mind tumbling into outright panic.

> My dear Miss Rafferty,
>
> We have never met, but I write to you with my family's approval and indeed with their encouragement, and feel I can do so in a spirit of friendship since your father was such a part of the world of the theatre – which is my own world.
>
> Recently, a play, almost certainly penned by your late father, but its existence previously unknown, came into the possession of the Gilfillan Theatre Company. News of this will shortly be appearing in newspapers, but I am hoping this letter will reach you before you read them.
>
> We are making it clear that we have no definite guarantee that the play was written by your father, but we are as sure as we can be that it is his work. It is certainly filled with his wonderful dark eeriness, and we feel privileged to have acquired it.
>
> We intend to bring the production to Ireland for the Dublin Festival – the four-day *Féile*. I am sure you will know of this event – the newly created celebration of theatre, which will include works by many famous Irish dramatists. We hope you can attend the *Féile* as our guest.
>
> The title of the play is *The Murderer Inside the Mirror.*
> Very sincerely yours,
> Viola Gilfillan
> for and on behalf of the Gilfillan Theatre Company, London.

Ethne sat with the letter in her hands, staring at it for a very long time. 'A play almost certainly penned by your father. Its existence previously unknown . . .'

Ethne knew every line her father had ever written. And if it had not been for one thing in Viola Gilfillan's letter, she would be able to dismiss this play completely – to say someone had mistaken a script for her father's work – that papers had become mixed up, and some play by an unknown author had ended up with Phelan Rafferty's name attached to it. Even to politely suggest it could be a deliberate fraud.

She could have done all of that had it not been for one thing. The title.

The Murderer Inside the Mirror.

Because only someone who had been in Dublin Castle on that long-ago night could have written a play with that title. Only someone who had been there – someone who knew the truth.

Ethne was no longer aware of the letter, still clutched in her hand, and she was scarcely aware of the present. The memories were winding themselves around her, dragging her back across the years. All the way back to the day, five years ago, when Montague Fitzglen had come to Westmeath.

He had arrived just one week after Ethne's father had discovered the letters sent to Seamus Rafferty about the rebuilding of Dublin Castle's Clock Tower.

'Didn't I tell you he was coming?' her father said to Ethne. 'I thought I had. But you can see about getting a room ready, can't you? You might look out that small ottoman, as well – the one Seamus brought back from Venice. Montague always likes that for his lame foot.'

Ethne could not recall her father mentioning this visit, but perhaps it had slipped her memory in the emotion of what had happened in the old orchard. There was nothing very unusual about the visit, though, for Mr Fitzglen came to Westmeath at least once a year. Ethne's father enjoyed his company – they had many things in common. Scholarly things in the main, things relating to the theatre. She was not in the least jealous of their friendship.

But three days after his arrival, a second guest appeared at Westmeath House – a man who was a stranger to both Ethne and her father, but who had been invited by Montague Fitzglen, and who it seemed had found out a considerable amount about the Rafferty family. His name was Todworthy Inkling.

Mr Inkling was a gentleman of rather small, slightly stooping stature, and he might have been any age between sixty-five and eighty-five. He was wearing an astonishing garment, rather like a surcoat of purple plush with embroidered panels, and on his head was a crimson velvet smoking cap. His face was seamed and the colour of old parchment, but his eyes were bright blue and extremely alert. He shook hands with Ethne, and, offered refreshments in the library after his journey, accepted a glass of Phelan's Amontillado, which he said was very welcome.

'I seldom travel far from my home these days,' he said. 'I care for so few aspects of today's world.' But he inspected his surroundings with interest, eyeing with a definite gleam the library shelves and the large table with its piles of books and documents.

'Tod really belongs to the middle of the last century,' said Montague, seating himself near the fire, which Ethne had built up for them. 'I've often suspected he's actually a character from one of Mr Dickens's novels – that he fell out of an 1860s plot by mistake and never managed to find his way back in.' He smiled at Mr Inkling, who was sipping his sherry with composure.

'However,' went on Montague, 'he's recently acquired an interest in a shop in Dublin – a shop that deals mostly in maps and manuscripts. I persuaded him to travel to Ireland to inspect it – as you know, Phelan, I have always had a . . . an interest in manuscripts and old documents. Purely academic, you under-stand.' His eyes slanted with amusement as he looked at Phelan, and Phelan grinned, as if understanding something, and refilled their glasses.

Mr Inkling appeared to understand this rather curious exchange as well, but he only said, 'Mr Fitzglen made the arrangements for me to travel to Dublin. I found the journey surprisingly smooth, and very comfortable.' This was said with a nod of approval, causing the tassel on the velvet smoking cap to swing jauntily. 'And I was indeed able to visit the Dublin shop – and inspect much of its contents.'

'I helped him,' said Montague Fitzglen. 'And the thing is, Phelan, that Tod found a very interesting bundle of letters in that shop.'

'Largely thanks to you, Mr Montague. You were most industrious in exploring the premises and examining the stock. It transpired that an earlier owner of the emporium – a former Maguire – had stored particular correspondence with considerable care,' explained Mr Inkling. 'I should not like to say Mr Maguire had hidden it, but—'

'But it was all shut inside a commode,' said Montague Fitzglen, with what Ethne thought was uncalled-for indelicacy. 'The lid was partly stuck down with age,' he added. 'But we got it up in the end because, as Todworthy said, you never know what you might find, or where you might find it . . .'

He paused, and Phelan, sounding amused, said, 'Ah, now we're having the famous Stage Pause, designed to heighten suspense. But don't overdo it, Montague.'

Montague said, 'There were several packages in there – most of them tied up with legal tape, or folded into oilskin packets. The majority were not especially interesting, but—'

He glanced at Mr Inkling, who said, 'But several of the missives bear the Rafferty name. Letters,' he said, his eyes very bright and alert, 'almost all dating to the mid-1700s.'

'Seamus Rafferty,' said Ethne's father, at once. 'Have you brought the letters with you?'

'I have.'

'And you thought we might be able to transact business over them? Am I right?'

'You are. But for – shall we say practical, preliminary purposes? – I have made a summary of them which I have with me now.' He patted a pocket.

'Which,' said Montague, 'is Tod's way of saying he won't be letting you get within grabbing distance of the documents until you've agreed to buy them, and at a price he considers acceptable. I told you he was a wily old bird, didn't I?'

Mr Inkling said he was sure some amicable arrangement could be reached. 'In the meantime, Mr Rafferty, if you would like to hear my précis . . .?'

'I would indeed.'

Mr Inkling reached into a capacious pocket, produced a sheaf of notes, refreshed himself with a sip of wine, and began to read.

To Ethne, one of the curious aspects of listening to this unexpected guest reading his notes, was the way in which his voice – as well as his appearance – pulled them so firmly into the past. Into the time of Seamus, who had tumbled his way through life, mischievously sprinkling disruption – and the Rafferty money – as he went.

'It seems,' said Mr Inkling, 'that Mr Seamus Rafferty commissioned Maguire's bookshop to make a fair copy of a map – from a sketch which he had sent him.'

Phelan said, 'Seamus's proposals for the new Clock Tower in Dublin Castle, that would be. I know about that – Seamus sent the map to the Surveyor General when the tower was being renovated.'

'He did indeed,' said Mr Inkling. 'And, rather strangely, the letter he sent to the Surveyor General, enclosing the map – or, more likely, a copy of the letter – found its way into Maguire's shop.'

'Probably Seamus wanted Maguire to know what exalted correspondents he had, and made a copy of the letter and sent it to Maguire,' said Ethne's father, caustically.

'Perhaps. Whatever the reason, among other things, Mr Seamus wrote this to the Surveyor General:

'"You will note, my good sir, my sketch plan showing how a hidden compartment could be incorporated into the walls of an upper passageway just below the great clock itself. I venture to say that anyone holding office in the castle – having responsibilities for guarding valuable and historic items – might consider such a secret recess extremely useful. May I draw a comparison with priests' holes in English manor houses during the reigns of the Catholic monarchs there – also, with the panels hiding cupboards within Borgia palaces, where poisons were kept for ease of administration to enemies. Not, you understand, that I am suggesting there are ever likely to be enemies of that calibre within any of Ireland's castles, but strange times befall all countries, and there is no knowing what may become necessary . . ."'

Here, Mr Inkling looked over the top of his pince-nez, and waited. Ethne's father said, slowly, 'So Seamus was trying to get them to incorporate a secret room into the castle, was he?'

'So it would seem.'

'Why on earth would he do that?' asked Montague Fitzglen, and with the question, Ethne saw an expression flicker across her father's face that startled her. It was not a sly expression – he could never look sly in a hundred years – but it was almost as if he might be secretly calculating something.

And then it was gone, and he said, very lightly, 'Oh, he was a terrible old hoaxer, that Seamus. It could have been part of some elaborate joke.' He paused, then leaned forward, in a different tone, said, 'But the map? Mr Inkling, did you find the map that Maguire made for Seamus?'

There was considerable force in his tone, and for what seemed quite a long time, Mr Inkling did not answer. Ethne felt a sudden tension in the room, and she thought Mr Inkling was assessing her father very carefully, before deciding how best to answer.

Then he said, 'The map Maguire provided was, of course, sent to Dublin Castle. But I found what I think is Mr Seamus's original draft.'

'Did you indeed? And—?'

'And it is upstairs in my suitcase.'

After dinner, an amicable arrangement as to the purchase of the various documents having apparently been reached, Mr Inkling brought from his suitcase the map that Seamus Rafferty had drawn up.

They spread it out on the library table. Ethne had never seen a drawing or a map of this kind before, but it was fairly easy to understand. Montague Fitzglen certainly seemed to understand it; he and her father studied it for a long time, murmuring to one another, pointing out various things on it. Mr Fitzglen said something about this being the main entrance to the castle, and that on this side was what would be the east gate.

'It's clearer than I expected, and it looks as if it's to scale,' he said. 'You see how he's put a scale there in the top corner? As for the secret room itself – that'll be it just here.'

'Outlined in red ink,' said Ethne's father.

'Yes, he wanted it to be very clear, didn't he? I'd think it was about the size of a very small room, wouldn't you?'

'More like a large cupboard,' said Ethne's father. 'The kind you'd walk into, but not have much room to turn around.'

Mr Inkling retired to the deep armchair on the other side of the library hearth, and began turning the pages of his notebook, occasionally nodding in a pleased way at some entry. Silence descended on the room, broken only by the faint crackle of the fire and the occasional rustle of paper.

Then Ethne's father straightened up from the table, and said, 'Well, Montague? What's your opinion? Was Seamus really involved in the castle renovations?'

'It certainly seems as if he tried to be,' said Montague. He glanced across at Todworthy Inkling who was still apparently immersed in his own notes, and then at Ethne, who had picked up a novel more or less at random, and was appearing to be reading it. 'Although whether his secret room was ever actually created . . . But it wouldn't be so difficult to do it, you know. These sections here – where the passage turns sharply to the left, d'you see? – they would allow sufficient space. Seamus mentioned priests' holes in that letter, too. I have an idea that the construction of those was often surprisingly simple. There was a man called – dammit, my memory . . . Oh yes, Nicholas Owen, who created a great many of them for the aristocracy. I think there were wall panels that swivelled – sections that appeared to be solid stone, but could be moved across. Concealed entrances in chimney shafts, even. Simple but effective, and seldom discovered. But, see here, Phelan, if Seamus had something he needed to hide, why wouldn't he have hidden it in this house? There are plenty of attics and cellars and sections of panelling that could be removed.'

'There are. And it's still highly likely that this whole thing was some elaborate prank anyway,' said Ethne's father. 'Unless . . .' He broke off, then, as if he was feeling his way along an idea – or was it as if he was deciding whether or not to disclose something? Then he said slowly, 'Unless there was something Seamus wanted to hide that he couldn't risk being found in this house.'

'Is that likely?'

'All old families have a secret or two,' said Phelan, in a vague kind of voice.

'Even so, it seems quite dramatic to hide something at such a distance.' Montague appeared to wait, but when there was no response, he said, 'Phelan, if your ancestor did get his secret room built . . .' He stopped, glanced to Mr Inkling, still absorbed in his notes, and to Ethne, apparently drowsing over her book, then said, in a much quieter voice, 'Are we sharing a thought?'

Ethne sensed her father look across at her, then he said, softly, 'I think we are.'

'That we might get into the castle and find the secret room – always supposing it exists – and discover what Seamus hid? It wouldn't be easy,' said Montague, thoughtfully. 'It would take cunning and stealth and a good deal of contriving.'

'But if anyone can contrive, it's yourself, Montague.' Ethne's father came back to the chairs around the fire, and, as Todworthy Inkling looked up from his notes, said, 'Inkling, are there any more significant documents you haven't brought out yet?'

'Nothing that would throw any light on the secret room in Dublin Castle,' said Mr Inkling. 'Although there does seem to have been a somewhat heated exchange between Seamus Rafferty and Maguire about a sixteenth-century gentleman who sounds as if he could have been part of your family's lineage. I found that quite interesting.'

'Thomas of Kildare,' said Ethne's father, and Ethne only just managed not to jump. 'The Tenth Earl of Kildare, he was. The Silken Earl, some called him, and I believe Seamus regarded him almost with reverence. But it was a long time ago – over three centuries – and it's impossible to know at such a distance whether he was anything to do with the family. Things become exaggerated,' he said. 'Distorted. Especially when it's my ancestor Seamus who has the telling of them.'

Ethne wanted to say that Thomas must surely have played some part in the family's past – how else would his portrait have found its way into this house? But she did not speak; instead, she listened to Mr Inkling, who was saying that the correspondence between Seamus and Mr Maguire regarding Thomas of Kildare had been very forthright.

'I have my notes on it here.' He turned a few pages of his notebook, then said, 'In one letter, Seamus wrote this to Maguire: '"I take issue, sir, with you calling Thomas of Kildare a naïve idealist who led hundreds of good men and true to their deaths. It was no such thing. Thomas was brave and gallant.

"'I am no willowy romantic, and I do not know all the facts, but I do know that Thomas's life was eventful, and his end was probably inevitable. In addition, there is a legend of a lady whom he loved and who loved him in return – but who met a terrible destiny of her own. Her very existence is believed to have been suppressed, and it is possible she was simply a romantic legend. But traces of her are there for the enquiring mind to find, although sadly her name does not seem to have survived the centuries".'

A lady whom he loved and who loved him in return . . .

The words were like a blow. Ethne had deliberately never tried to find out if Thomas had had a lady in his life. She had not wanted to think of her beloved Rebel Earl having a dull, domestic side to his life – she especially had not wanted to think of him having a wife to whom he paid loving attention . . . But if he had, he would not have behaved to her as the deceitful actor had behaved to Ethne. Thomas would not have made love in such a hasty way, in a place where anyone might have wandered along and caught him; he would have had a deep soft bed with perfumed sheets, firelight, candlelight . . .

She pushed the images away and managed to bring her mind back to the conversation. Mr Inkling had set down his notes, and her father was saying, in a thoughtful voice, 'The lady who loved him and met a terrible destiny . . .? There's a whiff of dark romance there, isn't there? You found no other mention of her in any of the letters, though?' He glanced from Mr Inkling to Montague Fitzglen.

'We did not,' said Mr Inkling. 'Is there no reference to her in any of your own papers?'

'If there is, I've never found it,' said Ethne's father, in an almost dismissive tone.

Ethne did not want to listen to her father and Mr Fitzglen picking over the results of the foraging in Maguire's Dublin shop. They would most likely go on discussing it for hours – working out some ridiculous plan to sneak into the castle on the slender chance that the disreputable Seamus had hidden something in there. Montague Fitzglen would pretend he could get into any building he wanted, and Ethne's father would start spinning stories about Seamus and Thomas's unknown lady.

She said goodnight, went up to her bedroom and got undressed, but instead of getting into bed she sat in the chair by the window, a shawl wrapped around her shoulders, her thoughts in chaos.

The lady whom he loved, Seamus had written about Thomas, according to the letter Mr Inkling had found. *The lady who loved him in return, but who met a terrible destiny . . .*

It was not really likely that Seamus's story about the lady was true, though. It would be some half-woven, quarter-remembered tale, traces of which Seamus would have found and gleefully seized on, and embroidered.

The clock in the hall below was chiming midnight, and Ethne went quietly out of her room and along to the gallery. The portrait would not reveal anything about Thomas she did not already know, of course. If there had been anything to be gleaned from it, Ethne would have done so long since. But nothing about it gave any clue to his life; there was no inscription or artist's name; no date or place written on the back, and no background showing – only a carved high-backed chair and the blurred impression of a panelled wall behind it.

There was certainly no hint of a lady who had been in Thomas's life – a lady who, according to Seamus Rafferty, Thomas had loved.

But a lady who had met a terrible destiny of her own, resulting in her name being wiped from history.

ELEVEN

Ireland, 1534

Catherine Ó Raifeartaigh often wondered whether her descendants – always supposing there were any descendants – would ever know about her. Would her name even be remembered? But even if it was, it was likely that people in the future would only say, 'Oh, Catherine Ó Raifeartaigh – hadn't she a dull old life?'

It would be terrible to be remembered as somebody who had had a dull life; Catherine would much prefer people to say, 'Ah, Catherine Ó Raifeartaigh – don't they tell a few grand stories about that one?'

But by the time she was seventeen it was beginning to seem as if there would not be any stories to tell about her at all, because it did not look as if her life would ever change. She would probably end up marrying some dreary neighbour's dreary son, and have a child each year, and grow fat and plain, and boredom would take her over like a fungus.

And then, one week before her seventeenth birthday, something did happen that promised to be far from boring. It came from her brother, Liam.

People often observed that it must be great for Catherine to have a brother who was an artist – someone who could set down images on paper, or even wood or canvas. Houses and trees and faces, so that they would be there for all to see many years in the future. The nuns at St Joseph's thought Liam was wonderful, but the nuns were impressed by most men, largely because very few came their way. Sister Bernadette was always thrown into a flutter when farm workers went into the convent grounds to help gather in the autumn fruit, or when work had to be done to the convent's fabric that meant men with ladders and hammers.

Catherine was immensely proud of Liam, but she did not think he was a very good artist. The people he painted always looked

to her a bit lopsided, as if they had a swollen jaw or a bad toothache, and buildings seemed to be on the verge of toppling over.
It was an irony that Liam's paintings might survive, while the
memories of Catherine herself and her family might not.

But even if she could think of a way to leave Westmeath, she
would never bear to leave Liam on his own in this big old house
with the memories that had a way of pouncing on you when you
least expected it. Most of those memories were of their parents,
who had died two years ago in what people said was the worst
plague ever to befall Ireland – adding, wouldn't you expect the
country to suffer plague with Henry Tudor on the English throne,
the greedy malevolent toad that he was. Even at fourteen, struggling with the grief of losing her parents, Catherine had not
understood how Henry of England, no matter how sinful or greedy
he might be, could be responsible for plague in Ireland. It did
not do to say so, though, and since everyone hated the English
king anyway, Catherine always joined in with the hating.

Liam spent most of his time in the attic room under the roof,
which he called his studio, and which was littered with half-
finished paintings and sections of canvas and board, and with
palettes and brushes splodged with paint, as if a rainbow had
melted over them.

But out of the blue he said he thought they should celebrate her
forthcoming seventeenth birthday in a special way. He smiled in
the way that always made her remember their father, although
Catherine thought she had better not become too excited, because
Liam probably only meant they would hold one of the displays of
his paintings. They did this once or twice a year, with all his work
carried down from his studio, and displayed in the hall and the
library of Westmeath House. Neighbours were invited – they all
always came along enthusiastically, because it was grand to be
going into the Ó Raifeartaigh house and getting a look at their
belongings, and being given a bite to eat and a glass of wine, as
well. Hardly anyone ever bought a painting, and most people only
wandered around the rooms murmuring that wouldn't you think
Liam and Catherine would have had that tapestry cleaned, or that
settle re-covered, and picking suspiciously at the food that Catherine
and the two scullery maids would have spent at least two days
preparing. Still, the events were something to look forward to.

But Liam said, 'I thought we could go to Dublin.' And, as Catherine stared at him, her mind tumbling with disbelief and hope, he said, 'I heard yesterday that Himself of Kildare – Thomas Fitzgerald, the Tenth Earl, the Lord Deputy of Ireland, if we're to be respectful to the man – is to speak in St Mary's Abbey. A very big event it will be – and, Catherine, it's on the very day of your birthday. We could go to the abbey, and see Dublin, and it would be your birthday adventure.'

Catherine had just about heard of Thomas Fitzgerald, but she had not heard very much about him, so she listened to what Liam had to say.

'People are calling him the Rebel Earl,' he said. 'They hauled his father off to the Tower of London a few months ago – a fiery old gentleman he was by all accounts, and it's said that he quarrelled once too often with Henry VIII. The King finally lost patience and shut him up inside the Tower of London.'

The Tower of London. The words brought into Catherine's mind the image of a massive grim fortress – faint echoes of doors slamming and locks being turned; the sounds of marching feet from men who would drag you out to the block . . . If you were thrown into that dreadful prison-house, you never came out – or at least you did not come out alive and probably not with your body in one piece.

As if echoing these thoughts, Liam said, 'They also say it's in God's hands – or more likely, Henry Tudor's – as to whether old Kildare comes out of the encounter with his head still on his neck. Don't shiver, Catherine – none of it affects us.'

'No, of course not. It's a shame for the old Earl, though.'

'He made a fair few enemies during his time here,' said Liam, at once. 'Rampaging around and trying to trample down the greedy English landlords. But a lot of young men who rushed off to join his armies were killed – cut to ribbons and left to die in fields and ditches. Still, the old man's son is vowing to challenge Henry over his father's imprisonment. He's even created his own army,' said Liam. 'Gallowglasses, they're called – wait, and I'll draw one for you, and you'll see what a fine warlike appearance they have.' He was reaching for paper and charcoal sticks as he spoke, and sketching a figure. There was armour and there were tabards and breastplates with emblems on them. 'And you see the silk fringes they have on their helmets?' said Liam.

'I do.' Catherine thought it would be as well not to say she thought the silk helmets struck a peculiar note for warriors, especially as Liam's imagination had so clearly been caught.

'Thomas is bringing the gallowglasses to Dublin,' he said. 'He's going to rouse people up to join with him in the fight against the English.'

A wholly unsuspected fear came scudding out of nowhere, and Catherine said, 'You – you aren't thinking of joining Thomas of Kildare's fight?'

'God, no,' said Liam at once. 'I don't want to join his fight. I want to paint him.'

He was perfectly serious. He said Thomas of Kildare was destined to occupy a place in Ireland's history.

'And whatever the outcome, he'll be remembered long after his death, and that's why I want to capture his likeness. Imagine it, Catherine – setting down history so that people in the future will be able to see what Thomas looked like. They'll be able to look back across the years – across the centuries, even, and there he'll be.' His eyes took on the faraway look that Catherine knew meant he was inside his own private world – the world that was filled with images he had made of people and places.

She said, warmly, 'Of course we must go. I'd love to. Will we be able to get near enough for you to see the Earl? Would we even get a place in the abbey?'

'We'll make sure we do,' said Liam. 'We'll set off early on the morning of your birthday, and we'll be inside the abbey ahead of the crowds – in good time to find places.'

Catherine thought it was to be hoped that if Liam did paint this Rebel Earl, he did not make him appear lopsided or as if he had toothache.

Liam packed his sketching things in a large carpet-bag. He had milled paper and charcoal sticks, and he wrapped pots of paint and brushes in soft cloth. Almost as an afterthought, he put in a clean cambric shirt and stockings.

Catherine thought it was difficult to know what to wear to

hear a vengeful young man defying the English King in an ancient abbey, but she decided on her blue gown – Liam said it was the colour of sapphires and it brought out the colour of her eyes and almost made them violet. One day he was going to paint her wearing that gown, he said.

The gown had a square neck, not too low but just low enough to be becoming, edged with deeper blue velvet, and Catherine had an aquamarine pendant which had been her mother's. She would take the cloak with the deep hood and the silk lining, as well. For the actual journey she had a plain gown – it was a subdued greyish brown, so it would not matter if it got mud-splashed.

It was not very likely that Thomas Fitzgerald would notice her in the crowded abbey, of course – he would be taken up with being defiant and rousing his listeners to insurgency. But on the small chance that he might see her, Catherine would look as fine as she could manage.

TWELVE

The journey to Dublin was the longest she had ever taken, but Catherine found it full of interest. The huge coach seemed to bounce along the high-roads at a very fast rate indeed, although the other travellers grumbled and told one another that you could almost have walked to Dublin on your own two feet in the time this was taking.

It was almost dark when they arrived. It seemed as if street flares had been lit everywhere in the city – was that done every evening, or was the city preparing for the arrival of the Earl? Whichever it was, the flares cast pools of radiance over the cobblestones and the buildings, and in addition candlelight glowed warmly in almost all the windows they passed. Catherine, round-eyed with curiosity, had to keep reminding herself that she was not going to let anyone guess that she was not used to cities or travelling. Her mind was tumbling with delight, because this could be the start of the adventure she had wanted for so long. Dublin was alight and humming with life, and the thought that tomorrow she might see a piece of history unfold in front of her eyes was so thrilling she could hardly bear it.

Liam had arranged for them to stay for two whole nights in a tavern, which was exciting in itself. It was called the Black Boar, and Liam seemed to know what to do about their rooms. They were to have a bedroom each, with a connecting door. This was apparently the height of luxury, and the girl who carried their bags up for them treated them very respectfully, and said they hardly ever had people booking a whole room each, to sleep in all by themselves, and wasn't that the finest thing ever. And here were the rooms, which both had views over the square. Hot water would be brought up for them; supper would be ready very soon, and would there be anything else?

'No, thank you.' Liam passed her a coin, which Catherine did not know you had to do on these occasions, but which was something she committed to memory, because you never knew what situation might arise in the future. The girl bobbed a curtsey, and cast an approving eye over Liam as she went out. Catherine sometimes had to remind herself that her brother was very nice-looking – he had the Ó Raifeartaigh glossy dark hair and deep blue eyes, and he would seem a very attractive prospect to most ladies. And although Westmeath House might be getting some-what shabby, as well as crumbling a bit here and there, it still stood in several acres of their own land. Also, if you cared for such things, which Catherine did not especially, the Ó Raifeartaigh name was considered an honourable one.

The following day they walked to St Mary's Abbey, which was quite near to the Black Boar. There was a sense of anticipation everywhere, and cheering crowds.

'Although,' said Liam, glancing about him and then speaking very quietly, 'I suspect that among them are Henry Tudor's spies, on the watch for trouble.'

It had not occurred to Catherine that there might be any kind of trouble attached to this adventure, and she looked warily about her. But no one in the bustling crowds seemed to have the furtive sly air she thought spies and plotters would have.

St Mary's Abbey was a marvellous place – Catherine had not expected it to be quite so impressive, and she stood for a moment at the entrance, staring up at the soaring spires, trying to make out traces of the ancient Cistercian monastery it had once been. Sister Bernadette, impressed and delighted at the thought of her dear Catherine visiting such a famous sacred place, had told her about its history, and said she must be sure to commit all the details to memory to tell them all. And perhaps her brother would be making sketches as well, said Sister Bernadette hopefully. They would all like to see them, if so.

At first Catherine thought they would not be able to get inside, because there were so many people everywhere, but they managed to squeeze into seats on one side of a wide aisle. There seemed to be people from all walks of life present – some were rather poor-looking and ragged so that Catherine wanted to go over and give them money or food. But others were richly garbed, so she was glad she had worn the blue gown. A number had children with them – the children were clearly awed by their surroundings, the younger ones pointing to stained-glass windows and statues, older children being told to keep quiet by their parents – didn't they know this was a church, and churches were places where you had to be quiet and respectful, because you were in the sight of God.

No one seemed to know the exact moment when Thomas of Kildare would appear, but Catherine could feel the anticipation that was gripping the abbey. When soldiers came into the building, the anticipation intensified and people craned to see better, some of them standing up and leaning forward. There were twenty or thirty of the soldiers, and they walked in an orderly fashion through a high, soaring archway flanked by immense stone pillars and columns, and took up positions on each side of it. A murmur went through the assembly, for weren't these the famous 'gallow-glass' army of Silken Thomas himself. They pointed out the silk fringes on the soldiers' helmets.

Catherine liked the image of the softness of silk against the hard defiance that was being ascribed to Thomas. She was starting to hope that he would be as rebellious and wild as the stories told, because it was going to be the greatest disappointment ever if he was just some feeble milksop.

The abbey was humming with expectancy. It was almost as if the tall candles were blazing up more brightly, and as if the stained glass glowed and shone like clusters of jewels. Musicians came through the archway – trumpeters who took up positions on a high balcony as if some kind of triumphal music was going to be played to herald the arrival. With them were harpists and lute-players. Liam murmured to Catherine that Thomas was known to be an accomplished lutist, which Catherine thought an unexpected trait in someone with a reputation for such outright defiance. A young boy – perhaps thirteen or so – took up a place with the lutists; he was clutching a parchment scroll and, even from where she and Liam sat, Catherine could see the delight and pride in his face at being part of all this.

There was the feeling of something thrumming on the air, as if someone was drawing a finger round and round an immense glass bowl. The moment stretched out and out, and just as Catherine was thinking she could not bear it any longer, between one heartbeat and the next he was there, framed in the soaring pillars and columns, standing quite still, but looking about him, as if he was drinking in the sight and the sound and the whole atmosphere of the vast abbey and the people in it.

He had the eyes of a poet and a dreamer, but he also had the look of a warrior – of someone prepared to fight the entire world for what he believed. And of someone resolved to win that fight no matter the cost, thought Catherine, staring at him spellbound.

Thomas Fitzgerald, the Tenth Earl of Kildare – in the Gaelic tongue, *Tomás an tSíoda*. Silken Thomas. The Rebel Earl.

He was plainly dressed, but at his belt was a scabbard with a sword – the sword's hilt caught the candle flares and glinted. Catherine could not take her eyes from him. If the entire abbey had suddenly become engulfed in flames, if the devil's brimstone had rained down from the vaulted ceilings, she still would not have looked away.

He took his place at the head of a long table that had been placed just below the altar – Catherine had the impression of a very formal meeting. But when the Earl began to speak, all sense of formality or ceremony vanished.

His voice echoed and spun around the great abbey. The echoes picked up some of the words, lending a strange other-worldly air to what he said. His voice was beautiful – it was like velvet, but there was a strength to it. Velvet over steel, thought Catherine. And even though, to begin with, the speech was conventional, she felt as if a spell had been flung out and as if it had wrapped itself around her and trapped her.

Thomas thanked them all for coming. He paid tribute to the abbey's ancient tradition, and he touched briefly on its history, on the monks who had lived and worked and prayed in these walls.

'They prayed for God and for their souls, but they also prayed for Ireland,' he said, and with this last word it seemed to Catherine that a sigh of contentment went through the listeners. Then he moved from the table, and came to stand at the head of the aisle.

'Ireland,' he said, and he almost made the word into a caress, so that Catherine felt it brush sensuously across her mind. The flames from the sconces and the candles seemed to be burning within his eyes now.

'Once, Ireland was called the blue and green misty island,' he said. 'Did you know that? Did you know how men sailed the seas just to catch glimpses of it, for tales of it had spread half across the world. But of course you did – I see in your faces and in your eyes that you did.

'But so much has been lost to us. The legends and the lore and the myths. We shall always hold them in our memories, though.' He walked along the aisle, studying the faces, all of them intent and absorbed, all of them leaning forward, not bearing to miss a word of what he said. Catherine leaned forward as well, willing him to look at her, wanting that direct stare to fall on her.

But he returned to his stance, framed by the stone pillars. 'Ireland is yours,' he said, and he looked round the abbey again, doing so slowly, as if he did not want to miss a single person. 'It's yours by blood and by battle and by inheritance. All of it – the legends and the myths and the memories.' Then, in a voice that rang through the great building, he cried, 'And we shall not let Henry Tudor have it!'

A murmur of assent went through the abbey, and Catherine realized she was clenching her fists so tightly that her fingernails were digging into her palms.

'My father is dead at Henry's hands,' said Thomas, 'and I will die valiantly and in liberty, rather than live under Tudor bondage. Here, now, in full view of you all – in complete knowledge and understanding of what I do – I renounce my allegiance to the English King. I renounce all commitment and all duty to Henry Tudor.'

Even though everyone had expected this, even though most of them had been told it was what he would say, Catherine thought no one had believed he would actually say it, and a shocked gasp went through the listeners. Then someone from the group of people standing with Thomas came forward, moving quickly and agitatedly, and took his arm. A man in the seats behind Catherine and Liam whispered that there was about to be trouble.

'Trouble?' said Liam, half-turning his head.

'That speech was outright treason on Thomas's part,' said the man, his eyes on the people surrounding the Earl. 'He's courting death, and a bad death – it looks as if they're trying to persuade him to retract that renunciation of Henry Tudor.'

'He won't retract it,' said Catherine, and as she spoke, the Earl snatched the sword from its scabbard, and, his eyes blazing with fury, threw it down on the ground.

In ringing tones, he said, '*That* is what I think of the Sword of State – that it is fit only to be flung to the ground. As for Henry ap Tudor, I shall fling him to the ground as well, and trample on him for the greedy, selfish murderer he is!'

Before anyone could stop him, he turned and went out of the hall, his steps ringing out on the old stones. The entire congregation were on their feet by this time, and Catherine was standing with them. Then, before she realized it, she had moved out of the aisle where they had been sitting, and she was going after him.

She had only taken a few steps when Liam's hands grabbed her and pulled her back, and she was aware of the man who had been sitting behind them, saying urgently, 'That was the most outrageously dangerous . . . Sir, I think you must get your lady out to safety at once.'

'She's my sister – and I will get her out,' said Liam. 'But she acted impulsively – unthinkingly. It was nothing more than that—'

'Look at those men over there – they're watching you,' he said. 'See that thin-faced one? That is Sir William Skeffington.'

'The wizened old man, hunched over as if he's about to fall down?'

'He may look hunched-over and wizened, but he's Henry Tudor's man to the last drop of blood,' said the man. 'And after the speech Thomas has just delivered, Skeffington will be one of the Earl's fiercest enemies. Certainly eager to seize anyone who might be a threat – who might be one of Thomas's spies. Don't you see how he's looking about him – he's trying to spot the Earl's supporters.' A pause, then in a low, urgent voice, 'He's looking this way,' said the man. 'Believe me, friend, you should get your sister out of the abbey . . .'

He gave Liam's shoulder a friendly pat, and moved away, as if to distance himself from them. Catherine, bewildered, her mind still echoing with Thomas's impassioned words, saw that the soldiers were running across the abbey, towards the massive doors through which their leader had gone. The silken fringes on their helmets stirred with the movement, and their faces were grim and fixed. The old man pointed out as Skeffington was still in his place, scanning the congregation avidly. Was he really looking at her? But of course he was not – there were hundreds of people here, and she would not be in the least noticeable among so many.

Even so, she was glad when Liam managed to force a way through the crowds for them, and they stepped out into the sunlight. And, of course, everything was all right – there were no avid-eyed men anywhere and the crowds were already dispersing. Of the Earl there was no sign. It had been ridiculous to think he would have remained near to the abbey, though.

'We'll go straight back to the Black Boar,' said Liam, taking her arm.

'Do we have to? Everywhere seems safe – everyone is quiet and ordinary. Can't we look around the city? It's the first time I've ever been here – the first time I've ever been in a city.'

'Catherine, those men in the abbey – they thought you tried to go after Thomas. They were watching you. That man, Skeffington, looked straight across at you. His men could be somewhere in these streets.'

Catherine found this difficult to believe. It was more likely that Liam was being his usual unworldly self. She said, firmly, 'I don't think anyone was looking at me. It was all too crowded and too confused, with everyone trying to get out, and no one knowing what was happening.' As he hesitated, looking about him, she said, 'There are no soldiers anywhere now. The Black Boar is just along the street there. You go ahead and I'll follow in a few moments. I only want to go into this shop to buy a length of that golden-brown silk. I shan't be very long, and you'll want to be starting on sketches of the Earl – while it's all still clear in your mind?'

She could see that this prospect was indeed in his mind – his eyes already had the look she knew so well – so she said, 'I'll come straight back to the tavern, and we'll have supper in that oak-panelled room that looks onto the square. I'd like that. And I can see your sketches. I'd like that, as well.'

Before he could say anything else, she smiled at him again,

wrapped her cloak more firmly around her, and went into the shop.

The golden-brown silk, spread out for her inspection, was the most beautiful fabric she had ever seen. Oh yes, certainly, she could purchase enough for a gown, said the lady who had unrolled it for her. And they had brocade lace that matched the colour, and some lengths of silken fringing in a darker shade that would enhance the colour. Could that be added to the purchase?

Silken, thought Catherine. Silken fringing. She smiled and nodded.

The silk, along with the lace, wrapped up, and the whole package stowed in the deep pocket of her cloak, Catherine went outside, then paused. Should she go into one of the other shops before returning to the Black Boar? The Dublin street was fascinating – she had never been anywhere so lively before, and she had never seen so many shops. Their windows were crammed with goods – there were bookshops, where printed books were all set out for you to see, and apothecary establishments, where, the instant you stepped through the door, you would be aware of the scents of the oils and perfumes and potions. Leather shops, too, with shoes and belts.

But the light was starting to drain from the afternoon, and Liam would be waiting – although more likely he would already be immersed in sketches for the portrait of Thomas. Would he manage to capture the force and the passion of the Rebel Earl, the poet and the dreamer and the rebel, in his painting? Catherine suddenly wanted to find out.

As she walked towards the Black Boar, a group of men came running towards her, six or eight of them, shouting the name of Thomas Fitzgerald, imbuing it with derision and vicious hatred – calling him a traitor, an enemy of the King, who must be seized and cast into prison.

'Hanged, drawn and quartered,' shouted one of them. 'That's what'll happen to him, the black-hearted villain. We'll make sure of it – Skeffington will make sure of it.'

'And his spies with him!' cried another of the men. 'And isn't there one right in front of us now! See her there – the one we marked out in the abbey. The one who tried to follow him and had to be pulled away – we all saw it.'

'I saw it,' said another man eagerly. 'Get her now before she can scuttle away,' he shouted, and before Catherine realized what was happening, they were around her, grabbing her arm, holding her so tightly it was impossible to pull away. She could smell stale sweat from their bodies and the sour ale on their breath – and what was almost worse was that she could smell their excitement, as well. Fear and panic welled up.

'Wouldn't old man Skeffington be glad to have this one,' said the man who had called her a spy. 'Grady, will we take her to him now?'

Skeffington. At the name, terror closed around Catherine even more strongly. The man in the abbey had pointed out Sir William Skeffington, saying he was Henry Tudor's man and Silken Thomas's fiercest enemy – saying he was looking about him for anyone who might be one of the Earl's spies.

One of the men was saying there was only one thing to do with spies, but the man called Grady pushed him aside, and in a voice that was suddenly thick and blurred, he said, 'Two things to do with them.' He grinned, and his hands came out to Catherine's bodice, thrusting inside it. 'Before we throw spies into the dungeons,' he said, 'first we *warm* them a little.'

There was a cheer of assent. 'Drag her into that alleyway along the side there,' said one of them. 'We'll take turns while the others keep watch.'

'You first, Grady, but don't be long about it, for we all want a turn,' said another, with a wet chuckle.

'And when we're all done, we'll carry her off to Sir William's men.'

Grady pushed Catherine into the narrow alley that smelled of rotting vegetation, and thrust her against the wall. She could feel his thick fat thighs and a hard warmth pushing against her, and she began to feel sick – it would serve him right if she was sick right in his face.

But she managed to struggle against him, shouting for help, knowing it was hopeless, knowing no one would come to help her, because the men were rough and strong and no one would dare challenge them . . .

Someone did dare, though. Catherine, her head swimming with panic and confusion, no longer entirely aware of what was

happening, heard hoofbeats – several sets of hoofbeats – ringing
out on the cobblestones. There were shouts, and then the sound
of footsteps running towards her, then Grady was suddenly pulled
violently away from her. There were sounds of blows and curses,
then Grady was tumbling back, falling against the stone mullions
on the side of the building. He gave a kind of grunt, then lay
still, blood coming from the side of his head, his face the colour
of tallow.

'Dead!' cried one of the men. 'By God, Grady's dead . . .'

'Murdered in the open street . . .'

'And would you see who the murderer is, for pity's sake!'

'By Christ, there'll be a reckoning for this—'

Then, through the dizzying mists, the voice Catherine had
earlier likened to velvet over steel, was saying, 'Give me your
hand, lady – quickly now, if you value your life and mine. For
I believe I've killed your attacker, and his companions will be
baying for my blood and yours.'

She was lifted as easily as if she was a feather, and carried
across the street. There was the feel of leather – a saddle? – and
of reins and a bridle being pushed into her hand. Then someone
was behind her, and an arm was enclosing her waist to keep her
from falling. None of it could be happening – she must have
tumbled into a dream; her own or somebody else's. Because it
was as if she had conjured him up to come to her rescue – and
in the dream he had pulled her free of them, then scooped her
up in his arms, and now he was riding off with her like a knight
from an old romance.

But it was not a dream. It was happening. Thomas of Kildare,
Silken Thomas, the Rebel Earl, had his arm around her, and with
them rode a small detachment of the gallowglass soldiers, and
they were galloping away from the men who had been about to
rape her before carrying her off to dungeons as a spy.

The journey was the wildest Catherine had ever known. The
wind was in her face, whipping her hair into disarray, and overhead, clouds were massing like huge purple bruises. The horses'
hooves were pounding on the ground; she had lost all sense of
time, and she had no idea where they were going.

As if he had picked up this thought, the man with the velvet-
on-steel voice said, 'I'm taking you to safety, lady.'

'Where—?'

She could not see his face, but she had the sense of a sudden reckless grin. Then the Rebel Earl said, 'We're going to a place where the people who believe in my fight can be safe.' A pause, then he said, 'You do believe in my fight, don't you? In my cause? You are for Ireland?'

The frantic gallop through strange countryside was snatching the breath from Catherine's lungs, but she managed to gasp, 'The cause – Ireland . . . Oh, yes, yes, I am. I do believe in it.'

The arm that was holding her tightened briefly, and she thought he said, 'I knew you were with me.'

She managed to say, 'Where—?'

'To my stronghold. To Maynooth Castle.'

And either by sheer good fortune, or because the fates were with him, with the words the castle seemed to rear up in front of them – as if out of nowhere. It was surrounded by the thickening twilight, but even from this distance Catherine could see lights burning inside it – warm, glowing oblongs that might be candlelight or lamplight or even firelight. She thought: I'm being taken to a dark castle, and I'm in the power of a man who I don't know, except that he's defying the King of England and rousing up the people to fight.

Then they were riding hard across a narrow bridge, towards what was presumably a portcullis, although Catherine had never seen one in her life, and it was being raised for them, and beyond it was a courtyard. People were running out to take the horses – the one that Catherine and her rescuer had ridden, and also those of the soldiers who had followed them – and there were shouts for food to be brought, rooms made ready, fires to be banked up, and sharp about it, for the master was home.

Catherine was lifted easily down to the ground, and the eyes that had blazed with such fervour in St Mary's Abbey were smiling down at her.

'Thomas Fitzgerald of Kildare at your service, my lady.'

In a voice she scarcely recognized as her own, Catherine said, 'My name is Catherine Ó Raifeartaigh. And I'm very grateful indeed to you, sir.'

THIRTEEN

Inside the castle it was warm and there was a feeling of life and liveliness. Catherine was taken by a maidservant to a large bedchamber with a deep soft bed, rich hangings at the windows, and copper jugs of hot water set out for her.

The sense of unreality was increasing with every moment, and it almost overwhelmed her when she found herself with her host – her rescuer – in a stone-flagged hall, with a huge fire burning in the immense stone hearth. There were carvings over it, and as Catherine inspected these, tracing the letters with a fingertip, her companion said,

'One of my family's mottoes. *Non Immemor Beneficii*. It translates, more or less, as, "Not forgetful of a helping hand". The Fitzgeralds don't forget those who help them.' He raised his wine as if in tribute.

Catherine sat down at the table, facing him. She said, very firmly, 'I can't stay here – sir – sire . . .' She broke off, realizing she had no idea how she should address him.

He seemed to understand, because he said, 'Between the two of us, Catherine, I am Thomas.'

'It seems disrespectful to call you that,' said Catherine dubiously, and he laughed.

'Respect is something I care very little for.'

'Then – Thomas – I can't stay here for very long. My brother—'

'You have a brother? And other family? No? But a message can be sent to your brother without delay. Where is he? And can he be trusted to keep secret that you're here?'

'He can be trusted completely,' said Catherine, at once. 'He'll be at the Black Boar still. We were to stay there until tomorrow. Our home is in Westmeath.'

'Maguire shall take a message to the Black Boar without delay,' said Thomas. 'If your brother is not there, he can go to Westmeath.' He went to the door and called out to someone, and when Catherine made as if to protest, Thomas said, 'Maguire, too, is to be trusted. He's worked well and loyally ever since he came into my service, and . . . Ah, come in, Maguire.'

Maguire, who had what Catherine thought of as a face like a bloated ferret, glanced at her, and listened to what was required of him.

'You're to take a note to the Black Boar in Dublin – to a gentleman by the name of Ó Raifeartaigh,' said Thomas, then paused, looking at Catherine, who said,

'Liam. Liam Ó Raifeartaigh.'

'You're to set off at once, and you're to make sure you place a note I shall give you into his hands.' As he spoke, Thomas crossed to a massive desk in an alcove by one window, and reached for paper and inkhorn. 'You know the Black Boar, I daresay?'

'I do.'

'If Ó Raifeartaigh has left when you get there, you're to travel to Westmeath to find him . . .' Again the look of enquiry to Catherine.

'He'll be at our home – Westmeath House,' said Catherine, who was feeling as if she was being swept along by a whirlwind. 'It isn't very far.'

Maguire said he knew the road to Westmeath. His rather small eyes regarded Catherine in a way she did not much like. It was as if he was studying her, almost trying to decide if she could be made use of. But Liam must certainly be told where she was – he must be told what had happened and reassured that she was safe, and of course Thomas's servant could be trusted. Thomas had said so.

'Westmeath House, you hear that, Maguire?' said Thomas. 'And you must make sure Ó Raifeartaigh has the note without delay.'

'I understand.' Maguire waited respectfully, and Catherine thought that after all it had only been the firelight that had cast that curious expression over his face.

Thomas folded the note, held a stick of sealing wax over a candle flame for a moment, then allowed a few drops to fall on-to the paper, pressing his signet ring onto the softened wax.

'Don't fail me, Maguire. Don't fail this lady.'

'No, sir.'

As Maguire went out, closing the door behind him, Thomas

said, 'I explained to your brother that I had rescued you from a group of ill-intentioned ruffians. Villains who had taken it into their heads that you were a spy. That I had injured – perhaps killed – one of them, but that the others had got away, and so for your safety I brought you here. I also said that your brother had my word you were safe, and I would look after you – oh, and that on no account was he to come here, in case it led a trail for the men to follow, and to find you.' He regarded her, then said, 'Those accusations, that behaviour; they would all be intended to harm me, Catherine. They would be my enemies – there are people who want to stop me from what I'm hoping to do.'

'Reclaim Ireland,' said Catherine, softly.

'Yes. You understand about that, don't you?'

The firelight was behind him, so that he was silhouetted against its glowing brilliance. The light seemed to have got into his eyes, exactly as it had done in the abbey, and the radiance from the wall sconces seemed to be pouring over his hair and the glossy beard that framed his face, turning them to melted copper . . .

With a huge effort, Catherine said, 'Yes, I understand. But – Thomas – if that man was killed, wasn't I part of his murder?'

'If anyone was a murderer today, Catherine, it was me,' said Thomas, sitting down next to her.

He had a way of saying her name that sent little rivulets of delight scudding across her skin. Catherine thought: his voice, his eyes, his very presence are like no one's I've ever met.

She said, 'They thought I was a spy. Your spy.'

'Yes. That is why it might be safer for you to remain here for a while,' he said, thoughtfully. 'Until matters in Dublin are calmer. Can you do that?'

'I can.' Catherine would not for worlds have said she would have walked into hell and taken up residence with him there if he had asked her to.

'If you write to your brother more fully tomorrow,' said Thomas, 'Maguire can take the letter to him.'

'I should do that. Thank you.' Liam would worry, but not as much as if Catherine was at home in Westmeath where the King's men might march in and accuse her of being a spy for the Rebel Earl. He would believe her safe inside Maynooth Castle.

It was actually remarkable how safe she did feel, particularly when she remembered that it was such a very short time since she first set eyes on Thomas Fitzgerald.

'Do you care for music at all?' he said, suddenly.

The question startled her, but she said, 'I – yes, I do. Very much.'

'Then we shall have some,' said the Rebel Earl. 'To calm us after the disruptions of today.'

He went over to a hook near the stone hearth, and took down a lute whose polished surface gleamed. Catherine remembered Liam saying he was an accomplished lutist.

'Come and sit with me by the fire,' he said, his hands already moving over the strings as if he knew and loved them. Catherine thought: how would it feel if those hands slid over me in the same way?

When he began to play, it was as if the music drifted out of the firelight of its own accord, and filled up the room. It was not music Catherine recognized, but it was music that beckoned, and that you wanted to reach out and cup between your hands and keep forever. This, then, was the other side of the man who could stir rebellions and challenge kings – this was the poet and the spinner of dreams.

When finally he stopped playing, the silence stretched out, and for some moments there was only the crackle of the fire.

Then he said, softly, 'You enjoyed that?'

Catherine said, 'How can I put into words how very beautiful it was?'

He came to sit next to her, and somehow his arm was around her waist, and his free hand was in her hair.

I mustn't allow him to do this, thought Catherine. I've only just met him. I certainly ought not to be feeling exhilarated, and I definitely ought not to be looking forward to whatever happens next. Except there mustn't be any next. I should go back to Westmeath – to the things I know, and once I'm there, life will go quietly on as before. Because of course nobody will follow me and shout that I'm a spy and try to drag me into an English dungeon.

But she knew she would not do any such thing. She knew that she would do anything Thomas wanted, tonight, now, here in this very room. This was shocking and exciting.

When he bent to kiss her, it was as if a star exploded within her, and she clung to him, and wanted him never to stop. But at last he removed his lips from hers, although one hand remained within her hair. Catherine felt as if she was inside a dream.

'And now,' he said, softly, 'don't you think it's time for me to take you to your bedchamber.'

Her heart lurched all over again. Had it been a question? Was it a signal that they would both go to her bedchamber?

But he said, 'And to wish you goodnight, Catherine,' and she knew it had not been a question at all, it had been a dismissal. He was telling her there was to be nothing more. She did not know whether to be relieved or disappointed.

They walked through stone corridors and up a narrow winding flight of stairs, his arm around her waist again. 'You'll be safe here,' he said. 'There'll be no danger.'

'Thank you,' said Catherine, who had been starting to hope that one very particular kind of danger would happen to her. 'Goodnight, Thomas,' she said.

The bedchamber was welcoming and already familiar. Even with the door closed, she could hear distant sounds of footsteps, doors opening and closing, people coming and going. But there must be a great many people in this castle who she had not seen. Tomorrow she would explore it a little. Probably it would be all right to do that, and probably she would not need to stay here for more than a few days, anyway.

She took off the blue gown, pleased she had worn it today, because it was certainly the most becoming garment she possessed. The package with the silk material and the fringing and lace had been placed on an oak settle – seeing it brought an unexpected sense of security. She would not be here for long enough to need another gown, of course, but it was comforting to think she had the means to fashion one if she had to.

The bed was deep and soft and comfortable. It was very wide, too – easily wide enough for two people – no, that was a dangerous way to think.

As she drifted into sleep, she heard somewhere below voices and the sounds of horses' hooves and the jingling of harnesses, and she felt a jab of fear, in case the men from Dublin had followed her here after all, or had sent William Skeffington's men. But even as the question formed, the conviction came that – whatever happened – Thomas would protect her.

And she could hear now that the voices below were friendly. There was a burst of laughter, followed by a snatch of someone singing what Catherine suspected might be a bawdy verse. They would be Thomas's soldiers or his servants down in the courtyard – this room must overlook it, but she was too warm and too comfortable to get out of bed and look through the window.

Drifting into sleep, she wondered if Thomas's man, Maguire, was down there. He had not seemed to be someone who would join in raucous laughter or bawdy songs, although you never knew. But he was most likely already on his way to Dublin and the Black Boar.

As she drifted into sleep, she heard again the laughter from the courtyard below.

As Dubhgall Maguire rode past the stables and the low-roofed buildings where the gallowglass soldiers were housed, he heard the laughter as well. It would be the soldiers celebrating the Earl's appearance in the abbey earlier in the day, of course. Some of them had started up an extremely rude song, too – Maguire could hear it as he rode across the courtyard. He did not even know what some of the words of the song meant, but it was disgusting and depraved behaviour, and the Earl ought to know about such behaviour, although Maguire would not be the one to tell him.

The gallowglasses would be telling one another that Silken Thomas had given a fine speech today, and saying wouldn't the whole of Dublin City – the whole of Ireland, in fact! – be rallying to the call. It was gall and wormwood to Maguire when people became spellbound by the Earl and vowed to do anything he asked of them. Reclaiming Ireland for the Irish was a praiseworthy cause – Maguire would acknowledge that – but it would mean a great many people dying in the process. As Maguire's own father had died, abandoned and virtually penniless . . .

Maguire had never forgotten the day his father rode out at the Battle of Knockdoe in the service of the old Earl of Kildare. He had left the small house and the struggling little smallholding, saying hadn't they to stop the powerful English landowners trampling the Irish tenancy? And he'd return a hero, he said, and as for their bit of land and the crops – why, Himself of Kildare had promised to reward all his faithful followers richly. Grants of money there'd be – enough to buy more land for the Maguires, and for them to become prosperous. Wasn't that worth fighting for?

Riding through the spiteful rain towards Dublin, the memory of his father's eagerness that day scalded Maguire's mind afresh. Because his father had not returned a hero – he had not returned at all, for he had died on the battlefield. Soon afterwards the old Earl had been imprisoned by Henry Tudor's men in the Tower of London, where the English put their villains. Almost certainly to be executed, people said.

And the struggling Maguire smallholding had failed altogether, and Maguire's mother had died of despair and grief.

But then Silken Thomas had stepped up to the fight. He made impassioned speeches, and he promised to save Ireland – to take the English by the scruff of their necks and send them to the rightabout. He had paid homage to the men who had served his father as well – Maguire had been instantly grateful; he had thought his father had not died in vain after all, and before long the Maguire land could be reclaimed.

He had waited and hoped and trusted, but when nothing happened, he had come to understand that the new Earl was not going to honour his father's wishes. Nothing could bring back Maguire's father, slaughtered in battle, or his mother, dead of grief, of course, but the conviction that Thomas should be made to pay – and not just in squalid coinage – took root in his mind.

That had been when he had managed to get into the new Earl's household. It had been easier than he had dared hope; it seemed there were always opportunities for willing, hard-working men prepared to serve the nobility – for a pittance of a wage albeit! – and, once in Kildare's service, Maguire made himself not just useful, but indispensable. He found he could be as two-faced and as double-tongued as any belted earl. He bided his time and watched his chances, and wove his plans.

The Earl frequently came and went between Maynooth and Dublin, of course. Sometimes Maguire was required to accompany him, but generally the journeys were military, and it was the gallowglasses who went with him. Maguire supposed that if you were an occupying army, you had to make sure the place you had occupied remained under the sole of your boot. He had no quarrel with Dublin City having been reclaimed for the Irish – dear goodness, of course he had not – and the absences meant he could make a thorough search of all the papers and documents in Thomas's library and also his bedchamber. At first, he found nothing except notes for plans and strategies; letters from various fighting men giving advice. But he persisted, because he needed to know for sure what the old Earl had said or promised, and he would not damn Silken Thomas without being sure of the facts. So he went on searching, and, at last, after several attempts, he found what he sought.

It was a dim old document, carelessly written, spattered with ink and wine stains and blobs of sealing-wax, but as soon as he had carried it over to the window to read more easily, his heart began to thud, because the intention within the document was perfectly clear.

> *To the faithful men who served me in the Battle of Knockdoe in County Galway in the Year of Grace, 1504, and very especially to those who died on the battlefield, I promise that on my death the sums herein named shall be settled . . .*

There followed a list of names, and Maguire, reading as quickly as he could, listening for anyone outside the door and his heart racing with apprehension, finally found what he wanted. It was halfway down the list:

> *To Diarmuid Maguire, the sum of one hundred crowns for faithful service in battle in the army of myself, Gerald Fitzgerald, the 9th Earl of Kildare.*

At the foot of the document, the same writing stated, very clearly:

> *I lay this charge on my son, Tomás an tSíoda, that is Thomas Fitzgerald, who one day will inherit my title and become*

the 10th Earl of Kildare, that if I have not fulfilled these
promises at my death, he afterwards honour my wishes
faithfully and fully.
   Hereto I set my hand and my seal.
   Gerald Fitzgerald, 9th Earl of Kildare, Lord Deputy of
Ireland.

The seal had been affixed to the page – bits of the wax had flaked off, but Maguire knew it for what it was.

One hundred crowns. It was not a fortune, but it was a very substantial amount indeed – more than most men of Maguire's standing would be able to amass in a lifetime. And it was a sum that would have bought back that lost piece of land and allowed it to be worked and cultivated – or perhaps would have realized Maguire's own dream of founding a small business, something that would endure and that could be passed down in the family.

It was now over a year since the old Earl's death had been reported – Maguire did not know if he had been executed or if he had died from his battle wounds. But he knew – everyone knew – how Silken Thomas had vowed to avenge his father's death. Maguire could certainly understand that, for hadn't he been planning all this time to avenge his own father's death?

But it was clear by now that Thomas was not going to honour his father's promise, and a conviction began to take hold of Maguire that not only must he get the money promised to his family, the Earl himself should be brought to a reckoning. The more he thought about this, the better he liked the prospect.

The Earl had the occasional female entanglement, of course, but Maguire had never paid them much attention, or especially worried over them. There was said to be – or maybe to once have been – a wife in England. It was vaguely believed it had been one of those child marriages frequently arranged between noble families, but nobody in Maynooth seemed to know much about the lady, although Maguire had heard a whisper that she had not regarded him with any especial favour. He certainly did not worry about the random females who came fleetingly in and out of the Earl's life. Until today, when the whey-faced little bitch, Catherine Ó Raifeartaigh arrived at Maynooth. Because even in the first hours, Maguire could see that the Earl regarded her as different.

He supposed you would have to say the circumstances of the meeting had been romantic, with Thomas galloping to the rescue of a beleaguered maiden (always supposing she was a maiden in the true sense), and carrying her off to his castle. Maguire was not one for such nonsense, but he would allow that it had a place in the world.

What he would not allow, though, was the skew-eyed female getting her claws so deeply into the Earl that she would also get her hands on his money, to the extent that there would be none left for those people to whom it had been promised.

But Maguire was more than equal to dealing with the likes of Catherine Ó Raifeartaigh.

FOURTEEN

After the first few days, Catherine found the time inside Maynooth Castle began to drag. It had been foolish to imagine she would be spending each evening with Thomas – to have visualized the two of them supping together, listening to his music by firelight, sipping wine, becoming ever closer . . .

Or had it been so foolish? He had kissed her that first night, and although it was actually the first time Catherine had ever been kissed in that way, it had seemed to hold deep emotion. And there was nothing wrong with a kiss, and Catherine would not believe there would be anything wrong if matters developed beyond a kiss. She had no idea if Thomas had a wife – nobody had mentioned her, and there did not seem to be any trace of one in the castle. Catherine had not searched for traces, but she had opened one or two cupboards, and there had not seemed to be any items that could be regarded as feminine.

There was plenty of time for her to search if she had cared to, though. Thomas was not at Maynooth very much; he spent a great deal of his time with his soldiers, frequently riding off with them, generally setting out in the early morning. Catherine did not like to ask where he went, and when he returned – usually late at night – he was often exhausted and drained, and clearly it would not be right to start asking questions at such an hour. You're afraid, said her mind accusingly. You're afraid that if you start questioning and asking about what he does and where he goes, he'll decide it's safe for you to return to Westmeath, and you'll find yourself back in the boring life and you'll never be free.

She began to measure and to cut the silk fabric to fashion a gown for herself. In one of the cupboards were several bales of cloth, as well – perhaps they would be intended as gifts for the servants – but Catherine thought she could use some of them to make a day gown for herself. It would be something definite to do.

She explored the castle, and she spent a great many hours in the dim, dusty library. It had an air of being set apart – sounds from the courtyard did not penetrate it, so it was always quiet. Catherine liked the feeling that over the centuries people had come here to study and be undisturbed, and she liked the shelves of books – many in Latin, Irish, French and English, and many of which did not appear to have been opened for years. There were sermons and journals, written by long-dead, religiously inclined Fitzgeralds, which were the dullest things Catherine had ever read, but there were also old legends of Ireland and a few books detailing the history of the Fitzgerald family. There, again, was the motto that had been carved into the great hearth in the hall. *Non Immemor Beneficii* . . . 'Not forgetful of a helping hand'.

It was on one of the afternoons when she was exploring these books, thinking she should call for the wall sconces to be lit because it was growing dark, that the library door was flung open. Thomas's voice said, 'Catherine! I've been looking every-where for you.'

It suddenly seemed unnecessary to call for lights, because it was as if he had brought a brilliance and a glow into the room with him. Catherine saw that there was such triumph and such delight in his expression that she wanted to run across the room to him. But he was already coming to her – holding out his hands, seizing her own hands, his eyes alight with triumph.

'Dublin is ours,' he said. 'We have wrested it from the English, and it's in Ireland's possession again at last.'

His voice thrummed with such joy and triumph that Catherine felt it engulf her. She said, 'Oh, how marvellous. It's what you've wanted all the time, isn't it? Can you tell me about it?'

'I can,' he said, pulling her across to a deep settle drawn up to the fire, his hands still holding hers tightly. 'Riding home just now, I was planning how I would tell you everything. I wanted you to know it all, Catherine.' He pulled her closer, and his arm went around her shoulders.

'It was the finest battle you'd ever imagine,' he said. 'We swept everything aside – the soldiers were with me all the time; they fought like heroes, every last one . . . Oh, we lost some and others are wounded, but they'll be taken care of, and their families. Most of them are celebrating now in their own part of the castle.' Then, for a moment, a shadow fell across his face, and in a different voice, he said, 'But it isn't complete. Dublin Castle held out against us.' His free hand clenched in anger. 'We couldn't break them down.' Then the light flared again, and he said, 'But I shall have that castle, Catherine, I shall take it all – all of Ireland for the Irish. I shall avenge my father completely one day.' He looked down at her. 'And this has been a great victory,' he said, and pulled her closer.

The blood had begun to sing through Catherine's veins. She knew quite surely what was about to happen, and she knew she should be afraid and that it was a sin – that it was the act you did not do unless you were married – but she no longer cared.

His hands were exploring her body now, slowly but with assurance, sliding over her shoulders and inside the bodice of her gown . . . His fingers felt soft and sure, and his eyes were dark with passion.

Catherine managed to say something about the servants – Maguire, about someone coming into the room without warning, and he laughed, and got up and dropped a latch on the heavy old door that led out into the big hallway. Then he pulled her down onto the thick fur rugs in front of the fire, and as the warmth and the glow fell over her body, she felt as if the fire had leaped out and enclosed her. He was reaching beneath her skirts, and murmuring that wasn't this what they had both wanted and intended from that first moment . . .? Catherine heard herself whisper that, yes, from the very first moment.

His hands were gentle and strong, and the room was beginning to spin and blur all around her, and of their own accord her hands were reaching down for him. She heard her own voice again, this time gasping something about never having done this – of not knowing how . . . But he only gave a soft laugh and said it did not matter, the body had its own knowledge anyway, and the only thing that mattered was that they were finally together like this.

When he entered her, it was with the same gentle, strong assurance, and Catherine gasped, and then clung to him, because she would not bear it if he stopped now. The fire burned up even more brightly, and she had the wild thought that it would pull them both into its depths, because it felt as if she was drowning in the fire, except she did not care, as long as he was there with her.

Through the spinning, whirling waves of delight, she thought one of them was saying they would never let go of this feeling – that there had never been anything like it in the world, and there never would be ever again . . . She had no idea if it was his voice or her own, though. And then the fires burned up even more fiercely and the whirlpool took them up and up, as if it had seized them and was carrying them out of the room and out of the castle and out of the world . . .

Thomas moved convulsively and cried out, and in the same moment Catherine felt the whirlpool explode in a cascade of purest delight, and then descend softly around them like a melted rainbow. And after all they had not left the room – the fire still burned brightly and they were still lying before it on the thick rugs. Thomas's head was on her shoulder, the soft bright hair like velvet against her skin. She reached up and took his face in her cupped hands, and kissed him, because even though he was strong and brave, like this, he was suddenly very young and dreadfully vulnerable, and she could bear him being strong and brave, but she could not bear his vulnerability . . .

She supposed that what they had done would be regarded as mortal sin – Liam would be horrified, and the nuns at St Joseph's would be shocked to their toes and forecast that the fires of hell would be waiting. Catherine did not care if she was forced to enter the fires of hell, as long as Thomas entered them at her side.

Maguire could hardly bear it. There they were, the two of them, clearly locked in a disgraceful and sinful love affair – Maguire would not use a stronger term than that – and whatever the outcome, the ending would be that the skew-eyed little cat would get her hands on Fitzgerald money, and there would be none – or precious little – left for Maguire himself. And, of course, for those other families listed in the old Earl's pledge.

Going about his daily tasks in the castle, he gradually became aware that a number of the soldiers believed that although Thomas had taken Dublin, he would not keep it. He had not managed to take Dublin Castle, said these doubters, and whispered behind their hands that there was a growing belief that the Earl would end in being captured by the English.

Maguire considered this. Thomas's capture would certainly result in his execution for high treason. And then what would happen to his estates and his possessions – what would be left of them? Maguire had little knowledge of the law, but he knew there was a half-brother who he thought would inherit the title. Titles were what he believed was called entailed – they passed straight to the legal heir without question or argument. There were those murmurs about a wife, too, although he had never been able to find out where she was or even if she was still alive.

The half-brother would most likely inherit Maynooth Castle along with the title, but there was other property. Maguire knew there was, because he had been to some of the places with the Earl. Could heirs and wives inherit those properties and lands without specific instructions set down? Maguire had no idea.

What he did know, though, was that in an excess of emotion, or gripped by love or lust or both – faced with death, the Earl might direct that everything that was not entailed, and everything that was left in his coffers passed to Catherine Ó Raifeartaigh. And she would seize it all greedily, and live richly on the proceeds for the rest of her life. Which would mean Maguire would never get his hands on anything, and his father's death would have been a worthless one.

Thoughts coiled and uncoiled in his brain for a very long time, until, eventually, one clear thought emerged.

Supposing that, if the Earl were arrested for treason, which some people were murmuring was likely, the whey-faced cat who was sharing his bed was found to have helped him?

Supposing Catherine Ó Raifeartaigh were also to be arraigned for treason?

FIFTEEN

Ethne had often thought that final visit of Montague Fitzglen to Westmeath had seemed, at first, to be just another of the visits Mr Fitzglen often made to Westmeath. But it had not. It had been the start of the nightmares.

Todworthy Inkling had not remained for long; after only two days, he left in a polite flurry of note-gathering and document-tidying.

'I have greatly enjoyed my stay,' he said. 'And it has been a pleasure to have met you, Mr Rafferty – and Miss Rafferty too, of course. You made me very welcome.' He shook their hands. 'And a most amiable arrangement we reached, regarding your ancestor's correspondence,' he said to Ethne's father. 'Entirely satisfactory.'

Ethne, watching Mr Inkling clamber into Grogan's cart, to be driven to the local halt for the train, hoped this remark did not mean a large sum of money had changed hands, which might mean difficulty in settling household bills. People thought a famous playwright, lauded and acclaimed in Ireland and England – never mind living in a fine old manor house in its own grounds – must be rich, but her father was not rich at all. It never worried him, though; if appealed to about money, he usually said airily that something would come along, and that in any case he was writing a new play.

After Mr Inkling's departure, her father and Mr Fitzglen spent most of their time in the library. This meant having to call them when meals were ready, although Ethne often had to do this with her father, who would frequently become so absorbed in his work he would forget about eating.

What was curious now, though, was that each time the two men came out of the library, either to go into the dining room, or up to their beds at the end of the day, her father locked the door. Ethne could not recall him ever doing this before, but probably they were reading old family papers, and he would not want the girl who came in every morning to read them and perhaps gossip in the village. He would be sure to forget to lock the door one of the times, anyway, which meant Ethne could go in and clean the room herself. She would not pry into whatever they were working on, of course, but left to himself her father would turn the room into a shocking muddle. Tidying up would be a considerate and daughterly thing to do.

The opportunity came two days later. Ethne's father was taking Montague to see the old sundial that Seamus Rafferty had caused to be placed in the orchard. Mr Fitzglen could not walk very far because of his lameness, but the orchard was only a short distance, and there were grassy paths.

'You used to go out to the old orchard quite often, my dear,' said Ethne's father to her, as they set off. 'Although I don't believe you've done so for some time.'

It was impossible to say that even the thought of the orchard brought back the night with the actor – the man who had expressed undying love, then had vanished with the coming of the morning. Or that the mere mention of the sundial brought back to her mind his voice reading the line about voyage, travel, and change of place imparting vigour. It had certainly imparted a particular kind of vigour to him, and it was a vigour on which Ethne now looked back with shuddering resentment.

But she smiled at her father, and said there never seemed time for a quarter of the things she wanted to do. She stood at a window, watching the two men going along the paths, Mr Fitzglen wielding his stick to point out various things he found interesting. Was this a good time to try the library door? It would most likely be locked again, and it did not matter if it was . . .

It was not locked. As the door swung open, the scents of old leather and dust, mingling with tobacco smoke and the dregs in the port decanter, greeted her. The room was shockingly untidy and disgracefully dusty. The curtains were three-quarters drawn across the tall windows – had they wanted to shut out anyone who walked past? – and the leather-topped table was stacked with sheaves of notes and books, and bundles of old paper, some of which were tied up with bits of tape, most of which were yellowing and curling at the edges. It was a good thing Ethne had brought two large dusters and the tub of polish. She set to

work, pleased to think of her father and Mr Fitzglen coming back
into the room and finding it neat and orderly, with the scent of
lavender furniture polish on the air. She would not disturb the
papers, or not very much.

But it was impossible not to see that on one side of the table
was a sheet of pristine and very impressive-looking writing paper,
with the pen and inkstand alongside it. The paper was lavishly
water-marked and partly covered with elaborate handwriting. At
the top was a Dublin address, with what seemed to be some kind
of coat of arms or insignia above it.

Ethne was not going to pry or read anything that might be
private, but you could not polish a table without lines of handwriting catching your eye. Also, you would not be human if you
were not curious about such an important-looking heading to a
letter – especially when the letter looked to be only
half-written.

She glanced towards the windows, but there was no sign of
the two men returning, and she would hear them coming back.
Footsteps always echoed loudly on the creaking old floors of the
house, and Mr Fitzglen's steps were uneven and instantly recognizable anyway.

The heading on the notepaper said *Office of Surveyor General,
Dublin, Ireland.* Beneath this was the name of what sounded like
a building, and a street Ethne had never heard of, although there
would be many streets in Dublin she had never heard of. The
insignia was colourful and looked very grand, although it did not
actually mean anything to her.

There was no date, but the letter was addressed to Sir Arthur
Vicars. In brackets after this name were the words, *Ulster King
of Arms.*

Ethne stared at this, and then began to read the letter
properly.

> *Sir,*
>
> *I respectfully beg to draw to your attention a vital require-
ment for a visit to Dublin Castle by representatives from
these offices.*
>
> *You will be aware that in March 1750, His Majesty, King
George III of England, granted the sum of £9,277.9s.2d to*

be handed to Viceroy Lord Harrington, for the restoration of parts of Dublin Castle – in particular the Clock Tower, which is now more usually known as the Bedford Tower. As you know, work began in the summer of that year, and included the demolishment of the medieval gatehouse and of the remaining sections of the curtain wall.

You will also know that a requirement of this Restoration Grant was that the structure be thoroughly inspected every fifty years. This requirement was duly adhered to in the year 1800 and again in the year 1850. However, our records show that no such inspection was made three years ago in 1900, as it should have been. Therefore, we beg to inform you that the survey will be carried out forthwith.

I am pleased to inform you that our two representatives – Maurice Flanders, Esq. and Philip Rawnsley, Esq. can undertake this without delay. They are both qualified and experienced surveyors and are members of the Royal Institution – indeed, Mr Flanders was created a Fellow only last year, so it is most fortunate that he can make himself available.

I will ask that you set aside an entire day for the inspection, and can inform you that the date on which the two gentlemen will call on you will be . . .

Here the letter ended.

Ethne stared at it in bewilderment. She could not see how anyone, other than her father or Montague Fitzglen, could have written this letter, but she could not understand why they had done so.

She had never heard of Maurice Flanders and Philip Rawnsley, but Seamus's correspondence had certainly included letters to or from the Surveyor General about the restoration of Dublin Castle's Clock Tower, and there had been the map, as well.

But this letter had clearly been written recently – in the last day or so. She was about to investigate the other papers lying on the table, when there were voices outside, and her father and Montague Fitzglen appeared, walking slowly, engrossed in discussion. Ethne was about to dart back out to the hall, but they stopped outside the library windows to light cigars – it was to

be hoped the smoke did not drift into this nicely polished room
– and she heard her father's voice clearly.

'I still maintain it's a hell of a risky plan, Montague,' he was
saying. 'But, by God, haven't you of all people the brazen-faced
impudence to get away with it!'

It was not eavesdropping to stay where she was and listen.
Ethne was in her own home, engaged in ordinary household
cleaning, perfectly entitled to be here.

Mr Fitzglen was chuckling. 'D'you know, Phelan, I'm rather
pleased with Mr Maurice Flanders and Mr Philip Rawnsley,' he
said. 'I do like to give these fictional characters names as near
to the real ones as possible. Use the same initials, you know. Bit
of a tradition in the family to do that.'

'I liked being made a Fellow of the Institution,' said Ethne's
father. 'What institution would it be, by the way?'

'Haven't the faintest clue, dear old boy. But neither will anyone
at the castle have the faintest clue, and it'll impress them mightily.'

'Will we finish the letter now?' asked Ethne's father. 'And
send it to Vicars as soon as we've done so? He'll agree to the
visit, I suppose?'

'I'll date our letter three days ago, so it will look as if it was
delayed,' said Montague. 'And I'll put in a date of three days
from now for the actual visit. Vicars won't have time to write
back with a refusal, and you and I will simply arrive at the castle
before he's able to do anything about it. Oh – what about your
daughter, Phelan? What will you tell her? You won't tell her the
truth, I imagine?'

'God, no. I'll say we've arranged to meet some theatre people
in Dublin,' said Ethne's father. 'She won't question it.' And then,
as Ethne was beating down a spurt of fury, because how *dared*
he brush her aside like that! – he said, in a softer tone, 'She's
very trusting. And a good girl, as well. I don't know what I'd
do without her, Montague,' and Ethne relaxed, because she had
known, really, how much she meant to him.

'Phelan, wasn't your name originally spelled Ó Raifeartaigh?'
said Montague, suddenly. 'I daresay I haven't pronounced that
correctly, but was it written like this?'

There was a faint rustle of paper, and Ethne risked edging
closer to the window, in time to see Mr Fitzglen pass a small

notebook to her father. He looked at it, then said, 'Yes, that's right. I believe a marriage was proposed some generations back, with an English family. The English family were nouveau riche, and they liked the idea of being allied with an ancient bardic line. My family liked the idea because they were broke and they needed the English girl's dowry. But the English lot didn't care for the idea of Popery, and I believe there were terrible old rows. In the end my family offered a sop – they would not renounce their Catholicism, but they would simplify their name to a more English version.'

'Interesting,' said Montague. 'Do you know the English family's name?'

'Something about cakes comes to mind.'

'Bun? Scone?'

'Not even the English would have a surname like Scone,' said Ethne's father. And then – 'Or would they? I have a vague memory that the name was something to do with some northern delicacy they have in your country. Griddle, I think. Is there such a thing?'

'I don't think . . . Oh, but there's something called girdle scones.'

'That sounds like it.'

'I might rummage around in the family archives later, if you don't mind, to see if I can find the Girdle Scones.'

'Rummage to your heart's content.' A pause, and Ethne saw her father look about him, as if making sure no one was in earshot. Then he said, quietly, 'Let's have this out in the open, Montague. Is it Seamus's secret you're after? Or is it something much older? You listened to old Inkling and Seamus's letters with far more attention than you wanted us to realize, didn't you? Isn't it really that long-ago Earl – what did you call him? The Silken Earl, wasn't it? Isn't he the one who's pulling you to Dublin Castle.'

Montague Fitzglen said, slowly, 'You're right, Phelan. It is Thomas,' and Ethne felt her heart lurch.

'Look at it clearly,' he went on. 'Don't the two things intertwine? We have your ancestor, Seamus, wanting to create a hiding place away from this house – a hiding place he needed to be so secure, so far away from the family, that he tried to have it built within Dublin Castle.'

'Shockingly impudent, of course, but from all accounts he was impudent, that Seamus.'

'I rather like the sound of him,' said Montague. 'We don't know if he did get his secret room – although it sounded as if the castle people gave it consideration – but don't you see that it might have had something to do with your Thomas? Those references to a lady who seemingly met a terrible death because of him . . . Supposing Seamus found out something about her – even about her and Thomas himself – and it was so potentially damaging, or even dangerous, that he wanted to make sure it remained hidden.'

'And hidden somewhere that couldn't be traced back to this house or this family,' said Ethne's father, almost to himself. 'It's still wild-sounding, but it could have happened.'

'Of course it could. And now,' said Montague in a brisker voice, 'let's finish our letter to Sir Arthur Vicars.'

'It's looking very convincing, that letter,' said Ethne's father, as they moved away.

They were still just within hearing, though, and Ethne heard Montague say, 'I always am very convincing, my dear Phelan. And I'm never caught, as you know.'

She waited until they had gone around the side of the house, then went back out to the hall, closing the library door quietly. She darted into the morning room, and heard them come in, Mr Fitzglen's stick tapping on the oak boards as they crossed the hall.

Her father said, 'Dammit, I forgot to lock the library door. Ah, no matter. I shouldn't think anyone's been in.'

After supper that night, as Ethne was crossing the hall on her way to bed, she realized her father and Mr Fitzglen were still in the library. The door was slightly open, and it was impossible not to hear what they were saying.

Mr Fitzglen had apparently found an old letter earlier in the evening.

'I'll read it to you, Phelan – it's from the early 1700s, and the writing is very spidery and straggling. You were right about the girdle scones – although the name is actually Girdlestone. They sound shockingly prim and stuffy. This is what one of them wrote to one of your ancestors:

*You will by now be in receipt of the bank draft representing
the dowry agreed for your daughter's marriage to my son.
Documents are being prepared that will change, legally, the
spelling of your family name from Ó Raifeartaigh to Rafferty,
which my family finds more acceptable.*

*I am told your daughter is wishful to bring to Girdlestone
Hall some of your family's portraits. I, myself, am not
especially in favour of this, but am prepared to agree to it.
I recall the paintings from my visit to Westmeath when we
arranged the marriage; two will form an acceptable part
of the Girdlestone collection. The third, which is of a young
female in a blue gown, is poorly executed, but it can hang
in a corner of the upper gallery here, which is seldom
frequented, so is unlikely to be seen by many people.'*

The loss of a few paintings two hundred years ago seemed to
Ethne a trivial matter, although it was vaguely interesting to know
how the alteration of the family name had come about.

But her mind was almost entirely filled with the fact that
tomorrow, or perhaps the day after, her father and Mr Fitzglen
would leave for Dublin. That half-written letter – which clearly
Mr Fitzglen himself had penned – would allow them entry to
the castle and mean they could go wherever they wanted. They
had created false identities – Maurice Flanders and Philip
Rawnsley, and those identities would be accepted. Mr Fitzglen
was an actor, he would be convincing.

Once in the Clock Tower they would search for Seamus
Rafferty's secret room, and again they could be entirely open,
because they would seem to be accredited surveyors, authorized
to check the tower's structure. They would even have with them
Seamus's sketched map to help them find the room.

It was important to remember that what her father and Mr
Fitzglen were about to do was not actually criminal, or at least
Ethne did not think it was. But her father had said it was risky,
and Mr Fitzglen had talked about the possibility of Seamus having
discovered something potentially damaging or even dangerous,
making it necessary to hide it somewhere far from this house.
Ethne's mind had instantly flown to Thomas, because if there
were any secrets in this house and in this family, they must surely

centre on him. A slow anger at being excluded from something that might involve Thomas began to burn up, but alongside it was concern for her father. It had sounded as if Mr Fitzglen might be about to lure him into something questionable. And her father, who trusted the whole world and never believed ill of anyone, would allow himself to be lured.

As she had expected, the following morning the two men presented her with a careful explanation of having to travel to Dublin. A bit of a nuisance, said her father – Ethne was sad to see how his eyes slid away from her when he said this.

'But we'll only be away for a night or two,' he said.

Ethne, choosing her words carefully, asked if the journey was a theatre matter, at which her father donned his slightly bewildered, confused-scholar expression. But before he could reply, Mr Fitzglen said they were not absolutely sure of the details yet. It was going to be a question of exerting persuasion on some gentlemen who might be interested in a forthcoming production of one of Phelan's earlier plays.

'*The Iron Tongue of Midnight*,' he said. 'A marvellous piece, it was, and wasn't that the one that netted you the Sheridan Award, Phelan?'

'It was. Didn't you put it on at the Amaranth the following year?'

'We did. Jack's father played Medoc – a fine stirring performance he gave, as well. I believe young Byron wanted to revive it quite recently, although I don't know if anything will come of the idea.'

They were talking like this to distract Ethne from the truth, but they were lying. The truth was that they were going to Dublin Castle under false names and, once there, they were going to search for Seamus's secret room.

If they found it – always supposing it existed – there would not be anything shameful or discreditable to be uncovered about Thomas. Ethne knew that. But Thomas had had enemies; people around him who would have wanted to blacken his name. There could be something that Seamus – or maybe someone earlier than Seamus, perhaps even someone from Thomas's own time – had thought must be hidden in order to protect him. And if people had protected Thomas in the past, then it was for Ethne to continue to do so in the present.

Her father would believe anything Montague Fitzglen told him and suggested to him, and he would never see the hazards that might be involved. Ethne realized, with a fresh surge of fear, that the two people who meant most to her in the entire world could be at risk. Her father and Silken Thomas. That being so, there was only one thing to do. She would have to follow her father and Mr Fitzglen to Dublin and, if they really did find Seamus's secret room, she would have to follow them in there.

For a moment the fear spiralled into near-panic, but then within the panic was a sudden twist of excitement. This might bring her closer to Thomas than she had ever been – she might be about to enter a secret part of his life. The feeling of excitement shot up, engulfing her, bringing with it courage and resolve.

SIXTEEN

The following morning, Ethne helped the two men prepare for their journey – left to himself, her father would have forgotten essential items such as a nightshirt and washing things. She helped Mr Fitzglen, as well, of course; there were shirts to fold up, and shaving things and facecloths. There were also a couple of photographs of Mr Fitzglen's family, without which he never travelled. They were in silver frames, and he always said he liked to have them with him in a strange house or on a long journey.

'A very dear niece,' he had once said, when Ethne asked about one of the photographs, which showed him with a lady on his arm, clearly in wedding attire. 'I had the delight and the honour of giving her away at her wedding.'

Ethne wrapped the photographs in the silk evening scarf that Mr Fitzglen had brought, and placed them in the suitcase.

Immediately after breakfast, Grogan's cart took the two of them to Westmeath Halt for the Dublin train. Ethne allowed an hour to be sure they were well on their way, then packed a small bag for herself, and sent a message for Grogan to return to the house. It was easy to explain to him, and also to the current village helper, that Mr Rafferty and his guest had left some important papers behind.

'And they must have them for their meeting later today,' she said. 'So I shall have to take them to Dublin myself. There's a midday train.'

Once in Dublin, she hesitated, because she had forgotten how noisy and how bustling it was, but rising up behind the city was the silhouette of the castle, standing on its own high ground.

It was still only half past two, and Ethne set off. She did not ask anyone for directions, but the castle was impossible to miss. It was a longer walk than she had expected, though, and the nearer she got to it, the more apprehensive she felt. What, in

Westmeath, had seemed romantic and quite adventurous was starting to feel frightening.

There was virtually no trace of the castle's medieval origins, but there was still the aura of age and strength and a kind of mightiness about it. There had been a book in her father's library, telling how the original structure dated to the Norman invasion when the castle had been built as a massive defence by the order of the English King John. Reading that, Ethne had found it incredible that a hundred years ago, Seamus Rafferty had travelled to it and confronted the keepers. Seeing the castle now, she found it even more incredible.

But her father and Mr Fitzglen had believed Seamus's story – to the extent that they had created disguises so they could get into the castle and search for his secret room. And Mr Fitzglen might be a bit of a rogue, but neither he nor Ethne's father were likely to be easily fooled or seduced by improbable legends. As she drew nearer, she slowed her steps, trying to see which part of the castle she should approach. It looked as if you could walk round it for the best part of a day without finding the right entrance, or any entrance at all. But surely you could not mistake a Clock Tower, even in a structure of this size? And then without warning she saw it, rearing up against the lowering skies, octagonal in shape, and unmistakable. Each of the eight sides had a huge clock face on it – for a bad moment it felt as if they were living things, staring down at her.

As Ethne got nearer she saw that people were coming and going, in and out of various entrances. Some wore uniforms, while others were clearly soldiers on duty. She held on to the thought that she could provide a perfectly credible reason for being here, and walked firmly to a small outer room that looked as if it might be a guard room or sentry house. At any rate, a place where you would be required to state your business and probably show that you had permission to be allowed in.

Astonishingly, it was easy. She said she was assistant to the two men who were here to carry out survey work, and she had brought various important papers and notes they had left behind. An appointment had been made for Mr Rawnsley and Mr Flanders with Sir Arthur Vicars, she said, firmly.

No one appeared to find this in the least suspicious. Within a remarkably short time she was being taken along passages and up stairways by a youngish man in uniform. The stairs were very narrow in places and the stones were worn. Were they fragments left from the original castle? Was any of this from Seamus's design?

She was increasingly aware of the massive clock above her. It was as if its mechanism resonated through the old stones and thrummed out a message.

Let-the-past-stay-buried . . . Or was it even saying, *You-shouldn't-be-here* . . .?

As they reached a long corridor with doors opening off, her escort indicated an archway at the far end.

'The two gentlemen will be through there,' he said.

The corridor was quite dim, although thin light came in from the narrow windows. But there were gas mantles at intervals on the walls, and probably they would be lit quite soon and the shadows that lay like black pools over the stones would retreat.

Once beyond the archway the clock's voice came closer. *Don't-disturb-the-past-Ethne* . . . *Let-Thomas-stay-in-the-dark* . . .

Ethne pushed the voice away, because at the far end of the passage she could see her father and Mr Fitzglen. They had Seamus's sketch spread out on the floor, together with measuring tape, and notebook and pencil, and they were examining a section of stonework. It looked as if they were being entirely open about it, but they were believed to be surveyors and there would be no reason for anyone to question them.

Then her father looked up, and Ethne saw the shock and the dismay in his face.

'Ethne . . . What in God's name are you doing here?'

'Hoping to make you see sense and come home,' said Ethne. 'I know what you're doing – you're trying to find Seamus's secret room, and it's madness, because you'll be caught.' She glanced at Montague Fitzglen. 'I did preserve your disguises when I came in,' she said. 'Mr Rawnsley and Mr Flanders. I said I was your assistant and I had brought you some notes you had left behind. So you're safe so far.'

They looked at one another, then her father said, 'I'm not even going to ask how you knew about Rawnsley and Flanders. But Ethne, please just go home and leave us to do this.'

'Or,' said Montague Fitzglen, softly, 'you could stay here, Ethne, and help us. Help us to find the hidden room and what Seamus concealed in it.'

Ethne stared at him, trying not to show how his words added to the sensation of the past pulling her in.

'Seamus was your ancestor as well,' said Montague. 'Don't you want to know why he went to such trouble all those years ago? Aren't you curious about your family's past? About what secrets there might be in that past?'

Ethne was about to answer, although she had no idea what she was going to say, but sharp footsteps rang out beyond the stone archway, and a voice reached them, echoing slightly in the enclosed space, calling out that the castle was shortly closing – all guests must please leave in the next fifteen minutes, and make their way to one of the two guard rooms.

Montague Fitzglen waited for the footsteps to die away, then said, 'Well, Ethne? Your father and I have no intention of leaving, you know. I will not get this close to finding what Seamus Rafferty secreted in this castle and walk away from it.'

'We aren't walking away,' said Phelan. 'But Ethne, you have time to go back to the station and be home later today. There'll be plenty of trains still.'

'But if you stay,' said Montague, a note of persuasion in his voice, 'you'd be with us when we find whatever's been hidden. You might even be able to act as a look-out for us. Phelan, what do you think?'

Ethne's father said, slowly, 'A look-out. That would certainly be useful.' He frowned, then said, 'And as Montague says, you'd be sharing the secret, Ethne. Perhaps you have a right to do that.'

Sharing the secret, thought Ethne. The secret of whatever Seamus concealed all those years ago. But with the thought came the clock's relentless tapping against her mind again. *Don't-let-the-past-pull-you-back, Ethne . . . It's-dangerous-to-disturb-the-past . . .* Or mightn't it be saying, *Find-the-secret, Ethne . . . Find-Thomas . . .*

In a voice meant to push the clock's insistent voice away, Ethne said, 'I'll stay. I'll help. I'll be the look-out.'

In the hours that followed, the thrumming of the massive clock seemed to become part of the half-fearful, half-anticipatory pounding of Ethne's heartbeat. Several times the guards walked along the passages, but each time the two men and Ethne simply stepped into one of the little side rooms.

'Offices or storerooms by the look,' said Mr Fitzglen. 'We marked them out earlier, of course. The guards aren't likely to look into them all.'

'And they probably won't make their rounds more than once or twice through the night,' said Ethne's father.

'Which means we have almost the entire night to search,' said Montague Fitzglen.

'Should we wait until midnight until we start properly, though?'

'The "Iron Tongue of Midnight", Phelan? Be damned to that,' said Montague. 'Pass me Seamus's sketch again.'

But eventually, Ethne's father sat back, pushed back his hair impatiently, and said, 'It's not here, Montague. Never mind waiting until midnight, if we searched and tapped and pushed bits of stone until the Last Trump sounded, we still wouldn't find it. Seamus was simply playing a gigantic, elaborate joke.'

'Or,' said Montague, slowly, 'we're in the wrong corridor. Let's look at the map again. Yes, look there. There's a level immediately above us – and doesn't the layout look the same as this one? Phelan, there's an identical passage over our heads.'

An identical passage . . . A passage that took them closer to the massive mechanism of wheels and cogs and the ticking voice warning them not to disturb the past.

It was much narrower and much darker, and there was a lonely feeling to it. The only light came from two narrow windows, set high up; Ethne glanced through one and saw the dark countryside spread out far below. She shivered, because she had not realized they were quite so high up, so near to the beating clock. *Leave-the-past-hidden, Ethne . . . Leave-the-secrets-in-the-dark . . .*

But her father and Mr Fitzglen were already examining the walls, tapping and measuring, consulting the map, and murmuring to one another. Ethne remembered her role as look-out, and went to stand at the head of the stairs, from where she would hear if the guards came along.

She was just beginning to think that they were not going to find anything up here either, when Montague suddenly said, in a voice that held suppressed excitement, 'Phelan – I think there's something. Light a match, will you?'

'Dare we do that?'

'We'll have to if we're to see. We'll hear if anyone comes up here anyway – Ethne will warn us.'

From her post by the stairway, Ethne saw the tiny flare from the match burn up, magnifying the shadows of her father and Mr Fitzglen. Or were they different shadows – shadows who had stood up from their corners, and crept forward to watch . . .? Then her father swore as the match burned down, scorching his fingers, and the darkness closed down.

But as it did so, Montague said, in a voice of suppressed excitement, 'I think I saw something over to the left. You'd never realize it without Seamus's sketch . . . Ethne, would you come over here and strike the match again for us, so your father and I can both look more closely? I've brought a couple of candles, but I'm reluctant to light them unless we have to – it could attract attention.'

As Ethne struck the match, trying to stop her hands shaking, Montague said, 'Yes, I was right! See up here, Phelan? This piece of stone is separate – it will move to one side . . .'

'Would it move after so long, though?' said Phelan, leaning closer to see.

But Montague was already grasping the jutting stone near the ceiling. For a moment nothing happened, and Ethne was thinking that of course the stone would not work after so long, and feeling disappointment but also relief, because they would not have to open up the past after all, and they could go quietly home and forget the whole thing. Except she would never forget it.

Then there was a harsh hard grinding sound – a dry scraping, as if old *old* bones were struggling to move – and her heart lurched. After all, were they about to find something that had been hidden for more than a century? Something that Seamus had believed it was necessary to hide in here – something that might date back beyond his time, and that might date back to Thomas himself?

The rasping of stone-on-stone came again, and slowly and reluctantly, a section of the stone wall moved. A dry stench gusted out, like the breath of an ancient tomb. Was it a tomb they were opening up? What might lie inside?

Then Montague said, softly, 'That seems to be as far as it will go,' and before them was the yawning opening, perhaps four feet in height and three feet wide.

'Dear God in heaven,' said Ethne's father. 'Seamus's secret room. He told the truth.'

'It doesn't look quite big enough to be called a room,' said Montague Fitzglen, as if determined to keep matters on a practical level. 'It's more an alcove.'

They were speaking in whispers, not so much as if they were fearful of being heard, but as if they were afraid of disturbing something. Ethne's father knelt down to examine the ground, and said, 'There's some kind of sliding mechanism that's been sunk into the stones down here – d'you see? There are runners, sunk into the floor.'

'I do. And along the top, as well. It's ingenious. But that it should still work after all these years . . . I wonder if it can be operated from inside?' said Montague. 'It looks as if it can, but I can't see properly—'

'Ethne, come along here, and light more matches so we can see better.'

'But don't go too close, my dear, because there's no knowing what'll be in there. And there's no knowing what condition it's in. The floor could have fallen in, or anything . . .'

The movement of the wall had disturbed the thick layers of dust that lay beyond it, and caused grey veils of cobwebs to float outwards. Like beckoning fingers, thought Ethne, caught between fear and a compulsion to step into the waiting darkness and see what was in there.

Don't-go-in-there-Ethne . . . Leave-Thomas-in-the-past . . .

'I think we'll have to risk one of the candles, Montague,' Ethne's father said. 'It won't be seen, and we'll hear anyone coming up those stairs anyway. Ethne, light one for us, and hold it up.'

As Ethne took the candle, she had the feeling that the cobwebs stirred again, as if they were reaching out to wind themselves in her hair and pull her inside. But as the candle burned up, the cobwebs flinched. They don't like the light, she thought, and then – is there something else in there that doesn't like the light?

Then her father moved, and Ethne realized he was going to

step through the narrow opening, and horror rose in her throat. He mustn't go in there, she thought. The past mustn't be disturbed . . .

She moved closer to him, although whether she was intending to pull him away or to try to step into Seamus's room with him, she never knew.

Because as she did so, there was a movement from deep within the darkness . . . Ethne gasped, and reached for her father's arm, because it was a tomb they had opened, after all – only whoever had been buried in there was still alive; *it was still alive* . . .

The movement came again – something was unfolding itself – it was stepping out of the thick shadows, and coming towards them, putting out a hand as if to defend its hiding place – as if to challenge whoever was trying to enter this ancient, silent place . . .

Within the narrow stone tunnel, someone began to scream.

SEVENTEEN

G us was getting to know Russell Square and its surroundings quite well. There was a letter to be collected from Miss Tansy most mornings – often there was one to deliver to her as well, usually from Mr Jack, but sometimes from Mr Byron or one of the others. It was nice that they were writing to her and encouraging her, because it could not be easy for her to be within the enemy's camp, so to speak. Gus would have hated it, although he had to say Miss Tansy was being remarkably cheerful.

This morning, arriving at the garden flat, it seemed today's letter was especially important.

'It's to tell Jack and the others that I'll be setting off with the company for Ireland tomorrow – for the *Féile*,' she said. 'I don't think I've pronounced that right, although Timon Gilfillan has told me how to say it. But the pronunciation won't matter in a letter. Tell Jack I'll write from Dublin as soon as we get there, will you Gus. I've put the address in the note for him – it's a lodging house – quite close to the theatre, apparently. Is everyone all right? They're doing *The Philanderer* at the moment, aren't they? Is it going well?'

'Some very favourable notices, I believe,' said Gus. Miss Tansy had sounded a bit wistful, as if she felt outside all the excitement, so he stepped a bit nearer and told her about Mr Jack and Mr Byron's plan to return to Girdlestone Hall to examine the strange-sounding portrait.

'How marvellous,' said Miss Tansy, delightedly. 'What a good idea. Tell Jack to let me know what they find.'

It had, of course, been safe to tell Miss Tansy about the Girdlestone Hall plan, because she could be trusted, and Gus had made sure no one was around who might have been listening. He had realized he needed to be careful about that, after two occasions on which he had been mistaken for a genuine postman, and asked about deliveries of letters. And on his third day, a young woman had come up to him and said she hadn't seen him in this delivery area before, and wondered if he had just joined the Post Office. She herself was a telephonist at the nearby exchange, which was very interesting work, and she often went along to a friendly little club for Post Office workers which was just off Southampton Row. He would be made very welcome if he cared to come along one evening.

Gus said he was not permanently based in Bloomsbury; he had been drafted in from his usual delivery area as temporary help, and when the young woman asked where his usual area might be, he said it was Newgate, and you got some very strange letters and parcels to deliver in those streets.

The young woman then remembered she had to be on duty in half an hour and they were ever so strict about you being on time, and beat a retreat. Gus supposed it was gratifying to know that the disguise was convincing.

Tansy was glad to have sent the message to Jack letting him know she would be leaving London tomorrow. She would feel a bit far away from the family, but she was quite excited about going to Ireland, although some of the company had grumbled at the early start to the journey. It was the crack of dawn, they said, a positively unearthly hour, although Tansy thought it was a reasonable time, given that it would be a long journey – a train to Liverpool and then the ferry to Dublin.

Even so early in the day, Euston Station was crowded, with porters trundling laden luggage trolleys and travellers worriedly scanning arrival and departure times, and newspaper vendors plying their wares. Trains chugged in and out, enveloping the platforms in clouds of smoke and steam. Tansy was just wondering if it would somehow be possible to create this effect at the Amaranth – because it would be marvellous to have people materializing out of swirling smoke – when a figure did materialize out of the billowing smoke.

It was Florian. Tansy would not have put it past him to have lurked in the men's room or behind the newspaper stand, waiting for a suitable blast of steam in order to make a striking appearance. He was wearing a cloak, and he nodded graciously to the porters, and extended his hands to one or two passers-by, as if, thought Tansy, he was making a first-night entrance rather than walking across a railway platform on a dank October morning.

She went back to helping the stage crew, who were bewailing the difficulties of loading all the scenery onto the luggage van. They called Timon over, and told him that it was all very well to build spiral stairways and create dimly lit passages in their own theatre, and set them up on their own stage, but it was another matter altogether to transport flats and staircases piece by piece across a turbulent sea, on a ferry that would very likely sink halfway across – not to mention half the crew succumbing to seasickness. Then have to put everything together on an unfamiliar stage. Did anyone actually know anything about the facilities they would be accorded in this Roscius theatre?

'Oh, the Roscius is very well-equipped,' said Florian, who had wandered over to observe.

'You know it, do you?' asked Timon, straight-faced.

'By reputation only, dear boy. Although I was in Ireland some years ago – I have very fond memories of that, although matters there did not go quite as I had hoped. An affair of the heart, you understand . . .' He broke off, examining his fingernails sadly, then said, in a more robust voice, 'But everyone knows the Roscius was named for the great Roman comic actor, who was born into slavery somewhere BC or other—'

Timon said, 'Shall we find our seats? I think everything's safely on board now.'

As he walked away, he glanced back, and there was a moment when Tansy thought he half-winked at her. But most likely he had not, so she clambered onto the train, found her way to the two carriages occupied by most of the company, and was pleased when she managed to squeeze into a seat next to Florian. It was possible that he might be coaxed into imparting the secret of the hidden scene – or at least some of it – to an insignificant props person, whom he would not think would count.

In the event, though, he launched into a description of how, some years earlier, he had played Horatio to Beerbohm Tree's Hamlet at The Haymarket.

Tansy could remember her father playing Horatio, with her mother as Ophelia, and she could still remember her father saying that committing Horatio's lines to memory was a tour de force for the mind. She wondered if Florian had remembered all the speeches when he had played it.

The ferry crossing from Liverpool was entirely straightforward, and Tansy greatly enjoyed the new experience. There did not seem to be any mishaps, although it was a pity that halfway across, one of the inquisitive sisters had to retire rather hastily below deck.

The lodging house was bigger than she had expected. Tansy had a sliver of a room at the very top of the building – there was only just enough space for a bed and a chair, but at least she was on her own, for which she was thankful. A few of the company were sharing rooms, and she suspected some of them might have manipulated the sharing arrangements, although it was probably better not to enquire too deeply into that.

Timon and Viola Gilfillan were staying in a nearby hotel, which Tansy supposed was what you would expect. Chloris, confronted with the lodging house and the room allotted to her, had shuddered and declared she would not soil her feet by stepping inside, and Florian, who had come along to see where the serfs were housed, patted her shoulder, and said he would arrange a room for her at the hotel. He had booked himself in there as well as Timon and Viola, he explained, because if he had to be surrounded by chattering fools before a performance, his acting would be utterly smothered.

One of the inquisitive sisters told Tansy afterwards that the 'chattering fools' line was from the Bible, and the other observed that it was remarkable how Florian could remember lines from the Bible, but could not remember his own lines in rehearsal.

'But he looks up suitable quotations ahead of each occasion,' said the first.

After supper, which was substantial and friendly, Tansy considered going to bed. It was almost ten o'clock, but even though it had been such a crowded day, she would probably not be able to sleep. She thought she would walk along the street to see if she could find the Roscius, and if the stage door was unlocked, she would take a look inside while no one was around.

The Dublin streets were lively and bustling, and she found the Roscius quite easily. It was a vast old place – it seemed to sprawl out in several directions, as if, over the years, it had sneakily taken over several of the adjoining buildings when nobody was looking.

The stage door was in a side street, just beyond the theatre's main entrance. Tansy expected it to be locked, but it was not, and there was surely no reason why she could not go inside. If anyone challenged her, she could say with truth that she was a member of the Gilfillan company, and she wanted to see where her props corner could be set up ahead of tomorrow's early morning rehearsal. She had put the typed scenes she had now been given in a pocket, along with her own notes, which would be proof.

But no one challenged her as she went up an iron staircase, which was similar to the Amaranth's, and then along a corridor. She could hear distant voices and faraway sounds of hammering and thudding now. It might be the Gilfillan backstage crew, still unloading scenery, or even the Roscius's own people.

Did this corridor lead towards the stage itself? Yes, it seemed so. And here the stage was. It was in semi-darkness, with only a low light burning somewhere, and shadows clustering in corners. As Tansy stood in the wings, looking out, the sounds of hammering and the voices seemed to fade, and silence folded around her. After a moment she stepped onto the stage itself, and looked out into the auditorium. Even in this half-light it was clearly very large and plush. There was crimson carpeting and polished mahogany, and ornate gilding everywhere.

The stage itself was *vast.* You could put on immense, spectacular productions here – you could have armies fighting the Battle of Agincourt, or jeering French Revolution crowds storming the Bastille, and vivid *Commedia dell'Arte* pieces, with Harlequin and Columbine prancing around, and Pulcinella and Pantalone cavorting everywhere.

The images whisked across her mind; then, as if from nowhere, came others. And this time they were different – they were fleeting glimpses of figures so elusive they were like pencil drawings on the air. Ghost images, thought Tansy, trying to capture the outlines; imprints left behind by characters from all the plays that had been performed here. People who were never real – who never existed beyond the make-believe world of this stage. It was an entrancing idea to think they might be here, those shadow beings, watching and listening, hoping to hear their cue, wanting to be called back to the lighted stage, wanting to hear the applause, wanting to *live* for a few hours . . .

Maran would not be among those pencil-drawn creatures, though, and nor would Tomás or Catrina, because none of them had yet walked on this stage – or on any stage. Tansy suddenly very much wanted them to be here – she wanted to be able to reach out to them, beckon them forward, see them walk towards her.

Maran and Tomás and Catrina. And Mimi, too, of course.

Mimi.

It looked as if someone from the Gilfillan company had been here already, because chalked out on the boards were details of where various scenes had to be set, with roughly scrawled identifications. 'Alleyway', and 'Steps inside castle', and 'T's house'.

T's house. Tansy reached into her pocket for her script notes. The light on the stage was quite dim, but it was enough to read the scene in which Maran and Tomás met in his house. They had studied maps and planned their entry into the castle, then Maran came back into the cobbled alley. There would be flickering lamplight, and by it he saw Mimi curled into a doorway, waiting and watching.

Tansy looked out into the shadowy auditorium, then walked to where the cobbled alley was marked. As she did so, she felt she was becoming Mimi – that she was the girl Maran called an elfin waif.

Here were Mimi's lines, when Maran found her outside Tomás's house again – their second meeting, it was.

'Don't let him lead you both into danger, will you, sir? He's planning to commit a crime – I know it. I seen enough people doing that to know. There's something he wants to find – and you're helping him to find it, I know that, too. He thinks you can do so, too; you make him think he can do anything in the world. But I understand that, because you'd make anyone feel like that.'

Tansy heard, with a start of surprise, her voice ring out in the emptiness. She had not known she was going to speak the lines aloud, but she did not think they sounded at all bad. Just enough Cockney, exactly as she had attempted when she walked through the scene while Chloris was away. She tried the line again, with a different emphasis. '*Don't* let him lead you into danger . . .'

Without the least warning, the answering line came back.

'But supposing I want to be led, Mimi. Don't judge Tomás, will you? Don't judge either of us.'

Tansy's heart leapt, and she turned her head and saw a figure half-leaning against a flat, almost negligently, the arms crossed. For a moment she thought one of the pencil-drawn ghosts had stepped out of the shadows and that it was Maran who stood there. Then the figure said, 'You see, Mimi, Tomás will never rest until he does find what he's seeking. Until he possesses it. That's why I'm going to steal it for him.'

The silence stretched out, and the shadows seemed to creep nearer. The figure came closer, then Timon Gilfillan said, softly, 'Well? Aren't we going to finish the scene?'

Tansy stared at him, no longer sure whether this was actually happening – or whether Mimi and Maran had in fact stepped out from their ghost-shadow existence, and were here on the stage. Then she heard her voice – no, not her voice, Mimi's voice again.

'You said, "steal", sir?'

'My dear street waif, you must have realized by now that I'm an irreclaimable thief,' said the amused voice. 'Beyond saving. I can't betray Tomás's secret, and I won't, not even to you. But I will tell you this is about something he has striven to find all his life.'

'But if he's caught – if you're both caught?'

'We won't be caught, Mimi. I never am caught.'

'If you were, I'd rescue you, though. Both of you. I'd do anything.' This came out with a kind of angry defiance, and Tansy was so pleased to hear it was exactly how Mimi would have spoken, that the other-world sense of the situation became natural. She was Mimi, and this was Maran she was talking to, and they were standing in a lamplit cobbled square, surrounded by wizened buildings and dreary windows . . .

Then Timon said, in his ordinary voice, 'Thank you, Tilly Fendle. You really were Mimi then. It's a pity, isn't it, that—'

He broke off, as a door banged at the very back of the auditorium, and a small figure made a lively way between the rows of seats, whistling as it came, and calling out a cheerful good evening.

'Sorry to have startled you, sir. Only old Ben Barley, come to do my rounds, as usual.'

The figure came into view, and Tansy saw it was a small, fairly elderly gentleman, wizened as to face and slightly bent as to posture. The figure tipped a disreputable hat, and said, 'Night-watchman, I am, sir – and miss – although when I say night-watchman, I'm not here all night, you understand. Just look in every now and then, to make sure the old place ain't burning down or been taken over by rioters.'

'We aren't rioters,' said Timon, 'but I think there are a few of the backstage people working somewhere downstairs.'

'That'll be in the cellars,' said Ben Barley. 'Workshops they call them nowadays, but for all that they're cellars. Gloomy old places.'

'It's very good to know someone looks in to make sure the theatre is safe,' said Timon.

'I look in on several places, sir. Between times I'm at The Moonshine just on the corner.' He waved a vague hand.

Timon walked across to the steps leading down to the auditor-ium, and held out a hand to help Tansy. She did not really need helping, but she took his hand and tried not to think it tightened around hers for a moment.

'It's been good to meet you, Mr Barley,' he said, and there was a chink of coins. 'Will you drink a glass on me at The Moonshine later tonight?'

'I will that, sir, and pleased to do so. I'll be locking all the doors just on midnight. I daresay your people will all have gone by then anyway, will they?'

'I should think so.'

Ben Barley nodded, tipped his hat again, and took himself off, whistling once more.

After a moment, Timon said, 'Well, Tilly Fendle? Now you've seen the Roscius, what do you think of it?'

Tansy was back in the present, and able to realize they had only been standing on a bare, dimly lit stage and that her companion had not been Maran, but the distinguished Timon

Gilfillan. And she was not Mimi, at all, only Tansy Fitzglen –
except that he must not know that about her.

She managed to say, in what was a nearly normal tone, 'I like
it. I probably shouldn't have come in here so late, but I wanted
to see it – to prepare for tomorrow's rehearsal.'

'It's an interesting place,' he said. 'Although all theatres are
interesting, of course. This one's very old, and it'll probably turn
out to be appallingly inconvenient.' He looked about him thoughtfully, and said, 'I believe bits have been added on to the original
structure over the years – walls knocked through into adjoining
buildings; places that were once warehouses, and so on.' He
paused, glancing back at the stage. 'Have we left the ghost-light
burning?'

'Yes,' said Tansy, without thinking. 'There – on the prompt
side.'

'So it is.'

He appeared to wait for her reaction, and Tansy said, 'The
ghost-light should always be left burning somewhere in a theatre,
shouldn't it? Although whether it's to ward off ill-intentioned
spectres—'

'Or provide a lighted area for them to perform by, no one
knows,' said Timon, and he sounded pleased at her response. 'I
expect, though, that it's only to make sure nobody comes blundering in and falls over in the dark.'

'I'd rather think it was so that the ghosts could put on their
own performance while the living weren't around,' said Tansy.

'So would I . . . It's a pity it's a bit late for us to explore the
Roscius properly together now, isn't it?' he said as they went
out into the street. 'Look here, I'll walk back to your lodgings
with you, to make sure you get there safely.'

Tansy thought there was no need to mention any of this to Jack
in her next letter. The fact that she and Timon had played that
brief scene on stage did not mean anything, and nor did the fact
that he had walked back to the lodging house with her afterwards.
That had been a considerate act from a gentleman to a younger
lady in an unfamiliar city. There was nothing to be read into it,
which was why she would not bother to tell Jack about it.

In any case, Jack would have more than sufficient to cope with at the moment; Gus had said there was a plan to see if the old portrait in Girdlestone Hall contained any more information, and when Tansy got back to the lodging house after her trip to the Roscius, there was a letter waiting for her, which it appeared had come by the evening post. It was nice to see Jack's writing – it made her feel that the family were not so very far away after all.

'I'm glad you let me have your address before you set off,' he had written.

'Everyone is looking forward to hearing all developments. As for what's happening here, Byron and I are going to Girdlestone Hall in a couple of days' time. It will have to be a midnight drainpipe job, of course,' he said and, reading that, Tansy instantly had a picture of him swarming up a guttering as midnight chimed somewhere, and climbing through a window. He would be a dark-clad figure, blending with the night, silent and swift, and of course he would succeed, because he always did.

'Byron thinks he can scrape away a bit of the paint that's almost completely covering up the lute,' went on Jack's letter. 'As you know, Montague taught him a fair amount and it will be a delicate task, but all the implements are still at the Notting Hill house, so Byron will bring them along. It's a pity we can't resurrect the two French academics and go in openly by daylight – perhaps with some story about wanting to test the age of the paint. But Gertie the Girdle would stay in the gallery with us, and she's probably realized by now that those two gentlemen were bogus, anyway.

'I think I had better ask you to burn this letter as soon as you've read it. It's somewhat incriminating and you're in the enemy camp, let's not forget!

'All love, Jack.'

Tansy smiled as she consigned the letter to the fireplace. Jack was certainly fascinated by the wicked Catherine.

EIGHTEEN

A village clock was chiming the three quarters after eleven as Jack and Byron left Girdlestone Halt and walked down the tree-lined lane towards the hall.

'It was lucky we were able to get such a late train,' said Byron. 'I was worried that we might have to sit under a hedge waiting for midnight to toll its iron tongue. I've brought Montague's leather wallet with the tools of the forger's trade with me, of course. Scraping implements and little pointy instruments and blades. And a bottle of some solution for cleaning, as well. I have no idea what it is, but I've seen him use it, and I'm hoping it will work on that layer of paint that somebody added. And you've got the silk ladder, haven't you, in case the gates are locked?'

'I have.'

The ladder was folded inside Jack's overcoat. It was thin and light and immensely strong – his father had designed it with help from Rudraige, who liked to tell how he had broken into more houses in his youth than the rest of them would ever know. The ladder had slender steel hooks at each end, which, judiciously flung upwards, bit into stone or brick, allowing for a cautious ascent by way of the silk rungs. He answered Byron somewhat absently, partly because he was watching and listening for anyone who might come along this remote country road and remember seeing two strangers, but mainly because his mind was filled up with Catherine – with knowing he would shortly see that disturbing blue stare again, and that air of challenge and defiance.

It was just on midnight when they reached the hall. They paused, looking at the gates, then Jack reached out to try the latch. Unexpectedly it gave way, and the gates swung quietly inwards.

'Very hospitable of Gertie,' he said, grinning. 'Or is it that it wouldn't occur to her that anyone would have the impudence to walk in uninvited.'

They went inside, closing the gates behind them to avoid attracting notice. Keeping to the thick shrubbery that fringed the drive, they went towards the house, carefully avoiding the gravel paths and the patches of moonlight that silvered the ground.

As the house came into view, Byron pointed to its right-hand corner. 'Picture gallery,' he said, softly. 'Third window from the end. It's the window you unlatched – and left unlatched in case we did decide to return, you remember.'

'I do. But if there's even half-decent housekeeping in there, the window will have been properly closed and latched long since.'

'It didn't look as if people went into that part of the house very often, though. That drainpipe looks fairly secure – plenty of leering gargoyles, as well, for you to grab hold of.'

'Some of them look as if the stonemason used Gertie as a model,' said Jack, studying the wall. 'But there's a ledge just outside the gallery window up there – d'you see it? If we can get on to that we should be able to get inside.'

He reached for the guttering, tested it, and said, 'It seems safe enough. Wait until I've got in, then come up after me.'

'If any lights come on down here, shall I give the traditional owl-hoot as warning?'

'I don't care if you shriek like a banshee on Hallowe'en, as long as we aren't caught.'

Jack went up more easily than he had dared hope, finding handholds and footholds in the brackets that held the pipe in place. With every moment he expected lights to flare in windows and shouts to ring out, but the hall was quiet and dark, and he reached the ledge outside the gallery, and leaned across to the window. He had expected it to be latched, but when he grasped the edge of the frame it pulled outwards easily, almost over-balancing him. He grabbed the wooden frame, folded the window back as far as he could and inched his way across the ledge until he was able to swing one leg over the sill, and climb through. The remembered scents of the gallery closed around him – old timber and polished oak. And perhaps there were fragments of memories here, as well – long-ago hopes and fears and loves and tragedies, hoping someone would notice them . . .

He looked across to where the small portrait hung in its corner.
The enigmatic stare looked back, and Jack stood very still. You
were almost certainly never here, Catherine, he thought, but when
your likeness came into this house, I think it brought something
of you with it. Is that why Uncle Montague wanted to get in
here? To find you – to find out more about you so that Phelan
could write his play? But did Phelan write it at all?

He leaned out of the window, gesturing to Byron to come up.
Watching him swarm up the drainpipe, Jack thought, not for the
first time, that despite the languid demeanour Byron liked to
present to the world, he was actually remarkably lithe, especially
when it came to climbing into a house by night.

'Everything all right?' said Byron, softly, as he climbed over
the sill, and brushed a few specks of brick and wood dust from
his shoulders.

'Yes. But we'll be as quick as we can. How much light do
you need?'

Byron looked about him. 'I'd like to take the painting to the
window,' he said, 'but if someone does come along, we'd need
to dart into immediate hiding.'

'And we'd lose precious seconds if we had to put it back on
the wall,' said Jack, understanding.

'Yes. We'd better make do with working on it where it is. But
we'll need to use candles. Be ready to snuff them out, though.'

He produced two small candles from his pockets, both in tiny
metal holders. Once lit, he set them close to the portrait, moved
it slightly to examine the back, then shook his head, indicating
there was nothing there.

'I'll stay by the door to listen for anyone approaching,' said
Jack, and Byron nodded, and unfolded the small leather pouch,
taking from it a tiny stoppered bottle and cloth.

'This stuff smells disgusting,' he said. 'But I've seen Montague
use it, and it generally works.' He spread a silk square on the
floor beneath the portrait, and for some time there was no sound
except for the soft scratching from the tiny silver blades.

'The paint's starting to flake off,' he said, presently. 'I'll try
to ensure no one will notice anything's different, though.'

'I shouldn't think anyone looks at the painting from one year's
end to the next, anyway,' said Jack, watching him. The candles

flickered, and there was a moment when he thought Catherine's eyes flickered too, as if she was looking across at him.

Finally, Byron stepped back, and said, softly, 'Oh, my. Come and look.'

He lifted up one of the candles so that its light fell more directly onto the painting. And there, in the corner, brought into clear view, was almost the whole of the lute. Jack thought it would be one of hundreds of lutes that had existed in Catherine's time, but when Byron moved the candle even closer, the light fell on to three words that had been engraved or painted – or perhaps even only scratched – into the main body of the instrument. *Non Immemor Beneficii.*

Byron said, 'I'll see if I can get a translation of that when we're back in London. But you see what else was under that thick layer of paint?'

'Oh, yes.' Jack was staring at the painting. Lying next to the lute was a second object.

A music score.

It had been painted to show it as slightly curled over, with only what looked like the top quarter visible. But the musical notation was clear enough, and Jack thought anyone who could read music could probably even play the notes. Beneath the notation was writing.

'Can you read it?' said Jack, in an urgent whisper. 'It's medieval script, isn't it? Practically unreadable now.'

'At least it's in English, though.' Byron frowned at the portrait. 'The title is "Cat's Lament. A farewell to the Martyr of Silk".'

'I've more or less made that out,' said Jack. 'Give me your notebook – if you can translate, I'll write it down.'

Byron frowned, moved one of the small candles closer, then, after a moment, said softly, 'My God, whoever wrote this had a passion for his wench. As near as I can get, it says this:

"'She who uprighted me with such desire –
She whose name could twist my heart/And wrench my very
    soul apart
I must forswear, but gladly so
For my Love is safe, she cheated Fate".'

He paused, and for a moment the entire gallery and the shadows blurred and receded. Then he became aware of Byron saying, 'The second verse seems to be almost a command. Listen.

> '"This charge I lay on all who come –
> Veil her name, her story hide.
> Speak not her name, let memory fade.
> Let history not recall my Love".'

Jack was no longer aware of the shadowy gallery. His eyes were on the painting, and the painted fragment of music. *She whose name could twist my heart*, the musician had written. But then he had laid that charge – as Byron said, almost a command – about not remembering her. *Veil her name, her story hide . . . Let history not recall my Love.* Catherine, thought Jack, what did you do that caused someone to write that – and for it to be set down in your portrait?

But Byron was now clearing up the traces of his work, wiping away the tiny flakes of dry paint, so Jack went to help him.

Neither of them spoke, as they snuffed the candles, and climbed silently back through the window and down to the ground.

NINETEEN

When finally they got back to London, by way of a milk train that seemed to rattle around most of the south of England for several hours, they went straight to Byron's rooms since, as Byron said, he had all the books and reference material to hand there. Jack left him scouring the shelves that lined most of the walls, and managed to find coffee beans in the tiny scullery, from which he brewed a pot of coffee.

Byron had spread several books over the table, some open, with bookmarks slotted in. He took the coffee gratefully, and said, 'I'm trying, first off, to find that Latin tag scratched into the lute in case it identifies the musician.'

'*Non Immemor Beneficii.*'

'Yes. It sounded like a family motto, but . . . Oh, this looks like it. And it *is* a family motto. There are one or two interpretations, but the general meaning seems to be, "Not unmindful of favours".'

'Is it the Ó Raifeartaigh family motto?' Jack sat in the chair facing Byron, drinking his own coffee.

'No, it isn't,' said Byron, frowning at the page. 'I was expecting it to be, but it's the motto of an Irish family called Fitzgerald.'

'Who?'

'Fitzgerald.' Byron turned back a page, re-read it, then said, 'They were earls of Kildare – and of various other places. Their principal home was Maynooth Castle, though – it was fairly near to Dublin, and it's described as one of the largest and richest of the family's dwellings. Destroyed in a siege by the British during Henry VIII's reign.' He frowned. 'There was a famous Irish rebellion against the English led by a Fitzgerald, wasn't there? It's bound to be mentioned somewhere . . . Yes, here it is. The rebellion was led by one Thomas Fitzgerald, the Tenth Earl. The dates given here are 1534/35, and it says Thomas was born in 1513. He'd fit with the portrait's date, wouldn't he?'

'Yes. And the portrait was dated "circa 1536",' said Jack. 'The date could have been added later, though – perhaps by someone who wasn't entirely sure when it was painted.'

'The Earl was often called Silken Thomas,' said Byron, returning to his book. 'I hadn't known that, but it was something to do with his soldiers wearing helmets with silken fringes.'

'Whoever composed the ballad calls Catherine the Martyr of Silk,' said Jack.

'True. Apparently, Thomas made a rousing speech in Dublin Abbey – highly treasonable from the sound of this,' said Byron. 'He publicly and very angrily renounced all allegiance to Henry VIII of England, and flung down the Sword of State by way of demonstrating his words. Then he led a major rebellion against Henry – you have to admit it would take a fair amount of courage to do that. It sounds as if it was partly to avenge his father, whom Henry had imprisoned in the Tower, but also to keep Ireland out of the hands of the dastardly British.'

'Is there anything about his family?' asked Jack. 'Was he married?'

'Are you wondering if Catherine was his wife? There doesn't seem to be anything . . . No, here's something. It seems he married an English lady in London when he was very young. There's a cross-reference . . .' Byron got up to take down another book, flipped the pages back and forth, then said, 'This looks like it. The details are brief and quite vague, but there's an entry saying his wife died of plague "before 1529".' He turned a few more pages, then said, 'But there's another reference here, attributed to a different source, that says she remained in England and distanced herself from the rebellion and Thomas himself, "for fear of the King's wrath".'

'When you remember the fate meted out to traitors, you can't blame her,' said Jack.

'But then there's a footnote saying it's believed she took the veil and was never heard of again.' Byron leaned back in his chair. 'Her story could be any one of those, or none of them,' he said.

'If she's thought to have died before 1529, it can't have been Catherine, anyway,' said Jack. 'Not if someone painted her around 1536. What happened to Thomas?'

'According to this – and I'll look in other sources to make

sure – he fought against English rule with all the forces he could summon,' said Byron. 'He called out his own armies, and he pulled in local people, and employed spies. But the rebellion failed, and he was finally forced to surrender to the English. He was executed for high treason in – damn, where's the date?' He turned the page back, then said, 'Here it is. He was executed in 1537 on Tower Hill.'

'Executed,' said Jack, almost to himself. 'Byron, does it say how was it done? Wasn't it sometimes hanging, drawing and quartering for treason?' If Thomas of Kildare had indeed been the composer of Catherine's ballad, Jack did not want him to have endured such a vicious death.

'It doesn't say,' said Byron. 'Oh, but there's a legend that he sat beneath a tree and played his lute the night before his arrest, or possibly the night before he surrendered to the British – the accounts vary a bit. But it does say that very tree is still in Ireland. I like that story, don't you? I'll bet the Irish enjoy making capital out of it, as well.'

'Thomas is the one who wrote the ballad to Catherine, isn't he?' said Jack, after a moment. 'Don't look so sceptical, Byron, it's a reasonable assumption. And could that music in the portrait even be the music from the legend? The music Thomas played the night before he died?'

'You think the musician and Catherine are your shadow figures behind Tomás and Catrina in the play, don't you?'

'Yes, I do. If we're going to accept that play as Phelan Rafferty's work, can't you see him uncovering the story about Catherine – his mysterious ancestress – and a connection to Thomas of Kildare?' said Jack. 'And being inspired to base a play on it. For heaven's sake, Phelan even calls his main character Tomás!'

'It's a tempting idea,' said Byron, 'but, much as I'd like to believe it, I think you're making too great a leap. In any case, I don't think it's something that could be proved. And it still doesn't explain the secrecy around the play itself. Whoever that musician was, can you really believe that all these years later, Phelan was honouring his request to – what was it? To "veil Catherine's name and hide her story, and let history not recall her"? It conjures up tales about family secrets and promises handed down through generations. Like that Rider Haggard novel – *She* – where succeeding generations are charged with searching for the lost city in the desert, and finding the immortal woman who rules it.'

'But we're fairly sure Phelan was Catherine's descendant,' said Jack. 'It sounded as if Montague thought so, too. Could Phelan have written the play and then panicked because he thought he had betrayed the command in that piece of music?'

'And gave the play to Montague to hide? It doesn't chime with anything I've ever known about Phelan Rafferty,' said Byron. 'I think you're getting carried away, and I'm usually the one who does that.' He thought for a moment, then said, 'I should think Montague would have kept any promise he'd made to Phelan, but once Phelan was dead, wouldn't Montague have staged the play? But he didn't. He kept it hidden. And if he hadn't fallen down the stairs and broken his neck, we wouldn't have even known it existed.'

'And,' said Jack, 'we still don't know what's in that disguised scene – the scene written in Gaelic. We still don't know who wrote the play, either.'

'Or who stole it from Montague's house, or . . . Damn, that's someone at the door.' Byron glanced at the clock. 'It's a bit early for callers.'

'Probably the postman,' said Jack, getting up to refill their coffee cups.

But it was not the postman. It was Gus, apologizing for such an early morning call.

'You said you might come here after the Girdlestone Hall visit, Mr Jack, so I thought I'd take the chance. A letter came from Miss Tansy by early morning delivery. The postmark is three days old, and I know you like to see her letters at once—'

'Yes, I do,' said Jack, taking the letter. 'Thank you, Gus.'

Gus surveyed the room, then said, 'Begging your pardon, Mr Jack and Mr Byron, but it looks as if you've only just got back to London.'

'We have. We think we've found out one or two useful details, but we had a bone-rattling and very long journey on a milk train,' said Byron.

'Milk trains don't serve breakfast, do they?' said Gus, and his eyes went to the open door leading out to the tiny scullery.

'They do not,' said Byron. 'If you're offering to make us breakfast, Gus, your feet are as beautiful on the mountains as those of the prophet—'

'And,' said Jack, who was opening Tansy's letter, 'I saw eggs and bread in the cupboards, and since your scrambled eggs are fit to rival those of Escoffier—'

'Scrambled eggs it shall be, Mr Jack.'

'Good man. But keep the door open, Gus, so you can hear what Tansy has to say.'

'Well, I would like to know, Mr Jack, having acted as postman from here to Russell Square, so to speak.'

'Of course you must know,' said Jack. 'You're as much part of this as the rest of us.'

'I always think of you as one of the family anyway,' said Byron, and Gus, looking pleased, went off to find the eggs, as Jack unfolded Tansy's letter and began to read it.

Dear Jack and Family,

This morning at the Roscius, Florian said he was *so* sorry, Timon, dear boy, but he would have to leave rehearsal a little early.

'A luncheon engagement,' he said. 'An unexpected invitation I cannot ignore. Someone from my past – in fact a lady about whom I once cherished romantic hopes.'

'Ah,' said one of the inquisitive sisters, 'the "affair of the heart" you mentioned when we were all boarding the train in London.'

'The one that did not go quite as you hoped,' put in the other one.

Florian said, very grandly, 'When she read the newspaper reports of my being in Ireland – that's to say of the company being in Ireland – nothing would do but for us to meet again. The love of one's youth, you understand – something never forgotten.' He sighed, then said, 'I believe she has come to Dublin especially to see me, and she is very eager to find out about the intervening years since we met – and to hear our plans for the festival.'

'A romantic afternoon interlude?' enquired Timon, rather dryly.

'Luncheon at my hotel,' said Florian. 'I shall say no more – her reputation, you understand. I was ever a gentleman in such matters.'

There was a sarcastic snort from the corner where the carpenters were working, and Florian glared at them, then swept out.

Jack, I'm actually quite relieved to hear that Florian is caught up with a lady, because he's started to be rather embarrassingly attentive. He's taken to coming to sit with me at rehearsals, and he pats my arm and says I'm doing a splendid job. Yesterday he said he felt we were becoming close friends.

'I feel as if I am beginning to know you in a special way,' he said. 'And I've been wondering whether we might have a little late-night supper together?'

That, of course, was my cue to say, 'Oh, Mr Gilfillan, I am not worthy.' What I actually said (rather suspiciously) was, 'A late-night supper?'

'Some champagne and caviar, perhaps? A little smoked salmon? And then—'

Thankfully I didn't hear how the 'And then' line would have ended, because he was interrupted by Timon, crossly calling out that Florian had missed his cue.

I don't think there's any way in which Florian could know who I am, so I can't think this is anything other than plain old-fashioned lechery – and I'm sorry if Cousin Cecily is with you when you read this. I wouldn't actually have expected any lechery aimed at Tilly Fendle – what with the patchily dyed hair and an assortment of clothes that look as if they've come from an East End rag shop. What I do think is that in my attempts to get information about the hidden scene, I've overdone the eager admiration role, and the vain old goat has interpreted it as romantic admiration.

I shan't, of course, accept the supper invitation – or only if it's likely to be somewhere with plenty of people around.
Tansy

Jack put the letter down, and said, 'I hope that old roué, Florian Gilfillan, isn't suspicious of her.'

'But he couldn't know who she is. Ah, Gus, is that our breakfast?'

'Have you had something to eat yourself?' asked Jack, as Gus carried in a laden tray.

'I had some at your rooms before I came out, thanking you kindly. The eggs are in the covered dish, and I've made toast, and brought the butter dish. And, begging your pardon, Mr Jack, but did I hear something in Miss Tansy's letter about champagne and caviar?'

'You did, Gus. Involving a certain Mr Florian Gilfillan.' Jack waited, and Gus said,

'Well, I'll take leave to say that might have been a good seduction line in Edward VII's giddy youth, but I shouldn't think a champagne and caviar approach would be very effective with someone of Miss Tansy's generation,' said Gus. 'Oh, and Mr Byron, there was a pot of marmalade in your cupboard, so I've brought that as well.'

TWENTY

Ethne had believed she had put a safe distance between herself and the play said to have been written by her father. She had written a polite reply to Miss Viola Gilfillan's letter, telling her it could not possibly be Phelan Rafferty's work and that she did not want her name attached to it in any way whatsoever. It had crossed her mind that there might be an approach from one of the newspapers – from reporters who might want to talk to Phelan's daughter about the discovery – but there had been nothing, and after a while she had begun to feel safe. Perhaps, after all, the title had simply been an odd coincidence. And perhaps the play had already been discovered for the forgery it undoubtedly was, and would no longer be performed, anyway.

But now had come a newspaper article, mostly about the Dublin Festival in general, but making particular mention of the play.

MOUNTING SPECULATION ABOUT PHELAN RAFFERTY'S RECENTLY FOUND PLAY – AND THE 'DISGUISED SCENE'

There is increasing excitement about a play which is to open the *Féile* in Dublin, and is believed to be a recently discovered work by Phelan Rafferty – the distinguished playwright who died five years ago.

The play bears the enticing title *The Murderer Inside the Mirror,* and this week, Miss Viola Gilfillan, from the Gilfillan Theatre Company, gave a brief interview to us, in which she reminded readers of the 'mystery' within the play.

'As I told your newspaper recently, there were four pages of the script which in effect were disguised,' she said. 'They were written in Irish Gaelic, and had to be translated. We do now have that translation, of course.'

[Readers can see this earlier interview in our edition of last month.]

Asked about the content of the disguised scene and the possible reason for it having been wrapped in such mystery, Miss Gilfillan would not be drawn.

'I shall only say it is a very strong piece of theatre,' she said. 'And to honour what we believe may have been Phelan Rafferty's wish, we are preserving the aura of mystery. The scene will not be viewed until the festival's opening night at the Roscius. We are rehearsing it in secrecy – behind locked doors, even. The only people who presently know what it contains are the three actors who appear in it – that is myself, Mr Timon Gilfillan, and Mr Florian Gilfillan.'

Asked about the play's title and the old stage superstition that it brought bad luck to have a mirror on stage during a performance, Miss Gilfillan laughed.

'We aren't in the least worried about superstitions,' she said. 'That one is purely a safety concern in any case. A mirror can reflect a light, which could temporarily blind an actor – who could end up blundering into a piece of furniture or even walk off the edge of the stage.'

On page 8 our readers can see photographs of the three players, taking the leading roles of Tomás, Maran and Catrina in the play.

When Ethne finished reading this, her heart was racing and her hands were shaking. She had the feeling of the past closing suffocatingly around her.

She had tried to dismiss the play's title, but this could not be dismissed. The revelation of what Viola Gilfillan had called a disguised scene, taken in conjunction with that title, could surely only mean one thing. That the play really was the story of that long-ago night in Dublin Castle.

Miss Gilfillan had said only the actors appearing in the scene knew what it contained, but if Ethne was right, there were three other people who would know. The three people who had been there – who had played the scene in real life. Phelan Rafferty, Montague Fitzglen, and Ethne herself. It therefore followed that only one of those three could have written that play.

Ethne had not written it, of course, and her father's death had been announced barely a week after that night in Dublin Castle.

That left Montague Fitzglen. He was certainly enough of a man of the theatre to understand how to structure a play, but Ethne could not believe he would have allowed the truth about that night to become known, any more than she would have done so herself. Or would he? He was an actor, and actors were vain. Mightn't he have wanted to set down the events of that night? To make sure they were not lost – even that his own part in it was recorded for history? Then, once the play was finished, he had hidden it, intending it to remain secret until memories had died down and suspicions had faded. She could easily visualize him doing that, hugging the secret gleefully to himself. But he had died suddenly, and the script had been found.

Although could Montague have written this disguised scene, which apparently was in Irish Gaelic? He had stayed at Westmeath often enough to acquire a smattering of Irish; her father liked to sprinkle his conversation with Irish phrases, and Montague, with his sharp intelligence and inquisitive mind – you might even call it a prying mind – had listened, and frequently replied in the same language. The two men used to laugh over it, Phelan correcting his friend's pronunciation, Montague demanding to know what this word meant or that one, trying out phrases, jotting down spelling and accents. Viola had told the newspaper that the scene was only four pages long, and Ethne did not think it would have been beyond Montague Fitzglen's capabilities to write four pages of dialogue in passable Irish. She could almost see him smiling to himself as he did so, murmuring that even if anyone found the play before he was ready, before he considered it safe, this would fool them.

Ethne had long since destroyed everything that might reveal anything about that long-ago night in Dublin Castle. She had torn to shreds and burned every document ever written by Seamus Rafferty; all the letters to and from the Dublin antiquarian, E. L. Maguire, and all the correspondence with the surveyors about the restoration of the castle – including the sketch map. She had even burned the polite note of thanks from Mr Todworthy Inkling who had stayed at Westmeath House and been part of the discussions about those documents. After she had done all that, she had thought herself safe.

But she was not safe. She would have to find out what was

in the play being attributed to her father and, above all, she had to find out what was in the disguised scene. And if she was right about what it contained, she must find a way to stop the play being performed.

She read the article again, then looked at the photographs of the three people who would be in the scene. Viola Gilfillan, Timon Gilfillan and Florian Gilfillan.

Florian Gilfillan. The name jumped out at her.

You did not, if you had any pride, write to a gentleman who had seduced you in the orchard of your own home (and very uncomfortably and embarrassingly as well); who had held out a promise of marriage, and then vanished the next morning. She had told herself he was not worth the shedding of a single tear, and life had gone on very much as before.

But he was in Ireland again – as near as Dublin – and it might be possible to lure him into re-entering her life, and then make use of him. Ethne thought for a long time, then sat down to write two letters. One was to book for herself two – possibly three – nights in a small Dublin hotel near the Roscius theatre.

The other letter was to Florian Gilfillan.

Being in Dublin after so many years churned up all the memories, and as Ethne walked out of the railway station, she had the feeling yet again of the past pulling at her, trying to take her back over the years. But this was absurd, and she asked a porter to find a cab for her – she was pleased that she remembered how such things were done – and was taken to her hotel.

Florian had replied to her carefully worded letter almost immediately, expressing himself delighted to hear from her. Of course he remembered her, he said; he had thought of her many times over the years, always with affection and pleasure, but also with some sadness.

'For you will know your father forbade all further meetings between us, and regretfully I had to accept that. You were so young, dear Ethne, and I could not spoil your life by causing a rift between you and Phelan. I was deeply saddened to read of his death some years ago. Perhaps, though, times will be kinder to us now, and as I am in Dublin for the festival, and as you are

apparently also in Dublin for a brief visit, as you say it does
indeed seem ordained that we should meet.

'I see that your hotel is quite near to where I am staying, so
I wonder if you would like to come to luncheon in the restaurant
here? I am very much involved with rehearsals, but I could be
available tomorrow. I await your response with eagerness and
hope.'

Ethne sent a note of acceptance, and dressed carefully for the
encounter. As she walked into the foyer of Florian's hotel, he
came towards her, his hands outstretched, quoting Shakespeare
– saying that age had not withered her, nor custom staled her
infinite variety. Ethne smiled an acknowledgement and thought
it was a pity she could not say the same about Florian himself.
The years had not withered him – on the contrary, he had thick-
ened and coarsened. She wondered how on earth she could have
been so foolish as to be charmed and eventually seduced by him.

She had prepared careful remarks to introduce the subject of
the play, but he broached the matter himself over their lunch.

'A remarkable piece,' he said. 'I play Tomás – a wonderful
role. But you don't believe it's your father's work?'

'It isn't his work,' said Ethne. 'I would have known – I would
have found the manuscript – drafts – notes – in his papers after—'
She broke off, with a gesture expressive of distress, and Florian
reached for her hand across the table.

'My dear—'

'The play is a fake,' said Ethne, managing not to snatch her
hand back. 'And it makes me very angry to know that someone
has practised such a monstrous fraud – also that your family
have been so shamefully deceived.' She glanced about her, then
said, 'This is perhaps rather a public place for such a discussion.
Is there somewhere more private for us to talk?'

'There's my bedroom here on the second floor, if you felt you
could—'

'A business discussion, of course,' said Ethne, but she smiled
into his eyes. 'Although between such old friends—'

His colour deepened at once, and he said, 'I'll ask them to
send up another bottle of wine. Private discussions are always
so much more comfortable over a glass of wine.'

Once in his bedroom, Ethne sat in a chair near the window,

while Florian perched on the edge of the bed, and poured the wine.

'I believe I owe it to my father to find out who wrote that play,' she said, speaking very earnestly. 'To expose and denounce whoever is behind it all. But there is something that is raising a small doubt for me, and until I'm reassured about it . . . I felt you were the one person I could approach.' She leaned forward. 'Florian, this hidden scene the newspapers have written about—'

'Ah. The Murder Scene.'

The Murder Scene. The words struck at Ethne's mind as if they had been a blow. But she said, 'Is that what you're calling it? I didn't know. But I suppose from all I've read in the newspapers, I should have known there would be a . . . a murder.' She leaned over to touch his hand. 'Florian, if I could know just a little about the play, it might reassure me that I've been right to disown it. On the other hand, if it is my father's work, I must certainly acknowledge and accept it. You do understand, don't you? But of course you do – you were always so sensitive. That scene in particular . . . It sounds as if it's the real heart of the play. Its essence.' A pause. 'You're in that scene yourself, I think the newspaper said?'

'I am. But I've given my word not to discuss it. Even the pages of that scene have to be given back to Viola after each rehearsal,' he said, in an aggrieved voice. 'And rehearsals of it are only ever behind locked doors. In fact tomorrow evening we're even rehearsing it after everyone has left and the theatre is deserted. Eight o'clock call, if you please. Not even the backstage crew will be there. And there's a dear little soul who recently joined the company who's doing her utmost to be helpful and who I think should be included – Timon wants to try out some sound effects, and I think this girl could be trusted to manage them for the evening. Tilly, she's called. Tilly Fendle. She looks like a startled sprite that's lost its way in the forest and found itself in the twentieth century by mistake. Utterly stage-struck. I've tried to impart a few pearls of wisdom to her, as a matter of fact – from my wealth of experience in the theatre, you know. I think she has found some of our talks instructive and encouraging.' He examined his fingernails, casually, then said, 'I'm so sorry, my dear, but you do see, I can't tell you anything about the play – and certainly not about the Murder Scene.'

Ethne went to sit next to him on the bed. 'Of course I under-stand,' she said. 'But aside from that, this has been such a pleasant reunion. It's brought back those days in Westmeath.'

'You were very sweet,' he said, and pulled her against him, squashing her breasts uncomfortably. 'You still are,' he said, in a breathy whisper into her ear, and began to fumble at the fasten-ings on the front of her gown.

Ethne forced herself not to push his hands away. She would allow ten minutes for him to grope and jab, then she would say she had arranged a taxi to take her back to her hotel, and it was due quite soon.

He was pulling her down onto the bed now, and Ethne managed to conceal her revulsion at the feel of his thick body pressing against her. But after some heaving and panting, and a bit more fumbling and prodding at her bodice, Florian rolled back to his side of the bed, gave a heavy sigh, and said, 'I must not assume anything, must I? After so many years, I must not allow myself to think I would still be attractive to you.'

Either he had developed more gentlemanly habits than he had possessed six years earlier, which Ethne did not think likely, or he had drunk too much wine and rendered himself semi-unable – which she thought very likely indeed. She sat up, buttoned her gown, tidied her hair, and used her line about a car having been booked.

'But I hope we could have a further meeting very soon,' she said, reaching out to touch his face with a fingertip. 'I could stay in Dublin for another day or two.'

'Then we shall dine together,' he said.

Ethne had to endure a flabby kiss before she was finally able to escape.

But as she returned to her own hotel, her mind was working furiously. Florian had refused to be drawn about what he had called the Murder Scene, and if it had not been for that disguised scene, Ethne might have been able to dismiss most of her fears. Yes, but there's the play's title, said a sly little voice in her mind. *The Murderer Inside the Mirror . . .*

The words ran back and forth in her head, and with them, she felt the past pulling her back into that night five years earlier inside Dublin Castle's Clock Tower.

TWENTY-ONE

Ethne would never forget that night. She would never forget how the shadows had lain thickly everywhere, or the sense of danger . . . She would never forget the relentless ticking of the immense clock over their heads, tapping out its warning like hammer blows. *Don't-go-in . . . Leave-the-past-alone . . .*

When Mr Fitzglen found the jutting stone that would move the section of the wall, Ethne had wanted to say the words aloud – to tell them to leave the past sealed up – to let it keep its secrets.

But she had done what they asked, striking the matches, and then lighting the candle and holding it up so that it could shine into the yawning blackness. The small light had burned up in the dry, airless space, and then had come the moment that still walked through her nightmares.

From within the dark recess – the recess that Seamus Rafferty must have designed and that had been sealed up for a century and a half – had reared up the shadowy figure that had come towards them. The room, the entire tunnel, had reverberated with screams that sliced through the shadows, and it was several seconds before Ethne realized that the screams were her own. But even when she did realize, she could not stop, because there was someone in there, someone who had been sealed up in Seamus's room, and it really was a tomb . . . And whoever had been walled up inside it was coming towards them – a figure splintered with shards of light, the hands stretched out – a figure who wanted to kill them for disturbing the past and opening up the secrets . . .

The slap across her face came from her father, and it was like a dash of cold water. Ethne gasped, and half fell, shaking and sobbing, against the wall. Her mind was tumbling – she was dimly aware that they must try to get out.

But it was already too late. Running feet were coming toward them, commands were being shouted. Lights flared and guards – four, no five, of them – erupted into the passage, shouting to the intruders to remain still, not to move, they would be shot if they tried to resist. There was the black glint of what looked like guns.

Ethne felt her arm grabbed, and her father pulled her into the cobwebbed blackness of the alcove. She struggled, but he said, 'We must hide – it will buy us time . . . The mechanism operates from inside . . .'

'But there's someone in there . . .' Ethne flinched as he pushed her forward, expecting to feel the hands briefly glimpsed to reach out and close around her neck.

'There's no one,' said Phelan, and as he spoke they both fell into the yawning oblong of blackness.

Ethne stumbled against the brick wall, banging her head hard, so that the darkness spun and tilted all around her. But through the spinning confusion, she heard the dry rasp of the stones and blackness closed about them. She thought: he's moved the wall back. He's shut us in. We're shut in with whatever's in here.

But as she struggled to sit up, her father said, 'Safe for the moment.'

'No . . . There is someone in here with us – I *saw* him—'

'There's no one. Give me the matches.' He fumbled for them, and struck one, holding it up. 'See there? A mirror.'

Ethne's senses were steadying, although her head was throbbing where she had hit the wall, but she managed to look where he was pointing. Propped against the wall, facing the alcove's opening, was a tall, narrow mirror.

Her father said, bitterly, 'Seamus's last macabre joke. He must have wanted anyone getting in here to see what would be a figure walking out of the darkness as soon as the place was opened up.'

'I did see a figure—'

'You saw your own reflection. Or mine,' he said, and as he spoke, there was a tapping against the stone – sharp, insistent.

Ethne's heart leapt, and she looked across at the wall in sick terror.

'It's the guards,' said her father. 'They're trying to get the wall open again, but they can't see how to do it – they haven't got Seamus's map, showing the stone that works the mechanism. Montague's got it.' He moved to the wall and pressed his ear against it, listening. 'Montague's gone, I think,' he said, after a moment. 'But I can just hear what the guards are saying. They've sent three men after him, but with fair luck he'll be out of the castle and halfway down the hill by now.' Incredibly a note of amusement suddenly came into his tone, and he said, 'Or, more likely, he'll fashion for himself a disguise, and still be around.'

'Will he?'

'He won't leave us to our fate,' said her father, at once. 'But listen now, two of the guards are still out there, and they're trying to get in.' As he spoke, the tapping came again, louder, and moving across the other side of the wall.

'Will they get in?' Ethne could not stop shaking, but her whispered words came out reasonably calmly.

'If they can't find how to move the section of stone wall, they'll force it open with pickaxes and sledgehammers. They know we're in here, you see.' The match had burned out, but Ethne could sense him thinking very intently.

'Montague might stage something,' said Phelan, at last. 'But even if he doesn't, that wall will be opened eventually. We can do it from in here, though, which means we might be able to choose our moment. Wait, till I make another light . . .' The match-flame flared up again. 'There's the stone, d'you see?' he said. 'It comes through from the passageway outside. Now listen, Ethne, we'll give Montague a few moments, but if he doesn't come back, we'll open the wall without the guards realizing what we're up to. They won't know that we can work it from in here, and it'll startle them. But they'll come tumbling in, and if we're quick we can be out and running through the passages before they've got time to realize what's happened.' The match went out, but he struck another and, in its wavering light, he looked at her very straightly. 'It will be dangerous,' he said. 'And I might have to use force, although what . . .' He looked about him, then reached out to prise a section of the looking-glass frame away. The wood was old and partly rotting, and it splintered, sections of it coming away. 'I shan't need it,' he said. 'But if necessary it can be used as a bit of a defence. It will deal a fair blow – enough to stun the guards – and buy us time to get out. And we will get out, Ethne. I'll make sure you're safe.'

Ethne was shivering at the knowledge that the guards were on the other side of the stone wall, waiting for them, but she suddenly heard herself say, 'Why did Seamus create this room? What did he need to hide?'

At first she thought he was not going to answer, then he said, 'Haven't you seen?' and striking yet another match, held it up and pointed with his free hand to the far corner.

In the uncertain light, Ethne saw what lay against the wall.

A lute. An old, *old* lute, lying against the wall. Its surface was ingrained with dirt, but it was possible to see that it would once have been smooth and satiny.

The strings had long since rotted – there were only a few threads clinging to the wood, and the circular sound-hole at the centre of the body had fallen away.

At her side, her father said, very softly, 'It's Silken Thomas's lute. It's what Seamus created this room for. It's the hiding place.'

He moved the match's flame closer, and Ethne saw that wedged inside the lute were sheets of musical notation, with writing on them.

'Dear God,' said her father, leaning forward, speaking very softly, 'It's not just his lute, it's his music, as well.' He struck another match and, almost without realizing what she was doing, Ethne reached out and drew the fragile, curling papers from the lute. They felt dry and as if they might crumble to nothing in her hands. She stared at the elaborate writing, and thought she was closer to Thomas in this moment than she had ever been in her whole life.

The writing at the top of the page had been penned so forcefully that in places it had scored into the paper. But it was possible to make out what it said.

'*Cat's Lament. A farewell to the Martyr of Silk.*'

As her father leaned forward, phrases written beneath the music notation leapt out. Ethne was hardly aware of the proximity of the guards now; her whole being was focused on trying to read the words Thomas had set down centuries earlier.

'*She who uprighted me with such desire . . . She whose name could twist my heart/And wrench my very soul apart . . .*'

At first Ethne did not understand the opening line, then the memory of that evening in the old orchard came back, and she understood very well indeed. And even in this place, with the danger all around them, and the stench of age and sadness everywhere, she felt her cheeks suddenly hot with embarrassment, because her father was reading this with her. But he would not realize she understood the meaning, of course he would not.

He had already turned to the second of the two pages, but the match had burned all the way down, and darkness closed in.

But into the darkness, he said, softly, 'He was writing about his own execution. About someone having betrayed him – someone he thought he could trust.'

'I didn't see—'

'Didn't you? But there were lines at the end . . .' In a voice so low she had to strain to hear it, Phelan said,

'"In cold bleak dawn I soon shall die
Betrayed by one I thought to trust.
But he will walk with death's grim hood,
With tolling bell, with sawdust spread.
A faithless man, a faceless death . . ."'

The words dripped like acid into Ethne's mind, but with them came a brief moment of puzzlement. What was meant by death's grim hood? Was it simply a term used in those times?

The shouts from beyond the wall were suddenly louder. At any moment the guards would start to break it down, as her father had said. But he handed her the matches, and she managed to strike one and hold it high up for him to examine the upper part of the stonework. He was going to open it from this side, and that would be the moment when they would have to scramble out and run – the moment when force might have to be used against the guards.

Her father's hand closed around her wrist, and he pushed her back against the stonework. With his lips close to her ear, he said, 'Stay as still and as quiet as you can. And do whatever I tell you. I think it's going to be all right.'

'How—?'

'Listen,' he said, and, from beyond the wall a familiar voice rapped out a command.

'Dammit, you lazy good-for-nothings,' said the voice, 'get this wretched wall open, and let's get at the scoundrels hiding in there!'

Ethne gasped, because it was unmistakably the voice of Montague Fitzglen, but slightly tinged with an Irish accent. Her father said, softly, 'Didn't I tell you? Didn't I say he'd conjure up a disguise and be back to rescue us?'

'Oh . . .'

'He's snatched a cap or a jacket from somewhere,' said her father, 'and he's donned the guise of a very senior guard, issuing orders.'

Ethne managed a nod of understanding, then, almost as if obeying a silent command on her own account, she pushed Thomas's music back in the lute. It folded back into place, and she slid the lute into its dark corner with her foot. There was a movement from within the old mirror as she did so – almost as if there was another Ethne, another lute, inside the looking-glass that Seamus Rafferty had placed here over a century ago. For a wild moment she saw the lute's reflection, with the music and the writing weirdly reversed, looking almost like runic symbols, or an ancient code. The guards were saying something about not being able to open the panel, apology in their tone.

'A secret room,' said one of them. 'Who'd have guessed it? But none of us able to tell how to open it. Will we break the wall down?'

'You half-wits,' snapped Montague. 'Of course we won't break it down. Don't all ancient castles have secret rooms and stairways? And isn't the way in nearly always on the same principle? There'll be a lever – concealed behind a bit of stone – something that's out of true with the rest of the wall. Jesus, Mary and Joseph, what do they teach you on this job nowadays? When I was a young man . . . For pity's sake, hold up that light, and we'll soon find how to open this room.' His last words came much more loudly, and they were followed by insistent tappings.

'He's warning us,' said Phelan, softly. 'He's telling us he's about to open the panel and we should be ready to run for safety.'

'There it is!' cried Montague, triumphantly. 'That bit of stone, looking for all the world as if something's standing inside the wall, sticking its tongue out at us! That'll be the part that'll operate it – I'll wager my virtue – and no need to smirk like that, either of you, it's an honest enough wager. Let's see can I move it . . . Slowly, now . . . Is that a movement, there to your left? The *left*, man! That edge of the wall there, see it? Now then, if the panel doesn't move properly in a few seconds, then I don't know anything about castles. Ready?'

Ethne and her father were both on their feet, and he was gripping her arm with one hand, while the other held the length of wood torn from the mirror earlier, clearly prepared to hit out at whoever came into the room if he had to do so. Ethne seized the second piece of wood, and gripped it determinedly. It was astonishing how much courage it gave her.

There was the remembered sound of the stones grating, then the wall began to slide across as it had done earlier, and Montague gave a shout of triumph. 'Stand ready,' he cried. 'You two go in first – I'll stay here and grab the rogues if you fumble things, for they'll come bounding out, like pellets shot from a poacher's gun.'

Ethne glanced to where Thomas's lute lay quietly in its corner, made a half-movement as if to pick it up, then drew back, because no one need ever know what Thomas had written – that there had been a lady to whom he had written those impassioned words – and that he had been betrayed by someone he had trusted. The lute and the music should stay in its dark hiding place.

The stone panel slid back and the light from lamps and lanterns filled up the small room. The mirror's surface picked up the lights, and again was the brief, confusing impression of a second room deep within it – a room in which people moved and came forward, their hands held out, as if trying to break free. Then the first guard came at them, knocking Ethne's father back, then pouncing on him, his hands closing around Phelan's throat. Phelan gave a half-strangled cry, and pushed the man away, sending him against the stone wall. His head struck it hard, and he gave a half-gasp, his eyes rolling up so that only the whites showed, then lay still.

But Phelan had fallen with him, and he had fallen against the mirror, shattering it. Shards of glass flew out, glinting redly in the light from the lanterns, and Phelan gave a howl of pain, and flung up his arms in anguish. Ethne saw with horror that blood – dreadful dark blood was pouring across his face. Even in the uncertain light, she could see he had fallen against the wickedly sharp spears of glass – and that several had torn open his face, but, far, far worse, had pierced his eyes, *his eyes* . . .

There was a movement in the corridor, and Ethne spun round

to see the second guard with Montague behind him. Montague had taken in the situation at once – of course he had – and he was barking an order to the guard to run and fetch help.

'Fetch it yourself,' said the guard, snatching Ethne's arm and half-dragging her away from Phelan's barely conscious body. 'These two are my prisoners – that black-hearted rogue has committed a bloody murder and, by God, I'm going to make sure he pays for it. You're a killer, Phelan Rafferty!' he shouted. 'I recognize you, you evil sinner, and I'll see you hanged for tonight's work! And you'll come with me, girl, for you're part of this as well!'

Ethne fought to get free, but the guard held her too tightly. He was still shouting about bloody murder, screaming Phelan's name, and at any minute the other guards would come running, and they would catch them, and Ethne's father would be branded a murderer . . . But he was injured – dreadfully injured, and he had to be got out of this place, and hidden and looked after.

She still had in her free hand the length of wood from the mirror's frame. Fury and strength surged through her, and she raised her arm and brought the oak smashing down on the guard's head. He had no warning – he gave a grunt and half fell back, releasing his grip on her. Ethne at once brought the wood crunching down on his skull a second time. This time he fell against the wall, and as Ethne struck him a third time, he slumped, his head falling at an unnatural angle. The colour drained from his face, and she stared down at him, knowing instinctively that he was dead – knowing she had killed him – but feeling no remorse, because he had *had* to be silenced; he had recognized her father, he was shouting that Phelan was a murderer, that he would hang, and it could not be allowed . . .

Montague's voice came to her, low and urgent, telling her not to think about what she had done. 'Help me get Phelan out,' he said. 'With God's luck – or the devil's – we can carry him to the little back stair and get him out without being caught.'

Ethne said, 'Is he—?'

'I don't know,' he said, abruptly, turning to close the shutters of the lanterns and douse the flaring lights. Darkness folded around them, but through it, Ethne heard the scraping of stone. He's closed up Seamus's room, she thought, then Montague's whisper reached her again, telling her he had Phelan's shoulders, and for pity's sake to take his feet.

Somehow she did what he told her, and somehow between them they carried him along the dim passages. The shadows swirled around their feet, as if trying to trip them up, and the massive clock over their heads seemed to tick in exact time with every step. There were shouts and running footsteps everywhere, and with every second Ethne expected guards to appear. Her father was barely conscious – several times he groaned, but Montague said, softly, 'Don't try to talk, old chap. We're getting you to safety, and we'll get help for you. We're almost outside now – almost out.'

'So dark – everywhere's dark,' said Phelan in a blurred, bewildered voice, and Ethne's heart contracted, because the glass had gone into his eyes, she had seen it happen.

'That guard . . .' A hand came out, searching helplessly, and Ethne managed to reach out to take it. 'What happened? I only wanted to push him away—'

'I know it. And now you're safe and everything is all right,' said Montague at once. But his eyes met Ethne's and he gave a slight shake of his head, and very softly, said, 'Self-defence. All of it. Remember that, Ethne.'

Phelan tried to speak again, but fresh blood was welling up from where his eyes should be, and Montague paused for long enough to lean down and fold a handkerchief over Phelan's face.

Ethne's mind was filled up with anguish and fear for her father and for what might be ahead, but running beneath it was the knowledge of what she had done. It had not been self-defence as Mr Fitzglen had said. She had deliberately and knowingly committed murder. She had done so to make sure the guard could never speak of what he had seen – that he could never name Phelan Rafferty as a killer. She had dealt those blows deliberately and calculatedly, and she felt no regret or remorse about it. She would do it again if necessary.

But for now, they must get her father to safety without being caught.

Somehow they managed it. Somehow they carried him away from the castle – Ethne felt as if she was walking through a nightmare, but she was aware of Montague hailing a passing cab, and asking the man to take them the whole way to Westmeath. She thought the journey probably cost a great deal of money, but she was beyond caring. Montague laid her father on the long seat at the back, covering him with his own coat, and murmuring to the driver about drunken louts who had set about them, but saying matters were in the hands of the Garda.

'And here is something extra for making such a troublesome journey for us,' he said. 'Also for your discretion.' Coins were passed over, and the driver nodded, and hunched over the wheel for the entire journey back to Westmeath, not once looking back over his shoulder at them huddled in the back.

Without Montague Fitzglen, Ethne would not have been able to cope. But in the days that followed he dealt with everything. He advised and guided, remaining in Westmeath for some considerable time. Ethne thought he sent to Dublin to collect their things from the hotels – the one where the two men had been staying, and Ethne's own modest lodgings. 'Because we dare not overlook any detail if you're both to be safe from retribution,' he said.

'But there will be questions – the people at the castle will try to find out who broke in—'

'Have you ever heard of the concept of creating a diversion?' said Montague. 'Throwing a false item – a ball, a sphere, a globe – into the air to detract people's attention from the real one?'

'No.'

'Then think about it now. If you make the false item sufficiently glittering and vivid, no one notices the real one,' he said. 'It's what I'm going to do.'

Ethne was not entirely clear what he meant, but she was grateful to him, because by then she was too overwhelmed with grief to think very clearly.

Montague drafted a death announcement for newspapers, which Ethne sobbed over for a long while, because seeing the words in print twisted a knife in her heart.

'Suddenly and peacefully at his home . . .' 'Distinguished playwright . . .'

Montague went with her to St Joseph's, where the sisters were eager to help and provide support for dearest Ethne at such a terrible time. He even attended the service that the nuns held for Phelan at the chapel.

'And I daresay that if I get any of the Latin responses wrong, you'll prompt me,' he said. 'At worst, I can cover it up by sneezing.'

He did not get anything wrong, of course, and he used his stick to help him to genuflect in the correct places, as well, doing so with what Ethne thought was considerable panache.

At intervals throughout everything, she remembered the secret room in Dublin Castle's Clock Tower. She would always be grateful to Montague Fitzglen for closing it up, especially in the midst of such panic and fear. It had been the right thing to do, of course. It was better that what lay in there should remain hidden.

TWENTY-TWO

Maynooth Castle, Ireland, Autumn 1534

Dubhgall Maguire was becoming increasingly aware of a growing conviction within Maynooth that the castle would be taken by the English.

As the damp mist-shrouded autumn progressed towards winter, he heard the gallowglasses worriedly murmuring to one another that although the Earl had taken Dublin, he had not managed to take its castle. That stubborn old stronghold was still holding out for the English King, (may he rot in hell), and it was still firmly in the hands of the Earl's fierce enemy, Sir William Skeffington.

Still, weren't they equal to dealing Skeffington, said the soldiers, and who cared if he had vowed not only to recapture Dublin City, but to take Maynooth as well. They were equal to any attacks the sly old fox might mount, they said; they could deal with any number of guns and cannons, and those Frenchified things called *trebuchets*, which were no more than over-sized catapults, but which could inflict an astonishing amount of damage, and allow enterprising enemies to swarm up walls and storm battlements. They sank vast amounts of ale, and pored over battle plans, and pounced on any strangers who came to Maynooth in case they were spies. Didn't everyone know that spies flourished during wars? Several scuffles broke out, and a perfectly innocent carrier, who had been delivering a consignment of ale, was forcibly ejected from the sculleries on the grounds of him having a sly slant to his eyes. The carrier took himself off angrily, shaking his fist at the castle's battlements and shouting that he was not being manhandled by minions and scullions, and if this was what Ireland for the Irish meant, as far as he was concerned, Henry Tudor's men could come marching down Winetavern Street and occupy St Stephen's Green, and be done.

The incident brought the concept of spies to the forefront of Maguire's mind, and with it an awareness that spies could be very useful people, and not just for wars. If paid sufficiently well, spies might undertake other tasks . . .

On the Earl's next journey into Dublin, Maguire had to accompany him. This was quite a frequent occurrence, because often the Earl would want some errand running, or messages discreetly delivered.

He generally said, 'Make sure you call into a tavern as well, Maguire, and allow yourself a tankard or two of ale.' He said it this time.

Maguire had to try three – it might even have been four– taverns before he found what he sought. The tavern was near the main city centre; it was crowded and noisy, and thick with the smells of wine and ale and sweat, but he had talked to people and put out hints, and it seemed that this was where he would find what he wanted.

Partway through the evening, he managed to insinuate himself into conversation with two individuals, who were somewhat rough-looking, but who were instantly interested to hear he was in the Earl's service. They were even more interested to hear of Maguire's deep dissatisfaction with not only the Earl, but with his cause.

'And I'm not one to be on the losing side,' said Maguire, firmly. 'If I could find a way to put an end to Kildare's cause . . .'

This led to a much longer discussion, during which several tankards of ale were downed. Eventually one of the men said, 'You've talked a great deal of sense, friend. But how do we know you're to be trusted? How do we know you aren't playing a double game?'

'And setting a trap for us?' demanded the second.

'Haven't I already told you that as an earnest of good faith, I'm prepared to leave the courtyard door at Maynooth unlocked for you in two nights' time?' said Maguire. 'Kildare's soldiers live in an old stable block just off the courtyard; there's a long room where they drink every evening. If you stand outside the windows there – and there's plenty of corners and recesses where you can hide – you'll hear almost everything they say. You'll hear them making their battle plans. They do that most nights now, what with all the fighting there's been. You'd likely pick up a fine lot of information for you to take back to Sir William.'

'And for all we know, you'll hand us over to Thomas of Kildare the same night,' said the first man, scathingly.

'I have my own score to settle with Thomas of Kildare,' said Maguire, at once. 'But aren't you both friends of Grady? The one who was so badly injured by Thomas the day he gave that speech in St Mary's Abbey?'

They exchanged looks, then one said, 'How do you know that?'

'And what does it matter to you if we are friends of Grady's?'

Maguire was not going to let them know he had deliberately been looking for friends of the man, Grady, who had led the attack on Cat Ó Raifeartaigh, and been severely injured by Thomas because of it. He said, very deliberately, 'The woman Grady attacked that day – the woman who's responsible for the Earl damn near killing Grady – is inside Maynooth Castle as we speak.'

'Is she, by God!'

There was what seemed to be genuine surprise in the response, and Maguire said, 'Indeed she is. And she's as steeped in treason as Thomas himself. Her name's Catherine Ó Raifeartaigh, and he's bedding her every night.'

The first man said, slowly, 'Grady was badly injured that day. That bitch yelled for help fit to raise the devil, and Kildare heard and came running. He sent Grady smashing against a stone wall – he broke several bones in that fall. He'll always walk with a stick. I always blamed the bitch for it. I always said I'd find her one day and make her pay.'

This was exactly what Maguire had been told, and precisely why he had gone to such trouble to find these particular men. He said, eagerly, 'Would you see handing her over to the English as payment?'

'What would they do with her, though?'

'For pity's sake man, they'd use her as a hostage.'

'But would she be of any value? Just one girl . . .?'

'There's no knowing what the Earl might agree to if he believed she was facing a charge of treason,' said Maguire. 'And don't we all know the punishment for committing treason?'

There was a pause, then one of the men said, 'But . . . Silken Thomas to let a woman affect his rebellion to such an extent? To the extent of forcing his surrender?'

'He's besotted by her,' said Maguire. 'She leads him around like a pet dog.'

'Leads him around by his cock robin, sounds more like,' said the first man, and they both sniggered.

'I could make it easy for you to snatch her,' said Maguire, quelling his impatience. 'And take her to Skeffington. I could leave doors unlocked while Kildare is away fighting – he's away a good deal now. And I'd ensure there would be evidence with her for you to take.'

'Evidence? What kind of evidence?'

Maguire saw at once that this had given an added attraction to the plan. He said, 'Thomas's own battle plans. Maps and details of strategies. The placement of the gallowglasses. Even perhaps dates of attacks.'

'Those details would be there for us to take?'

'They would. When Thomas is at the castle, he spends almost every evening in the book room, pacing up and down like a caged animal. And the Cat writes everything down he says – all his plans and strategies. Everything is there – clear as a curse. You deliver Ó Raifeartaigh and that evidence into Skeffington's hands, and you'll be aiding the English cause more than anyone's done so far. And,' he said, 'Skeffington will surely reward you very richly indeed.'

They looked at one another, then the first said, 'Supposing we agree, when would we do it?'

Maguire had been ready for this. He said, 'As close to Skeffington's attack on the castle as possible. In the confusion and the panic of that, you won't be noticed. The girl's disappearance will hardly be noticed, as well.'

They thought for a moment, looked at one another as if for confirmation, then nodded. 'We'll send word when we can come,' said the one who had done most of the talking.

'Have a note delivered to the garden door,' said Maguire. 'You can address it to me quite openly. I'm the Earl's body-servant; I'm often sent messages about something he's ordered – boots or a cloak, perhaps. Yes – write that the leather boots ordered in Dublin are ready for collection. I will reply, letting you know when the Earl will be away from the castle.'

They nodded, and Maguire said, 'On the night we agree, I'll

make sure the plans and notes are all in the room with her. It had better be after midnight – the servants will all be abed, but the Cat sits for hours in the book room when the Earl is away.'

The men nodded, then one glanced over his shoulder, and in a much lower voice, said, 'You realize the English attack isn't likely to be for another two – perhaps even three – months?'

'February next year,' said the other. 'Even March.'

'I do know it. But I can wait.'

'You'll trust us until then?'

'I will. And in turn you'll trust me?' said Maguire. 'For I think I've proved my real intentions over that offer to let you into the courtyard two nights from now. For that alone I'm risking a lot, you know.'

They looked at one another, then nodded.

'We'll trust you,' they said.

Walking back through the city, Maguire noticed an empty house in one of the streets leading off a square. An attractive property it was, bow-fronted and with rooms at street level that might be used as business premises. There were rooms above where a man might live. It was a place that might serve for a very respectable concern which could be passed down to future generations. He stood looking at the house for a long time.

Then he went along to rejoin the Earl for the ride back to Maynooth.

Once they were back at the castle, the Earl went straight to the whey-faced creature's bedchamber. He always did. The latch of the door was dropped, but any servant who had to walk past often told with a knowing smirk how the bed creaked and protested and how the lady cried out with delight – not just once, but many times. The Earl's own cries of satisfaction were discussed in detail; Silken Thomas was clearly a very energetic, not to say imaginative, gentleman, and it was well known that the excitement of danger and intrigue often gave a man a stand like an autumn crocus. Hadn't you only to see him when he rode out at the head of his armies, his eyes glowing with reckless delight, obviously looking ahead with relish to the danger and the risks he would be taking.

Nobody blamed the Earl for the enthusiastic bed bouncing when he returned from one of his trips, and if a few of the female servants wished they could have been in the lady's place between the sheets, none of them actually admitted it. One or two remembered the youthful marriage that had taken place between the Earl and a lady in England. One of those arranged marriages the nobility so often entered into, it was thought, and no one could recall ever actually seeing the lady. But never mind what the arrangement had been, it was a shocking thing for a married man to be openly consorting with another female, and to call it *consorting* was to put it politely.

It tore Catherine to shreds to know that even his own people were prophesying defeat for Thomas, and it was a knife in her heart when he told her he was starting to believe he was destined to fail.

'And then the vow I made will be dishonoured,' he said in one of the misty dawns that shrouded Maynooth that autumn. He pulled her against him, as if trying to draw warmth and strength and hope from her. 'I'm going to lose Ireland to the English, Catherine. I promised to keep out that bloated monster, Henry Tudor, but his men still hold Dublin Castle, and I don't think I'll be able to honour my promise.' He held her so tightly that she could scarcely breathe. 'But whatever happens, I'll keep you safe, my dearest girl,' he said.

Catherine said, 'Are there others you need to keep safe? I've never asked you that . . .'

For a dreadful moment she thought she had stepped over a line, because his face darkened. But then he said, 'Once there was. But it was many years ago, Cat. Another country, another life even, and I was so very young . . .'

Later that day he led the gallowglasses out of Maynooth, and Catherine knew he was going to make one final attempt to take Dublin Castle. She wanted to beg him to let the statesmen and the politicians – and the English King as well – have Ireland, if it meant Thomas himself would remain safe, but she could not say it. She watched from a window as he led the soldiers out, all of them fully armoured, in mail shirts and the famous iron helmets with the silken fringes. The Kildare pennants fluttered in the breeze, and Thomas wore the robes of the Kildares over his own armour – scarlet and gold, silk on velvet. His head was thrown back challengingly, and Catherine had the sudden thought that this was how she would remember him: proud and defiant, and unswerving in his belief that what he was doing was right. His final endeavour to vanquish the English.

She would cling to the belief that he would succeed – that he would take Dublin Castle, and return to Maynooth in triumph.

But he did not succeed and he did not return. Two of his captains came galloping back three days later, with the news that the Earl's armies had been crushed, and that so far from taking Dublin Castle, they had lost the entire city to the English.

'And William Skeffington's men are swaggering around the city, boasting they created desertion in our ranks, the black-hearted liars,' said one of them, recounting it all to Catherine and the servants in Maynooth's great hall.

'Himself's still in Dublin,' said the second. 'He's hiding out, but he's laying plans and gathering information for another onslaught. For the time being, this castle is in the command of his man, Christopher Parese – the Earl trusts him to keep Maynooth safe.' But his eyes slid away as he said this, and Catherine saw there was not the faith or the confidence in this man, Parese, that there had been in Thomas.

'The Earl will come back to Maynooth as soon as it's safe,' said the first man. 'He wanted you all to know that.' It was a remark intended for everyone present, but he looked at Catherine as he spoke.

Catherine thanked the soldiers, and as soon as they had gone and the servants had returned to their own quarters, she shut herself in the book room, and huddled in a chair in the corner, shivering as violently as if she would break apart. She wrapped one of Thomas's fur-edged robes around her for warmth, and she pored over his maps and notes, remembering how they had talked – how he had eagerly poured out his plans and ideas, and how she had written everything down for him. She had loved knowing that he trusted her, and that in this very small way, she was helping him.

TWENTY-THREE

Maynooth Castle, Ireland, Early Spring, 1535

Catherine had talked to some of the soldiers – among them the captain who had brought the news of the defeat – and she had done her best to understand what had happened. She had tried to talk to the man in whose hands Thomas had left the castle – Master Parese – but he brushed her questions aside, and said all would be well. Catherine had the feeling of being patted on the head and told to run away and occupy herself with women's work, which infuriated her so much she wanted to fly at Parese and scratch his face.

She did not do so, of course. She retired to the library, where she always felt close to Thomas, and tried not to watch for the arrival of messengers, who might bring letters from Thomas. Twice, scrappy notes came, delivered by people who were described to her as the raff and skaff of the country.

'A tinker this time, come to ask if he can mend pots, mum,' said the kitchen maid bringing the second note. 'Mend pots indeed! As if we didn't look after pots in Maynooth Castle for ourselves! We sent him away with a flea in his ear!'

Even to know Thomas's hand had moved across the scrap of paper brought comfort. The notes were not very informative, only saying she must keep believing, and that he was safe. There was no way of knowing where they had come from or how long ago they had been written, and no hint as to when he would return to Maynooth, or even if he would return at all. Catherine tried to imagine a world which did not contain him, and could not.

She began to feel as if it had been in another life that she and Liam had gone to St Mary's Abbey. Her birthday, it had been, and the visit had been to mark the day – also, of course, because Liam wanted to paint the Earl. Catherine had written to Liam to let him know she was safe, choosing her words carefully, and he had replied, but his replies had been short and cautious, and she had understood he was concerned about letters falling into the hands of Thomas's enemies.

Several times, she wondered whether to leave Maynooth – whether she might get out without anyone realizing, or perhaps even caring. She could steal out under cover of night, taking one of the horses. It should be possible to reach Westmeath, and there was a faint, far-off comfort in the thought, but almost immediately she knew she would not do it. She would never desert Thomas. Even if she had to walk out to the block at his side, she would never desert him.

Often, during her evenings in the library, Maguire came in to ask was she all right, to bring her food or mulled wine on the colder evenings. This was kind of him.

Once or twice, he said he supposed he ought to tidy up the papers on the Earl's desk.

'Only somehow I haven't the heart. Leaving them there makes it seem as if he's only just laid them down, and he'll be walking through that door at any moment, and sit down to study them.'

Catherine still did not much care for Maguire, but she was grateful for his understanding. She said, 'Yes, please leave them there, Maguire.'

'I will indeed leave them there.'

It was shortly after the second note came that Catherine – sitting in the firelit room with the windows shuttered against the night – became aware of the stealthy movements and the whispering voices outside the door.

Even at this hour – midnight had just chimed in the stable yard – people in the castle did not move stealthily, or whisper, or creep across the floor like this. Servants came and went during the day, clattering pans or brooms, calling to one another as they went. And Thomas, whether he returned to Maynooth in triumph or defeat, was never stealthy or furtive, no matter the hour.

This was as if someone – several someones – had tiptoed along the passages to stand outside. Catherine pulled her thick robe around her, and went as quietly as possible to the door, pressing her ear against it to hear better.

Whoever was out there was whispering – the whispers reached her in fragments, and she thought there were three people.

'You're sure this is the room?' one was saying. 'We can't risk being caught.'

'It is the room. She sits in there every night. Waiting for him to come back.'

'Can we trust you, though? You're a servant of the Earl – we still don't know which side you're really on.'

A second voice said, 'And we already know you're a double-faced spy, Dubhgall Maguire.'

Maguire, thought Catherine, with a jolt first of shock, then of fear. He's out there, and he's brought men in, and they're after Thomas. Surely it could not be Maguire, though – not Thomas's faithful servant. But when the whisper came again, she knew it was.

'Aren't we all spies?' he was saying, anger in his tone. 'And didn't I leave that courtyard door unlocked for you, as I promised? And didn't you get for yourselves and for Sir William's men a good deal of useful information about the Earl's plans?'

'But what if you're taking us into a trap now, and you'll end up handing us over to Thomas of Kildare?'

'I have my own score to settle with Thomas of Kildare,' said Maguire. 'But you should remember that if you take this sly little cat to Sir William Skeffington, you'll be handing him something he can use to force Silken Thomas to surrender.'

'You really think the Rebel Earl will give himself up for a woman?'

'He will,' said Maguire. 'He'll surrender to Skeffington to save her.'

There was a brief pause, then the first voice said, 'Very well. We'll go in and get her. If we stand here much longer, we'll be caught.'

'We're quite safe,' said Maguire. 'The soldiers are in their own quarters – the ones who came back from Dublin, that is – and servants don't come up here unless they're called for. I've told you all that.'

There was a more definite movement from beyond the door, and Catherine backed away, her heart racing with fear, looking frantically around for a way to escape. But there was only the one

door and Maguire and the two men were on the other side of it.
Even if she dragged a heavy piece of furniture across it, barricading
herself in, they would break through. The windows were all high
up, and there were latticed strips of lead across them. She reached
for a fire iron from the hearth, which could be used as a makeshift
weapon, but the door had opened and the men were already in the
room – the two whose voices she had heard and Maguire himself.
And there was a look on Maguire's face that Catherine had never
seen there before – that she had never seen on anyone's face. Pure
hatred. But she lifted the fire iron and drew breath to scream,
because surely the servants would hear and come running . . .

But the men had already grabbed her arms and were pinioning
them behind her back, and Maguire was twisting a length of
thick cloth around her face and across her nose and mouth, tying
it so tightly that it was half-choking her, making it impossible
almost to breathe, let alone shout.

Through the sick dizziness she heard one of the men saying
something about leaving her legs untied.

'For didn't you say Kildare swives her every night when he's
here? Why shouldn't we do her, too.'

'No time,' said Maguire, shortly. 'We need to get her down
to the cart at once . . . Wait, though, you want the evidence of
Thomas's treason as well, don't you? The maps and the notes.'

'By God, we do,' said the man, and through the sick dizziness
and terror, Catherine saw Maguire cross to the big desk and gather
up sheaves of the papers that she had left out, seeing them as a
link to Thomas, believing that he must come back to take them.

'Good,' said the man, taking the papers and leafing through
them. 'Exactly what we wanted – and what you promised.' He
studied the papers for a few moments, then in a satisfied voice,
said, 'Oh, these will damn Silken Thomas, without any doubt.'

'All the way to the scaffold?' demanded Maguire, eagerly.

'All the way, my friend. But, dear God, was the man so stupid
he believed these wild ideas – these reckless plans – would take
him to victory? We were told he was misguided – rash – but seeing
all this . . . Had he no understanding at all of how wars are fought?'
He folded the papers into a pocket, smiling, then came to stand
over Catherine. 'This place will soon be in English hands,' he said.
'For your man, Parese, is of less account than Kildare himself.'

'More fool Kildare for leaving the weakling in command here, anyway.'

'Kildare is a fool,' said the first man. 'But he'll shortly be in the Tower – in the hands of Henry of England.'

He was saying something else – something about going across the Irish Sea – and Maguire was adding how Catherine would soon be joining her paramour on the scaffold. But the struggle to breathe was taking over, and their words were becoming distorted. Catherine felt herself spinning away from the firelit book room and tumbling into a deep, dark well, into a faraway place where there was nothing at all.

But before she fell all the way down, she heard Maguire say, 'Where will they take her?'

'Where do you think they'll take her?' said the man. 'The Tower of London, of course.'

'She'll go in by way of Traitors' Gate and from there into the dungeons,' said the other.

Maguire had thought he was prepared for the bombardment of Maynooth Castle by the English, but when it came, it was far worse, far more brutal than he had expected. It was unrelenting – constant shelling and firing of cannons against the old walls. And all the while was the appalling sensation of being trapped in the castle, and of knowing that the English soldiers would inevitably break through the outer walls, and storm into the interior of the castle itself. Not that Maguire intended to be still here when that happened, of course.

It was extremely gratifying to realize he had judged the timing of the Cat's kidnap exactly right. In the confusion and panic of the English attack, no one was taking much notice of the fact that the Earl's lady was nowhere to be seen. Who knew where anyone was? said people, rushing frantically around, trying to plan defensive manoeuvres against the marauders – occasionally pausing to ask where, for pity's sake, was the Earl himself all this time, for wasn't that lily-livered Parese, no use to man nor beast in all this, and wasn't a bit of strong leadership what they really needed now?

But the two Englishmen had kept their part of the bargain with Maguire – they had sent discreet messages that the Cat was in the hands of the English. The papers they had taken from

Maynooth's library were in the hands of the English as well, they said, and a number were in the woman's own handwriting, which would certainly serve to damn her.

They had also given Maguire carefully disguised information about the times of the attacks on Maynooth, and where Lord Grey's various detachments would be positioned. This meant that Maguire could choose his time to slip out of the castle – waiting until the bombardment was being repositioned to the eastern side, and then steal across to the courtyard to the stables, to take a horse.

There was a brief moment as he rode away when he risked pausing, and looked back at the devastation that had been wrought. It was dreadful. Massive holes had already been blown in the walls, and sections of bricks and stones and masonry had tumbled down and were lying everywhere. It was an appalling sight to see this great castle almost in ruins, but Maguire would waste no sympathy on it, for wasn't it only what that arrogant, selfish, untrustworthy Thomas Fitzgerald deserved.

He rode on, leaving the beleaguered castle behind. It was time to ensure that Silken Thomas joined Catherine Ó Raifeartaigh in the Tower of London.

He had to try several places before he finally found the Earl, who had been travelling half across the country, trying to raise help, trying to call up more men and arms. But he eventually ran him to earth in one of the houses of his allies, although he was shocked to see the ravages that recent events had wrought. Thomas was thin and – despite his youth – he looked almost haggard.

But he was still the man who had turned his back on the promise to Maguire's father – and also on those other men who had died fighting for the Fitzgeralds – and Maguire would stay true to his plan. He was respectful and even humble with Kildare, though, explaining that he had come straight from Maynooth itself.

'And a sorry sight you'd find it, sire, blown to splinters, and the English rampaging everywhere.'

The Earl said, 'Mistress Ó Raifeartaigh? Is she safe?'

Maguire had to repress a stab of fury, because even at such a moment, even with his rebellion in tatters and his family's ancient castle all but destroyed, Thomas's thoughts were for the bitch.

He said, sorrowfully, 'Oh, sire, she's been taken – before even the siege started, it was. An English captain and one of his men sneaked into the castle in the middle of the night, like the sewer rats they are, and took her to London without anyone knowing.' He was pleased to hear how well this sounded. 'They say they're holding her in the Tower of London for treason – for aiding you in the rebellion,' he said.

He would not have thought it possible that the Earl could turn any whiter, but he did. In a voice Maguire had never heard him use, he said, 'Sweet Christ, I must get her out,' and then, 'Is Parese still at Maynooth? Ah, well, I suppose I never believed he would hold out against the English? Is Lord Grey still commanding the English?'

'He is, sir. He's been appointed Lord Deputy of Ireland.'

'Has he, by Christ,' said Thomas, with what was almost a snarl. 'By God, I'll spit his liver if he harms Catherine.'

'Sir, they're saying Lord Grey intends to offer you a pardon. He's sending you a guarantee of safety, if you surrender to him.'

'Surrender . . .' The word came out in a breath of sound, as if it had been forced from him. Then, with a brief return to his old spirit, Thomas said, 'Oh, the offer has been sent, but I've told them I'll never surrender!'

Maguire had expected this, and so, choosing his words with care, he said, 'Sir, there's something you should know. I've talked to people – in the English army, I mean. I acted the spy, I suppose you'd say, but it was all for our cause, and in times like these—'

'In times like these you use whatever weapons come to hand. So, you played the spy, did you, Maguire? Well?'

'I think the information can be trusted,' said Maguire. 'And the word is that if you surrender, as well as pardoning you, Lord Grey will give an assurance that—'

'Yes?'

'That your closest allies will also be given a full pardon.' And, as the Earl turned to stare at him, Maguire said, very deliberately, 'Even those they have already taken prisoner.'

They looked at one another, then Thomas said, very softly, 'Catherine. That's what they mean, isn't it?'

Maguire looked his master straight in the eye, and said, 'Yes. If you surrender to Lord Grey, Mistress Ó Raifeartaigh will be set free.'

TWENTY-FOUR

Thomas of Kildare's surrender was no real surprise to anyone. No one was sure what had happened to him or where he was, but most people agreed that the promise of a pardon would very likely turn out to be as hollow as a blown egg, and the Rebel Earl would find himself facing a very brutal justice indeed.

Maguire took unobtrusive lodgings in the city, and waited for the wildest of the rumours to die down a little. Then he made a cautious way to the castle. The English had left, but they had wrought such devastation that in places it was almost in ruins. Maguire thought it was not quite the heap of rubble people were saying, and parts of it were certainly still habitable, but there was certainly the impression that if anyone did live in there, they would not be doing so for much longer. He was able to go through the massive iron-studded door unchallenged, which could never have happened before the siege, and although there were faint sounds of life from the sculleries, he made his way to Thomas's rooms without seeing anyone.

Once there, he made a careful search, opening drawers and cupboards and desks, listening for anyone who might come along. But no one did come, and Maguire found a great number of items that clearly were valuable, and could be sold profitably. There were things such as amulets, and signet or seal rings. There were several drawstring bags of coins as well, stashed in the back of a cupboard. Several times the amount of the original hundred crowns his father had been promised. Maguire pocketed these, along with several pieces of the jewellery.

In a corner cupboard he found more jewellery – clearly that of a lady, this time: necklaces, bracelets, pomanders, fashioned from gold or silver and studded with jewels. The forgotten wife, thought Maguire, staring at these. But wherever she was now, she was not going to miss these trinkets. He scooped them up.

Once the Earl was dead, his title, together with his lands and his castles would pass to his half-brother – Gerald Fitzgerald, that was, and it could not be changed. Maguire did not want castles and lands, though; he was very satisfied indeed with the hoard he had collected today, and, riding back to Dublin, he thought his future was beginning to look very hopeful indeed. Tomorrow he would go into the jewellery quarter in Dublin. In times such as these, the selling of jewellery was not likely to raise comment or bring forth awkward questions as to rightful owners.

And after that . . .

His mind went to the bow-fronted house on the city's fringe that he had marked out not so very long since. Now, looking at the memory of it, he could see a name quite clearly above those bow windows. *Maguire's.* Something that would endure long after he himself had gone.

One week later, he sat in a rather untidy room, facing a gentleman wrapped in dusty, knee-length black silk robes. He was rather elderly, but he seemed knowledgeable, and he said that certainly he could arrange for a lease to be drawn up on the house described. It could be ready in one week's time, he said. It would be necessary to know the nature of the business for which the premises were intended; oh, and please to name a legatee – by which he meant an heir – who would take over the property in the event of any . . . ah, unfortunate occurrences.

After thought, Maguire named his nephew. He intended the boy to join him in the venture, anyway. It was unlikely he would need to actually take over the premises, though, for Maguire had no intention of succumbing to any unfortunate occurrences. But he liked to think of the name of *Maguire* being painted over the shop and the name being handed down. He said the business should be designated as dealers in books and manuscripts, and as offering copying and letter-writing services. His nephew would be very good indeed at such things; Maguire was very pleased to think of all this.

One week later, he signed the document that made him what was termed the lessee of the bow-fronted house. He had to pay an entire year's rent in advance – a sum that once would have struck dismay into his heart, but which now, with the proceeds of the Fitzgerald jewels and the coins stashed in the drawstring bags, allowed him to do so with equanimity. The fee requested by the gentleman in the black silk robe shocked him, but there was a further shock to come.

As the robed gentleman added sealing wax to the document, he said, almost off-handedly, that he had been interested to hear Master Maguire had been in service to the young Earl of Kildare.

'A bad business, that,' he said, frowning at the parchment, waiting for the wax to cool and set. 'A gullible young man, though. There was that business with his lawyer a year or so back – you'd know about that, of course?'

'Oh, of course,' said Maguire, who was not going to let anyone think he did not know everything there was to know about the Fitzgeralds.

'It is galling to me when a person in my own profession is found guilty of such gross deception,' said the man. 'Misappropriation of clients' funds, that was the charge, and of course, it turned out the wretch had misappropriated a great deal of money from the Kildare estate. Sly, you know.' He clicked his tongue disapprovingly, then tilted the document to make sure ink and sealing wax were properly dry.

'The scoundrel was taken to Newgate, of course. A shameful fate for a man of the law.'

Maguire managed to say, 'Shameful, indeed. And your profession normally such an honourable one.'

The silk-robed gentleman, apparently encouraged by this, became confidential. 'It was whispered that some of the money had been promised to the men who rode to battle with the old Earl,' he said. 'You won't have known him, I daresay, but I remember him, and he would have been deeply shocked to think his pledge had not been fulfilled. Of course, people said the new Earl – your Earl – ought to have realized what was happening and put things to rights.'

Maguire stared at him, then managed to nod sadly.

'And now,' said the lawyer, 'here is your part of the agreement, and I wish you all success in your venture, Master Maguire.'

Walking back to his lodgings, Maguire's mind was tumbling. Was it possible that Silken Thomas had been genuinely deceived? That he had believed the promised money had reached the men to whom it had been promised? But if he had not known the truth, he should have done. The lawyer had said that, and Maguire saw it was true. Thomas should certainly have made sure that the men who served his father received their due rewards. But he had not, and why had he not? Because, thought Maguire, viciously, he had been more concerned with riding off to battles and stamping around as arrogantly and as imperiously as if he was some kind of god descended from the clouds.

Maguire was not going to waste time wondering if the present situation could be altered. It could not be altered at all, and it did not need to be. Thomas Fitzgerald had been careless and selfish and self-centred; he had been heedless of his obligations, and as a result people had suffered loss and distress. He deserved to be where he was – inside the Tower of London. His paramour deserved to be there with him too.

It was annoying when, a few days later, Maguire's nephew said the house would need a considerable amount of work before it could be acceptable to potential customers. There must be book-shelves from floor to ceiling everywhere, he said, and also the creation of alcoves with tables where customers could discuss their business requirements.

This would involve spending more money than Maguire had visualized, and he hoped his nephew would not turn out to be a spendthrift. However, there were the several bags of coins taken from Maynooth, and a fair amount of the jewellery was still unsold. It was a good thing he had been able to take almost all of it.

Time had blurred for Catherine, but fragments of her journey to this stone room swam in and out of her mind. The lapping of water against a boat, with herself lying, still tied up, in the bottom of it. Smeary lights, blurred by mist. And then a huge building rearing up out of the swirling fog. Flaring torches burned in twisted iron brackets on its walls, and as they drew nearer there had been the sound of immense machinery clanging into life above them. Catherine remembered looking up, and seeing a huge portcullis slowly rising. She thought she had struggled all over again at that point, but it had been of no use. The boat was rowed beneath the portcullis, and once beyond it, there had been the sound of its immense iron teeth descending again and biting viciously into place.

She tried to keep these images at bay, and to keep hold of reality and sanity, despite everything. I won't despair, thought Catherine. I will believe help will come.

And incredibly it had, although in an entirely unforeseen form. But hadn't dear Sister Bernadette in St Joseph's taught that, 'Help seldom comes in a guise you expect.'

The help came with the unlocking of the door of her room, and the guard calling out that there was someone to see her.

A voice said, 'Catherine – oh, Catherine, my dearest girl.'

Next to Thomas, it was the voice in all the world Catherine would have wished to hear. She gave a half-gasp, and said, 'Liam.' And ran forward into his arms.

It seemed the Constable of the Tower of London had written to Liam, as Catherine's nearest kin, telling him of his sister's arrest and her imprisonment.

'I travelled to England at once,' he said. 'Of course I did. Whatever is ahead for you, I must be here with you.'

'Will they let you visit again?'

He smiled. 'They will,' he said. 'For I told them I wanted to paint your portrait – Catherine, I had to say it was so that I had a . . . a last image of you to keep.' His hand closed around hers. 'We'll hope it needn't be, though,' he said.

'They agreed to the portrait painting?'

'They thought it was a strange request,' he said, 'but they agreed.'

Despite the fear and the grimness of her surroundings, Catherine smiled, because of course the people here – the guards and the Constable of the Tower – would think it a strange request. But Liam did not quite live in the ordinary world as others did, and perhaps this had been understood, and that was why permission had been given.

On his second visit he brought easel and paints, which he set up in a corner of the room. 'I really am going to paint you,' he said. 'And I shall show you wearing the blue gown you wore on that day we went to Dublin,' he said. 'You remember?'

The words sent Catherine's mind back to that afternoon outside St Mary's Abbey. She had indeed been wearing the blue gown – she had worn it when she met Thomas. Thomas . . .

Without realizing she had been going to say it, she said, 'Thomas is in here as well, isn't he?'

Liam was frowning at the board he had set up on the easel, but he looked up, hesitated, then said, 'He is.'

'Could I see him?' said Catherine, eagerly. 'Could you find a way? It needn't be for long. Half an hour would be enough.' To herself, she thought that ten minutes – five even – would be enough.

She expected Liam to say it would be impossible, but he said, thoughtfully, 'If I were to say I wanted to paint his portrait, as well as yours, it might be allowed. The famous Rebel Earl – Silken Thomas – to be set down for posterity.'

Incredibly, permission was granted for Liam to make a single visit to Thomas's room. He did not actually tell Catherine he had represented himself as an English loyalist, keen to set down an image of the infamous Irish traitor, but Catherine guessed it was what he had done.

'But a sketch only,' the Constable of the Tower said. 'And just the one visit, and for no more than an hour.' He took her hand. 'You must pose as my assistant for that hour. If you wear a long cloak, no one will suspect. You will have to cut your hair, though, to look like a boy. I'm not sure how— Oh, but you could try the scraping knife. It's small, but the blade is quite sharp.'

'But if we can walk through the passages openly like this, can't we simply walk out of the Tower itself?' said Catherine, taking the small knife which Liam used to scrape smooth the surface of a board.

'I wish we could. But there are too many heavily locked doors between this part of the Tower and the way out. And the guards at the main gate know I did not arrive with an assistant. There are inspections – records kept of who comes in and out. If I tried to leave with someone who was not written on their list for the day, they would know at once it was an escape attempt.'

'I understand. And I'll cut my hair and all the other things.' Catherine would have shaved her hair and gone barefoot over broken glass to see Thomas.

'Good girl.' Liam smiled. 'And I will leave you alone with the Earl for that hour, of course.'

As Catherine and Liam were led along stone passages two days later, her heart was beating so furiously she thought it might explode.

Seeing these passageways – walking past low doors with small grilles in them – made her realize that her own captivity was not as severe as it could have been. Her room was stone-floored and stone-walled and it was chilly and unfriendly. But it was a reasonable-sized room and there was a slit of a window overlooking a small, grassed piece of ground. Catherine looked out of this window several times each day, but there was never anyone out there. She had a pallet bed and a small table and chair and even a square of carpet. One of the more sympathetic guards had brought in books and writing materials and extra blankets. Hold on to hope, thought Catherine, as she and Liam made their way through the dim corridors. Remember, to despair is the worst sin of all.

And remember that you're being taken to see Thomas . . .

Thomas.

She never knew, afterwards, whether, once the guard had unlocked the door, Liam went back into the passage to wait there, or whether he did not even come into the room in the first place. As soon as the door swung open, she was aware only of one person.

He was waiting for her, standing with the light from the high, barred window behind him, so that in those first crowded seconds she saw him as she had first seen him in St Mary's Abbey – with the pouring brilliance of the stained-glass windows showering over him.

But when he spoke, his voice was blurred with such emotion that for a moment Catherine could almost have believed it was a stranger who stood there.

Then he said, 'Catherine – oh, my dear love . . .' She saw him struggle for mastery of his emotions, then he said, 'I thought I had saved you . . . They said if I surrendered . . . I believed if they took me instead—'

Catherine said, unsteadily, 'They deceived you. They took us both.'

'If I had known you were in here, I would have torn down the walls, brick by brick, to get to you—'

Catherine had no awareness of having moved, but his arms were around her and, as he bent his head to kiss her, she felt salt on her cheeks – she had no idea if the tears were hers or his, but she did not care.

Time ceased to matter. They were seated on the narrow bed, and Thomas's arms were still around her. He turned her to face him, cupping her face between his hands, looking at her intently as if trying to print her features deep on his mind.

'Were two lovers ever in such a dismal situation as this, Catherine?'

'I don't care where we are. For now, I don't care about anything.'

'I care that I failed, though,' he said, and there, briefly, was the rebel, the defiant young man who would challenge the world, and who had taken on an English King to fight for a cause in which he believed passionately. 'And I care that it's ended in you being in here.' He traced the lines of her face with the tip of a finger; then he glanced around the room and, without warning, the smile that was so very precious lighted his face.

'Do you suppose,' said Silken Thomas, softly, 'that anyone has ever made love in this place? I mean really, completely, made love?' He looked behind them at the bed, then raised an eyebrow quizzically.

Catherine felt her heart start to beat faster. 'I shouldn't think so,' she said, at last.

'It would create a new memory – another layer of history for the Tower of London,' he said, his eyes never leaving hers.

'It would. But – would it be possible? I mean, in such a place, could you—?'

For answer, Thomas pushed her back onto the bed, and pulled her hard against him.

'Well, my lady? Doesn't it feel entirely possible that I could?'

'Oh, yes.' But Catherine glanced across at the door. 'But, what if someone comes in—?'

'I don't care if the entire Guard of the Tower come in, or if the whole of the English army marches through the door with

Henry Tudor at the head of them,' said the Rebel Earl. 'Let's make history.'

Catherine thought – when she could think clearly again – that Thomas's love-making on that snatched, secret visit, had been far more intense than ever it had been at Maynooth, if that were possible. Was that because he had known it would be their last time together? That was not a thought that must be allowed to linger, though.

Liam was allowed into her room, to work on the portrait. Twice he worked on a sketch of Thomas: taking it from the rough drafts he had made during the visit to Dublin, when Thomas had made his extraordinary speech in St Mary's Abbey. He was making good the excuse provided for visiting Thomas's room, of course.

He worked with absorption. Catherine did not think that her portrait or anything he might eventually paint of Thomas would be very good, because Liam's paintings never were very good, but she did not say this.

Once, he showed her a rough sketch he had made of parts of the Tower – 'Only the parts I have seen for myself,' he said, 'for it's a vast old place. But to have an idea of its layout could be useful.'

He looked at her very straightly, and Catherine said, carefully, 'I expect it could.'

She did not dare ask anything else, just as she did not dare ask anyone what might be ahead for her. She certainly did not dare ask what might be ahead or Thomas.

There was starting to be a dreamlike quality to life, and it was difficult to measure time any longer, but gradually Catherine became aware that the body had its own way of measuring time. That there was something her own body was no longer measuring. Something that should be happening to her, but was not.

At first she did not dare trust the tiny hope – it was too fragile; it was as if it was a cobweb that would dissolve if brought into the light. And surely to goodness, being captive in this grim place was more than enough to disturb the body's rhythms. But presently, the faint hope strengthened, and gained substance. She was going to have a child. Thomas's son or daughter. The realization poured through her like cascades of molten gold.

A child. A boy with Thomas's fiery hair, and with eyes full of light and life and rebellious spirit. Or a girl – an elfin-faced daughter, with mischief and delight and eagerness in her smile.

When one of the guards asked if she would like to have visits by a priest, she said at once, 'Yes – yes, I would.'

The priest was elderly and inclined to be severe, but on his first visit he heard her confession without interrupting. When she finished, he used the word fornication in relation to what she had done with Thomas, and said it was an abomination in the sight of the Lord. Catherine flinched, because the word did not seem to bear any resemblance to what had happened between them, but the priest gabbled the words of absolution, added a blessing, and said he would visit her again.

At his second visit she told him she was going to have a child. He compressed his lips, and Catherine thought if he used words such as bastard, or child of sin, she would refuse to see him again. But he did not. He said he would make sure the Constable of the Tower was told of her condition, and that the proper arrangements would be made. The hope Catherine had tried to keep alive grew stronger and, encouraged, she told the sympathetic guard as well. He said he would tell people who needed to know. You could never entirely trust the clergy, he said.

Catherine had no idea if any of this meant she would be released, and she did not dare ask. She could not believe she would be left here to give birth, though. She did not dare to ask if Thomas could be told, in case they refused.

TWENTY-FIVE

Ethne Rafferty knew that she must find out what was in *The Murderer Inside the Mirror* as soon as possible. Above all, she must know what was in the scene that was being kept secret. The Murder Scene. Florian Gilfillan had failed her, but there must be some other way.

Montague Fitzglen had never used the word 'murder' about the two killings in Dublin Castle that night – her father's killing of the first guard, and Ethne's killing of the second one. He had said, with great firmness, that both had been self-defence. Ethne had never known if he believed that, but she certainly knew what she had done had not been self-defence; it had been outright murder.

When the second guard – the man who had grabbed her arm and was holding it too tightly for her to get free – shouted that he would tell the world that Phelan Rafferty was a murderer, she had known he must not be allowed to do so. There had been no hesitation and no doubt in her; she had raised the thick shaft of wood from the mirror she still had in her free hand, and brought it smashing down on the guard's head. He had slumped at once, releasing his hold on her, and she had struck him a second, and then a third time, because she had had to make sure. She had to protect her father. It had unquestionably been murder – she had always known it, just as she had always known she would not flinch from killing again if the truth ever seemed likely to come out. It would be partly to protect Phelan's memory, of course. But it would be to protect Ethne herself, too.

And now, it seemed, the truth might indeed be about to come out, and in a way Ethne could not possibly have visualized. She was almost sure what the play would contain, but she was not absolutely certain. She needed to read the script – even to see a rehearsal.

A rehearsal . . .

Florian had said they were rehearsing the Murder Scene

tomorrow night at the theatre. Could Ethne slip inside and hide
somewhere to watch? Perhaps in one of the boxes? And if it
turned out that she was right . . .? What then? The answer came
at once. She would have to prevent the play being performed
– stop it from telling the story to the world. But how? She
thought for a long time and gradually the glimmerings of a plan
began to form. What if someone were to be attacked in the
Roscius – not fatally, but sufficiently severely to result in an
investigation? Wouldn't that mean a postponement of the play,
at the very least? The possibility took stronger shape in her
mind, then with it came the memory of Viola Gilfillan's interview, and how she had been asked about the theatre superstition
of mirrors on a stage bringing bad luck. Miss Gilfillan had
dismissed the belief, saying that the avoidance of mirrors on
stage was purely a safety measure. Ethne knew there were a
great many superstitions within the world of the theatre, of
course – how it was unlucky to say aloud the title of *Macbeth*,
how it was forbidden to whistle backstage. But if a member of
the company were to be attacked in the theatre shortly before
the festival's first night, as well as it causing an investigation,
mightn't it bring into prominence the mirror superstition? Ethne
knew from her father that theatre people were inclined to accept
such beliefs, and she thought it might not take much for this
play to become regarded as jinxed – as a kind of albatross that
presaged ill-fortune. If that were to happen, no actor manager
would touch it.

The more Ethne thought about this, the better it seemed. But
who could be attacked? It could not be Florian, and nor could
it be Viola or Timon Gilfillan, because that might end in someone
making the link between herself and any of those three. The play
bore her father's name, and her own friendship with Florian had
just been revived – and she knew him well enough to be aware
he would probably have talked about it.

But she did not know anything about the rest of the company.

Or did she? Hadn't Florian talked about some eager, wide-eyed
little girl – Tilly, was it? Yes. Tilly Fendle, who was dazzled by
the world of the theatre. Clearly he had developed something of
a *tendresse* for her, and Ethne thought it possible that Tilly Fendle
had been dazzled by the attentions of a senior member of the

famous Gilfillan family – and that she would find an invitation to a secret rendezvous intriguing.

Florian had mentioned the lodging house where most of the company was staying – near the theatre, he had said. It oughtn't to be difficult to find it, and unobtrusively slip a note through the letterbox.

Ethne reached for a sheet of notepaper from the supply set out for guests, careful to choose one that did not have the hotel's address printed on it.

It was not until after supper that Tansy saw a letter lying on the table in the hall of the lodging house with her name on it. But no one except the family knew this address, and it had been agreed that only Jack would write to her – they did not want to draw attention to her, but a single, occasional correspondent was unlikely to be noticed. But the writing on the envelope was not Jack's.

She took it up to her room and opened it. There was a single sheet – her name was at the top – just *'Tilly'* – then two lines of neat handwriting.

'We never seem to have chance to talk privately,' said the author of the note. 'As I think you know, I would very much like to do so. There is a rehearsal this evening at eight o'clock, so the stage door will be unlocked. Could we meet in the theatre at nine? Wait for me in the stage box.'

There was a squiggle that could have been anything, but Tansy's heart gave a huge leap, because it could be *T*. Or couldn't it as easily be *F*? Florian? Don't let it be Florian, she thought, but her mind had already gone back to his sly sugges- tion about supper. Champagne and caviar, he had said, as if he was a lecherous relic from the Victorian era, for heaven's sake.

It might be a *T*, though. 'You really were Mimi,' Timon had said, after they had played that brief scene in the deserted Roscius. And later, 'It's a pity we didn't have time to explore the theatre properly together,' he had said.

Tansy reached for a coat, pulled on the butcher-boy cap, and went quietly down the stairs. As she left the house, a nearby clock chimed half past eight.

The stage door was unlocked as promised, and Tansy slipped

inside and went up the stairs, along the dressing-room corridor, and through the heavy doors that led to the boxes.

Timon had told her the Roscius had been built in the early 1700s, and had staged work by many notable Irish playwrights.

'They would come to watch their plays being performed,' he had said. 'Sheridan, and Oscar Wilde, of course. Oliver Goldsmith, too.'

Tansy liked the thought of those famous people coming here. Would they have been apprehensive, or would they have been excited and pleased to see their work and the characters brought to life? Would whoever had written *The Murderer Inside the Mirror* be sitting here in a week or so, feeling any of those emotions? But then she remembered that it still might be Phelan Rafferty who had written the play, and that he was dead and would not see the people and the story he had created walk on to a lighted stage. This was extremely sad.

The stage box was at the far end, nearest the stage, of course. No one seemed to be around, so Tansy went cautiously in. On the left was the auditorium, shadowy and dim, the ghost-outlines of the rows of seats, and the gilt railings of the balconies and circle only just visible. But on her right was the stage. And the rehearsal was in progress.

Ethne had reached the Roscius shortly before eight o'clock. She had worn a long dark raincoat which would cover her and not attract attention. With it she had a deep-brimmed oilskin hat – the kind people often wore during inclement weather. Once in the theatre, the brim could be turned down to almost completely conceal her face. In the deep side-pocket she had a heavy marble paperweight, brought from Westmeath House.

The stage door was in a busy side street, but passers-by were intent on their own affairs, and no one gave Ethne a second look. It was unlocked, as she had expected, and she thought it should be easy to find her way to the theatre boxes – hadn't she accompanied her father to all those theatres when she was younger, and weren't theatres all built more or less to the same plan? She found the way easily. It was just on eight o'clock – too early for Tilly Fendle – and she went quietly into the box next to the stage box itself.

Florian, Timon and Viola were already on the stage, with a working light burning and shadows clustered at the edges of the stage. A half-completed stairway stood near the centre, and there were flats painted to represent stone walls. Even in the dim light there was the impression of a forgotten, shadowy corner inside some ancient castle.

Timon Gilfillan – as Maran – was saying the room they sought was behind the wall.

'And up here is the mechanism that will open it.'

'But Maran, if we're caught—'

'Tomás, haven't I told you, I've never been caught yet. This will be the smoothest filch I've ever worked.'

Timon Gilfillan switched briefly back to his real self, and pointed out where the wall's mechanism would be and where it would slide across.

'It should do so with a nicely teeth-wincing scrape of stone against stone,' he said. 'Although we'd better pray to the gods of theatre that the mechanism and the sound effects work. Let's go on. The panel's open now. Viola?'

Viola Gilfillan took several paces forward, then stopped and thrust out a pointing hand.

'Tomás – look there. In that corner . . . Lying by itself in the shadows – half covered by layers of dust, as if it's trying to hide . . .'

The words sliced deep into Ethne's mind, and in that moment she knew she had been right – that the play was an almost exact echo of that long-ago night. She pushed away the panic that was clutching her, and forced herself to keep watching and listening.

Florian – Tomás – had moved forward. 'It really is there,' he said. 'I've tried to find it all these years and finally and at last I've done so. The murderer's lute, my family called it. No one knew what happened to it, but they all knew my ancestor played it as he walked to the scaffold – to be hanged for committing murder. His name was suppressed – I've never known what it was.' He turned to the other two. 'That's the nightmare,' he said. 'That's what's been with me ever since I can remember. That final dreadful walk by a man whose name was wiped from history – a man who walked to where the executioner waited, his music walking alongside him.'

Catrina said, 'Tomás, did you want the lute so you could find out about your ancestor? About his music?'

'No! Never that! I learned to play a lute – or at least, to play a stringed instrument. Only in a very basic way, but enough to understand it. What I needed to do, though, was to find this lute and destroy it,' said Tomás. 'To be rid of the nightmare. But all I ever knew was that it would be lying by itself somewhere – hiding . . . Shrouded in its own darkness . . .'

This time the panic almost overwhelmed Ethne. The dim theatre spun sickeningly around her, and she was seeing again Thomas's own lute lying in the dim secret room, his last ballad folded inside it. The ballad that could only have been his own death song. *In cold bleak dawn I soon shall die*, he had written. But no one except for Ethne herself and Montague Fitzglen had ever known about it. Before they escaped that night, carrying her father's unconscious body, Montague had closed up the secret room. No one would have known how to get into it. No one – *no one* – could have known the lute or the hidden music were in there. But whoever had written this play – this scene – had known.

It was some moments before she could bring her mind back to what was happening on the stage, but she managed to do so at last.

They appeared to have moved on to a later part of the scene, and Ethne had the sense of having missed some of the dialogue.

'We haven't got the walk-on who's playing the guard,' Timon Gilfillan was saying. 'But he'll fall about here.' He indicated a place near the steps. 'On you go, please.'

'Murder,' said Tomás, and Florian's hands came up to half-cover his face. 'Murder's a hanging offence. You walk to meet your punishment, with music playing . . .'

Then Maran, his voice cutting sharply through Tomás's line: 'Tomás – Catrina – we have to close this room up, and we have to do it at once. If we push the body back in there it could be years before anyone finds it . . .'

'But can't you see!' Viola, as Catrina, had backed against a wall, and in a low voice – but a voice that reached Ethne with dreadful clarity – she said, 'Can't you see? There's someone inside the room. Someone's been sealed up in there—'

'Catrina, there's no one—'

'Tomás, he's walking towards us . . .'

'There's no one – we must get out, because if we're caught now, we'll all be damned . . .'

'We're damned already, Tomás. Listen.'

'What . . .?'

Then Florian broke off, because into the dim old theatre, shocking and discordant, came the sonorous chiming of a bell.

There was a second or two of what was clearly genuine shock, then Tomás's voice came again. 'It's the warning bell. It's the alarm.'

Ethne did not hear the next lines, because her mind was reeling with terror, and the memories were churning up again. There had been no alarm bell that night in the Clock Tower, but there had been the immense clock itself, crouching immediately above them, relentlessly pounding its own giant's-heartbeat rhythm.

The chiming had stopped, and Ethne realized then that Timon Gilfillan had moved unobtrusively to the side of the stage, and that he had created the chiming.

Florian said, crossly, 'Timon, we knew there was going to be a bell sounding, but you might at least have warned us you were going to try it out tonight.'

'No, I might not. I wanted you to portray shock,' said Timon, coming back onto the stage. 'And you both did. Remember that feeling – those reactions – for the actual performance, will you, because it's exactly the reaction that's needed. It's the moment you realize you're cornered – that you aren't going to escape.'

Viola Gilfillan said, almost to herself, 'And the moment when we realize the condemned cell almost certainly awaits because we couldn't hide the body of the murdered guard.'

'Yes.' Then, in a brisker tone, Timon said, 'The chiming was good, wasn't it? We found a kind of ship's bell in the cellars here – somebody said it was used for a production of *The Tempest* years ago. It's mounted in a wooden frame, but the musicians are going to set up some kind of echo chamber – I don't entirely understand the details, but they promise it will rip through the entire auditorium, and that it will be ominous and very sinister. Like a huge heartbeat, or an immense ticking clock.'

A huge heartbeat or a ticking clock. Ethne's mind flinched all over again, then Timon frowned, glanced at his watch, and said, 'I had hoped we might do the next scene tonight as well – it's quite short – but it's already getting late. And I think we need the mirror to work out the exact positions. I'll get backstage to chalk them out for us in the morning. They need to be right, because the reflection Catrina sees must be visible from all corners of the auditorium. The audience won't realize what it is at this point, and the main intermission comes there, so they'll be going out to the crush bar surrounded by shivers of fear. It'll only be when they're back in their seats that they'll hear the explanation in the next scene about there being a mirror in that room, and they'll understand it was the reflection of one – or both of us – that Catrina saw.'

Florian said, 'Timon, dear old fruit, don't you think Tomás would fall to his knees when the bell starts its frightful clamour? Slump against a wall and cringe and sob with horror and fear?'

'No, I don't. You're to stay in position, Florian, and if you do anything else, I will personally drop you over the edge of the stage into the orchestra pit,' said Timon.

'Are we repairing to that tavern on the corner?' asked Viola, who had gone to the side of the stage to examine the bell mechanism. 'Can ladies go into such places in Ireland? Because I could certainly do with something to drink after all that emotion and darkness and alarm bells.'

'Yes, let's,' said Timon. 'But we'd better carry some of this scenery down to the basement first. The stair flat – and certainly the mirror and the bell – could give away too many details of the scene – it would be a great shame if the details became known so close to the performance. I'll take the mirror – it isn't very heavy. Florian, can you bring the small flat? Don't scowl, you can manage it, surely?'

'All the way down that iron staircase—'

'It's only canvas on a plywood frame,' said Timon. 'And the stairs are quite wide.'

'I'll take the bell thing, and I'll go ahead and switch on lights for you,' said Viola. 'Those underground rooms are like the caverns of doom, and they stretch under the street for ever – one of the carpenters was complaining that it took ages to carry stuff back and forth, never mind having to drag everything up the iron stairs. If we get lost in the gloom, we'll meet in the tavern. Who's got the key to lock the stage door?'

'I have,' said Timon. 'I'll lock up. But there's a night-watchman – he looks in around half past ten, I think, so he'll make sure everywhere's secure.'

As they went out, Ethne sat back, trying to pull her emotions into place. The sound of the alarm bell was still reverberating inside her mind, exactly as the sinister ticking of the massive old clock had done that night. But it was vital to remember none of this made any difference to the plan, and after a few moments she managed to lean cautiously forward until she could see the stage box. She had not heard any sounds from it, and if the Fendle girl had not responded to her note, the plan would be ruined.

But it was all right. She could see the faint outline of a figure. Tilly Fendle was here. She must have slipped in quietly a little earlier. The plan was unfolding exactly as Ethne had planned.

TWENTY-SIX

As Timon, Viola and Florian made their way from the stage, Tansy sat back, realizing that she had been so tense all her muscles were aching.

It was a remarkable scene – even though she had not seen it all, and even though she had not seen the murder that had clearly been committed early on. But Viola's line about something lying in the shadows – 'Half covered by layers of dust, as if it's trying to hide' – was extraordinarily chilling. And the sudden intrusion of the alarm bell would send the entire house into fits.

It was now well after nine o'clock, and there was no sign of her suitor. Ought she to go in search of him? Scenery had had to be carried down to the cellars, which was not something that could be done in five minutes, but there had been time to dismantle the entire set of *The Murderer in the Mirror*, stack it in the cellars three times over, and for the note-writer to come back to the stage box. If her anonymous admirer was so interested, he had better come into the open and admit it, and they could have a proper romance. Providing it did not turn out to be Florian. And if it turned out to be Timon, Tansy was not inclined to embark on a romance with somebody who sent furtive notes for a secret rendez-vous, then did not turn up. Or went blithely off to The Moonshine as if he had changed his mind, or even forgotten altogether.

She went out of the stage box and headed for the stairs and the stage door. Timon had said something about locking it, but Tansy thought it would not be a massive disaster if she had been accidentally locked in. At a pinch, she could go into one of the offices or the gilt and chrome box office at front of house and use the telephone to ring someone to let her out. She had only actually used a telephone twice, but she knew what you did. And there had been that jaunty night-watchman who drank at a corner table in The Moonshine – in fact Timon had mentioned him just now, saying he thought the man looked in at around half past ten every night. If she was still here by then, he would let her out.

She was halfway along the dressing-room corridor when a door opened nearby, and a voice called softly, 'Tilly . . . Tilly Fendle . . . Over here . . .'

Tansy looked about her, trying to work out where the voice had come from. It had sounded muffled, as if the person did not want to speak too loudly for fear of being heard. But wasn't the theatre empty now? Her heart began to thump erratically, because it was eerie to hear a whispery voice calling to her like this. It might be the kind of ploy Florian would try – he would think it was mysterious and romantic, not realizing it was frightening. But Tansy was definitely not going to respond to somebody who whispered chillingly and furtively like this; what she was going to do was run down the stairs and get out into the street as quickly as possible. Providing the stage door had not been locked, that was.

But the minute her hand closed around the stage door's handle, she knew it was locked. She dragged fiercely at it, jiggling it up and down, willing it to give way, but it remained stubbornly immovable. Jack or Byron or almost any of the family would have been able to get it open, but they were not here, and Tansy had no idea how you picked a lock.

Could she stay here and wait for Ben Barley to make his rounds? But it was not even ten o'clock yet. There was no other way out that she could see; the main doors from the auditorium and the foyer would be locked, and in any case to reach that part of the building she would have to go back up the stairs. And the whispery voice was up there. Tansy no longer cared if the voice belonged to Florian or Timon or the ghost of Hamlet's father; she did not want to meet it.

Was there anywhere she could hide until Ben Barley arrived? Timon had said they would carry the scenery and the mirror down to the cellars – Florian had objected, mentioning the iron stairway. Surely he could only have been referring to this stairway, which meant the cellar entrance must be down here.

It was. A little way along, almost at the end of the passageway leading from the stage door, were double doors that must lead to the cellars. It would be dark in there, and probably quite spooky, but it would not be as spooky as waiting for the whispery voice to come down for her. Would the cellars be locked, though? No – she could see that one of the doors was slightly ajar. As she went towards it, there was the sound of footsteps overhead, and the voice reached her again.

'Tilly . . . I've been waiting for you . . .'

Tansy no longer believed that this was Florian, and it certainly was not Timon. Either of those would have called out who they were – 'Tilly, it's Florian . . .' Or, 'Tilly, it's Timon . . .'

This was someone who had slinked into the theatre and was lying in wait with some mad, unfathomable intent. But what was really dreadful was that it was someone who knew her name – at least, the name she had been using in the Gilfillan company. But Tansy could not believe that any of the company would do this – not the nice gossipy, inquisitive sisters, or the police sergeant, or any of the backstage crew she had become friendly with – or even Chloris.

The voice came again. 'Tilly . . . Where are you, my dear . . .?'

Absurdly, but terrifyingly, it was that 'my dear' that sent the fear sky-rocketing. The words had a slurred treacly sound – she had watched and read enough melodrama to recognize them as belonging to the classic villain lines. 'Come inside, my dear,' the murderer would say, enticingly, to his victim. By which he usually meant, *Prepare to meet your doom – or a fate worse than death – my dear . . .*

Tansy was not going to risk meeting doom or a fate worse than death at anybody's hands. She went straight through the partly open door, closing it. The scents of paint and glue-size and sawdust closed around her, and she heard the clang of footsteps coming down the iron stairway. She began to retreat very cautiously down a short flight of steps, but the cellar door was already being pushed open, and a figure was framed in the dimness. It was wearing a long dark coat, with a deep-brimmed hat pulled down to hide its face, and it could have been anybody. The darkness was not absolute – trickles of light came in from somewhere and lay across the ground, showing up the corner of a painted flat, or the edge of a piece of furniture. As the figure began to descend the steps, Tansy backed away – twice half-stumbling against where a wall had been knocked through, but each time regaining her balance.

She had no idea if there would be another way out of the cellars, or what would happen if she was cornered. But what possible motive could this person have for attacking her? Other than the fact that it's a madman, said her mind.

As the figure advanced, Tansy, her hands thrust out in defence, backed away again. In moving, she stepped into one of the thin patches of light from overhead, and the dark figure cried out and recoiled. Incredibly, there was shock in the cry, and even something that might be fear. The sound echoed all around the cellars, then the figure recovered itself, and bounded forward, one hand raised. And Tansy saw to her utter horror that a second figure moved with it.

A figure that was coming from out of the depths of the mirror. That was walking out of the glimmering dimness, one hand raised menacingly. It's the play coming alive, she thought, terror engulfing her. The nightmare waking – Tomás's darkness stepping into the light.

I'm seeing the murderer inside the mirror – but he's stepping out of the mirror and coming towards me . . .

Ethne had experienced an exultant satisfaction when the Fendle girl scuttled into the cellars, because she was playing right into her hands. She moved towards her, watchful in case the girl suddenly sprang, but she did not. In any case, she was a little bit of a thing – Ethne would easily overpower her. She touched the heavy marble in her pocket.

And then the girl moved into a thin spill of light from overhead, and as it fell across her face, Ethne felt as if something had dealt a blow across her eyes. She heard herself cry out, because this was no longer some unknown girl chosen almost at random to fit into the plan; this was a face she knew – it was a face that had often looked out at her from a silver frame in Westmeath House – from the dressing table in the bedroom always allotted to Montague Fitzglen.

'A very dear niece,' he had said, when Ethne asked about the photograph. 'I like to think of her accompanying me on my travels.'

That photograph could not be this girl, of course. It was too far back – the creature standing in front of Ethne could not be much more than twenty. But – the daughter of the woman in the photograph? Even a younger sister? Whichever it was, she was unquestionably a Fitzglen, and there was only one reason for a

Fitzglen to be in this theatre – and under a false name. She knew the truth about the play, and she was here to expose that truth. That being so, Tilly Fendle – or whatever her real name was – must be silenced.

Steely determination gripped Ethne, but as she moved again something moved with her – something dim and shadowy, picked up by the vagrant spears of light. A figure emerging from the blurred darkness of the glass . . . Like the figure she had seen that night in Dublin Castle – the figure she believed had shared the darkness with Thomas's final ballad about walking to where men awaited him with hood and axe . . .

Ethne cried out, and the darkness began to whirl all around her, the screaming slicing through it, as it had done that other time . . .

She thought the Fendle girl – no, she was Fitzglen – started forward, but the cellars were spinning dizzyingly, and the figure inside the mirror was blurring, and Ethne was falling headlong towards its waiting hands . . .

Tansy had gone, almost without realizing, towards her attacker, with a confused idea of pushing him away from the glass, because he had not realized it was his own reflection that was moving towards him, and he was clearly about to fall against the mirror.

But it was already too late. There was a scream that echoed all around the enclosed space, and with it the sound of glass shattering as the figure fell back. The deep-brimmed hat slipped half off, and a quantity of hair fell free, and Tansy saw with shock that her attacker was a woman.

Whoever she was, she had not been knocked completely unconscious, though. Thick shards of glass protruded from her neck and jaw, and her face was covered in blood, but she was conscious and struggling to get to her feet. But even as Tansy instinctively went towards her, the looking-glass, dislodged from where it had rested against the wall, toppled over, crashing down onto the woman. The heavy mahogany frame crunched against her head, and there was a kind of half-scream, then silence.

Tansy had no idea how long she stood there, the shadows creeping around her like reaching claws. She must try to get help somehow – the phone upstairs . . . Yes, she could call for help on that.

But the mirror had fallen across a section where a wall had been broken through, and it was almost completely barring her way to the door. To reach the door she would have to climb over it – and over what lay under it. She began to shake again at this prospect, but she could not ignore the prone figure, lying there, one hand flung out as if in entreaty.

She finally managed to kneel down and grasp the edges of the mirror's frame, and to partly raise it. It was not as heavy as she had expected, but it was a large mirror; broken glass was sticking out everywhere, and splinters were still showering down. She scraped her hands several times, but finally managed to drag the mirror partly clear.

The woman's eyes were closed, and blood was still coming from the glass lodged in her neck. People did not bleed when they were dead, did they? Tansy glanced across at the door, and thought she might manage to reach it now. She leaned over, and said, 'I'm going to get help for you. You're a bit injured, but I don't think it's serious.'

The woman's eyes opened, and she stared into Tansy's face. Tansy said, 'I'll be as quick as I can.'

In a whisper so laden with hatred that Tansy flinched, the woman said, 'You're a Fitzglen . . . A Fitzglen . . . *You know . . .*'

Her hands came up and locked around Tansy's throat. Tansy fought to drag them away, but they were like steel clamps. She struggled and tried to cry out, but no sound came.

The darkness was becoming shot with crimson, and then from somewhere beyond it came the sound of running footsteps and shouts. Hands grabbed Tansy and tore her free and she was held in an embrace so tight she thought it would never let her go.

Timon Gilfillan said in a voice she had never heard him use, 'My darling girl, thank God I got here in time.'

And then he began to kiss her so fiercely that Tansy thought he would never stop. She did not want him to stop. She clung to him and kissed him back.

'Why did you come back?' said Tansy, seated on the Green Room sofa, his arms still about her, Garda tramping around the theatre. 'You saved my life in doing so.'

'You would have got free. She was badly injured.' But his hold on her tightened.

'But what brought you back?'

'It was dear old Mr Barley,' said Timon. 'You remember him – the night-watchman? He came into The Moonshine where Florian and Viola and I were having a drink after our rehearsal, and said he had heard crashing sounds coming from the cellar when he made his round. He thought likely a tinker or a tramp had got in to spend the night, so he would be grateful if we would go back in there with him to turf the man out, on account of you couldn't trust the Garda to get here inside of an hour, not at this time of a night.'

In spite of the grimness of everything, Tansy smiled, because it was the instinctive player, taking on Ben Barley's role, speaking with a tinge of Irish brogue. She relaxed, then suddenly wondered if he intended to kiss her again, or if it had simply been something he had done in the cellar in the remarkable emotion of the moment.

'Of course I intend to kiss you again,' said Timon, and smiled, and said, 'You have a very expressive face,' and bent over her once more.

But when he finally released her, he said, suddenly, 'I'm not going to lose you, am I? Because I don't know how I'd bear that.'

Tansy did not dare say – not yet – that she would not bear losing him, either. Instead, she said, carefully, 'You don't need to lose me. Unless you think I'm too young for you.'

'I don't think that at all.' One hand came out to trace the outlines of her face, as if he wanted to absorb her through his fingertips. 'I'm afraid of losing you because you're a Fitzglen,' he said.

They looked at one another for a long time. Then Tansy said, in a whisper, 'How did you know?' It did not occur to her to deny it. Not to Timon, who in any case appeared to have the ability to step into her mind and pick up her feelings. 'Oh, wait, though – did you hear that woman in the cellar call me that? Although how she could have known—'

'I didn't hear her say anything,' said Timon. 'But I knew who you were almost from the first. Because, my dearest, absurd

Mimi, around fifteen years ago a young, naïve, wide-eyed boy sat in the Amaranth theatre and saw on its stage a lady who lit up the entire auditorium with her acting. A lady who had your eyes and your colouring and your voice. And your delight in life. I never forgot her.'

Tansy stared at him, then in a half-whisper, said, 'My mother. Did you know her?' she said, eagerly. 'Meet her?'

'No. The famous enmity between the two families was already well established. But,' he said, with an air of choosing his words with care, 'I was genuinely sad when I heard of her death. In Canada, wasn't it?'

'Yes. She and my father were touring.'

'A great loss,' he said. 'But it meant I recognized you. What I don't know, is your real name.'

'Um, it's Tansy.'

'Tansy.' He appeared to savour the name, then said, 'I would never have thought of that for you.'

'As a matter of fact,' said Tansy, realizing crossly that she had turned bright red, 'it's really Thomasina, only nobody ever uses it, and I don't think many people know.'

She looked at him anxiously. It was not the moment to tell him she had been named for Highwayman Harry's daughter, the infamous Thomasina Fitzglen, who had filched a pair of miniatures from the King of Prussia's entourage when he was visiting George III.

But Timon only said, gravely, 'I promise never to tell.' The smile came again, and he said, 'To me you will always be Mimi.' He paused, then said, slowly, 'How likely is it that your family will let you step into wedded bliss with someone who's part of the enemy?'

Wedded bliss . . . Tansy stared at him.

'We've only known one another a short time,' he said, 'but I knew at once . . .'

'I knew at once, too,' said Tansy, and he smiled.

'Shall I try to persuade them, then?' he said. 'Your family? And if I can . . . Would you accept it if I can?'

Delight was running all over Tansy. She said, in as down-to-earth a voice as she could manage, 'Oh, yes, I would accept. Please – Timon, *please* – let's try to persuade them.'

TWENTY-SEVEN

G us always experienced a jab of apprehension at the sight of a telegram – horrible orange things, which everyone associated with bad news. Opening the door of Mr Jack's rooms this morning, he was alarmed to be handed two of the doomful items.

'The boy asked if he should wait for an answer,' he said, carrying both missives into the sitting room, where Mr Jack was studying a playscript. 'But I said not.'

'Tansy?' said Mr Jack, taking the two envelopes. 'But wouldn't she have telephoned the theatre if something had happened? Don't go, Gus, if there's bad news, I'd rather have someone with me when I read it.'

He read the first telegram aloud, then read it a second time, because it was so astonishing, he was not sure he had entirely taken it in.

TO MR JACK FITZGLEN
YOUR COUSIN TANSY WELL AND SAFE BUT INVOLVED IN DISTRESSING DEATH AT ROSCIUS LAST NIGHT STOP BELIEVE SHE WOULD WELCOME YOUR PRESENCE HERE IF POSSIBLE STOP CAN BOOK YOU INTO HOTEL PLEASE ADVISE STOP LETTER FOLLOWING KINDEST REGARDS TIMON GILFILLAN.

Jack stared at the thin sheet of paper, and finally said, 'At least he starts by saying Tansy's all right. But – distressing death. What on earth can have happened?'

'Whatever it is, Mr Gilfillan knows who she is,' offered Gus.

'Yes, and probably why she's there. He says there's a letter to follow – that would arrive tomorrow, I expect. The second telegram's probably from Tansy,' said Jack, opening the envelope.

TO MR JACK FITZGLEN
I AM FINE DO NOT WORRY TIMON GILFILLAN
WRITING YOU BEST LOVE TANSY.

'Have we got a Bradshaw?' said Mr Jack, going over to his
bookshelves. 'Something with the times of trains to Liverpool
and ferries across to Dublin.'

'We're going to Ireland?' said Gus, trying not to sound too
dismayed.

'Sorry, old boy, but it's necessary. I always meant to get there
before the festival's first night, anyway. You'd better pack. Oh,
and will you take a note over to Byron? I daresay he'll want to
come as well – oh, wait, though, he's in this week's piece. But
he could follow on Sunday.'

Gus said, 'Will it mean going on the ferry, Mr Jack?'

'I'm afraid it will.'

'Then,' said Gus, resignedly, 'I'd better take a pot of Miss
Cecily's gooseberry jelly.'

'Gooseberry jelly?' said Jack, who had been reaching for pen
and paper to write the note to Byron.

'Miss Cecily,' said Gus, gloomily, 'swears by gooseberry jelly
as a cure for seasickness.'

Halfway between Liverpool and Dublin, Gus discovered that the
gooseberry jelly had been a waste of time.

'Bounced, did it?' said Mr Jack, sympathetically. 'I'll order
half a bottle of champagne. They say the fizziness helps.'

'I'll get hiccups.'

'Better hiccups than being sick over the side of the boat.'

Remarkably, the champagne worked, and Gus was able to step
off the ferry with reasonable dignity, and help with their luggage.

Mr Jack had sent a telegram to Mr Gilfillan, accepting the
offer of a hotel room. It turned out to be the one in which Mr
Gilfillan – also Miss Viola and Mr Florian Gilfillan – were staying.

'And Tansy as well,' said Jack, pointing to an entry in the
register when they arrived and checked in at reception. 'It sounds
as if the Gilfillans are looking after her very well—'

'I couldn't be better looked after if I was royalty,' said a delighted
voice behind them, and there was Tansy, hugging Jack. 'I've been

waiting for you,' she said. 'Watching the street and dashing out to greet the most unlikely people. I'm so glad to see you.'

But when Jack asked what on earth had been happening, Tansy said she would leave it to Timon to explain.

'It's dreadfully sad in parts, but he'll explain it much better than I could. He hopes you'll dine with him in the restaurant here tonight, and he'll tell you everything. He's booked a table for eight o'clock.'

'I didn't think, at the start of all this, I'd find myself dining with the enemy,' said Jack.

'Oh, he's not the enemy,' said Tansy.

Jack was increasingly curious to meet Timon Gilfillan, who had figured so frequently in Tansy's letters, and who was often said by critics to be one of the leading actor managers of the day. He was glad he had told Gus to pack his dinner jacket. It was not that he especially wanted to impress Timon, or any Gilfillan, and he was certainly not wondering whether Viola might be present. In fact, when he entered the restaurant he was quite glad not to see her, because it would be easier to talk to Timon with just the two of them and Tansy there.

Gilfillan was waiting for him, Tansy at his side. Jack, who had only seen him in newspaper photographs and never on a stage, thought he had an air of quiet authority. At first, he thought Timon was older than he had expected, but when he smiled Jack revised his opinion and thought he was much younger.

Tansy had clearly jettisoned Tilly Fendle; she was wearing a very stylish outfit, which was unlikely to have been part of the Fendle wardrobe, so it looked as if she had gone into one of the Dublin shops to purchase a ready-made outfit. The result was a pleasing combination of amber silk and what looked like topaz jewellery.

As Timon embarked on an account of the attack inside the Roscius, and the identification of the attacker as Phelan Rafferty's daughter, Tansy listened absorbedly, but Jack noticed that when she did speak, Timon at once turned to listen to her. He liked this.

They had reached the dessert stage before the story was finished, and Jack said, thoughtfully, 'Miss Rafferty was trying to prevent you staging the piece, wasn't she?'

'It's what we think,' said Timon. 'The police – Garda I should say, shouldn't I? – suggested the original plan was to injure someone enough to create an investigation. Which would have delayed – perhaps even prevented entirely – the performance.'

'Did she want to do that because she knew it was her father's play?' said Jack. 'Or because she knew it wasn't?'

'Whichever it was, she recognized me – right at the end,' said Tansy. 'It was dreadful, Jack – it was as if her mind had suddenly been wrenched off its hinges. I was bending over her, saying I would get help, and she stared up at me and said, *Fitzglen*, in a hate-filled, accusing kind of voice, and something about me knowing. But I don't know what she meant I knew.' She shivered slightly and Jack saw Timon take her hand briefly.

'We don't know why she went to such lengths,' said Timon. 'And it's unlikely we ever will. Jack – you do realize that I don't know where that script came from?'

Jack said, carefully, 'Someone must know.'

'It isn't me. And neither Viola nor I thought there was anything detrimental or scandalous in it.'

'There still could be something, though,' said Jack. 'Something you wouldn't recognize. Something that might go back several years. Miss Rafferty might have known about it and wanted to stop it coming out.'

'But detrimental to who?' Timon made an impatient gesture. 'You'll have to read the thing, of course,' he said, and Jack remembered how he had flinched from reading the play when he found it in Montague's house.

But that was before I knew Thomas or Catherine, he thought, and he heard himself say, 'I hoped you'd say that. Does it mean we're calling a truce?'

'Temporary cessation of hostilities, perhaps? And on that subject,' said Timon, 'I have to talk to you about something else.'

He glanced at Tansy, and Jack had the impression they both drew a deep breath, as if about to plunge into something extremely difficult. He looked at Tansy, whose face was glowing with more happiness than he had ever seen, and guessed what was coming. What he did not know was how he was going to react. But he was already remembering how distraught she had been when her parents were killed, and he remembered, too, that she was lovely and warm and kind and talented, and he knew he would never be able to put anything in the way of her happiness. Even with a Gilfillan? said his mind.

Timon had taken Tansy's hand again. 'You already know what I'm going to say, don't you?' he said, and Jack was aware, not for the first time in the evening, of the man's perceptive mind. 'We should like your blessing, Jack – and that of your whole family, of course. I think it might need your permission, as well.' He considered Jack, then said, 'I expect we can omit the obvious Montague and Capulet lines, can't we? "Two houses, both alike in dignity".'

Jack regarded him, then looked at Tansy again. 'How about, "For this alliance may so happy prove, to turn your households' rancour to pure love"?' he said.

'Wouldn't it be more like a plague called down on both houses?' said Timon, dryly.

'They'll certainly raise objections,' said Jack. 'Led, I suspect, by my Great Uncle Rudraige.'

'And you?'

Jack smiled. 'I can deal with Rudraige. And, "Let me not to the marriage of true minds admit impediment".'

There was a brief pause, then Timon said, 'I'm extremely glad to hear you say that,' and the youthful smile showed again. 'Even though I am possibly slightly mature for Romeo,' he added.

'It never shows from the front and with good make-up,' said Jack, gravely. It's all right, he thought, as Timon shook his hand warmly. I wouldn't have wanted a Gilfillan for her, but I think with this particular Gilfillan, it will be very much all right.

Tansy had leapt out of her seat to hug Jack. 'And we'll deal with Uncle Rudraige perfectly easily, and Cousin Cecily will be in transports.'

Timon was refilling the wine glasses. He said, 'Jack, I think we need to get something else out of the way.' He paused, then said, 'I know about your family's other profession.'

They looked at one another, and at last Jack said, 'I'm not sure how to answer that.'

'Perhaps a dignified and discreet silence on both sides might better.'

'You do know there are lines over which none of us will ever step?' said Jack.

'I think I do. That makes it almost acceptable.'

'This must be one of the strangest conversations I've ever had,' said Jack. 'Does anyone else in your family know?'

'Viola probably does,' said Timon. 'It's never been mentioned, though. Nor will it be, I suspect.'

He seemed about to say something else, when Tansy said, 'Oh – here is Viola now,' and Jack turned to see Viola Gilfillan regarding him.

She sat down in the chair that Timon pulled forward, and said, 'I've brought the script of *The Murderer in the Mirror.* We both thought you'd better finally read it, Jack.' She glanced at Timon and at Tansy, then said, 'Can I bring congratulations to the star-crossed lovers, as well?'

'You can,' said Timon. 'And in fact . . . God in heaven, look who's just arrived. What the devil do those two want?'

Jack turned, startled, to see two figures walking towards their table.

'"Spirits of health or goblins damn'd"?' murmured Viola.

'"And in such questionable shapes",' put in Tansy. 'Jack, it's Florian and Chloris.'

'So I see. But are their intents "wicked or charitable"?'

Timon glanced at Jack. 'It's so good,' he said, 'to be in company with someone who picks up the—'

'Unconsidered trifles of Bardic-ness?'

'Something like that.' He grinned, and Jack tried not think it was shockingly disloyal to his own family to like the man so much. Then he looked at Tansy's shining eyes, and did not care.

Timon introduced Jack and Chloris. 'And Florian I believe you already know.'

'Our paths have occasionally crossed,' said Florian, graciously.

'Most recently at the wake of my great uncle, Montague Fitzglen,' said Jack, cordially.

'But I am afraid this is by way of being a business meeting,' said Florian.

He clearly expected Jack to take this as his cue to leave, but when Jack stood up, Timon waved him down. 'Florian, you'd better know that Jack is about to become linked to this family—'

'I'm very sorry to hear that,' said Florian, coldly.

'Are you? The rest of us are extremely pleased. But it means anything you want to say can be said openly. I expect you'll have a drink, will you? Yes, I thought you would.'

'I will take a small potation,' said Florian. 'Have you any Calvados, waiter? No, I didn't expect so. Armagnac will do, then. Chloris, my dear, you'll have the same, I daresay?'

'Purely restorative,' said Chloris in a die-away voice, and Tansy grinned at Jack.

Florian sipped his brandy, then said, heavily, 'I have been very much distressed by what happened in the Roscius. Chloris was distressed as well. You see, I had known the – ah – lady. Miss Ethne Rafferty.'

Timon said, 'The lady you mentioned as having been the "love of your youth"?'

'That is a very unfeeling thing to say, Timon.'

'Not when you remember she tried to brutally murder Tansy,' said Viola, at once. Jack thought she brought out the name very deliberately.

But Florian said, 'Possibly there was some confusion. A gentle soul she was, Ethne Rafferty. But now, I am not sure how I can continue with the piece after such a blow to my senses. The memories . . .' He reached for Chloris's hand, and Chloris said,

'There is also the fact that blame must lie with – with this lady,' she said, glaring at Tansy. 'Whatever her real name is.'

'Tansy Fitzglen,' said Timon, at once. 'And Chloris, you and Florian are both talking utter rot.'

Jack was unexpectedly and rather endearingly reminded of Great Uncle Rudraige.

'No, we are not,' said Florian. 'She – damme, Timon, she's practised trickery of the highest order.'

'False pretences,' nodded Chloris. 'She even read in as Mimi. The impudence of it.'

'When you were unable to attend a rehearsal,' said Timon.

'I was unwell,' said Chloris, placing one hand to her brow. 'But I was told afterwards that you admired her reading of the part very much.'

'I did,' said Timon.

'But you do see,' said Florian, 'that taking everything into consideration, we feel quite justified in asking that Miss Fendle's – that is, Miss Fitzglen's – association with the company be terminated.'

'You want me to send her packing?'

'Yes.'

'Sorry, Florian, but it's out of the question. But if you find the memories of Miss Rafferty too painful for you to continue with the piece . . .' Timon waited, then, as Florian did not respond, he said, 'and if you have other offers waiting for your consideration—?'

'Oh, of course I do. Oh, I'm frequently approached by other managements. There are several at the moment, in fact.'

'Ah. And, of course, Chloris would be a welcome addition to any theatre company.'

This time the silence lasted longer. Then Florian squared his shoulders, and said, very grandly, 'It seems as if we are to part, then.'

'But as gentlemen,' said Timon, and stood up and held out his hand.

After they had gone, Timon reached for the brandy decanter, refilled the glasses, and looked at Jack.

'We find ourselves in an unexpected situation,' he said, and waited. When Jack did not speak, he said, 'Well, Jack? What would you feel about a collaboration?'

'I think,' said Jack, carefully, 'you had better be more specific.'

'And I think you know perfectly well what I mean. In the privacy of this table, I'll say Florian's exit is good riddance.' He made an expressive gesture with his hands. 'A matter of hoping to give one last chance to someone who . . . But that's in the past now. Will you take over as Tomás?'

Tomás, thought Jack. That strange, tortured creature. I've only encountered fragments of him from the opening scene and the notes Tansy sent, but I know him.

'You've never seen me act,' he said. 'How do you know I could do it?'

'I have seen you act,' said Timon.

'So have I,' said Viola.

'And you're more than capable of conveying the . . . the darkness of Tomás.'

'There's a very short time until the festival opens,' said Jack.

'There is. We would have to work like fiends. And I don't think you're very used to being directed.'

'I'm not. We'd probably clash,' said Jack. 'Disagree.'

'I'm sure we would.' Timon paused, then said, 'I've got the key to the Roscius's stage door with me. We could walk along there now, and you could at least see the place.'

Jack was not allowing into his mind the awareness that if he accepted this, he would be playing opposite Viola, but he looked at her, and said, 'Did you say you'd brought the script?'

'Yes.' Viola reached into her bag and produced a sheaf of papers. Jack pushed away the memory of how he had wanted to leave the play in its darkness in Montague Fitzglen's house, and managed to stop himself snatching the script of *The Murderer Inside the Mirror* from her.

He liked the Roscius at once. It closed around him, friendly and warm, but as he sat down on one of the front-row seats and began to read the script, he was aware of another set of emotions. I'm about to find out more about Tomás and Catrina, he thought. And perhaps about those twin shadows who stand behind them. Because Tomás is almost certainly the long-ago Irish rebel hero, Thomas of Kildare. Silken Thomas, who went to the scaffold for his beliefs. And Catrina? Isn't she Catherine Ó Raifeartaigh? He wondered briefly whether Timon and Viola knew about those two, and, if not, whether he would tell them. But he knew that of course he would, although not quite yet.

As he began to read, there was not quite a moment when he felt as if Tomás took his hand, but there was certainly a moment when he felt himself partly pulled into Tomás's world.

It was a shock to realize Timon had come to sit next to him and, as Jack looked up, Timon said, 'Well? Will you do it? Play Tomás?'

Tomás. The present and its reality blurred again for a moment, then Jack said, 'Oh, yes. Yes, of course I will.'

Timon nodded, as if he had expected this answer, then looked across at Tansy who was sitting on the stage, watching them hopefully. 'That only leaves the gap left by Chloris,' he said, and his face broke into a smile of sudden intimacy. 'Well, Mimi? What about it?'

As Jack and Viola walked back to the hotel, he said, 'I'd like to think that whoever did write this play could be present on the opening night.'

'I'd like it, too, but . . .' She stopped, then, speaking more seriously than he had ever heard her speak, she said, 'Jack, I'm going to trust you more than I ever thought I would – more than I've trusted anyone for a long time, I think.'

Jack was aware of a quickening of his pulses. 'Yes?'

Viola said, 'If you agree, I want to take you to meet the author.'

The noisy Dublin street faded all around them, then Jack said, 'That's the very last thing I expected you to say. You know who wrote it, then?'

'I've known all along. But Timon and the others don't.' She studied him. 'It would mean a journey, but not a very long one. We can travel by train, and I think we could be there and back in the same day.'

Jack's emotions were tumbling in such confusion he was not sure if he could make a sensible answer.

But he said, 'Tell me who the author is.'

'No,' she said. 'You need to hear the story direct – in full – or you won't understand. Actually, I need to hear it direct and in full, as well, because I only know fragments and I'm not sure I understand, either.'

After a moment, Jack said, 'Timon's rehearsing the scenes with the curious sisters and the policeman on Tuesday. We wouldn't be needed that day. You said we could get there and back in the same day?'

'I think the journey is about two hours – perhaps a little more.'

'And if it takes longer? If we encounter delays – if we don't get there and back in the same day—'

She said, slowly, 'That would mean having to stay overnight somewhere.'

They looked at one another, then Jack said, carefully, 'I suppose that would be all right.'

He waited, and after a moment, she said, 'Yes. I suppose it would.'

TWENTY-EIGHT

T he train tickets for Tuesday's journey, helpfully obtained by the hotel, stated the eventual destination to be Athlone. This was of no help at all, however, because a great many stops were listed along the way, and Viola refused to say at which stop they would be alighting.

'But we aren't going all the way to Athlone,' she said.

The train chugged out of Dublin at a quarter-past eight that morning, and it appeared that Viola had been fairly accurate in her estimation of the journey's length, because shortly after half past ten the guard came along the corridors, cheerfully calling that they were coming in to Westmeath Halt soon, and would anyone wanting to get out there please have luggage ready, since it was only a five-minute stop.

'That's our station,' said Viola, getting up. Jack reached for the small bags they had brought, and the train clanged into a small country halt.

A guard assisted them onto the tiny platform, touching his cap.

'And if you're wishful to be taken anywhere, Fintan O'Leary always meets the Dublin train with his cart.'

Before Jack could reply, Viola handed the guard a small piece of paper. 'Could Mr O'Leary take us there, do you think?'

'He could indeed,' said the guard. 'A short distance it is. I'll be off to make sure he's here, and . . . Oh, thanking you kindly, sir,' he said, as Jack passed over a coin.

'Viola,' said Jack, 'if you don't tell me where we're going, I'll get back on that train and return to London and you can find someone else to play Tomás.'

'No, you won't,' she said. And, as the guard returned, calling out that Fintan was waiting, she said, 'We're going to get us to a nunnery, Jack.'

As he turned to stare at her, she said, 'We're going to a place called St Joseph's Convent.'

* * *

Of all the scenarios Jack had conjured up around the mysterious play, a convent had not figured in any of them.

Fintan O'Leary, who had a face like a wrinkled nut and twinkly eyes, bade them welcome to Westmeath, which he said was the finest place God ever made, and as they climbed onto the trap, promised that once at the convent there'd be a grand welcome.

'We'll be there in the whisk of a glow-worm's tail,' he said, as the cart bounced across the slightly uneven road. 'At one time, of course, you couldn't travel more than half a day across Ireland without coming across a religious house. That was before the tyrant Henry VIII got a stranglehold on the country – that's begging your pardon, sir, and madam, for speaking ill of an English King.'

'Speak as much ill of him as you like,' said Jack. 'He's one of our less reputable monarchs.' But with Fintan's words, he had an abrupt sense of the past reaching out, and of Silken Thomas brushing against his mind – the Rebel Earl who had defied King Henry.

St Joseph's Convent stood on slightly higher ground than the main part of Westmeath. It was a long, grey building, with a modest tower partway along, containing what looked like a small bell.

'The main door is just here,' said Fintan, 'and that's the school entrance at the far side – only a small school, I daresay, compared to the fine places in Dublin or Athlone, but a fine education the sisters give local girls. Then there's the guest house on the other side.' He waved one arm, indicating a two-storeyed building that appeared to have been tacked on to the main convent, as if somebody had suddenly thought it might be useful to have an extra wing.

For the first time, Viola hesitated, and Jack said, firmly, 'The main door, if you would, Fintan.' He glanced at Viola, and said, 'We'll ring the bell or ply the knocker, and introduce ourselves in proper style.'

They were admitted almost at once by a very young nun, who listened to Jack's introduction, and then to Viola's explanation that they had come to visit a resident in the convent's guest house.

'I'll take you to Mother Superior's study,' she said. 'That will be the thing. Come along in, now.'

The convent had lingering scents of old timbers, good polish, and incense. It was scrupulously clean, and there was an air of serenity. Jack glanced through several of the windows as the little nun led them along the corridors, and wondered how it would feel to live here, away from the world, in tranquillity and seclusion.

'You'd hate it,' said Viola, softly.

'How did you know what I was thinking?'

'Because I was thinking it too.'

'You'd certainly hate it,' said Jack.

'The wimple might be rather fetching, though.'

'Miss Gilfillan and Mr Fitzglen,' said the convent's Mother Superior, studying them. 'You are very welcome.'

'We should apologize for intruding on you without an invitation,' said Jack.

'Mr Fitzglen, it is one of the very oldest traditions of religious houses that all travellers are welcomed in, given food and shelter, and, if required, a bed for the night.' A sudden sweet smile showed. 'And there was a telephone call,' said Mother Superior. 'So I know who you have come to see.' She reached for a bell rope. 'Later, you will perhaps take luncheon with us?'

Jack said, 'Thank you. I think we'd like that, if it wouldn't be too much trouble.'

'We would enjoy your company.' Then, as the door opened, she said, 'Sister Mary, these are the two visitors we were expecting.'

Sister Mary, who was young and rather academic-looking, took them through what seemed to be connecting doors between the main convent and the guest house.

Jack's emotions were in turmoil by this time, but a definite suspicion as to who they were about to meet was starting to unfurl – only I cannot believe it, he thought. It isn't possible. Twice he looked at Viola, but her face had a shuttered look.

The corridor beyond the doors had framed prints on the walls, and several doors opening off it. Sister Mary stopped in front of one of the doors, looked at Jack and Viola, then tapped on the door. Apparently hearing permission to enter, she opened it, and stood back.

'Go along in,' she said. 'I will come back when you wish.'

Jack reached for Viola's hand almost without realizing it, and was grateful when her fingers closed around his.

Sunlight poured into the room, and there was a brief impression of chairs, a desk, bookshelves, but Jack scarcely saw them, because his entire attention was on the figure standing near the window. He had dark, slightly too-long hair, streaked with grey. A beard framed a thin face, and dark glasses hid most of the upper part of the face.

Jack had the sensation of stepping into a whirling sunlit tunnel, where half-formed figures were holding out their hands to him. It can't be what I'm thinking, said his mind wildly.

Then in a soft, Irish-tinged voice, the man said, 'Good morning. Miss Gilfillan and Mr Fitzglen, I think?' He remained where he was, but said, 'I'm delighted to meet you both. Forgive me for not coming forward to greet you, but . . .' One hand came up to briefly indicate the dark glasses, 'but I have been blind for the last five years,' he said. 'Please sit down. I believe you've come to talk to me about my play. I am Phelan Rafferty.'

As the name dropped into the room, Jack was almost overwhelmed by the feeling of the past closing around them. But after a moment he managed to say, 'Mr Rafferty. I'm Jack Fitzglen.' He paused, then said, 'I'm not sure if I know the right words to use in this situation, sir. I'm not sure if there are any right words. I can only say it's a very great honour to meet you.'

'But also a very great shock, I daresay. You thought I was dead, of course.'

'The whole world thinks it,' said Jack.

'And the whole world must continue to think it. Except,' said Phelan, 'for the sisters here at St Joseph's.' He moved with care to a high-backed chair – not quite feeling his way, but making sure of where he was going. Viola went to sit by him, reaching out to take one of his hands in both of hers, and Jack was instantly grateful to her for the warmth of the gesture.

He said, 'Mr Rafferty – I don't understand any of this. I'm not even sure why I'm here.'

'No formality, Jack,' said Phelan. 'As for understanding – I believe you're here to learn the truth about my play. Viola, you're staging it at the Roscius as part of the *Féile*, yes?'

'Yes.'

'Sister Mary reads the newspapers to me,' said Phelan, as if by way of explanation. 'So I'm aware of much of what goes on in the world. She's my eyes – although I suspect her of sometimes being selective in the reading. But she's often been my sanity, too.' His head turned towards Jack. 'Will you forgive all the deceit, Jack?' he said. 'And will you accept that in the main it was created to protect several people. Myself, of course, and also my daughter. But your Great Uncle Montague, too. I was extremely distressed to hear of his death,' said Phelan. 'He was one of my closest and dearest friends. And he was an entertaining companion and a very perceptive man.'

'He was all of those things,' said Jack, at once. 'We'll all miss him for a very long time. Your play was hidden in his house – I don't know if you would know that? We found it when we were clearing his things out.'

'Then afterwards it vanished.'

'Yes. Phelan, now I'm here – now we're both here – can you explain all of this to us? All the secrecy—?'

'I can, of course. And you've time to listen?'

'I don't think,' said Jack, 'either of us would care if it took a day or a week or a year to hear the story.' He paused, then said, softly, 'Imagine that it's Tomás and Catrina who are here, talking with you.'

There was a brief silence, then Phelan said, 'Tomás and Catrina. Your Uncle Montague wasn't the only perceptive Fitzglen, was he? Yes, of course those two were strongly with me when I created that play.' He turned his head, almost as if searching the room, and Jack had the brief, disconcerting impression of sight where there could be none. 'They're still sometimes with me now,' he said.

'And those other two?' said Jack, softly. 'Are they ever with you? Those two people I think you lifted from another century?'

He was aware of puzzlement from Viola, but his whole attention was focused on the man in front of him.

Phelan said, 'You mean Thomas Fitzgerald, don't you?'

'Yes. Thomas of Kildare,' said Jack. 'Silken Thomas. I know a little about him. And I think he stands behind your Tomás. As for Catrina, I think a lady called Catherine stands behind her.'

He thought, but did not say: But I don't know who the shadow standing behind Maran might be – or even if there is a shadow there.

'Ah, Catherine,' said Phelan, with a kind of wistful affection. 'Did Montague find her portrait? In the English house? He found mention of it in letters at Westmeath House, and he was convinced a portrait existed.'

'It does exist,' said Jack. 'Montague didn't find it, but I did. And she's from Thomas of Kildare's time, of course.'

'She is. What was she like?' said Phelan, eagerly. 'She wasn't beautiful, was she? I never imagined her as beautiful.'

'She wasn't at all beautiful,' said Jack, slowly. 'Not even pretty. There was even what could have been a cast in one eye, although that might have been the painter's lack of skill. But I wanted to go on looking at her. I didn't want to leave her. It wasn't a face you would necessarily want to take to bed,' he said, 'but it was a face you might want to take into dreams.'

'Ah, you've a touch of the poet yourself, haven't you?' said Phelan. 'That describes how I've always thought of her. Could you see where the painting had been done?'

'I couldn't,' said Jack. 'But the lute was with her.'

'The lute,' said Phelan, half to himself. 'Yes, she'd have his lute in the portrait.'

'It's Silken Thomas's lute, isn't it?'

'I think it would be. And the music? The Lament?'

'A fragment was painted in,' said Jack. 'But someone had tried to conceal it – long after the portrait was done, I think. My cousin, Byron, managed to scrape some of the paint away, though.' He glanced at Viola, who was still looking questioningly from one to the other of them, then said, 'Between us we were able to read what Thomas had written – had asked—'

'Commanded more like, arrogant rebel that he was,' said Phelan. '"This charge I lay on all who come – Her memory to shroud, her name to forget . . ." Those were the lines, weren't they?'

'They were. And then, "Guard her guilt and enclose her memory . . ."' said Jack.

Viola leaned forward. 'In the play, Tomás and Maran and Catrina find the lute,' she said. 'Tomás calls it the Murderer's

Lute – the story is that he had an ancestor who played it on his way to being hanged, isn't it? But I didn't know the lute existed outside of the play.'

'It did exist. And Montague and I found it,' said Phelan. 'Not quite as the characters in the play found it, but near enough. Over a century ago, an ancestor – Seamus Rafferty – somehow persuaded or fooled builders or architects into creating a hidden room when Dublin Castle was being restored. I found some of Seamus's letters – he'd had maps and plans copied by a firm of antiquarian booksellers, *Maguire's* in Dublin – and some of the documents were in Westmeath House. Montague brought that old rogue Todworthy Inkling over, and I suspect the two of them had a rare old time in Maguire's shop. They arrived at Westmeath laden with tattered papers and letters.'

Jack said, 'And once Uncle Montague had put everything together—?'

'He was determined to find Seamus's hidden room,' said Phelan. 'And to get at the lute.' The smile was mischievous and indulgent. 'I didn't believe any of it at first, but the sketch plan Seamus had drawn up was clear enough, and Montague was right. We found the room, and when we got it open . . .'

He broke off, and Viola said, '"Lying by itself in the shadows – half covered by layers of dust, as if it's trying to hide . . ."'

'Thomas of Kildare's lute,' said Jack, softly. 'That's what you and Montague found. It's what inspired that scene.' He thought: And Maran is Montague, of course.

'It did inspire it,' said Phelan. 'Seamus had hidden the lute there, and with it the ballad Thomas composed to Catherine Ó Raifeartaigh. We found them both,' he said, and now his voice was faraway. 'I read most of the Lament before we were caught. And I never forgot it. But I never knew why Catherine – her memory, her name – had had to be so fiercely suppressed.'

'The guards caught you, before you could bring the lute and the music out?' said Viola. 'That's what the disguised scene is about, am I right?'

'Near enough. We fought the guards and somehow we got away. But I was injured.' One hand went up to brush the dark glasses. 'I fell against a mirror and the glass shattered, and . . . And my eyes were destroyed.' A shudder went through him, and

Jack understood that the memory was still vivid and painful – that it always would be.

'Montague and Ethne thought I was dead, but they carried me out, and brought me here,' said Phelan. 'I was probably not far off death, in fact.'

Jack knew he and Viola shared a thought: he doesn't know Ethne's dead. He doesn't know what happened inside the Roscius. But it's not for us to tell him – not yet.

He said, 'The nuns nursed you?'

'They were wonderful. They were given to understand there had been some kind of fight – a street brawl, I think – and that I had been injured. That was Montague – he could always spin a good story.' Phelan smiled wryly. 'The Roman Catholic Church is very accustomed to hiding secrets,' he said. 'The nuns would never have condoned theft or violence, though. They've always believed that it was losing my sight that caused me to renounce the world – to forsake it and my former life completely. They found that perfectly understandable – they know about renouncing the world. They respected my wishes, and kept my identity from everyone. I'm just another of the residents in their guest house. They look after me as much as I need to be looked after,' he said. 'But I'm able to be almost wholly independent, and I thank whatever gods are appropriate that I am. Ethne visits me, although not too often. It would draw attention to the convent if she was for ever coming here. It would draw attention to me – which is exactly what I don't want. I want the world to believe I really did die five years ago.'

'I understand,' said Jack, but he thought: there's more to this than he's telling us. He wrote a murder into that play, and he called it *The Murderer Inside the Mirror.* A murder happened that night in Dublin Castle, that's almost certain. One of the guards, maybe, as in the play? But the three of them got away. We can't question him about it, though, and we'll probably never know the truth.

Phelan was saying, 'My life here is better than you might think. There's work I can do and enjoy. Sister Mary has become a good friend – as far as nuns are allowed friendships. She's currently engaged in compiling a history of St Joseph's – it's a very old Order, and she's disinterring all kinds of ancient documents. She reads them to me – between us we manage to decipher the old Latin and the Gaelic – and she writes at my dictation. It's a great pleasure to us both.' He paused, then as if to lighten the mood said, 'Tell me, now, did Mother Superior invite you to lunch? If she did, I hope you accepted. You've time to stay a little longer before you go back?'

Jack looked at Viola, who gave a quick nod. He said, 'We were invited, and we have as much time as you want, Phelan.'

'And we'd enjoy having lunch here and talking with you some more,' said Viola, and Phelan, clearly pleased, felt for a bell rope that hung near his chair.

'Do the nuns know who we are?' said Jack.

'They know you as friends from my theatrical past. I suspect they were sent into something of a flutter at the prospect of a visit from two such distinguished people, and . . . Ah, Sister Mary, it's yourself, isn't it,' he said, as the door opened. 'I'd know the footsteps anywhere. Dainty as a dewdrop, and you come most carefully upon your hour.'

'A fine old flatterer he is, this one,' said Sister Mary, coming into the room. 'As I daresay many a lady has known to her cost.'

'That's between me and the confessional booth,' said Phelan, promptly.

'Is it indeed? Well, as for the hour,' said Sister Mary, 'isn't it everyone gathering in the refectory, and wanting to meet your famous guests.'

TWENTY-NINE

J ack sat next to Mother Superior in the refectory. He liked her, and he enjoyed the lunch, which was plain, but well-cooked and plentiful. Wine was offered – 'A little wine for the stomach's sake, so the Bible tells us, Mr Fitzglen,' said Mother Superior, gravely.

'A very good maxim,' said Jack, accepting the wine and finding it excellent.

'It's a vintage we reserve for visitors, Mr Fitzglen. We don't offer our guests the communion wine, you understand.'

'Ah.'

'We buy that wholesale from a supplier in Dublin,' she said, deadpan.

After the meal, they were served coffee in Phelan's room, and it was then that Viola asked the question Jack had been framing throughout lunch.

'Phelan,' she said, 'the break-in at the castle. You said there was a fight with the guards, and there must have been enquiries – investigations.'

'And the existence of Seamus's secret room would certainly have become known,' said Jack.

Phelan smiled. 'You're forgetting,' he said, 'what a wily old fox Montague Fitzglen was. He often called himself a master forger, but he could forge other things than paintings and jewellery. And there's no need to recoil, Jack – yes you did, I felt it. But Viola will be well aware of what Montague always called the Fitzglens' other profession.'

'Of course I'm aware of it,' said Viola, with a gesture as if to brush something unimportant aside. 'Phelan, how did Montague forge a distance between the two of you and what happened in the castle?'

'Montague could conjure up diversions,' said Phelan. 'Smoke-screens. You might not remember, but four or five years ago – around the time my death was reported – there were accounts in the newspapers of what was believed to be an attempt to steal the Irish Crown Jewels from Dublin Castle. The accounts were somewhat vague – Montague read them to me; in fact he left a couple of the cuttings here. There was a faint air of puzzlement in most of them. There was also,' he said, 'an air of glee in Montague's voice when he read them out.'

Jack looked at Viola, and a frown creased her brow. For a moment neither of them spoke, then Jack said, slowly, 'You're saying my Uncle Montague sent false information to newspapers? That he created a story that the castle had been broken into and an attempt made to steal the Irish Crown Jewels? Purely to cover up what had really happened?'

'That's precisely what he did. If you will look in my desk – it's just by the window, Sister Mary often sits there – you should find a folder of newspaper cuttings. And if my memory serves right, there's at least one that describes what it was believed happened.'

Jack was already at the desk, sliding open drawers. In the top one was a card folder.

'I've got it,' he said, opening the folder. 'The cutting is from the *Morning Post*.'

'Yes, but you needn't hold that against it. Read it out,' said Phelan.

Readers will recall how this newspaper recently reported that the collection known as the Crown Jewels or State Jewels of Ireland had been transferred to a newly constructed strongroom in the Bedford or Clock Tower. Security was stringent; seven latch keys were created, all in the keeping of Sir Arthur Vicars, the Ulster King of Arms.

It is a splendid and historic collection, and includes the collars of five Knights of the Order, and also the heavily jewelled star and badge regalia created in 1831 for the Sovereign and Grand Master or the Order of St Patrick (see page 6 for a more detailed description).

The Garda (Irish police force) say an attempt was made to enter the Clock Tower, and staff were injured in the process. However, no one was apprehended. Happily, though, the strongroom with the jewels was not breached, although, regrettably, Sir Arthur woke after a stint of night duty to find the jewels had been taken from the strongroom, and several pieces were draped around his neck.

The Garda issued a statement to say they do not yet know who was responsible.

'Did people believe that?' said Jack, putting the cutting down. 'That it was a . . . a bungled attempt to reach the Irish Crown Jewels?'

'Of course they believed it. Your Uncle Montague wove some splendid rumours – they kept the newspapers busy for weeks. And everyone said Vicars would have been drunk at the time – a shocking old soak, Arthur Vicars.'

Jack said, 'But weren't the jewels – or some of them – really stolen a few years afterwards? As recently as last year, wasn't it?'

'They were. I should have known you'd stay aware of any major filches,' said Phelan. 'And, of course, the real theft was huge news, and it strengthened Montague's story. He wrote to me about it – a very guarded letter it was, since Sister Mary reads all my letters to me. Montague simply described it as an item of interest – how it was being speculated as to whether the earlier break-in might have been some kind of rehearsal for the main theft. You understand I couldn't say whether Montague started that line of speculation,' said Phelan, virtuously. 'But I wouldn't put it past him.'

'Neither would I,' said Jack, replacing the cutting in the desk.

'And you do see how it covered up the truth about that night when the three of us got into the Clock Tower? And,' said Phelan, 'how it led the trail of suspicion away from Westmeath – from myself and Montague, and also from Ethne. My main concern, of course, was to protect Ethne.'

There was the sense of evasion again, and Jack thought, as he had earlier, that there was more to Ethne Rafferty's part in all this than Phelan was disclosing. But whatever it had been, it could not matter now.

He said, 'And out of all of that, you created Tomás and Catrina and Maran.'

'I did. When I recovered,' said Phelan, 'I had the writer's

compulsion to set down the story of what had happened that night. Montague was still here, and I dictated it to him – most of it in this room – in the form of a play.' There was a brief gesture with his hands. 'I know of no other form of writing,' he said. 'I suspect it was a Herculean task for Montague, because I dictated at white-hot speed. All the bitterness and the anger poured out of me like a scalding torrent. I used the Rebel Earl's story at the heart – and his lute, with it.'

'The Murderer's Lute,' said Viola, softly.

'Yes. In that hidden room I had seen, and read, part of Thomas's ballad to Catherine. Whatever the reason for his request to guard her memory, I honoured it,' said Phelan. 'Seamus had honoured it, as well. He was a raffish care-for-nobody, that Seamus, but I believe it was because of what Thomas wrote in that ballad that he hid the lute so far from Westmeath House – somewhere he thought it would never be found and there could never be any link to our family. To Catherine. I wish,' he said, 'that it could be discovered what happened to Catherine. And why Thomas laid that charge on her descendants.'

'I wish so, too,' said Jack.

Viola said, 'Phelan, you created extraordinary characters in that play. It's a deeply moving piece – full of emotion and atmosphere. I once told Jack I didn't think he could ever play King Lear – I didn't believe he could conjure up darkness. But I was wrong. Seeing him in rehearsal as Tomás, it's as if he can hear him at some level the rest of us can't. He will give a remarkable portrayal. A memorable portrayal.'

'I'm glad. Your father would have been proud of you, Jack,' said Phelan. 'I met him once, many years ago, did you know that? A very gifted man. A great loss to the theatre.'

Jack managed to say, 'Thank you,' and then, in a more level voice, 'I greatly like the little light touches you've woven into the piece.'

'The gossipy sisters and the policeman and the lamplighters,' said Phelan, and smiled. 'I enjoyed writing those. You have to have the lightness to emphasize darkness, of course. You can't feed your audience unremitting angst and agony. But you're both people of the theatre – you understand about that.'

'We do. And I think,' said Viola, 'that *The Murderer Inside*

the Mirror is probably your finest work. I'm immensely proud
to be playing Catrina.'

The smile came again. 'Your voice is exactly how I wanted
Catrina's to be,' said Phelan. 'But you do see that when the script
was finished, I didn't dare keep it here. I trusted the nuns
completely, but I couldn't risk it being found. There were too
many parallels, too many similarities to what Montague and I
had done that night. We could so easily have been identified as
Tomás and Maran. So Montague took the script back to England,
giving me his word he would never allow it to be staged until it
seemed safe.'

'And when Montague died,' said Jack, 'you thought the safe
time had come?'

'I did.'

'Phelan, who stole the script from Montague's house?'

The question dropped into the room, and for a moment Jack
thought Phelan was not going to answer. But then he said, 'It
was Tod Inkling, of course.' He smiled. 'Tod was the only other
person who knew about my deception,' he said. 'He's as close
as an oyster when he cares to be, and Montague convinced me
it would be safe to admit him to the secret. Taking the script
would have been easy enough for Tod,' he said. 'I daresay he's
picked up a few tricks from the Fitzglens over the years, anyway.
I telephoned him when I heard about Montague's death. The
telephone rather flusters the nuns, but secretly they're proud of
being in touch with the modern world. As for Tod – you wouldn't
think he would be sufficiently in tune with the twentieth century
to even possess a telephone, but he does.'

'I know he does,' said Jack. 'I've seen it on his desk.'

'I told him to retrieve the play, and try to get it staged.'

'You wanted to give the world one last Rafferty play,' said
Viola.

'Well, I did, but I'm afraid there was a stronger reason.' Phelan
made the classic gesture of rubbing his thumb and forefinger
together. 'The sordid subject of coinage, my dears,' he said. '"If
money go before, all ways do lie open". St Joseph's charge a
relatively modest sum for guests, but my funds were starting to
dip alarmingly. I couldn't ask Ethne to sell Westmeath House,
of course – she has never known any other home, and it would

have been too cruel. She lives a very quiet, very retired existence; I don't think she even takes a newspaper, so I wasn't worried that news of the play's performance would reach her. But if it did, I intended to dismiss it by saying someone was trying to cash in on my name.' Then, in a tone that was suddenly sharper, he said, 'Tod told you the truth, didn't he, Viola. He told you the play really was my work – and that I was here. Still alive. He must have done – how else could you have known to travel out here? Come now, we're tumbling all the secrets out today – let's have this one with them.'

'He did tell me,' said Viola, sounding reluctant. 'Under pains of all kinds of promises and vows and threats and caveats.'

'Blackmail and extortion, too, I shouldn't wonder. He wouldn't have carried out a one of them, of course. But Tod is the only one alive now who knew the truth.'

'Not your daughter?' said Jack, carefully.

'Oh, Ethne will have no idea I wrote the play – she'd never see how I could have done it – or even that I would have wanted to do it. The concept of me dictating it wouldn't occur to her.' Phelan paused, then said, 'Viola, I'm glad you felt you could trust Jack with the truth now, though. I would have liked the Fitzglens to have the piece – for Montague's sake, you know. But I told Tod we couldn't risk it, and I suggested he approach you, my dear. Tell me, did you have to haggle with him?'

'Oh, I did,' said Viola, with a sudden grin. 'Very vigorously.'

'The old miser.'

'But he kept the secret,' said Viola. 'And so did I. No one knew how I acquired the play, and Tod suggested we give the impression that it was almost certainly a very clever forgery – but that no one could be sure. He said it would create speculation, and that it would be very beneficial for publicity. And I have to say he was right,' she added. 'I think we'll be playing to full houses.'

'That pleases my vanity all over again,' said Phelan.

Travelling back to the railway halt in Fintan's cart, Viola said, 'We'll come back quite soon, won't we? To see Phelan?'

'Of course,' said Jack. 'More than once, too.'

'And the play? Do we try to persuade Phelan to let us smuggle him into the Roscius on the night? Could it even be done?'

'It probably could,' said Jack, thoughtfully. 'Byron would most likely work out a very elaborate scheme – and he'd love to meet Phelan, of course. But—'

'But you don't know if Phelan would want it?'

'I think he might want to keep Tomás and Catrina and Maran to himself,' said Jack. 'In his own make-believe world. I'm not sure he'd want to hear them speaking in a theatre with an audience listening and watching. I think he underwent a massive change on that night he lost his sight. I think whatever happened – and he told us a good deal, but I don't believe he told us everything – altered him very radically indeed.'

'Something to do with Ethne? Clearly she played some significant part in it all.'

'Yes. But whatever it was, I think we'll have to let it go,' said Jack. 'And he's got her death to face, and however it's put to him – whatever story is pieced together – it will be a massive blow and a huge shock.'

'The nuns won't want to lie to him.'

'No, but the Garda might lie to the nuns.'

'True. In fact no one in St Joseph's – in Westmeath, even – might ever know the circumstances of Ethne's death,' said Viola. 'But it's better that way, isn't it?'

'It is.'

She frowned, then, making an impatient gesture as if to push the thoughts away, said, 'Mother Superior told me we would have been welcome to stay the night there if we wanted.'

'We did say if we encountered any delays we might have to stay overnight somewhere.'

'We did.'

'But I don't believe we envisaged that being inside a religious house.'

'I don't think we did,' said Viola, not looking at him. 'Isn't there a quotation about "never the time and the place"?'

'Robert Browning,' said Jack, pleased he could identify the line. '"Never the time and the place/And the loved one all together". Not that all of that sentiment applies, of course.'

'Certainly not,' said Viola, promptly. And then, 'This looks like our train. I hope we can find an empty compartment, then you can tell me about Thomas of Kildare and Catherine.'

They did find an empty compartment, and she listened with absorption to the story.

'I would love to see that portrait,' she said, at last. 'To see what Catherine looked like. But I can't think of any way of getting into that house – Girdlestone Hall.'

'Nor can I. And I don't suppose there are any other portraits of her,' said Jack. 'There's bound to be one of the Earl somewhere, though. We'll try to find it.'

'Jack – what do you think happened to Catherine?'

Jack hesitated, then he said, 'Lady Girdlestone said she was regarded as the family murderess. Thomas of Kildare was executed as a traitor. If Catherine aided him, she could have been arraigned as a traitor and executed with him.'

'They would have hanged her? Or beheaded her?'

Jack did not immediately reply. Then he said, 'This will sound strange, but – I hope it would have been hanging or beheading. I hope it wouldn't have been anything worse.'

THIRTY

Catherine knew most people hated winter, but at Westmeath she had loved it. She had liked sitting in the window seat, seeing snow blanketing the ground, and frost tracing lace patterns on the windows. They had always had roaring fires, and the scent of the burning fruitwood would fill the entire house.

Thomas's child should have been born at Westmeath House. Catherine did not let herself think of the birth being at Maynooth Castle, because Maynooth had been ravaged and partly destroyed by William Skeffington's armies. She knew that. It had been said that almost everyone died in the siege.

Winter inside the Tower of London would be grim and bleak, but the guard who had brought her extra rugs and blankets, now smuggled in extra food and pitchers of milk – occasionally even some fruit. He had a wife himself, he said, and three children, and he knew that ladies at such times needed looking after. Eating the apples, and a little later the pears, brought back to Catherine the memories of the orchard at Westmeath.

Whenever Liam came, he brought warm clothing and often extra candles; they gave out a faint warmth as well as light, which was comforting. He had not been able to arrange a second visit to Thomas, and Catherine did not dare try sending a message about the child, because she was afraid it would alert the guards or even the Tower Constable to that secret hour they had had. It was absurd to wonder if discovery of that could bring down punishment on two people already facing execution, but execution could take different forms.

On a morning when the grey light from the small courtyard lay drearily everywhere, the Constable, Sir William Kingston, came to Catherine's room to tell her that her execution was to be at the beginning of February.

'I am advised that you will have recovered from the birth of your child by then,' he said, not looking at her. Catherine sensed he was disliking what he had to do and say very much.

'Yes.' She did not dare ask what form her execution would take.

'Thomas of Kildare is to be executed on the same day,' said the Constable. 'You will go to the scaffold together.'

Together one last time, thought Catherine.

'The child is to be taken and cared for by your brother, I believe?'

'Yes.'

'Mistress Ó Raifeartaigh, I ask again if you will name the man responsible for your condition.'

'I will not, sir,' she said, looking at him very straightly, and Kingston shrugged and went out.

Catherine supposed it would be thought that one of the guards had either seduced or possibly even raped her. When she confided this to Liam, he said this was very likely something that happened in this place more often than anyone realized, then told her there was an extremely nice and kindly woman who owned the lodging house where he was living; she would take care of the babe, and find a wet-nurse for it until Liam could take it back to Westmeath.

'But don't lose sight of the hope that I may be able to take you back to Westmeath with me,' he said.

Catherine thought he was trying to give her some hope, and although she knew it was a very fragile thread, she was grateful to him.

The sympathetic guard, whose name was Rufus, brought a small flagon of something he said would help at the birth.

'You won't need much,' he said. 'But my wife took it when our three children were born. She says you will only need a few drops. She's asked me to make sure you're looked after.'

It was unexpectedly comforting to hear of this unknown woman wanting to make sure Catherine would be looked after. She hid the flask under the rugs on her bed. The liquid it contained was thick and syrupy, and it had a scent of poppies. Probably it would not help much, but it had been kind of Rufus and also his wife.

But when it came to the birth, the syrup was of considerable help. It drove back a good deal of the pain that tore through her, and it felt as if a calming hand was smoothing her whole body, as if caressing it with silk. The woman who had appeared to deal with the birth – she turned out to be the woman from Liam's lodging house, and Liam had been right about her being kind – nodded approvingly as Catherine managed to sip it.

She swam in and out of awareness, and she had no idea how long she lay on the rugs, gasping and fighting to bring Thomas's child into the world. Through it all she tried not to know it would be taken from her almost at once, and that afterwards Catherine herself would only have a very short time of life left.

There was a final dreadful wrench and she cried out, and felt blood on her lips as she bit through them, and then there was an indignant cry, and the woman was saying the babe was a boy, healthy and strong, and angry at being so abruptly thrust into a strange world.

Catherine felt her bitten lips curve in a half-smile, because of course Thomas's son would be angry – he would be defiant and ready to challenge everything.

The woman said, 'I had to promise to take him with me at once, my dear. I'm so sorry. He will be well cared for, though, you have my word on that. And I know your brother will love him dearly for your sake. Hold him for a short while, though.'

Looking down at the small creature wrapped in a blanket, Catherine felt such a flood of emotion wash over her she could hardly bear it.

She held the child against her, and said, very softly to him, 'I promise if I can find a way to get out of here and be with you, I will find it – if I have to commit murder to do it, then I will. But whatever happens, I *promise* you will be safe and loved and you will be told all the marvellous stories of the man who fathered you. You will be told how he was a rebel and a fighter, prepared to die for what he believed right – but also that he was a lover and a musician.'

The woman stood quietly at her side, and as Catherine looked up at her, she said, 'His name, mistress? What is he to be called?'

Catherine said, at once, 'Thomas.'

Maguire, going about the business of setting up the shop called *Maguire's*, was surprised to receive a letter bearing Liam Ó Raifeartaigh's signature.

He took it to the bow window of the shop where the light came in from the street, but which was a little removed from the main premises, allowing a degree of privacy.

'Master Maguire,' Ó Raifeartaigh had written:

> I trust you will forgive this approach. I was able to obtain your direction from one of the servants still living near to what is left of Maynooth Castle.
>
> These have been strange and troubling times, but I recall your kindly understanding when you brought to me news of how my dear sister had been rescued from a group of louts in a Dublin street by the Earl of Kildare, and how you promised she would be safe in his care at Maynooth Castle. I was reassured and heartened by your kindness – also that of the Earl himself.
>
> You will know, of course, that a terrible retribution has overtaken both the Earl and my beloved sister, and that they are held within the Tower of London, facing execution for treason.
>
> For the time left to them, I am living in London, since I must be with my sister as often as I am allowed during her final days.
>
> There is a small hope that it may be possible to help her escape before execution – also that the Earl, too, might be brought out, although that is a very small hope indeed. I dare commit no more details to a letter which could fall into ill-intentioned hands. I find, though, that the help of a trusted ally will be needed if the plan has any chance of success. I know you to have been a faithful and good servant to the Earl, and I am therefore encouraged to ask if you would help in what lies ahead.
>
> I should of course recompense you, and would make acceptable arrangements for your journey to London. I am staying in very comfortable lodgings, and a similar arrangement could be made for you.
>
> Only one week – at most, two – would be necessary. Both executions are set for the first days of February. At no time would you be in any danger or at any risk. Only a

single visit to the Tower would be required of you – on the day of the execution. It is unlikely you would be recognized, and even if you were, it would merely be seen as the visit of a loyal servant wishing to bid his master a final farewell.

I await your reply with hope.

Signed by my hand,

Liam Ó Raifeartaigh

Maguire read this extraordinary letter three times, then stood for a long time staring at the crowded street outside *Maguire's*.

His first reaction was to ignore the letter, or, at most, send a polite reply, saying what was being asked was impossible.

But was it? And oughtn't he to know what Ó Raifeartaigh was planning? The prospect of either of those two being smuggled out to freedom was deeply concerning. The whey-faced cat must certainly not be allowed to escape her fate – Maguire's mind went back to that night when he and the two English spies had got into her room and taken her away, gagged and bound. He did not think the bitch had talked about that – he thought he would have been sought out long since if so. People believed that almost everyone from the castle had died in the siege, and it would be what The Cat would believe. Even so, Maguire could not risk her being freed.

He could not risk the Earl being freed, either, because it must never be known that it was Maguire who had helped ensure Thomas's surrender to the English.

He went up to his bedroom, and sat for a long time, thinking what he should do. In the end he wrote to Liam Ó Raifeartaigh that he would be honoured to help in whatever was planned, and that if it were to fail, he would at least have the comfort of knowing he had been able to bid his beloved master a final fare-well. He felt this struck a staunch and loyal note.

He worked out a good story for his nephew – how an English branch of the Kildares needed temporary help while their disgraced relative was awaiting death, and how they felt they could trust the Earl's former faithful servant. He thought it was plausible, and unlikely to create suspicion in his nephew's mind.

It did not create suspicion at all. The boy accepted it, then asked if suitable recompense had been offered. When Maguire said it had, adding that, dear goodness, had his nephew ever known him to do anything without proper payment, the boy smiled, and said, no, indeed he had not. It was not said with the least trace of sarcasm, of course.

Catherine had always known that Time played tricks, and it played them now, so that the days between the birth and the execution – the double execution – sometimes dragged, pulling all the light and the hope from the world. But then it would gallop on, so that you wanted to shout to it to slow down, because every hour, every minute, brought closer that terrible walk to the scaffold.

Liam understood. Once he said, 'Try not to count the days, Cat. Try to trust me.'

'I am trying,' said Catherine. 'I do trust you.'

But she was counting the days, of course. Very soon she would be counting the hours, and finally the minutes . . .

Two days before the execution came the news that neither Catherine nor the Earl would face the worst traitor's death.

A rush of thankfulness swept over her. Without realizing, she reached for the Constable's hand, and stammered, 'Thank you. I am so relieved.'

Sir William Kingston's hand closed around hers, and when he spoke, for the first time his tone was gentle. He said, 'The executioner is skilled and swift. It will be merciful, Catherine.'

The use of her name was so unexpected that tears rushed to Catherine's eyes, but she brushed them away at once, because she would not show any weakness to anyone.

THIRTY-ONE

Ａnd now the hours had finally run down and a bleak dawn lay over the Tower, grey and hopeless, filled with sadness and despair.

Catherine had not known if Liam would be allowed to come to her room at such an hour, but he was here, taking her hands and putting his arms around her.

Then he said, very softly, 'Catherine, there is a plan. The guard – Rufus – is part of it. But you must do exactly what I tell you, and you must not question anything.'

'An escape?' Catherine scarcely dared frame the word.

'I hope so. But only for you. Not for Thomas. If there was the least chance of rescuing him, I would take it. But there is not.' He held her a little away from him, and looked at her very directly. 'Listen, though,' he said. 'Last evening they let me see him – a final farewell. I told him of the plan for you. He was more grateful than I can describe. Catherine, that was a very great, very deep love you had together.'

'Yes,' said Catherine in a whisper.

'I was able to tell him about the boy – that he has a son,' said Liam. 'He did not know, and he was almost overwhelmed.'

Even though, from the day she had been brought here, Catherine had vowed not to display weakness, emotion overwhelmed her, and she clung to Liam, trying not to sob, but sobbing anyway.

He held her firmly, and said, 'Kildare wrote out a form of legacy. A bequest to the boy – not to you, because if we succeed in getting you out, you – and even your name – will have to vanish altogether. Thomas said he could not leave the child as much as he would like, because most of his lands are entailed. There's a half-brother, I think.'

'Yes.' The knowledge that Thomas had been told about the child – that in his last hours, he had tried to ensure his son would be provided for – brought the emotion flooding in all over again.

It was several minutes before Catherine could listen properly to what Liam was telling her about Maynooth.

'I went out there after the siege,' he said. 'A pitiful sight it was. So much damage to such a marvellous place. But I walked in, and I entered some of the rooms unchallenged. I found Thomas's room – and, Catherine, I found his lute.'

'Oh . . .' The memories came scudding in, of Thomas playing music to her on that first night, and of all those other nights when he had played, and then had taken her to his bedchamber and made love to her.

'He took it from me so gratefully,' said Liam. 'He said he would spend his last hours composing a ballad – a farewell to you, he called it. We will find a way to get it after – after all this is over.'

'Yes. Thank you. But Liam – the plan? Dare you tell me?'

Liam glanced over his shoulder to the closed door, then drew her over to the small window at the far end. He said, 'You remember the Earl's servant, Maguire?'

Catherine stared at him. 'I do,' she said. 'He was the one who arranged for me to be taken prisoner. I told you about that. I thought he would have died in the siege, though. I thought almost everyone did.'

'Most did, but Maguire survived like the sewer rat he is,' said Liam, and there was more anger in his voice than Catherine had ever heard. 'He betrayed the Earl as well – Thomas told me that. But if matters go as I hope, Dubhgall Maguire will meet his just fate today, and you will be free. There's no time to tell it all now – although please God there will be time later. Will you give me the poppy syrup Rufus brought for the birth of the boy. Mandragora, isn't it?'

'It's still under the rug there. But why—'

'It's part of the plan,' said Liam, reaching under the rugs near the bed for the flask.

Catherine did not dare question him. She sat on the edge of the bed, and began to feel unreal – as if she was seeing the room and everything in it from a distance. It was like looking into a dim old looking-glass, and seeing uncertain reflections gazing back at you. One of the reflections was of the door of the room opening, and two people entering. With a shock that drove back some of the unreal feelings, she saw one was the guard, Rufus, but that the other was Maguire. Maguire – the man who had brought the two men to her room that night at the castle, and had boasted to them that he would use her capture to force Thomas's surrender. She still remembered how one of the men had questioned it – how he had been disinclined to believe Thomas would give himself up for a woman.

And Maguire had said at once that he would. 'He's besotted by her,' he had said. 'He'll surrender to Skeffington to save her.'

A wave of anger rose up at seeing the man responsible not only for her imprisonment but also Thomas's, but Liam and Rufus were half-pulling Maguire into the room, and to interrupt might spoil whatever fragile plan was being unfolded.

Maguire looked round the room, at first clearly puzzled, then he saw Catherine, and fury and fear flared in his face. He made to push Liam aside and reach the door, but Rufus was barring the way and Maguire was trapped.

Liam said, 'At last, Master Maguire, I can make you pay for what you did to my sister.' He moved nearer and Maguire took an involuntary step back. 'You're to take my sister's place on the scaffold,' said Liam. 'We're going to switch your clothes, and you're to die in her place. It's a very simple plan, but usually the simple plans are the ones that work best.'

'Impossible,' said Maguire. 'Even if you manage such a substitution, I will shout to everyone what's been done. In any case, it would be seen at once that it was not your sister.'

'Not if you were wearing the death hood,' said Liam, and Catherine looked at him, startled, because she had never heard of such a thing. 'Nor,' went on Liam, 'will you be able to shout, for you will be almost completely insensible – apparently half-swooning from terror, as any young girl would be, faced with the axe.'

Maguire said, a note of new fear in his voice, 'The death hood?'

'An English custom,' said Liam, smoothly, and glanced at Rufus, who at once said,

'Little known outside this place, but we know of it in here. It is reserved for the nobility who can request it. It covers the entire head and face – hides them from the stares of the crowds who come to executions to jeer and taunt. It is,' he said, 'quite a merciful practice; it prevents the condemned prisoner seeing what's ahead.'

'Such as the traitor's death, with the noose hanging down, ready to half-strangle a man, and such as glinting knives waiting to disembowel him after he's cut down,' said Liam, softly, and Catherine saw the colour drain from Maguire's face, and thought: he does not know that the sentence is for beheading. He believes he might have to face being hanged, drawn and quartered. She felt a stab of pity.

But Maguire was saying, blusteringly, that this had not been the plan put to him.

'You said I would be disguised as a musician at the scaffold,' he said, furiously. 'That the Earl had demanded a death march for his last walk—'

'I did,' said Liam, gravely. 'And it is exactly what Kildare might have done.'

'Arrogant to the last, the reckless, cheating villain,' said Maguire, with such venom in his voice that the jab of pity Catherine had felt earlier vanished. 'You said as one of the musicians I was to create a diversion,' he went on. 'To shout that the rebels – the gallowglass soldiers – were at the courtyard entrance – about to come pouring in to snatch the Earl from the guards' hands. And under cover of the confusion, you would take the Earl from the scaffold and get him to safety.'

Liam said, 'Did you really believe that after all you did I would trust you? You would have watched the execution and done nothing.'

'Yes, I would,' said Maguire, spitting the words out with fury. 'And exulted to see the creature die.'

'It was a plan that would never have worked,' said Liam, as if Maguire had not spoken. 'But this will.' He studied Maguire, then said, 'You will have a small chance of escaping the axe,' he said. 'If you can draw the guards' attention to who you really are. Make them realize there has been an exchange and they have the wrong person—'

'I shall,' said Maguire, at once. 'Sweet Christ, of course I will. And they will release me, and come straight to this room. And then,' he said, with vicious relish, 'your precious sister, sinful

cheating little whore that she is, will be taken to the scaffold,
and you shall see how she likes facing the axe and the noose,
and very likely both.'

'The guards will certainly come in here,' said Liam, smoothly.
'But by that time my sister and I will be gone – I have a map
of the Tower and I know the ways through the passages. With
me will be the good friend who came to bear me company in
the ordeal of my sister's death.' He glanced at Catherine, and as
he did so, somewhere deep within the Tower, a bell began to
chime. Liam looked at Rufus and, as Rufus came forward,
Catherine saw he now held in one hand a thick iron bar.

As Maguire half-turned, Rufus raised the iron bar, and Maguire
threw up his hands in defence. But it was already too late. The
bar crunched onto his head, and, with a guttural grunt, he fell to
the ground.

'Now the syrup,' said Liam. 'Help me hold open his mouth
and pour it down. Make haste, Rufus.'

But Rufus was already kneeling over the prone body, and the
mandragora was going, drop by drop, into Maguire's slack, partly
open mouth.

'Now for the clothes,' said Liam, bending over Maguire.
'Catherine, there's no time for modesty – you must take off your
outer clothes so that we can dress this creature in them.'

'And you have to don his garments in place,' said Rufus, dragging off Maguire's breeches and stockings and then his jerkin.

Catherine tore off her outer things, and seized Maguire's. His
clothes were large and loose on her, but it did not matter. She
pulled the belt tightly about her waist to keep the breeches in
place, and jammed on the cloth cap, pulling it well down to shade
her face, grateful that her hair was still short. There were woollen
stockings and duckbill shoes, also much too big, but she folded
the stockings over several times, and thought she would be able
to walk in the shoes.

The Tower bell was still sounding its dreadful note – filling
up the room. What would it be like to walk outside and be led
to the scaffold with that relentless chiming all around you? She
shuddered, and clung to the belief that her brother's plan would
succeed.

'Tie one of the blankets around Maguire,' said Rufus. 'Around his shoulders and down to his waist. We need to hide where it gapes at the back – I couldn't fasten it . . . Yes, that's good.'

'Should we give him more of the syrup?'

'No. He needs to be sufficiently awake to be able to stand partly upright and walk a few steps. Hand me the hood, will you? Quickly, now – the guards will be here soon.'

'God, I wish that bell would stop,' said Liam. 'Pull the hood well down over his face – we dare not risk it slipping off and the executioner realizing it isn't Catherine.'

The hood was fashioned from thick, greyish canvas, and once in place it gave Maguire a faceless, blind look. It was macabre and it seemed to turn him into a different creature. Catherine found she was shaking so badly she thought she might fall apart, but she must keep up the pretence that she was Maguire – she must play her part. She sat on the edge of the bed, trying to adopt a masculine pose.

Footsteps were coming along the passage, and Liam stepped back from Maguire's figure. To Catherine, he said, softly, 'And now, pray to every saint you ever heard of that this wild plan works.'

Catherine was still feeling as if she was in the grip of a dream. She had no idea if any of this was really happening, but she was holding on to the thought that she might be free very soon, and that although she had certainly lost Thomas, she would be with his son.

Maguire came partly back to consciousness and to the awareness that something was half-smothering him and almost completely blinding him. He coughed, causing pain to throb through his head. He reached up to whatever was covering his eyes and his face, but he was only able to make a weak, ineffectual attempt. It was like trying to claw through mud. When he attempted to stand up, his legs were like threads of cotton, and he half fell.

There was the sound of marching feet and then of men's voices saying something about having to more or less carry the prisoner, but the sooner it was done the better. And would you look at that hood arrangement – wouldn't it make you shudder at the faceless creature it had created, but seemingly it was an Irish tradition and had been especially asked for.

'Can't ignore the last request of a condemned prisoner,' said another voice.

They were taking hold of his arms now – not brutally, but firmly, and half-dragging him along. Somewhere a bell was slowly clanging – it throbbed inside his head. Maguire struggled to understand, but he was starting to feel sick from the pulsing pain of his head and the peculiar sweetish taste in his mouth. The chiming ought to mean something – he could not pin down what it was, but he had the growing sense of danger, of something waiting for him that he must escape . . .

Escape. Understanding was coming in. He was in the Tower of London – he had been asked to help with getting Thomas Fitzgerald free, and he had agreed, because he dared not let either Thomas or the Ó Raifeartaigh bitch escape. He had even been able to see how he could ensure that Liam Ó Raifeartaigh's plan failed. He remembered the pleasure he had felt at that.

But then he had been cheated – cruelly and viciously – and now he was being carried to the scaffold in the bitch's place. It was all right, though; he had only to let them know who he was. He drew breath to call out, but only the faintest mewling sound came. The sick feeling swept over him again, and he had to swallow several times to force it down, because it was unthinkable that he should be sick inside this hood.

Hands – two pairs of hands – were pulling him to his feet, but his legs gave way and the hands lifted him, and carried him. There was a clogging smell of dankness and dirt and of stagnant water, and the sickness threatened again. A murmur of voices reached him – men's voices, one saying wasn't it a heavier burden than you'd expect, but the other saying you could never tell.

Maguire struggled, but he could still only make feeble movements, and although he summoned all his resolve, when he tried to call out again – to say this was a huge mistake – there was only a sound like a cat mewing.

Cold air was reaching him now, and voices from what was clearly a crowd of people. Maguire tried to listen, but he could not make any sense of what they were shouting.

He was being forced to half-stand, and there was a grittiness under his feet. After a moment he identified it as sawdust, and his senses spun in confusion, because why would sawdust be spread on the ground?

Now he was being pushed into a semi-kneeling position, and his hands were dragged behind his back and a rope wound around them. Realization was flooding his mind in huge, terrified waves, because he was remembering what had been said in the Ó Raifeartaigh bitch's prison room – that they were sending him to the scaffold in her place. He struggled and tried to cry out – if only he could get the disgusting covering off his head . . .

But he could still only make small weak sounds, and his hands were too firmly tied for him to move. He was being forced forward, and now there was the feel of a hard lump of wood under his neck and a scooped-out section into which his chin had fallen . . . He struggled again, and the sickness overwhelmed him, so that he vomited helplessly against the hood, gasping and choking, shuddering. Dreadful. Close to him a voice said, 'Guts thrown up, from the sound of it.'

'Often one end or the other,' said a second voice. 'And we've cleared up worse. Keep the head down – press on it, will you? You know what happens when they fight.'

The sickness came again, flooding the dark inside of the hood with dreadful wet sourness. But the spasms dislodged the hood slightly, and in Maguire's direct sight was Thomas Fitzgerald, standing a few feet away, flanked by guards, his own hands bound. He was waiting to walk to his own death, Maguire understood that at once. But he also saw that Kildare no longer cared about dying. There was a look in his face that suggested he had accepted what was ahead and had come to some kind of inner peace and acceptance. In that moment, Maguire understood Thomas knew the plan had succeeded, that Catherine Ó Raifeartaigh would be safe – and that in some way it had given meaning to the Earl's own death.

He made one last attempt to cry out, but there was already a movement behind him. There was a swishing sound and the axe came hurtling down.

For Catherine, Westmeath House was a sanctuary, a haven. The scents and the familiar furniture and the views over the gardens and the orchard closed round her like a blessing.

She sat in the deep window seat overlooking the orchard, the child in her arms. His eyes were bright and alert, and Catherine smiled.

'You've come home, Thomas,' she said, and then looked to where Liam had taken his familiar place in the deep chair by the hearth.

He said, 'I made sure none of the helpers – the village girls – would be here for at least two days.'

'Two days is time enough for us to plan what we have to do. But Thomas belongs here,' said Catherine.

'He does. I have the sketches of his father,' said Liam. 'The ones I did when we first went to St Mary's Abbey, and the ones from the last days in the Tower. I shall create a painting of him from them.'

'Will you? I should like that.' Catherine paused, then said, 'It would mean that Thomas would be here – his son would know him, just a little. And so would their descendants. All those Ó Raifeartaighs still to be born. I like knowing that. But I can't be here, can I?'

'You already know it.'

'I do know it. For my sake, but more for yours and even more for Thomas's son, no one must ever suspect I did not die in the Tower. Would they have discovered the substitution, do you think?'

'Not necessarily.'

He did not say that execution was a messy business, or that the remains of those put to death by the axeman were not treated with particular respect, but Catherine knew it. But Liam would not want to put images of what could have happened to Thomas into her mind.

'Whether they discovered it or not, I won't let them find you, Cat,' he said.

'I shall have to leave this house, though – it could be some-where they would look. I shall have to leave Thomas with you – and remain hidden, perhaps for the rest of my life.' She looked at him, then said, 'And I think you already know where I shall go.'

'I do,' said Liam. 'I told Kildare where you would go. He smiled and said he was glad to know you would be in that safety, that tranquillity. He also said the Roman Catholic Church has hidden many secrets over the centuries. And he believed it could hide one more.'

The sisters at St Joseph's were horrified and shocked to hear the story that Master Ó Raifeartaigh unfolded for them. They listened intently and, at the end, said wasn't it a tragic, sorry tale. But how wonderful that there had been a courageous guard who had been able to smuggle dear Catherine to safety.

When this was said, Catherine did not dare look at Liam. The nuns must never know the whole truth about how she had escaped from the Tower – how Liam and Rufus had sent that vicious creature Maguire to the scaffold in her place.

Mother Superior was talking about a Mass of Thanksgiving, then, characteristically, saying they understood there had been some sinning along the way, but they would pray to the good Lord to understand and be forgiving, and absolution would surely be granted. Sister Bernadette said that wouldn't the Lord know that retribution been made – more than made. As for the little one – ah, he would be great solace to them all, said the nuns delightedly; they would be proud and grateful to have a part in his care and his growing up.

And of course they would help their beloved girl – wouldn't they do whatever was needed to keep the truth from the world. Told of the money from the Earl, they said that to be sure the vow of poverty was a very worthy one, and they kept scrupulously to its tenets, but it had to be said they had never been an affluent House, and there were always expenses to be met, along with trying to help the destitute. The Earl's dowry would be thankfully received.

As for the concealment of dearest Catherine, said Mother Superior, well, they would not lie about it, but who was going to come out here to their quiet little convent to ask questions? All would be well.

THIRTY-TWO

As *The Murderer Inside the Mirror* wound its way to the play's culmination, Tansy, standing at the side of the Roscius's stage, could feel the audience's tension as they waited for the final scene – to find out whether the hangman's noose awaited.

Maran and Tomás were in the stone room with the barred window, the stage lights angled to enclose them in a pool of bluish light. Timon looked as he had looked earlier – he *was* Maran, thought Tansy – but Jack was so deeply in the grip of Tomás's darkness he was hardly recognizable. He looked as if he had not shaved for days – Tansy knew it would be a careful application of make-up, but it was immensely effective. He looked angry and uncaring and defiant. His hair, dark with sweat, tumbled uncombed over his forehead, and his narrow eyes glowed with emotion.

> *Tomás:* The time's almost run out, hasn't it, Maran? Can't you feel it has? Can't you sense an immense clock ticking away the minutes – or is it only my own heart beating?
> *Maran moves to door, listening:* Someone's coming—
> *Tomás:* Is there to be a final farewell, then? And then it will be the last walk – the murderer's walk – but there'll be no music as there was for my ancestor—
> *Maran:* No music, Tomás. But I have permission to be there until the last moment. It won't be a solitary or a lonely death. You have my word on that.
> *Maran exits.*

Catrina appeared in the open doorway, silhouetted against the backdrop, guards just behind her. Tomás went to her at once, and took both her hands in his, and the two of them stood motionless, looking at one another.

Tansy was aware of a soft movement beside her, and then of Timon's hand taking hers. Then, as Tomás's arms went around Catrina and he pulled her against him, Timon said, abruptly, 'That isn't how we rehearsed it. That close embrace . . . My God, it's a good thing no one from the Lord Chamberlain's office is here tonight.'

Tansy, her eyes still on the two people locked in each other's arms, said, 'It's remarkable acting, though.'

Timon said, softly, 'I don't think they're acting.'

At last Catrina stepped back, and the guards moved, taking her arm and leading her away. The lights changed slowly, a solemn monotonous drumbeat began to sound, and the outline of a noose gradually became visible against the back wall – clearly recognizable for what it was. The drumbeat continued for five – six – more beats, then stopped. Into the silence came the unmistakable sound of a trapdoor crashing down. As it did so, Tomás sank into the chair, and slumped forward, his head coming to rest on his arms.

There were gasps from the audience. It worked, thought Tansy. They believed it was Tomás who was under sentence of death – Tomás who was about to be hanged. The final twist of the story.

Then Timon said, 'Ready, Mimi?'

'Yes.'

Tansy moved around the back of the flats to the doorway on to Tomás's room. She paused, took a deep breath, then stepped into the blue-grey spot, and at once she was aware of the audience's warmth. A wave of tremendous emotion washed over her. They liked Mimi. They wanted to know what she was about to say.

She walked slowly to Tomás, and, as she sat down at the table, he raised his head and looked at her.

> *Tomás:* Mimi. My guardian angel of the street. The last
> person I expected to see— You know it's over?
> *Mimi:* Yes. Maran told me. He was there until the end. She
> refused the hood, he said. And she kept her eyes on him
> until the final moment. She didn't die alone, Tomás. She
> knew Maran was there. I think she would feel that in a

way you were there, too. Sort of holding her hand. That
sounds fanciful, don't it?

Tomás: No. I was holding her hand, Mimi. I'll be here for
four years – did you know that? Four years for breaking
into the castle and trying to destroy the Murderer's Lute.
I wanted to quench its darkness, you see. But I failed.
It's still there, in that dim secret old room.

Mimi: But it isn't still there, Tomás. It's here. I followed
you that night. I told you I'd always look out for you. If
I could've saved you – and your lady – I would have.
But they took you and they took her, and there wasn't
nothing I could do. Maran got away, though.

Tomás: Maran would always get away. He always boasted
that he was never caught.

Mimi: Nobody saw me. I can slip through a building like
a shadow. People don't notice a shadow. And I found it.
Your darkness. I brought it out with me.

Tomás: The lute. The Murderer's Lute. Dear God . . . *Takes
her hand.* Mimi, will you destroy it for me?

Mimi: I'll destroy it. But before I do, will you play it? Now?
One last time? For Catrina?

Hands him the lute. He takes it slowly, and looks at it.

Tomás, very softly: For Catrina.

*Pause, then slow curtain to sound of Tomás playing lute
music.*

Byron and Jack stood just outside the Green Room, watching
the critics and actors milling excitedly around.

Jack was strongly aware of Tomás still close to him, but he
must push Tomás back, and enter the Green Room, to greet the
distinguished people who had been in the audience – the theatrical
luminaries and critics, and the people who were so illustrious
they were very nearly legends. The Fitzglens were here in force
as well, of course – he was glad about that. He was especially
glad they had been able to see Tansy's performance as Mimi.
They would be tremendously proud of her. Jack was tremendously
proud of her, too.

Aunt Daphnis was wearing an astonishing hat which would
certainly have screened the view of the stage from anyone sitting

behind her. Cecily was pink-cheeked and round-eyed with delight, and Ambrose looked as if he might be calculating the profit the evening was going to make. Uncle Rudraige was very dashing in a velvet dinner jacket – Tansy had said earlier that he had promised to be polite to the Gilfillans, but she did not think they should rely on this.

At Jack's side, Byron said quietly, 'You'll have to go in and face the adulation in a moment, won't you? But before you do, I would like to say you gave a remarkable performance tonight, Jack. I don't think I'll ever forget it. I don't think anyone who was in the audience will ever quite forget it.' He hesitated, then said, 'Do you want to stay in Tomás's world for a while longer, because if so I'll plunge into the seething crowds and leave you alone. Or can we talk for a moment about the play?'

'I'll face the crowds presently,' said Jack. 'I'd like to talk about the play for a moment, though.'

Byron said, 'I find it remarkable that in the end the play posed hardly any threat to our family.'

'But it did,' said Jack, at once. 'In the original script, Maran – which I've only recently realized is the middle syllable of Amaranth—'

'So it is,' said Byron, startled. 'I hadn't seen that.'

'—Maran is depicted as slightly lame,' said Jack. 'Apparently Mimi had at least one line where she asks if he can walk across the courtyard to Tomás's house, or if he needs her help.'

'How do you know?'

'Tod Inkling told me,' said Jack, who had told Byron the truth about Phelan the previous night, knowing that Byron, of all the Fitzglens, could be trusted. 'Tod had given Phelan his word that he would make sure the Fitzglens couldn't be connected to the play. But he thought Maran's lameness was too strong a pointer to the family. I had a long telephone conversation with Tod, and he explained how he'd copied the entire play out in his own hand – I should think the Gaelic scene took a bit of doing, even for Tod. It's doubtful if Phelan's writing would have been recognized, but Tod was taking no chances. And while he was making the copy, he removed every reference to Maran's lameness. Loyal of the old rogue, wasn't it?'

'Very. Jack – that business with Phelan's daughter. Will we ever know the truth about that?'

'I doubt it. I believe Phelan's been protecting her far more than he's let on – or ever will let on,' said Jack. 'I think that was the other reason he wanted the play kept secret. In the murder scene, Catrina kills a guard and is caught and hanged.'

'Ethne wasn't caught, though,' said Byron, thoughtfully. 'But Phelan wrote that scene echoing what she had done. Perhaps he was somehow compelled to write it – almost like a confession.'

'Or perhaps, like Tomás, he was exorcising it – trapping it on the page,' said Jack. 'It's my guess he went into hiding to protect Ethne. And it was only after five years he felt safe to let the play be staged.'

'And,' said Byron, caustically, 'when he needed the money.'

'That too. But we'll never know for sure, and we can never ask him, of course.'

'Will you discuss it with Viola?' asked Byron, as they walked towards the open door of the Green Room.

'Oh, no. In fact I don't anticipate having any deep discussions with her about anything,' said Jack, vaguely.

'That final scene on stage tonight—' said Jack to Viola as they walked back to the hotel some time later.

'—wasn't as we rehearsed,' she said, at once. 'It should have been a brief embrace and a chaste kiss on the cheek, shouldn't it?'

'Do you want me to apologize? You do know it was Tomás in those last moments?' Jack made an impatient, almost-angry, gesture. 'Tomás took me over,' he said.

Viola hesitated, then said, 'Catrina took me over, as well. You must have realized that.'

'I did.'

'Only for the duration of the play – of that scene,' she said quickly. 'Nothing like that's ever likely to happen again.'

'Of course not,' said Jack, at once.

'Several times tonight I had the feeling that Tomás and Catrina's shadows were quite close to us,' said Viola, thoughtfully.

'Thomas of Kildare and Catherine Ó Raifeartaigh,' said Jack, half to himself.

'Yes. Ridiculous, isn't it?'

'No. I felt the same.'

'Do you think we'll ever find out what happened to them? Or are they too far back?'

'Too far back, I should think. I can't see how it would be possible.'

But it was possible, and the start of the possibility was waiting in the hotel, in the form of a telegram.

MR JACK FITZGLEN
DETAILS OF CATHERINE FOUND IN CONVENT STOP
MUST SHOW YOU SOONEST STOP PLEASE COME
WHEN POSSIBLE IN HOPE PHELAN RAFFERTY.

Jack looked up from the telegram, and met Viola's eyes.

'Well?' he said, softly. 'Shall we reach for Tomás and Catrina one last time – see if we can go back into the past with them to find Thomas and Catherine?'

'Oh yes,' said Viola, her eyes shining. 'Oh, Jack, yes!'

Phelan's room in St Joseph's Convent was reassuring and familiar.

He sat in his usual chair, with Jack and Viola seated in front of him, and Sister Mary at the desk. Jack saw that several yellowing documents were laid out, covered with a sheet of glass, presumably for protection. Next to them was an open notebook.

Phelan half-turned towards her and said, 'Sister, this is your discovery. Will you let Jack and Viola see what you found, please.'

'I will. As you can see, the documents are all very old and very fragile. They seem to be from a long-ago part of Mr Rafferty's family.'

'When you say a long-ago part—?'

'There's no date, but the script on two of them suggests the sixteenth century, Mr Fitzglen.'

Jack felt his heart skip several beats, but he only said, 'You've been able to decipher them? I know writing from that era can be difficult.' He went to the table, and looked at the documents so carefully laid out.

'I think I've managed to get the content with fair accuracy,' she said. 'Only, you understand, because I studied a little in that area of history.' There was a deprecatory note in her voice, as if she were trying to minimize her own learning, although Jack suspected it was considerable. 'I have a translation written out – perhaps you would read it aloud so Mr Rafferty can hear it again.'

There were three documents. Jack thought he could have managed to make out a few words on the two oldest ones, but he was grateful for the translation.

But what was perfectly clear was the signature on the first of them. The name leapt out.

Liam Ó Raifeartaigh.

Jack stared down at it. Liam Ó Raifeartaigh. Had he been part of Catherine's life? He must have been. Husband? Father? Brother?

He turned to Sister Mary's notes and read aloud.

> My dear Mother Superior,
>   I send you God's greetings, and am able to tell you that very soon I will be returning to Westmeath. With me will be the boy.
>   Blessings on you and the good sisters of St Joseph's for being such staunch and true friends to my family.
>   Liam Ó Raifeartaigh

Jack looked up.

'The boy?' he said.

'This other letter gives more detail.' She turned the page of her notebook, and as Jack began to read again, he felt the past close around him again.

> To Sister Bernadette
>   I am allowed to send a final note in my last hours of life in this world.
>   It was with the deepest gratitude to a merciful God I received the news that I have a son. I give thanks for his life, and know that you will make sure he is kept safe and well.
>   I have been able to arrange for a sum of money to be

settled on the convent. To preserve secrecy, it will come to
you in the form of a dowry – you will know in whose name
the dowry really is, and you will understand that this is all
I dare write. All missives sent from here are read, and I
believe missives sent do not always reach me. I think,
though, that this letter will reach you.
  God's blessings to you all.
  Please pray for me.

There was no signature, but there was an initial, and when Jack
studied the original document, he saw it had been written with
a flourish that suggested defiance. And rebellion?
The initial was a very clear, strongly inked 'T'.

Catherine had a son, thought Jack, staring at the pages. Catherine
must have given birth to Thomas's son. It has to be that. But it
was Thomas of Kildare himself who wrote that letter, he thought
– that strongly inked 'T' could not be anyone else. And Thomas's
son was brought to Westmeath, and even though Thomas himself
had been about to face death, he gave thanks for the life of his
son, and made financial arrangements for the child's care.
  He looked across at Viola, and saw her put up a hand impatiently, to brush tears away. Then he pulled his mind back to the
present, to Sister Mary pointing to the third document.
  'A later one – dated early in 1735. Quite ornate writing, but
much easier to read.'

  My dearest Mother Superior and Sisters of St Joseph's
  Convent,
    I am an irreclaimable sinner, as all of you know, but I
  write in sincerity and gratitude for the two items you have
  given me. They are indeed links to my family's past, and
  are precious because of it. It is, as you say, remarkable that
  for so many decades they have been lying quietly in a
  shadowy corner of your sacristy – almost as if trying to
  hide from the world.

Reading that out, Jack knew he and Viola and Phelan were sharing
the knowledge of Catrina's line.

'Lying by itself in the shadows – half covered by layers of
dust, as if it's trying to hide . . .'
'The lute is, of course, valuable, as much for its antiquity as
for its original owner,' went on the letter.

> As for the ballad, I find it moving and beautiful, and it points
> strongly to the truth of Catherine and Thomas's legend.
> Both items, though, could still be deeply damaging,
> even after so long. The sisters who helped Catherine
> during those years understood it must never be known
> that she was still alive. They also understood – as I do
> and as you do, my dear Mother Superior – that the boy
> who grew up at Westmeath – partly in this house, partly
> at St Joseph's – must never know the truth about his birth.
> Those nuns were brave and steadfast; they protected
> Catherine and her son, and they themselves must be
> protected even now.
> You have my most solemn promise that I shall continue
> to keep this secret, and will find a safe place for the lute
> and the music. It is sad to contemplate that it might have to
> be returned to a dark place of hiding, but it may be
> necessary.
> Perhaps you will not be too horrified if one day I attend
> a Mass in your chapel? Increasingly, there are times when
> I believe I might welcome the sensation of being taken back
> into the fold. Isn't there 'more joy in heaven over one sinner
> who repents' . . .?
> Blessings to you all,
> Seamus Rafferty

Jack returned to his seat next to Phelan, and reached for his hand.
At the same time, Viola took Phelan's other hand.
Phelan smiled. He said, 'Tomás and Catrina here with me. Or
is it even Thomas and Catherine?'
'Aren't they the same people?' said Jack. 'Phelan, can we
piece all of this together?'
'We can. And haven't I done nothing but speculate ever since
Sister Mary found those documents,' said Phelan. 'Listen, now,
Catherine had a son by Thomas of Kildare – that seems clear. A

pity there will be no birth records so far back, but we can't have everything.'

'The boy was your ancestor?' said Viola, a bit hesitantly.

'I'd like to think so. I don't think it's a fanciful idea,' he said, almost hopefully.

'I don't think it's at all fanciful,' said Jack, at once.

'Nor do I,' said Viola, eagerly.

'Good. Now, between us, don't we know the lines of the ballad Thomas wrote to Catherine?' said Phelan, with the air of having settled a vaguely troublesome matter, and now being able to pass on to more important matters. 'You found most of it in that English manor house, and I found the rest in Seamus's secret room in Dublin Castle. Always supposing,' he said, 'that you can remember the part you found.'

Viola said, 'He's an actor, Phelan. And he had your Tomás's lines by heart within twenty-four hours.'

Jack said,

> 'She who uprighted me with such desire –
> She whose name could twist my heart/And wrench my very
>   soul apart
> I must forswear, but gladly so
> For my Love is safe, she cheated Fate.
>
> 'This charge I lay on all who come –
> Veil her name, her story hide.
> Speak not her name, let memory fade.
> Let history not recall my Love . . .'

'You have the way with the written word, Jack Fitzglen,' said Phelan. 'The final lines were not in the portrait, though?'

'No, only the ones I've quoted. There were more?'

'There were.

> 'In cold bleak dawn I soon shall die
> Betrayed by one I thought to trust.
> But he will walk with death's grim hood
> With tolling bell, with sawdust spread.
> A faithless man, a faceless death . . .'

There was silence, then Jack said, slowly, 'Thomas was awaiting execution when he wrote that. He was beheaded, if the accounts can be believed.'

'Please God those accounts can be trusted. Let's believe them.'

'Catherine had been imprisoned with him,' said Viola, thoughtfully. 'Why would that be? Had she helped him? Would she have been regarded as a traitor alongside him?'

'I think so. But somehow they got Catherine out of the Tower,' said Jack. 'And brought her back here. Phelan, do you think that's what happened?'

'I do. That word "betrayal" says a good deal, you know. I think they sent someone to the scaffold in her place – and I think it could have been the one who betrayed her. The one Thomas "thought to trust".'

'Faceless and with a hood,' said Jack. 'They fooled the executioners.'

'They cheated fate,' said Phelan. 'Thomas died, but Catherine lived on. I think she lived on here, in St Joseph's, for the rest of her life – Liam Ó Raifeartaigh and the nuns kept her hidden.'

'Who would Liam have been?' asked Viola.

'We'll never know for sure. Her father?'

'More likely her brother,' said Jack. 'It sounds as if he was part of her escape – that would be more a young man's work.'

'You're right, of course.'

'And so,' said Jack, 'Catherine lived out her life here.'

'Hidden away,' said Viola. 'Even her name erased. I find that immensely sad.'

'Her portrait was painted over, as well, so that Thomas's lute could no longer be seen,' said Jack. 'Someone – perhaps it was Liam – made very sure there was nothing that could lead to her ever being connected to Thomas.'

As the train rattled its way back towards Dublin, neither Jack nor Viola said very much.

But as Westmeath receded into the distance, Viola said, 'Jack – about Liam? Did you expect that?'

'No. But I'm glad Sister Mary and Phelan found those letters.

I think Liam's the third shadow, Viola. Just as Thomas of Kildare stood behind Tomás, and Tomás stood behind Phelan—'

'—and Catherine behind Catrina, and also that strange creature, Ethne Rafferty—'

'Yes, just as that, Liam was behind Maran,' said Jack. 'And therefore behind my Uncle Montague.'

Viola said, 'Do you remember me telling Phelan I thought you were hearing Tomás at a level the rest of us couldn't? I think when Phelan wrote that play, he was hearing Thomas and Catherine at a level no one else did. I don't think he was aware of it, but I think it's what happened.'

'And hearing Liam, too? Phelan knew about Thomas and Catherine, but he couldn't have known about Liam,' said Jack. 'Not then.'

'But if he sensed Thomas and Catherine – if they were his ancestors – wouldn't he have sensed Liam, too? Whoever Liam was,' said Viola, leaning her head back against the seat, her eyes inward-looking.

Through the windows the sun was gradually sinking in a blaze of copper and gold and crimson, and Jack said, almost absently, 'It's said nowhere has sunsets quite like Ireland.'

'It's beautiful,' said Viola, turning to look. 'Jack – where exactly are we? I missed that last station sign.'

Jack glanced at the train tickets, and said, 'This train takes several diversions, it seems. Oh, that's unexpected—'

'What?'

'It stops at Maynooth,' he said.

'Maynooth?'

'When Byron was searching for details about Thomas, he found a reference to Maynooth Castle having been the principal home of the Earls of Kildare.' He looked at his watch, then said, 'I think it's the next stop.'

'You're going to get off the train at Maynooth?' said Viola, as he stood up.

'Yes.'

'But it's already well after five o'clock. It will start to get dark very soon.'

'I don't care.'

She paused, then said, 'Do you want to be by yourself?'

Jack said, 'I don't know.' He considered her for a moment. 'I don't know how far from the station the castle is. Or whether there'll be another train back to Dublin tonight . . .'

He stopped. Something seemed to hang in the balance – something that could tip one way or the other. Then Viola reached for the small bag she had brought with her. 'Unless you strongly object, I'd like to come with you,' she said, and waited.

Jack said, slowly, 'There are worse fates than being stranded in Thomas's home for a night.'

Maynooth was a university town, lively and energetic, and filled with purposeful people.

They asked for directions to the castle, which was, it seemed, the shortest of walks. There were enthusiastic gestures, pointing out the way. But there were generally cabs coming and going, if the gentleman and the lady preferred.

Viola said, 'Let's walk, shall we? It doesn't sound far, and I'd like to see a bit of the town.'

The castle did not exactly dominate the town, but it was a definite presence. You must have walked these streets, Thomas, thought Jack – or would you have been on horseback? Would the people have cheered you? Or would there have been little groups quietly plotting to bring about your downfall? Including the faithless faceless one who walked hooded to his death . . .?

What remained of the ancient Norman fortress, once the seat of a powerful family of Irish noblemen, was lit to lonely splendour by the sunset. Jack stood very still, staring up at it, trying to hear echoes from the past. But they're too far back, he thought. And too little remains of the castle. Even so, here and there were impressions of a lost grandeur – of soaring towers and vast halls and courtyards. He thought there were the remains of what might have been a keep too, and Viola pointed to what had clearly once been a towering entrance gateway.

'But Thomas isn't here, is he?' she said. 'Nor is Catherine. Or are they? I almost have a feeling that something does linger. Like a – like a ghost-whisper. As if, just very occasionally, one of them might come here—'

'Each searching for the other?' said Jack. And then, because she must certainly not be allowed to see the emotion the castle had created in him, he said, lightly, 'Miss Gilfillan, you surely aren't giving way to romanticizing?'

'Only daydreaming for a moment.'

They walked on, but now Jack thought that with them walked the images of those two long-ago people who had loved and lost, and who might still occasionally try to find one another . . .

Somewhere in the town a clock chimed seven, and Viola said, 'I suppose we can go back to the station and ask about a train to Dublin.'

'That would be the sensible course of action,' said Jack. He paused. 'Or we could even spend the night here. There seem to be several quite nice hotels and taverns. Thomas and Catherine,' he said, very softly. 'Together again at last?'

'Thomas and Catherine,' said Viola, slowly. 'Nothing more than that, of course.'

There was an unmistakable question in her voice, and Jack said, 'Nothing more in the least.' But when he reached for her hand, her fingers clung tightly to his. He said, 'But for tonight—'

'For one night only—'

'—let's allow Thomas Fitzgerald and Catherine Ó Raifeartaigh to be together.'

AUTHOR'S NOTE

Placing the irrepressible Fitzglen family in an Irish setting for their newest venture, seemed almost to make it imperative that they played a part in the famous theft of the Irish Crown Jewels.

The theft took place in 1907, and neither the perpetrators nor the jewels themselves were ever found. However, a curious story relates how, in 1903, there was an earlier attempt to capture them, after they had been transferred to a new strongroom. The Ulster King of Arms of the day – Sir Arthur Vicars, who it seems was known to partake of a drink or two while on overnight duty – awoke one morning to find the jewels draped around his neck. Reports as to likely motives – and, indeed, to the actual truth of the event – vary wildly.

While searching for a motive for the insouciant and inventive Montague Fitzglen, the 'master forger' of the clan, this earlier and somewhat mysterious theft attempt helpfully presented itself. Even the contemporary reports about it hold an air of puzzlement, almost as if no one quite knew what to believe. It seems, though, that when the theft was successfully accomplished in 1907, amidst the speculation about political activities and suppressed scandals surrounding leading figures, there were muted suggestions that the 1903 episode could have been a dummy run. A rehearsal.

How easy, therefore, to weave Montague and his collaborators into those speculations and rumours.

As for the other Irish plot strand . . .

History in all countries is sprinkled with heroes and rebels, and with defiant men and women who have challenged and protested and mutinied. Some have been successful and have toppled reigns and regimes. Others have been vanquished, and had their heads toppled instead.

But while working out the story of *The Murderer Inside the Mirror,* one rebel in particular seized my attention, and, once he had seized it, refused to let go.

Thomas Fitzgerald – in the Irish tongue, *Tomás an tSíoda*. The 10th Earl of Kildare. The Rebel Earl often known as 'Silken Thomas', because his army of soldiers – the 'gallowglass army' – wore helmets adorned with silk fringes. The name is a derivation of the old Irish word *gallóglach*, a combination of the term *gall*, meaning foreign, and *óglach*, meaning youth. The soldiers were regarded – and certainly regarded themselves – as elite mercenaries.

It's difficult, at this distance, to know whether Thomas was the rebel hero often portrayed in history books – a young man intent on saving Ireland from the rule of Henry VIII at all costs, hurling armies into battles and sieges – or whether he was, as some accounts say, ill-advised, naïve, and rash. His action in St Mary's Abbey, Dublin, in 1534, when he renounced all allegiance to Henry VIII, and flung down the Sword of State before the shocked congregation, certainly indicates a flamboyant and defiant nature.

Among the many fragments of information that have come down from his contemporaries, Thomas is described, variously, as 'brave, generous, but wanting in discretion . . .', as 'a headlong hotspur, not devoid of wit – were it not that a fool had the keeping thereof . . .', and as having underestimated the resistance of the English and overestimated the likelihood of foreign help to his cause.

There are brief, tantalizing glimpses of his private life. Halfway through writing the book, I discovered the existence of a wife, who seemed to have vanished or died 'before 1529'. Try as I might, I was unable to find out anything more. I had to resist the temptation to weave in a sub-sub-plot about her, and I eventually presented her as a shadowy figure, about whom hardly anything was known.

But, fighter and rebel, or heedless and wild, there are unexpected indications that this undoubtedly brave, possibly rash Earl was also something of a romantic. He was a musician, an accomplished lutist. According to the Irish Tree Council, on the night before he surrendered to Henry VIII, he sat beneath what is now the oldest planted tree in Ireland, and played his lute. The tree has long since been known as the Silken Thomas Yew. The surrender itself is wreathed in suspicion and speculation, but most accounts seem to agree about the infamous 'Maynooth Pardon' – the promise to him that – were he to surrender to the King's mercy – his personal safety would be guaranteed. It was a promise that was not kept.

It was this strange blending of a romantic with a rebel who led armies and sacked castles and towns that drew me to Thomas Fitzgerald, and provided the basis for the sixteenth-century sections of the book – which is primarily the story of the (fictional) Catherine Ó Raifeartaigh.

The Fitzgerald family was attainted and disinherited for their treason. The Attainder of the Earl of Kildare Act, 1538, permitted Thomas's execution and the confiscation of most of his property.

But, despite that, the Rebel Earl – who led the Silken Rebellion – earned a remarkable place in history.